Laurence

CW01184480

The Incredible Eddie Reynolds: Escapologist (and Womaniser)

LOS GREEN WRITES

Los Green Writes

Copyright © 2024 Laurence Green

All rights reserved.

The story, all names, characters, and incidents portrayed in this production are fictitious. No identification with actual persons (living or deceased) is intended or should be inferred.

Book Cover by Jude Wainwright

2024

To Linda, always – and every other member of the family, past, present and future . . including Uncle Eddie, of course.

Contents

Author's Note

In the 1980's my Uncle became concerned that there was a huge swathe of family history that would be lost when his mother – our Granny – passed away. By that time she was in her 80's, though there was some debate as to her actual birth date as her birthday hadn't been celebrated during a tough Sheffield childhood. Granny dutifully and with some difficulty wrote out a list of the family as far as she knew it. The exercise was a struggle as she had been born left-handed (like me), but had her left arm tied behind her back at school to make her use her right hand (not like me). Still, she completed the task. We all read the list and I think everyone in the family paused when they saw the following entry:

Uncle Eddie: escapologist and womaniser!

From that point on I felt almost an obligation to write his story. What follows is entirely a work of fiction, but I'd like to think that it does Uncle Eddie some justice, whoever he was.

Laurence Green

Chapter One

"That's it!"

Eddie Reynolds looked down on Ada and saw a reflection of magic in her eyes.

"There!"

As she said it, they both felt the mystery quicken and he smiled to himself. Ada Morris - the girl from the Sky Edge estate, where the Sheffield gangs had run their business a decade before and who was born the day before the nineteenth century tipped into the twentieth - was trying to control the moment in the sticky heat of a June evening. The image she had taken from the features of Marion Davies, Jean Harlow and Greta Garbo was now beginning to moisten as Eddie wrestled above her. She had been a perfect picture at the start of the evening when she had made her entrance like walking onto screen for the first time. Now, her hair was ruffled on the pillow, her eyeshadow bloated with perspiration and her lipstick was smudged fat from kissing. No soft fade-out would make her whole again.

Eddie pushed down into her and she urged herself against him – just when the sound of the front door opening snapped the moment and she shuddered.

Eddie's eyes widened. The excitement was heightened and he continued his rhythm, unsure if he couldn't stop, or just didn't want to.

"Eddie," she whispered, in a stage hiss. "He's back."

Downstairs, the heavy, clumsy boots of Ken Morris clumped across the carpet and came towards the stairs.

Eddie sucked in a breath. He was so close. A little wind blew in through the window and caught the sweat on his back, making it sing. The moment, though, was over and gently as he could, he rolled over and off her, staring towards the doorway.

He was smiling.

"Bloody hell, Eddie," Ada's face was sharpening, squeezing out some of the lines that had formed in her journey of scraping her way from the grime of Sky Edge to the ease and comfort of Dore: six miles by road, thirty-four years of hard living.

The steps had started to hit the stairs now and they came like single drumbeats. Eddie would have preferred a roll. He liked the drama and the spectacle. Ada snatched the sheets to cover her body, hiding herself and the act of their lovemaking. She glared at Eddie, needing to be away from him. She was preparing her apologies. She was ready to beg, but she couldn't have Eddie so close. Eddie always told her how important it was to leave the right image in someone's mind when you're playing a trick on them. Eddie had to be out of the picture.

And now he was, up and out of bed, catching his clothes as the rap of nails from Morris's shoes kicked through the thin carpet to strike the wood beneath. He was home a good hour earlier than expected, an hour earlier than every Saturday. You could set your clock by his routines. He was a man of pattern and order. He was just so. It made him money and made him successful and his money shone like a light. Ada had seen it and flown in close. By the time you're twenty, if you've gone to bed hungry six days out of seven, you can swallow your pride and put up with dull trade talk and think of Eddie Reynolds when your husband occasionally found the time, the inclination and the energy to grunt his way through three or four minutes of passion. It wasn't a sacrifice she made. It was a bargain.

Morris was in a good mood today. He had done well and as he opened the door he was smiling. The good mood froze a little as he saw Ada. Her shoulders were bare as she took off her make-up. It stopped him for a moment, until the wind picked up again and made him turn to his right and the open window.

***

Eddie was gone.

By the time Morris had done his customary double-take, Eddie was skipping off the pavement and onto a tram to carry him into town. It was half past eight on a Saturday evening - far too light and far too early to be heading home.

Town was dusk-lit as he stepped back to the streets where the soft tone and still light made the new Library building up ahead of him seem more mystical still. In a city built on old designs and cheap materials, the deco lines were sharp and dazzling. The Portland stone made the image glow. Eddie liked to see it and looked forward to stepping inside early next month when royalty came to the city for the official opening of the building.

That was still some weeks off. More immediate and right in front of him was the Brown Bear pub, which was buzzing as he pushed inside. With the football season over, conversations had shifted, words of war and peace becoming the common language. The twentieth anniversary of the start of the

Great War was stirring up memories of things past and thoughts of things to come, none of them good. Japan's bombing of Manchuria three years earlier still reverberated and reminded everyone still brutalized by four years of European war that the world hadn't settled.

Eddie pressed forward, unconcerned. Half a dozen faces turned to see who had broken their spell as he opened the door. More than a few of them knew him. They nodded. This was where the theatre crowd gathered before and after shows and Eddie was a regular. When they congregated, he made sure he got in close so that he could share the air with them. They were working where he wanted to be and he felt the connection was helpful.

In the meantime, he was putting in regular shifts at Ward's Brewery as a drayman and the girl behind the counter knew it, slapping a pint of a rival bitter on the bar with a smile.

"Sorry it's not one of yours, Eddie."

"It looks nearly as good as you, Alice."

They shared an electric smile of two people who never quite knew if they would find themselves together somehow, sometime. Alice was pretty, but Eddie was something else. His face was perfectly cut and he took care of himself. During the day he laboured, so that in the evening he could shine. Nearly ten years younger than Ada, the attraction wasn't just his youth and energy, it was the tug of beauty that was never easy to resist. Eddie took a sip then swung round to survey the tables. He could hear a voice and wanted to pin it down.

Stan Kitteridge liked to work a crowd. Now his tongue was clicking like a steam-hammer at the heart of a group of half a dozen. He was a promoter at the Empire theatre and he never missed an opportunity to sell. Stan was late into his thirties now and every year took a little of his hair and added a lot more to his waist. He wore a moustache as a way of telling people which way up his head should be if there was any doubt.

As he jabbered away, Eddie noticed a middle-aged man he only knew as "Friendless Eric" hang at Stan's shoulder, waiting for a moment to get in a few words. The words were always the same, begging for a chance to slide a bit of work at the theatre his way. Eric was a violinist by trade and had worked across the city in the cinemas before the *talkies* came in. But now, no one needed an orchestra. Now, people wanted to listen to the actors and actresses speak in their clipped British or nasal American tones. Eric was part of the past. Eddie believed that *he* was still part of the present and the future, though the theatre was starting to feel the long effects of moving pictures, radio and – some said – television.

Stan stopped talking and Eric wasn't paying attention. He missed his chance.

"Stan!"

The sound of Eddie's voice worked like a hook on a fish. Stan looked up, smiling. He had a big round grin that always reminded Eddie of half a Yorkshire pudding on a Sunday dinner plate. Stan slipped away from his captive audience to join Eddie at the bar.

"You all right, Stan?"

"Bad times, Eddie. Bad times."

"Hard times?"

"*Bad.*"

"How come?"

Stan motioned to Alice for a drink. He took two fingers of whisky and cracked it over his tongue.

"Did you ever know Mary? Mary Riley. Worked in the office and covered ticket sales when we were short."

Eddie knew everyone in the Empire. He had made it his job. He wanted to work and live in the theatre and was prepared to put in the hard shifts to earn his entry.

"Yes. Nice. Quiet." By which he meant he had never been drawn to her, or her to him.

Stan tugged at the whisky again and let the alcohol snap out level across his mouth.

"She's dead."

"Hey, I'm sorry."

"Yeah, yeah. That's not the worst of it."

"How's that?"

"Suicide." The word came off his tongue as if it took some of the skin as it went.

"Oh, bloody hell."

"That's right. And she's Catholic."

"So?"

"So, they won't bury her! It's a sin, they're saying. So, they can't bloody bury her. I know her mother. She's in bits."

"That's tough."

Stan looked up at Eddie, halfway between hope and fear. "Why can't they bury her?"

"It's complicated."

"How come? Hey? How come? How's it complicated?"

At the age of twenty-five, Eddie had been heading out to mass with his Mum and Dad since the day he was born and he still hadn't quite figured out much about the Catholic church. But he knew what he knew. Suicide was a mortal sin. Everyone knew that and rules were rules. For a moment, he thought about sex and adultery, but the moment passed.

"Well. . ."

"I just want to help her poor mother. She just wants a Christian burial. That's not a lot to ask, is it?"

Eddie came out of the fog of theological doctrine and saw things clearly. Stan Kitteridge, booking agent for the Empire, wanted some help and Eddie Reynolds – desperate for a booking and a chance to get onto the stage - was right beside him, ready to console him and offer some light in the dark.

"I could talk to the local priest, Stan. Where did she live?"

"Up West Bar way."

Eddie nodded and smiled. His old parish. "St. Vincent's. I know the priests. I can catch them tomorrow, maybe. I've just got to work round my rehearsal schedule."

"Rehearsal? Yeah, yeah. Of course. Your act. What was it again?"

"Escapology."

"Escapology! That's a good show. How's it's coming on?"

Eddie shrugged. "It's ready, Stan. You don't have any gaps, do you?"

"For you? Course I do. I can work something. You want a drink?"

Eddie turned to Alice and winked.

An hour later he was moving again, pausing by Orchard Square to pick a pack of matches from Horace Lingard, who worked the area as if it was his shopfloor space. He was an old actor, who'd trod the boards up and down the country, trying his hand at every sort of show and every kind of character until he got too old and too tired to keep hold of the magic. When it finally slipped through his fingers he was out on the street.

"No luck tonight, Eddie?"

"Oh, some, Harry. Some." He burst a match alive and sank his cigarette into the flame.

"You'll get caught one day, you know."

"That's what you'd think." He shrugged. "It nearly happened tonight."

He enjoyed telling the story and Harry – who had been living vicariously for a decade – liked hearing it. Eddie slipped him a cigarette and they both smoked slowly.

"So, what did you do? He's up the stairs. You're on the first floor. You didn't jump, did you?"

Eddie smiled. "Misdirection, Harry. I pushed the window open wider. He came in, saw the window and headed straight for it. I was still in the room. I walked out behind him and straight down the stairs."

"It sounds dangerous."

Eddie shook his head.

"It *is* dangerous, Harry." He smiled. "That's the point."

Chapter Two

Eddie ran another tram home, letting it spark its way out of town all the way to Meadowhead, all the while moving as far away from the east of the city as it could and heading out into what used to be Derbyshire. Sheffield Corporation had started something of a land grab in the last few years and the Norton area, where Eddie lived, had just become part of the city. Space was needed to fit in the new housing that was planned to accommodate the steel working families that forged the city. A huge new building programme had commenced, aiming to sweep away the sludge of back-to-back slums that blotted the cityscape like dog dirt. It was an act of re-imagining and vision, they said. Times were changing and Sheffield needed to change with them. Eddie wouldn't argue with that. The city had a fragile feel to it, as if one strong gust of wind might knock all its febrile buildings to the floor to make the landscape flatter, leaving a cloud of dust to mingle with the ever-present industry smoke.

Eddie lived with his Mum and Dad in a row of newer housing built for veterans, moving in some years previously, hauling their few belongings from an area known as "the Crofts" out towards the edge of the city. The time was ticking past ten when Eddie opened the door and stepped in quietly. As he slipped off his jacket, he could hear the wireless playing soft in the living room. The door was just open and a little light crept through.

"Hi, Dad."

Frank Reynolds looked up at him over his paper and smiled. “Evening, Eddie. Has it been a good day?”

Eddie nodded. “All right.”

He had worked in the morning, but the afternoon and evening had been his.

“Have you been out and about?”

“In and out,” he said and thought of Ada. A blush of her perfume still tugged at his skin and he enjoyed the memory. “What are you reading?”

“Oh, you know, the same old stories.”

His Dad loved the newspaper, reading the Sheffield Independent cover to cover every day and keeping a stack of back issues beside his armchair. When he was done, he passed them to Mum to cut up into toilet paper. He regarded the papers as an extension of himself and a way of stretching to places he had never been or would never go. Money would always be a problem. That and having one less leg than most men he knew.

Eddie sat down and the smell of perfume disappeared, overpowered by an ever-present scent of *Germolene*, which his Dad used incessantly, part of a constant habit of trying to keep his world clean and disinfected. It started after the war and wouldn’t stop.

“Any news?”

“Plane crashed up at the aerodrome, at the show.”

“Bloody hell. Anyone hurt?”

“Two women.”

“Killed?”

“No, thank god. Tommy Nicholson saw it happen. *I* heard it. I was out front and I heard a bloody great explosion. Planes, eh?" His Dad was wistful, not quite able to know how he felt about them. They were part of the new age, he knew, but he couldn't shake the memory of them in the war. They were tied to battle in his mind.

He had lined up alongside his friends and family to sign up for the *Sheffield Pals* regiment then taken a trip to France. The regiment was far left of the front that formed part of the Somme Offensive and was cut to ribbons in hours. His Dad lost a leg. Eddie knew that he never talked about it. He'd lost a leg. What was there to say?

"Dad?"

"What is it, Eddie?"

"Why's suicide a sin?"

His Dad took a breath, to show that it was an important question and to give him time to think. His Dad was conceived in Ireland, his mother had told him, but born in Sheffield, as part of the early waves of migrators, leaving poverty and famine behind them. He was born into a Catholic world and raised not to question it too much.

"Because the Church says it is."

Eddie grunted. "Is that good enough?"

"Why?"

"Oh, just . . a friend of a friend was telling me something."

"Are you all right?"

"I'm fine, Dad. I just said I'd try to help someone's mum. Her daughter killed herself."

"How can you help?"

"They won't bury her."

His Dad sighed. "Talk to your Mum."

That was always good advice.

***

Sunday started sweetly soft. Eddie woke up feeling fresh. He could smell Mum's baking from downstairs and he followed the scent. Mum and Dad were tucked up tight in the kitchen, Mum asking for updates on people she knew in hospital – each one with their own personal number, which she kept in a diary – and Dad fishing through the paper to find the report. Mum checked daily then said prayers where she needed to.

She was just crossing herself as Eddie walked in. "Morning, love," she said as she kissed him.

"Morning, Mum."

"Cornflakes?"

He nodded.

"Can you manage a bit of bread and jam?"

"I'll do my best."

She smiled as he lifted the tea cosy from the tea pot to check that the water was still hot before pouring, sieving out the leaves and peering down into the pattern they left. He couldn't see any answers.

His Dad looked over at him and nodded.

"Mum?"

"What is it?"

Eddie bit his lip before starting. "I was talking to someone about suicide."

"Whatever for?"

"Friend of a friend."

"Oh, that's terrible."

"I know. I was going to talk to a priest about it. What do you reckon?

"Who was it?"

"Mary Riley?"

"Was she in Vincent's?"

"That's right."

"Well, Father Casey's very good. Or talk to Father Cleary at Our Lady's. What do you want to know?"

Eddie nodded at the suggestion. He liked Father Cleary. "Why is it a sin?"

She turned to him. "You're giving up on God, Eddie."

"Yes, but if things are bad. I mean, *really* bad."

Mum put the bread on the plate and passed him the butter and the jam. When she knew he wasn't looking – she glanced over at his Dad.

"How bad? You're giving up hope, Eddie, love. What's worse than that?"

He took a drink of tea. "I suppose."

***

With breakfast done, they readied themselves for church. His Dad had been using his crutches for nearly twenty years now and managed to move faster than Eddie most of the time. He seemed to swoop through the air with the ease of a chimpanzee and wouldn't take preferential treatment at any price. When someone offered him a seat, he refused.

"I've still got one good 'un," he'd say.

The church, Our Lady and St. Thomas, was a roll away down the hill. From some way off, they looked down where the people were congregating and it was a good feeling. There was a lot of chatter, a lot of smiles. The church was still new and fresh, part of a recent wave of missionary zeal that had come across from Ireland.

Eddie daydreamed for most of the mass, occasionally brought up sharp when the incense tickled his nose and made him think about using smoke on stage. Then, when Father Cleary upbraided the congregation for impure thoughts, Eddie couldn't stop an image of Ada's breasts slipping into his mind. Almost immediately, the image disappeared and he saw the face of Louisa Cassanelli. She was smiling. Eddie smiled too, then frowned, conflicted. Louisa. That was another story.

With mass finished, many of the families stayed back to share a cup of tea and a piece of cake. Sunday was rest day. The factories were shut and the chimneys were still. People wanted to relax. Eddie had to bide his time until they'd all gone, two by two and one by one. Then there was only Eddie left - and Father Dennis Cleary.

"Hello there, Eddie. You still here? The cake's all gone."

He pulled a pack of cigarettes out of his pocket and offered Eddie one.

"Thanks. *Craven A*?" He said, looking at the packaging.

Father Cleary smiled. "Good for the throat, they tell me."

They moved outside, where the sun was summer soft and sat together.

"What can I do for you, Eddie? Is it women trouble?"

"They've never been any trouble to me, Father."

Father Cleary laughed. "Ah, but you be careful there, Eddie." He looked at Eddie sharply. "If you know what I mean." He took a puff of smoke and hung out to it. "Your Ma tells me you've a nice girlfriend. Is that so?"

Eddie nodded. "Louisa." He shrugged. "We grew up together."

"In the Crofts?"

"That's right. But it's not that, Father."

"What is it then?"

"Suicide."

"Ahhh." Father Cleary tugged on his cigarette hard. The tip exploded into a life of fire.

"Why's it a sin, Father?"

Father Cleary didn't speak for a few seconds. Eddie knew him well enough to know. He was thinking – and thinking of what to say. He waved his arm out towards the hill that was Meadowhead, climbing up from the valley and out towards the fields and farms of Derbyshire. They were different worlds once. Now the tram connected them. Now the houses were coming, wave after wave.

"Things are changing, Eddie. They're getting out of control."

"How's that?"

Father Cleary took another drag to let the smoke play round his lungs until it found a soft spot to work on. "Do you read the paper much, Eddie? I know your Dad does."

"Not much."

Father Cleary nodded. "Take a read some time. See what people are saying. Have you heard them talk of this *eugenics*?"

Eddie shook his head. It rang some sort of bell, but it was distant.

"Perfect people, Eddie. Perfect races. Perfect nations."

"Wouldn't God want that? I thought we were made in his image."

Father Cleary smiled. "Ah, you might think that, but, no, Eddie, we're *all* part of God's image. Every one of us. The young and the old. The strong and the weak. And they'd be changing that, they would. They'd be killing them if they could."

Eddie listened. He liked to listen to Father Cleary when he wasn't talking about sex or adultery. But he couldn't make a connection with suicide. Father Cleary looked at Eddie and realised as much. He smiled before trying another tack.

"Your Dad fought in the war, didn't he? I was a chaplain out there for a couple of years, you know?"

"Where were you?"

"I was front line. They let the Catholics go all the way with the boys. I was with the Royal Irish most of the time." He smiled. "We got around."

"Not much fun."

"Not a lot, Eddie, no. But it was clear, at the time. Us against them. British against the Germans."

"But you're Irish. I thought you hated the English?"

"We hated them like family, you know. Germany was different. We wanted to change things with the British. But we wanted to *break* the Germans. It was bloody, though. The things you see, you don't forget. Does your Dad ever say anything?"

"No."

"He's a wise man. But, anyways, we won, didn't we? And that was that. Back to normal, maybe.

A bit of peace. But it's all gone wrong, Eddie. It *is* breaking. Bit by bit. You've got Mussolini in Italy and God only knows what in Germany. And that fella Stalin in Russia."

"I thought he was on our side."

"Ask the people there, Eddie. They can't say what they think. They can't believe any more than what they're told, so where does that leave God? Where does it leave their faith? Where does it lead the Church?"

"We're all right here, though, Father, aren't we?"

"Don't be so sure. That Oswald Mosley's working up and down the country, whipping up a storm for the fascists. More power, more control, more Godlessness." He stubbed out his cigarette. "It's a battle, Eddie. And we're not winning it."

"We?"

"The Church, Eddie. We're set apart right now. Countries are going in one direction and we're either tied to their apron strings or we're cut adrift. We need a change. We need order. We need to build on something solid, eternal. The great and the good of the Church used to dream of a Christian world, but that seems a long, long way away. We need something closer and surer and lasting. And that's the *family*, Eddie." Eddie looked into Father Cleary's eyes and saw passion and zeal. "Father, son, mother, daughter. It's our daily life. House and home. The things that remain." He took another swipe at his cigarette, as if it sustained him and gave him faith. "They're all under attack. Did you read that book by your man Huxley?" Eddie shook his head. "He's saying it's all about the future, but who's he kidding? It's about *now*. What's left?" Another tug at the cigarette. "Personal responsibility. The *family*. And so, suicide? That's such a sin. Despair. Giving up on your family. Giving up on God. It's the worst of the worst."

Eddie let the words settle for a while, in the way you would let water find its way to ground after a storm. "And there's nothing you can do?"

"Do?"

"It's a . . friend of a friend. They can't get a burial."

"Not on sacred ground, no. We need rules, Eddie. God's going to do all he can for us, but we've got to make our own effort too. There's a price to pay for sin."

"But if she was, you know, unhappy and stuff?"

"That's when you need God most."

"I suppose."

"How did she die?"

It occurred to Eddie that he didn't know, so he shook his head. "Who could tell me?"

"Where was it?"

"St. Vincent's."

"Was it Mary Riley?" The Catholic community was small enough that every priest could know everything. "I heard It was disinfectant. Common enough stuff. *Lysol*, I think. Father Casey would have some more details. Or Doctor Gilmartin."

The name hit his ear like a strike of the bell. Doctor Gilmartin had brought Eddie into the world twenty-five years ago. It seemed like they were about to be reacquainted.

"Thanks, Father."

"That's no trouble at all. By the way, how's your act?"

Eddie smiled. "It's good. Thanks."

"Good enough for a garden party next month?"

"Well, it's magic rather than a miracle, but I'd be happy to do it."

"I look forward to it. God bless you, Eddie."

Eddie nodded and walked away.

Chapter Three

Monday was wash day. As Eddie eased out of bed, he could already hear his Mum downstairs as she wrestled with the laundry. The weather was light and warm. It was going to be a nice day. More importantly, it was going to be a good drying day. Monday morning was the time before the factories heaved themselves back into the harness to work again to make the chimneys belch. The clear air was something to savour and up and down the streets people were pegging clothes on the line.

"Morning, son."

"Morning, Dad."

Eddie cut himself a couple of doorstep slices of bread and was generous with the bread and jam.

"You busy at work?"

Eddie nodded.

"It's picking up. People are drinking again. New licensing laws and all that."

In fact, the industry was still shifting less beer than it had before the war, but the bottom that had fallen out of the barrel had been pegged and things were moving in the right direction, for the brewers at least.

"What about you? Royal visit next month?"

"That's right. Everyone's in a flap, but it's good for business. People start noticing you." His Dad took a sip of tea. "They've even got some *head* doctors coming in to have a look at us. Lots of new ideas, apparently."

Psychology had started to thread itself into thinking across the West, with the sick and savaged from The Great War providing perfect specimens for a whole new slew of theories.

"Are you going to see them?"

"What do you think?" He snorted. "They'll take a look at me and say, what do you think the problem is?" He laughed. "I've lost a bloody leg, you daft bugger."

"Frank!" Mum snapped.

"Sorry, love, but it's not that complicated. Is it?"

"If you say it isn't, that's good enough for me."

He smiled and his Mum smiled too as she went to collect another basket of washing. The Royal visit would be something indeed. The Duke and Duchess - coming to open the city Library - were taking in a stop at Painted Fabrics, where Frank Reynolds worked. The Duchess was a patron.

His Dad returned to his paper, folding it down every now and then to peer over the top to tell Eddie what had been happening in the city, the country and the world.

"Five more dead on the roads this weekend," he tutted. "That was a smart move, wasn't it? Getting *rid* of the speed limit. That really worked."

He had accepted that the war happened and that he had lost his leg and a lot of friends out there in France, fighting a war that no one really understood. But with that came a knowledge that leaders mostly didn't know what they were doing. He was stoical and to be stoical was to accept that the world wasn't just and wasn't kind.

"The drivers are idiots and pedestrians don't watch out for them. It's a bad mix."

"I hope *you're* careful."

"Course I am," said Eddie, "but you don't get much speed up on a *steamer*. They're slower than the horses!" They both laughed. The steamers had only been in use for a couple of years at the brewery, introduced to harness mechanization in the beer delivery process. They were heavy, awkward and certainly not as reliable as the horses. The brewery used them for the longer trips out of the city or when the weather didn't suit the horses so well. But change was coming. The steamers would stay, it seemed. The horses would go.

"And as for the cricket! They want Larwood now, don't they? Lose the first Test against the Aussies and *now* they want Larwood back and he doesn't have to say sorry for *bodyline*. Why should *he* say sorry? He was following orders. They always told us that that's what you have to do. Bloody typical."

"Will he play?"

"*I* wouldn't."

Uncle Dick had told Eddie that his Dad used to be a good cricketer.

Mum put a fresh cup of tea in front of Dad and that quietened him.

"Have you got a busy day today, love?"

"I might have to cover some of the rounds with Bert Oxley. Archie's done his back."

"Doesn't Bert . .?"

"Drink? Yeah. More than he delivers, usually."

"You take care."

He smiled. He always took care.

***

He took the tram down towards town, then walked when the route started to steer away from his destination. It was a nice day for a stroll and he was happy to stride through Nether Edge to get to Ecclesall Road, where Ward's Brewery sat fat and happy.

Ward's wasn't the biggest brewery in the city by any stretch, but it was local and building up a solid following. Eddie had breezed through half a dozen bits-and-pieces jobs before he'd found his way to the brewery, where a combination of obvious good health and a smart mouth impressed the people who were recruiting. If the role of a drayman wasn't the most exacting in the world Eddie didn't mind. Shifting barrels kept him fit and gave him time to think about his act. Besides, given the choices out there – mostly involving molten metal in foundries the devil might steer clear of – life on the open road wasn't too bad.

Monday morning at the brewery had started with a buzz. Eddie was right when he told his Dad that times were getting better for brewers. Taxes had started to shift so that bits of money were beginning to spill through the businessman's hand into the fingers of the population. They spent it fast and loose with drink as good a purchase as anything.

As he walked through the brewery, a stale cloud of beer fumes starting to thicken gave him his first welcome, followed by choruses of "'ey up, Ed", "na then, Ed" and "y'all reyt, Ed".

"You're on the wagon, with me," Bert Oxley told him, wiping his hand across his brow to clear the first of his morning beer sweats.

"*You*, Bert? On the wagon?"

"Cheeky sod," Bert said, but he smiled, which put a crease in a worn-out face.

"Not using the *steamer*?"

"It's buggered again."

It always seemed to be buggered. Eddie didn't mind. He preferred the horses, giving them a stroke before climbing up then thinking about a lunchtime visit he had planned as well as a trip this evening. He was juggling, too, a time to get some rehearsal in with his stage partner, Nancy.

Bert pulled the horses into line before pushing out into the road where a few dozen cars were weaving along both sides of the carriageway.

"It's bloody murder out here. The horses get frit."

A car skidded past them, the driver holding on like it was a snake trying to bite him.

"It's going to be a long day."

Eddie was right. The morning was hard and heavy. They made a dozen drops to pubs, wheeling and hauling the casks to the cellars where the beer could settle before serving. The journey was interesting, though. They plugged their way out through Attercliffe, where the steel works bullied the only flat part of Sheffield into a wobbling submission, the pneumatic action of machinery making the earth shake and air tremble, thick waves of steam, smoke and pure white heat rolling out onto the roads so that the horses started as they passed.

"Easy, boys," Eddie whispered, leaning forward to pat them.

The route took them across town and it was strange to watch a city rebuild itself, great swathes of tenement blocks ploughed into dirt piles, while in other parts of the city a furious building workforce laid brick on brick to create the next generation of living.

They were back by lunchtime and while Bert slid off to the Pomona for a pint and some scran, Eddie headed along Ecclesall Road, to make a social call on a childhood idol.

***

"Hello, Eddie!"

The words came loud and clear and tickled in his ears. There was nothing unusual about that. What was strange was that the lips of the woman looking right back at him didn't move.

"You're getting better, Wynne."

"Thank you!"

"Work going well?"

"Yes, I'm busy."

Her smile was wide as she ushered him in, showing a perfect row of teeth. The lips didn't move as the words came about, but the curls in her hair bounced just a little. She led him into the parlour where her father was sitting: George Fox in person and the great magician Professor De Lyle on stage, Eddie's first idol.

"Eddie!"

There was affection in the voice, more than the simple fondness a performer has for their audience. Eddie had been watching him for over twenty years. Fox was getting old, mostly only performing for children's parties these days. Now he sat relaxed and in his civvies, rather than stage gear, but the face was still fine and sharp, the eyes had a touch of crystal about them and his silent movie moustache looked like the cat's whiskers. His daughter, Wynne, had grown up to become an artist in her own right, carving out a solid career as a ventriloquist. She was hard-working and focused enough not to be distracted by Eddie, as so many women seemed to be. She liked him, nothing more.

"Sit down, sit down."

The house was a treasure trove of memorabilia and stage props. Eddie loved simply sitting there, taking it all in.

"You never say no to a cup of tea, do you, Eddie?"

"He never says no." Wynne winked at Eddie. He grinned back.

"I've not managed to get out so much recently. Have I missed anything good?" He was in his sixties now and slowing down a little.

"Didn't you catch Gene Dennis?"

"Ah," he said and smiled, "that I *did* see."

"She was amazing," Wynne purred. "How does she do it?"

Eddie shook his head. "The psychics all have their systems. Houdini tried it for a while, but it's just trickery."

"It's *all* trickery, Eddie. It's just a question of how good the trick is. The audience isn't paying for the truth. They want a show."

Eddie slumped. "That's not what I want."

"What *do* you want?"

"I want to thrill people. And I think I might to get on the bill at the Empire."

"Well, that's magnificent." The benevolence poured out of him. There was no envy. "Is there a problem?"

"Making the act work."

George chewed his lip. "Is it magic?"

"Escapology."

"You've stuck with it?"

"I've stuck with it."

"Is it difficult?"

"Yes."

"Is it dangerous?"

"I think so."

"Good. Have you spoken to our friend?"

"Randolph? Yes, I was out there a few months ago."

"Interesting place he's made for himself."

Randolph Douglas – who carried the stage name of *The Great* Randini – was a local escapologist who had moved out to Castleton and built a world of wonders, a huge collection of items that he had gathered over the years or fashioned himself, piece by piece. As well as being a master escapologist in his own right, Douglas was a consummate miniaturist and had created his own small kingdom of constructions. The cottage museum pulled in a slow, but steady stream of visitors. He was polite with them all. When an enthusiast came along, he purred like a cat.

"It was amazing."

Douglas was a perfectionist, sketching out every trick he knew. Watching him, Eddie learned the importance of design, as well as noting the obsession with escape and a morbid fascination with confinement and torture. Houdini had met Douglas and told him things that he discovered on his mysterious trips round the world, where some said he was in the pay of the US government as a spy. Whether or not that was true, Douglas was more than happy to receive pictures of the original iron maiden and a slew of other torture devices. The greater the trap, the bigger the threat and the greater the escape.

George nodded. "What did you learn from him?"

Eddie smiled. "He said: only go back to the tricks that always work for you."

George laughed. "Anything else?"

"He had an idea."

Wynne brought the tea and joined them as Eddie talked through his act.

"He always has ideas."

It was truer than most people knew. When Douglas got a medical discharge from the war, his career was over. The slow impacts of rheumatic fever robbed his body of the strength and agility to perform what his mind could imagine. While he slowed, Houdini carried on and when he wowed the world with his first upside down escape, he didn't let on that the idea came from Douglas in one of the notepads he always kept handy.

Eddie explained the trick he was considering.

"I like the sound of it," Wynne said.

"But?" Eddie knew that there was a but.

Fox picked up the point. "It's dangerous, Eddie. *You* know that. But the audience don't really. *They* need to know it's dangerous. Don't focus on the technicality. No one understands that except you. Focus on the danger."

That rang bells with what Douglas had told him and what he'd read from Houdini.

"If you manage to convey the terror, Eddie, you've got a winner."

Wynne sat on the edge of a sofa, passing Eddie a plate with a piece of cake.

"They love the mystery. But they want the danger. They don't want to see someone die. They want to see someone *almost* die."

Eddie nodded, thinking about what they were saying.

"I want to try what Houdini didn't manage."

The words seemed to pour ice into the air. "Be careful, Eddie. There was a reason Harry didn't do those things, or didn't do them more than once."

"That's why they'd be special."

Wynne put her hand on his arm. "There's dangerous, Eddie and there's exciting. And then there's stupid."

Fox smiled. "Did Randolph say anything else?"

"Practice."

That was the mantra. From the first time his Uncle Dick had shown him a card trick he had wanted to understand it then repeat it. The shift to escapology was simply a move to a different medium. He exercised hard and stretched his body, all the while developing his stage patter and stage presence with card tricks and illusions, performing for parents, aunts, uncles, friends and girlfriends whenever he could.

George nodded. “If you’ve got the act and you practice hard, what else do you need?”

Eddie pulled a face. He knew that he needed to confirm the booking with Stan. To do that he needed to find out more about Mary Riley.

Chapter Four

The factories were working hard and fast again as Monday peaked. The day had seen the opening of a new Tool Factory at Firth Browns, down at the Atlas Works. It was sited on the spot where Bessemer had first started to make his money out of steel, an act of practical magic in Eddie's eyes. Eddie and Bert had swung by to catch the tail end of the celebrations.

With the factories fully in swing, three things accompanied the fact like dark angels: the sight of sparks exploding past the open doors or through the open windows of buildings as you passed; the sound of hammers creating a beat and rhythm that brought a sense of apocalypse into your everyday life; and the smoke.

The mood was mostly jovial. The men and women who worked the machinery knew that they were less important than the big metal cogs, but the work brought them wages which paid the bills. You took what you could get. Even though the crash in Wall Street had happened three thousand miles away, the aftershocks made their way across the water and took money out of wage packets or stopped them altogether. Things were picking up a little. Most people were pleased at that.

As Bert shared a celebratory glass of beer – the Management wanted to make everyone feel part of the party – Eddie stood at the back and heard the rasp of a sharp little man, whose features had been worn away by six- and seven-day weeks.

"They can say what they like, but they're sailing the Titanic."

Eddie pulled a face. "How's that?"

"Capitalism's finished, son. It hit the iceberg in '29 and it's sinking. Did you not read your Marx?"

Eddie shrugged. "No. Why? What do you mean?"

"It's revolution, isn't it?" The little man grinned. "Not like they've done in Russia. Not like they do in France every now and then. A quiet one." He had a glint in his eye. Eddie remembered his Dad talking him through poetry some years ago. Yeats, Eddie, he'd said. He's your man. He's a Dubliner, but we can forgive him that. He said: "the best lack all conviction, while the worst are full of a passionate intensity". Eddie looked at the clock on the wall and made his goodbyes, pulling Bert back to the wagon and back to base.

As he finished up, he caught Dick Hutchings in the office. Dick lived a few hundred yards down from Eddie and family.

"Hey, Dick. Can you let my Mum and Dad know I'll be back late? Everything's fine, I just need to see someone."

"Is it about a lass?"

Eddie nodded. "Sort of."

***

The Crofts was a little gentler in the summer sun, the heat just managing to crawl through the cracks in the houses to shift some of the residual autumn-winter damp. The sun, too, brought out the children, who skipped across the cobbles to run towards Gus Cassanelli's ice cream wagon, some to buy and some to beg.

"Hey, Eddie. You come back to join us?"

Augusto worked the streets morning to night in competition with a handful of other Italian ice cream merchants. As a child, you heard the rattle of the cart on the cobbles and came running, hoping that the men like Gus, or Angelo Fantozzi, might look kindly on you and give you a scrap of ice cream or a crumble of wafer.

"Not today, Mr C. Is Louisa home?"

"Sure. She's with her Mama. She helps to iron."

"Thank you."

As Eddie lapped at the ice cream a tag of boys and girls formed behind him, little ducks all in line. Because he'd bought an ice cream, they sensed he had money and so they stuck close to him.

"Clear off," he muttered as he went. He didn't mean it too much. He'd spent enough time in crowds like that, waiting for miracles to fall out of pockets into your hand.

Eddie tugged up Scotland Street, trying not to look left or right at the crumbled brick of the blackened houses, trying to keep a straight path on a road and pavement that wobbled with uneven cobbles and stones. A mother of two hung in a doorway and stared out, somewhere into the distance. It was hard to know what she was looking for. Behind her, a commotion of voices started a row that escalated from words into punches and kicks and fingers pulling hair. The sound burned fast and bright, then quietened again.

"Eddie!"

Louisa stepped back as Eddie pulled round the corner and into the back yard. He couldn't help but smile to be there. Her face was so full of welcome he softened to see it.

Her mother, Rosa, appeared at the doorway and saw Eddie, her face flipping between happiness and worry. Eddie could take Louisa away from all this.

Rosa waved her arm. "You look after her, Eddie!"

Louisa kissed her cheek and skipped up to Eddie, taking his hand and he liked the feeling.

"I will."

He itched a little at the responsibility, turning away and leading Louisa up the hill.

"Where are we going?"

Eddie set his face forward. The children were gathering again. "Out of here."

June evenings could be kind and this was one of them. Eddie mirrored the mood of the weather simply by holding Louisa's hand and walking at her pace. He normally liked to walk fast, as part of his pattern of keeping his limbs strong and supple. Tonight, he strolled.

He led them up to Crookes Valley Park, where they took a turn round the dam and then sat to watch the men roll their bowls across the carpet-soft crown green. There was a gentleness to the evening that was comforting. The sound of bowls connecting gave off a reassuring chink and the applause that followed was simple and civilized.

Louise squeezed Eddie's hand then turned to face him.

"You know I'm going away soon," she said. Fruit-picking over in Wisbech, she'd told him. Seasonal work. His fingers tightened on hers.

The fruit-picking season always cast a wide net across the country to pull in people – mostly like Louisa – who could spend a few weeks in the fields, picking the harvest. It was hot, hard, dirty work.

"I'll miss you."

Even as he said it, he was thinking of time with Ada – and yet he meant what he said.

"We need the money."

He sat back on the park bench and puffed out his cheeks. "How will I survive?"

She laughed. "You'll cope."

"I'll write every day."

"Don't make promises."

He looked at her hands. They were fine fingers and were oh-so-soft once. Hard work, dirt and malnutrition sullied them.

"Look after these."

"That's not going to be easy. How do you pick fruit without using your fingers?"

He smiled. "Use your tongue."

He leaned in towards her to kiss her. She didn't resist and didn't want to. For just a moment, Eddie felt completely at ease as he felt the skin of her face touch his, tasted her tongue and caught a scent of her deep inside him. She was different to everyone else he'd known. And for just a moment, he wondered if he was going to propose to her. He guessed she'd say yes. Perhaps that's why he didn't ask.

Her face puzzled. "What's wrong?"

He shrugged. "It's this woman."

"It's always a woman, Eddie."

He laughed.

"No. A woman I knew . . sort of knew. She worked at the theatre. She lived in the Crofts." Suddenly the image of her tipping disinfectant into her mouth, down her throat and into her belly filled his mind.

"Are you all right?"

"She killed herself."

"Mary Riley?"

"That's right. Did you know her?"

"Everyone knows everyone, Eddie. You know that. Why are thinking about her?"

"Stan, the booking agent, knows her mother. The church won't bury her because it was suicide."

"What are you going to do?"

He shrugged. "I don't quite know, but I said I'd help."

"How?"

"Find out what I could. What are people saying?"

"Is he paying you?"

"No," he said sharply, her words pricking his conscience. "I just said I'd try to help."

"She killed herself."

"I know, but why?"

She laughed. "Why do women ever kill themselves, Eddie?"

Eddie felt a thrill. "A man?"

"*That's* what people are saying."

"But why? Who was he?"

"I don't know. *They* don't know."

"But everyone knows everything."

"Not when the streetlamps aren't working."

"There *was* somebody, though?"

Louisa pulled a face. She didn't like gossip. "There was somebody there. But she kept herself to herself."

"Someone staying with her?"

That was a quite a thing in the middle of a Catholic heartland.

"Not permanently. He came and went. There was some trouble. Politics."

"Politics?"

"That's what I heard. The usual." Louisa wasn't a social commentator, but she was part of an Italian family, which couldn't help looking over the water to Benito Mussolini's new order. "Right and left."

Eddie sat back on the bench and looked out over the boating lake that the designers had dug out of the earth. A few boats skimmed across it. When he turned to look at Louisa, he saw that her eyes were set somewhere in the distance.

"What's wrong?"

"I thought you wanted to see me."

He took her hand and smiled, changing the subject. They sat for an hour, before walking home. They kissed – just out of view of her parents' house – and Eddie felt a tug for something he didn't know if he could ever have.

"I'm going to miss you."

She had a tear in her eye and Eddie found his throat was tight. He kissed her cheek.

Then she smiled. "You won't know I'm gone."

Eddie watched her disappear. It was like watching a trick in reverse, with the magic obscured as the door closed.

When she had slipped inside, Eddie traced some quick steps to the road where Mary Riley had lived. Number 38 stood as drab and dull as the others. He had almost expected a sign on it to show that someone had died – and lived - there. He stood and watched. In the corner of his eye he noticed the figure of a boy, a lean and stunted body wrapped in some or other rags.

"You live round here?"

The boy nodded.

"What's your name?"

"Peter."

"Hello, Peter. I'm Eddie. What have you got there?"

Peter was clutching something in his hands. With most people he would have cowered or maybe run away. Eddie had a gentle voice: calm, but commanding. The boy opened his fingers up to show a *John Player* cigarette card collection of the England and Australia Ashes teams.

"How many have you got?"

"I haven't got Grimmett or McCabe."

Eddie grinned. "Well, you're not doing badly then. I'll look out for you."

"Will you?" His eyes burned with hope.

"Course I will." He didn't smoke *John Player*, but he knew a few people who did. "You live round here?"

The boy ducked his head to say yes.

"Did you know Mary? Mary Riley?"

"A bit."

"Did you ever see anyone with her?"

Peter froze.

Eddie leaned in and let his stage show voice take over. "It's all right. You can tell me."

"There was a man."

There was a man. How many stories started that way?

"What did he look like?"

The boy was starting to freeze. He didn't like answering questions.

Eddie smiled. "Let's have a look at that collection of yours."

He took the cards easily and did a card-sharp shuffle that made the boy goggle-eyed. "Grimmett and McCabe, was it?"

The boy sparkled. "The police were trying to find him."

Eddie ruffled the boy's hair – and then pulled a halfpenny from out of his ear. He laid it in the palm of his hand so that the boy's eyes fixed there and then he lifted it onto the side of his finger and flipped it up high with his thumb, sending it into a shaft of the sun's last light and making it sparkle.

He caught it quick in a fist, then rolled out his fingers, offering it to Peter.

"See you around."

***

The day was starting to darken and Eddie hadn't eaten anything more than an ice cream for an age. He started to feel the hunger knot inside him. He was used to it. That was how you grew up and he'd learned that if he could control that, then he could control everything. There was a lot said about lust for liquor or women. He'd never come across anything that hurt so much as hunger.

By the time he got back, it was after nine o' clock. His Mum was flapping, part scolding him, part fussing.

"Where've you been? Your dinner's cold!"

"I asked Dick to let you know."

"I know, but . . ."

A portion of meat and potato pie sat on the table as she made up some gravy.

"It looks great."

His tongue was wet with salivation as his hand reached for the *Henderson's Relish*.

After eating, he sat back in parlour with a cup of tea, his Dad working through the last part of the day's paper.

"Good day, Dad?"

"All right. You?"

"All right."

"Where've you been?"

"Seeing Louisa."

"How is she?" His Mum piped up.

"They're off to Wisbech for a month. Fruit picking."

"Oh, that's a tough job. They all sleep together in these huts. It's like a barracks."

"Nothing wrong with a barracks," his Dad said.

"You'll miss her, won't you?"

He would. "I'll survive. Anything happening?" He asked his Dad.

"*New Britain* talking at the City Hall tonight," he said, off-hand.

"What do they want?"

"The clue's in the name, Eddie."

"I suppose."

Then his Dad turned to him. “Keep an eye on them.” He picked up his pipe and took a pull. “Never trust radicals.”

Eddie nodded. He carried his plate back to the kitchen and started washing it before his Mum could get in behind him to squeeze him out of the way. When he was finished, curiosity caught hold of him and he glanced along the ragged line of cleaning goods his Mum had stored up. He found a bottle of disinfectant and lifted it up.

“What’re you doing with that?” His Mum couldn’t keep away.

“Why don’t you use *Lysol*?” Eddie asked.

“*Lysol?* No, it’s too strong. It’s dangerous.”

There was something in her tone that made his heart skip.

“Dangerous?” He looked at her and she was blushing. He pushed. “What is it, Mum?”

“Why do you want to know?”

“Nothing. Just . . . Someone drank some.”

“Oh, they do some daft things, Eddie. It’s terrible what they tell them.”

Eddie was puzzled.

“What do you mean?”

She didn’t want to say anymore. Her head told her to be quiet. But she couldn’t. The stories you hear have to get out somehow, sometime.

“Girls.” It was all so obvious to her. “When they’re....” Her voice became tight. “You know?” Another pause. “Pregnant.”

Chapter Five

Eddie caught Stan Kitteridge close to his home in Woodseats, just a mile or so away from Meadowhead, propping up the bar in the Chantrey Arms and – as usual – creating his own centre-stage for whoever would listen. Lily, the landlady, had no choice as she smiled a practiced smile while he told his regular tales of theatre land as if he was describing the West End. When Eddie entered, her smile became real. Memories stirred of a hot September day two years ago.

"Eddie Reynolds!"

"Hello, Lily." He was never sheepish. She loved that about him. That and the blueness of his eyes, which reminded her of summer. She remembered that Saturday afternoon, when her husband had shuffled off early to Bramall Lane and Eddie had been stuck by himself, wrestling with the mess of a cellar that her husband kept. She'd offered him a glass of lemonade as the least she could do. She watched him drink and thought of the most.

"Eddie!"

Stan had had a few already. He ordered drinks for both of them, wrapped his arm round Eddie and pulled them away to a table in the corner.

"I had Mary's mum in today, Eddie." The alcohol was starting to make Stan's words rub together. "That was very upsetting." The drink was making him morose.

"I might have found something out."

"Really?" Stan's face exploded with hope. "Eddie, you bloody little wonder. What?"

There was a part of Eddie that thought he should tread carefully and not be too dramatic, but then the showman in him took over.

"There was a man, Stan. And I think she might have been pregnant."

Stan rocked back in his seat. "*Mary*?" He shook his head. "Mary?" He took a drink.

"Birds do it, Stan, and bees."

The song had shocked his Mum when it came out. His Dad liked it. A spell in the ranks broadened your mind. Eddie thought it was wonderful.

"Yes, but . . . *Mary*? Bloody hell." He took another drink. "Did the note say anything?"

Eddie froze. "What?"

"The note? They usually leave a note, don't they? When they . . . do that."

The note? Eddie took hold of his glass. Stan wasn't the only one who needed a drink.

***

"Where's the note?"

For the first time Eddie could remember, Dr. Gilmartin looked flustered.

"Eddie, I'm seeing patients, you know?"

"They leave a note. I asked my Mum and Dad and they say that people leave a note."

Eddie was standing in the hallway and the few patients who were cluttered in the waiting rooms managed to stop their coughs and sniffs long enough to listen. That made the silence between Eddie's words and Dr. Gilmartin's feel very long and sharp.

"This isn't the time or the place, Eddie." Dr. Gilmartin was trying to bring treacle back into his voice and hadn't quite succeeded.

"They're going to bury her in a pauper's grave, Doctor." He paused for effect. "Unconsecrated ground." He threw the words out like holy water.

Dr. Gilmartin rocked back on his heels. He turned the movement into a spin as he headed to his office, waving to Eddie to follow without saying anything.

Eddie was close behind and shut the heavy door firmly.

By that time, Dr. Gilmartin had made his way to his desk. He sat down hard.

"There isn't always a note, Eddie."

"Isn't there usually?"

"It's not that simple. For example, if there's no one to read it."

"There's always *someone*. The person who finds the body." Eddie looked at Dr. Gilmartin long and hard. The Doctor was a showman and sometime shaman. Eddie understood that. He wanted to be the same. This was a test for him, to see if he could best the man who'd brought him into the world and had played his role for over forty years.

"Could it have been an accident?"

Doctor Gilmartin looked up at Eddie in some surprise, as if he was trying to work out what Eddie was trying to do.

"Why do you think it might have been an accident, Eddie?"

Eddie had him where he wanted him. "Because she was pregnant."

And straightaway the doctor fell back in his chair as if he was Peter and the cock had crowed for the third time. There it was. Eddie had played his trick perfectly.

"Who told you that?"

"There was a man. She was a Catholic. There you go."

"I wish life was always that simple."

His voice had that smooth Irish roll of soft butter over warm bread, but Eddie knew a slip when he saw one. He studied people as they performed. That's how you learn – what to do and what not to. "If it was an accident, it's not a sin, is it?"

"Eddie, she's going to be buried tomorrow in the City cemetery."

"They can move her back."

"I don't think they will."

"But they *can*. It's about what's *possible*. Not just what happens, but what could."

Dr. Gilmartin was flustered, which didn't happen often. "Eddie, drinking disinfectant isn't a common way to . . sort these things out. But times are changing fast. I'm always catching up."

"Who'd know?"

Dr Gilmartin lowered his eyes, making his world darker as he thought about what he'd heard and what he knew of the back-street butchers. "The people who get paid to do it."

"Do you know them?"

"No – and I don't want to. I try to help people, Eddie. I try to heal them."

Eddie stood up and smiled. "I understand."

He felt a little sad for the Doctor. He had started his practice in a different century and ever such a different time, with Victoriana still tight like a straitjacket on society. Now the buckles had burst as surely as if Eddie had been popping them as part of his stage act.

"You need to be careful, Eddie. These people . . . they're already breaking the law."

"I'm always careful." It might have been his catchphrase.

***

Eddie zig-zagged back home then straight out again, swinging past Nancy's house to let her down gently that he couldn't make the rehearsal they had planned.

"*Eddie!*"

She was disappointed more than angry, sulking now that the night she had planned wouldn't happen. She wanted to work with him, be up close to him. The movements of his body made her shiver.

"I'll make it up to you." His eyes flashed with promise and she fell for them. A kiss on the cheek helped – and then he was away, walking in the gentle evening air, thinking about Mary Riley and how it must have been for her to be pregnant in that place, in that situation. That's not what happens to good girls, his Mum might have said. That was why he was heading to the opposite end of town to Louisa.

***

"What are you doing here?" Ada was flushed. She didn't like the fact of him being there at all. That wasn't part of her make up and her make-up was perfect.

"I want to talk to you."

"He could be back any time, Eddie."

"I'll be quick."

"That's a shame." She did her best Mae West grin. "Well, come in then."

She shoveled him off the doorstep, worried that the neighbours might have caught a glimpse of him slipping in.

Eddie paused in the hallway, caught her hand and pulled her round. She was still angry, but his smile had a way of loosening the screws of every tight face.

"Come here."

They pressed up close so that the blood under the skin began to bubble. He slid his hand down the dress that cut out her shape in cotton. His fingers smoothed from her hip to her inner thigh and instinct made her teeth snap at his lip.

Ada pulled herself away, tugging at a breath to slow her pulse and give her sense again. "What do you want, Eddie?"

He kissed her on the cheek. "I want to talk."

She hustled him to the back of the house, where no one could see and sat him down. She was making dinner, following a recipe her sister had given her.

"Smells nice."

"You're not getting any."

"Food?"

"Cheeky!"

"That's fair enough," but as he said it, he lifted himself up and picked up a bottle of stout from a stack just inside the pantry.

"What are you doing?"

"It's hot."

"He counts his bottles. Watch it."

"Tell him you drank it. Dr. Gilmartin prescribed it for my Mum. Helps with the nerves."

She pulled a face. "What do you want to talk about?"

He watched her work. She was a good cook, with an eye for detail and a mind for adventure. That went for life as much as food, so that as she moved around the kitchen, she couldn't help but shift her body into shapes that would provoke him. She was an artist every bit as much as he was, only her stage was smaller and ever so much more intimate.

"Where would go for an abortion?"

He might as well have slapped her.

Too many thoughts to manage bounced into her head, round and out again as she tried to make any sort of sense of what he'd just said. She turned to him and her eyes were broken. "I can't believe you can ask me that."

Too late, Eddie realised his mistake. He'd never had the arrogance to imagine he was the first secret liaison for Ada. It had never bothered him. He lived in the moment. Now, though, a long, hard past opened up and in it a time when Ada had a need to call on the back-street butchers herself.

"Hey, I'm sorry, Ada. I didn't think you - - I just thought you might know someone."

There were big tears in her eyes. The way her face was squeezed it seemed as if they'd been cut out of her with scissors. He was up beside her, pulling her into his chest as pain and anger turned to slower sobs, then a deep, heavy and hard weep, shaking her. He held on, wrapping her up in himself and saying he was sorry over and over again.

Behind him, water bubbled and food baked and the room grew hot and dense.

"Why do you ask me that?"

The tears cut holes in her make-up and the mask she wore every day started to fray. Eddie looked in and saw the person Ada had been and had been trying to forget.

"It's not about you, love. Something happened."

"I'm sorry."

She was soft with him now, forgiving him and needing him equally. They sat down. "It was a long time ago, Eddie. I don't want to think about it. I don't want to remember it."

She couldn't, of course, forget it. That was the only child she was ever going to have. The things they did to her horrified her mind on nights when she couldn't sleep.

He nodded and didn't need to say anything. This was her time to talk.

"And the people who . . *did it* . .They're not around. I know they're not."

They'd hurt her. Her husband, ignorant as ever, put it down to whatever she told him and whatever the doctor said: nerves, exhaustion, women's troubles. They were all one to him. Recovery wasn't quick or easy. Her body was damaged and part of her heart as well. Twelve months after her visit she heard that the police had caught them, charged them and shut them up in prison. She thought of all the harm they'd done in that twelve months.

Eddie didn't say anything.

"Ask your own kind, Eddie. Ask your Catholic girls. They're not as good as you think they are. We can all get into trouble, you know? Whether we believe in your God or not."

She was bitter with him. She envied him his youth and his hope and the opportunities he still hadn't wasted. He kissed her on the cheek and then nibbled his way to her lips. She resisted straightaway, then weakened.

***

"You're back, then." His Mum never quite knew how to handle her son, whether to pamper him or use the rod every now and then. So, she barked occasionally. It didn't mean anything.

Eddie kissed her, made a cup of tea for everyone and sat down.

His Dad was listening to the radio. He had become entranced by jazz bands playing for him in his own home as he sat by the wireless. It made him think of the times in the trenches when he had only heard anger and hate and fear, bound in explosions and shrieks. Now he could push back in his armchair, as Rudy Vallee sang *Love is the Sweetest Thing* and he could look at his wife and son and think things could be much, much worse.

"New Britain speaking at the City Hall yesterday."

"Yes, you said."

New Britain? It had an old ring to it.

"They're getting jumpy."

"Why's that?"

"Mosley and his lot."

Eddie sipped his tea. "Is he coming to Sheffield?"

"Next week. He's up and down the country. Bringing trouble."

"Are you going to see him?"

"I'm bloody not! And you'd better not, either."

"I wasn't planning to."

Eddie never bothered with politics. They hadn't stopped the Great War, or halted the Depression.

"Good."

His Mum came in and sat down. They were silent for a time, letting the pulse of *Got the South in My Soul* buzz through them.

Eddie licked his lips. He was waiting. He was choosing a moment and a way into a conversation. When his Dad pulled himself to head to the toilet – a task that was *never* very quick – Eddie leaned in towards his Mum.

"What was the name of that family at number fourteen. There were two girls."

"The Taskers? Maggie and Millie and Patrick, I think."

Millie Tasker! Of course.

His Mum was sitting forward on the edge of her seat. Millie Tasker wasn't a named she wanted on her lips. There had been more than rumours about Millie.

"Why?"

"Just trying to remember."

"You don't want to be remembering girls like Millie Tasker, Eddie."

She was wrong. Millie was *exactly* who he wanted to remember.

Chapter Six

Wednesday morning came with a nip in the air, which seemed to compact the particles of dust in the smoke over the city, turning it from a wave into a bullet. When Eddie took a deep breath, he felt like he'd been shot.

He was back on the wagon with Bert, wrestling barrels into cellars again. The steamer had been fixed and they rolled it out onto the road, the machine wheezing and coughing much the same as Bert. Eddie felt his muscles tighten and tone as he worked and he needed that, having missed his gymnastics class for a couple of weeks. He tried to think about his act and rehearsals, but memories of Millie kept coming back to him, taking him down different roads in his mind.

Now he thought back, she had been a sweet little thing at school. She was a few years his junior, but in the confines of St. Vincent's school yard that was – literally – just a hop, skip and a jump away. Her father was alcoholic and her mother had died young. Her elder sister, Maggie, did what she could to keep the kids and a drunken father in food and clothes. It was a struggle and there were never any signs of happy endings.

Fortune was kind to Eddie, though. As they swung past the Red House pub for a delivery, Bert reckoned it was time for a spot of something to eat. Millie's house was just a stumble down the hill from there. Eddie couldn't pass up the opportunity.

"I'll be ten minutes," he told Bert, who was happy with his snap and a pint the landlord pulled for him on the quiet.

"Take your time."

Eddie eased down the slope, again feeling the peculiarity of being back here so soon. He had a sense of a snake slipping back into the skin it had shed. Without a generous sun, which was buried in grey clouds that were coloured by the smoke, the neighbourhood was barren. The houses had slumped into angular shapes, matching the tilt of the pavements and the warp of the roads. There was no symmetry here.

The noise of the schoolyard bullied its way into the neighbouring streets, where mothers who weren't working bled their fingers dry to make something of the slums they were stuck in. The men who weren't working sat and watched, or drifted out into the streets to see if there was anything on the horizon: not necessarily anything to do, just something to see. They saw Eddie and watched him. They knew him. He knew them. They resented his escape. His Dad deserved it. Eddie was just hanging on his coattails and there was something smug about him. Something superior.

Eddie grinned. Bloody right, he thought. I *am* superior, you bunch of no-hopers. He thought of Ada, then, and what she'd sacrificed to claw her way up and across town into a world where *middle-class* was starting to mean something.

"What do you want, Eddie?"

Millie's sister, Maggie, guarded the door. Her face was tired from effort. If it had once been pretty it had lost softness, its curves and every sort of energy. Eddie's grace and charms were never likely to work on her. She didn't believe in dreams.

"I was looking for Millie."

"Why?"

"I wanted to talk to her."

"She's at work. Why do you want to talk to her?"

Eddie smiled. "It's all right. My girlfriend's going fruit picking. Over Lincolnshire way. She knew Millie at school. Thought she might want to go."

"She's got a job at the Abbeydale."

Eddie knew the picture house well enough.

"Thanks," he said. Maggie watched him warily. She didn't trust him. She wasn't the first woman to look at him that way.

"How's your dad?"

"Better if your lot stopped making beer."

He thought of his own Dad, with his one leg and the pains he kept to himself most days, except when it was just too much so that it pushed its way through the nerves to the skin to show in his face. He'd been like that this morning. When that happened, Eddie walked him to work at Painted Fabrics. He didn't help, just walked alongside talking, passing the new buildings of Norton that were stretching the city limits. His Dad didn't say much.

"He doesn't have to drink it."

He turned and left, checking his watch and taking the opportunity to drop into St. Vincent's church, just to see who was around.

Some of the women of the parish were sorting flowers or dusting down the pews. They worked like an army, fueled with pride. St. Vincent's was a mission for them as much as the priests, who had fought their way over from Ireland by boat late last century. At the time, there was barely but one place to pray in all of the city for the Catholics. Now, new churches were being born and the women of the parish were the mothers.

Father Shaun Casey was passing by as Eddie entered. "Hello, Eddie."

"Hello, Father."

Father Shaun was a satisfied man. He indulged a little too much in the beer and the food that the women of the parish liked to feed him. That had given him a halo of fat that he wore at waist level, which he'd pat on a regular basis, to remind him of gluttony and – oddly – pride. He'd come out of dark times in Ireland. Just to be alive was a sign of success.

"What are you doing back over here? Come to serve on the altar?"

"Not today, thanks. Have you got a second, Father?"

"Of course, I have."

They settled on a pew at the back of Church, sitting in the soft, cool gloom.

"I was talking to Father Cleary about suicide."

Father Shaun took a breath. "Well, that's serious stuff."

"I know, I know. It's a mortal sin."

Father Shaun nodded. It hurt him to admit it, but those were the rules. "It is indeed."

"What if it's an accident?"

"They didn't mean to kill themselves?"

"That's right."

"Well, how do you know?"

"If they were doing it for another reason."

Father Shaun sucked his hips, pushing a hand at the thinning curls of hair on his head.

"It depends on what that other reason is, Eddie. Some things that you might think of are as serious as suicide."

"Abortion?"

Father Shaun clucked his tongue. People weren't usually as forward as this. There was a delicacy to be preserved. "That. . might be. . one example."

"Why?"

"Because it's murder, Eddie. It's life and death."

"Father Cleary said that the family was all we'd got left now. You know, the Church?"

"These are hard times. We need to give people direction. Things are very confused."

"I suppose."

Father Shaun lent back and looked up at where the glass window sucked light into the building then breathed it down the nave. Life had been simple when the priests first settled in Sheffield. They had a battle to fight, but it was straightforward. There was an antagonism to their presence and nowhere easy or obvious for them to settle. They'd sorted all that out – and then came the war and then came all the time after. The 1920's had been a muddier battleground than the Somme. The Church, it seemed, was under attack from every side and when the likes of Marie Stopes began popularizing the idea of contraception it felt as if the Church was having to navigate unchartered waters.

Father Shaun could see that Eddie was starting to wrestle with the ideas.

"Eddie, it's wrong. You have to understand that. You need to believe it. Suicide is . ." He couldn't help but think of visits after the fact to the girls and women who'd died with their babies at the abortionists. "It's a terrible thing. And abortion is a sin. It's a terrible sin."

"Do you get ex-communicated?"

Father Shaun nodded. "Yes. Yes, you do."

"But there are people who've had them – and they still go to Church."

Father Shaun's face reddened and Eddie didn't know if it was fury or shame.

"You can't know that, Eddie. You shouldn't say it if you can't know it."

Eddie breathed gently. There was the answer. If you look away so as not to see something, you can all pretend it didn't happen. One day Millie was gaining some weight and a week or so later – having been out of sight and out of mind – her diet had worked. She was back in the fold. There were ways and means. He needed to find some for Mary Riley. He needed to find out exactly what her story was.

***

The Abbeydale Picture House was quick with couples as Eddie slipped into the queue. The main feature showing was *Dick Turpin,* with Victor McLaglen bouncing around the screen. To get people in the mood the staff were all wearing eye masks, by the look of them left over from a long ago showing of *The Mark of Zorro*. Eddie appreciated the gesture. He paid his money and climbed up to his seat, adjusting his vision to the dark to skim the faces of the girls who were serving food. He could still see their eyes and that was enough.

As the first feature started, the girls began to fade away and Eddie ducked out of his seat, his head catching the film pouring the pictures out of the projector and painting it black on the screen. Two men booed at him and he scuttled away.

Millie was catching up with the other girls in the foyer when Eddie found her. She gasped a little when she saw him. Her sister had told her that Eddie had been looking.

"Hi there, Millie."

Her head bucked at the sound of her name and she looked over at Eddie, caught somewhere between hope and despair.

"Eddie Reynolds?"

When she was growing up, she had liked Eddie. He had confidence about him – and charm and good looks didn't hurt. Of course, he was older than she was and that always counted for something.

"You're looking well, Millie."

She looked more than her years, that was for sure.

"I thought I saw you going in. Are you by yourself?"

"Sort of," he said with a smile. "I wanted to talk to you."

"I'm working."

"When aren't you?"

"I'm working afternoons and evenings."

"Tomorrow lunchtime?"

She nodded, weakly. She had no idea why Eddie Reynolds wanted to talk to her, but she liked his face, his voice and the way his eyes seemed to see her in the way that no one had for so long she couldn't remember.

Eddie's smile flashed again as he saw the door open, Ada walking tight and fast to the ticket office. "I'll see you tomorrow." He smiled again. "The milk bar on Pinstone Street. One o' clock."

With that, he was gone again, shooting upstairs to sneak into the seat he had left near the back. The first feature had finished and the second was spooling.

The crowd was busy and growing. The birth of the *talkie* had been a cataclysm in entertainment, along with the arrival of the radio and now – in some homes, somewhere in Britain – television. Entertainment was starting to sweep the world and every one of those new forms was a threat to the variety shows that Eddie grew up with. They said the days of the stage were over. Eddie didn't believe that, but he knew the theatre was in for a fight.

Even so, he loved cinema. While it wasn't as immediate as the stage, he marveled at the way it could carry so many dreams in so short a time. The last two years had been a miracle for him. He had sat with Ada through the potboilers she loved: Gable and Harlow kicking up a storm in *Red Dust;* Harlow again in *Red Headed Woman* and any number that included Bette Davis, Marlene Dietrich, Miriam Hopkins, Mae West and more. Eddie sat by himself through the gangster movies and snarled along with Raft, Cagney and Robinson and then watched in awe as Hollywood rolled out *Frankenstein, Dracula*, and *King Kong*. The first two were gothic fun, but the last was incredible. He was spellbound by the vision and the artistry. Film, of course, was another great trick of the eye and he loved it all the more for that. His Mum said that there were worse ways to spend your time. His Dad was unimpressed, sticking to the radio and his papers and – every now and then – warning Eddie that the more the films strayed from the ethical code they'd agreed, the more likely the censors were to come back with big scissors and start making cuts.

A sound beside him made him twitch, followed by the feeling of fingers resting on his thigh.

"You made it."

"I always make it," Ada said simply.

"Who does he think you're out with?"

"The girls. It's always the girls on film night."

He turned quickly and kissed her.

"Is this going to be any good?" She was waspish.

"It'll be fun," said Eddie.

The music grew, the lights brightened and within minutes Dick Turpin was doing what Dick Turpin did best. Ada slumped in her seat. She let her mind replay the last picture they saw, where *The Song of Songs* put Marlene Dietrich at the heart of everything and she crushed Eddie's hand at intervals. Dietrich was the embodiment of everything you could want to be. Most importantly – and all that mattered to Ada – she triumphed in the end over all her trials. There was always hope. *Dick Turpin* was dull, but she didn't say so.

They emerged out of the cinema in the hazy half-light of late evening, catching a tram to Millhouses Park then walking through the evening as it stilled. The park was quietening, the lido now shut and the boats on the pond locked away.

"You didn't like it, did you?" He asked.

"No, it was fine."

"*Fine*? It was daft. Or exciting. Or fun. It wasn't *fine*. But it wasn't Marlene, was it?"

"She's wonderful, isn't she?" Ada was glowing and Eddie couldn't help but feel the heat. He reached for her hand, something he rarely did in public. She let him take it and she squeezed.

"Do you think life can be like that?"

"Not our life."

"Why not?"

"It's all an illusion."

"You've got to hope, haven't you?"

He was gentle with her. "I suppose so. And what do you hope for?"

She was quiet for a moment. "Do you really want to know?"

"Tell me."

Again, she paused. "I hope my husband dies."

There it was. She'd said it. Eddie wasn't surprised.

"But you don't want to kill him?"

"What?" She pulled away. "No! No!"

"What's the difference?"

"Everything! You should know that. What with your God and all your rules."

"I think with my God and all the rules it might just be the same."

"It's *not* the same."

They walked again.

"You're not shocked?"

"No. You don't love him, or you wouldn't be with me."

"Don't flatter yourself."

"I don't. I'm not the first, am I?" She reddened at that. "And I won't be the last. That's all right, Ada."

She was still flushed. "You think you're special, Eddie, don't you? Think you're better than everyone. Living in a nice house now up in Norton. You've got your own room. Well, that's not down to you!"

"No, you're right." He turned to look at her and he was sharp. "I got the house because my Dad got his leg blown off and the room because my brother died young." She dropped her head. He carried on. "Those things happened. I didn't make them happen. That was the past. It's the future I'm bothered about. I'm going to achieve something."

"On stage?"

"Yeah. I've got things lined up. I just need the chance and the right people to see me."

"You talk a lot about your act. I've never even seen it."

"I've got a show in Millhouses pretty soon. Come along. You might like it. The costume's good. It's tight."

The words made her twitch. Eddie had a wonderful body. She tingled every time she touched it. The skin was so young and fresh and the muscles were strong.

They were past the park now, reaching the junction where Abbeydale Road would take Ada down to her house and where Eddie would swing left to start his final journey home. At the junction stood *Abbey Lane Motor Services*, a coach company advertising destinations to tempt. Eddie and Ada took a look at the adverts.

"Where would you go?"

Ada read them out loud. Cornwall. Scotland. The Lake District and the Lakes. North Wales and the coast. London, with all its noise and fanfare.

"London." She spoke the word with some longing.

"You're a regular Dick Whittington."

She squeezed his hand and pulled his arm in towards her. "I love you, Eddie."

He could have said he loved her too. After all, she was married and he was Catholic so there was never much they would ever be able to do about it and the lie wouldn't hurt her.

He wasn't thinking about Ada, though.

He was thinking about Millie and wondering just how to steer a conversation towards abortion.

***

Things worked well for Eddie in the morning. Bert had managed to drop a full barrel of beer on his foot and was caterwauling round the brewery, only a little calmed when one of the managers pushed a pint of beer towards him.

"I'll take the wagon," said Eddie.

"You can't do it by yourself," said Len Jeavons, an irritating man in Eddie's mind, who made himself out to be the general manager, but was never much more than a second or third in command. He was full of sound and fury.

"It's a light run." Eddie smiled. "And I'm in better shape in my sleep than Bert is."

They looked over at Bert, slumped in chair, spilling beer over his chin. "Are you sure?"

"Course I am."

The steamer was out of action again. Eddie smiled as he readied the horses, feeding them a couple of apples his Mum had given him and watching their jaws work the food round their mouths. He stroked and whispered to them. It was a secret language. He wanted them to go fast. He needed some time for Millie.

The journey was uneventful other than the now daily curse at cars skidding by, handled by drivers who didn't know how to fly a dragon. Eddie made good time, enjoying the trip as it wheeled him through the city's industrial heartland then swung away into new estates that were forming in great clumps, new worlds created out of the old bringing a sense of optimism to the people who could afford to snap them up. The east of the city was still an industrial furnace, but neighbourhoods were beginning to sprout beyond, planted out with trees that did what they could to gobble the carbon dioxide that poured over them.

You could see the change in the roads too. The horse-drawn days were coming to an end and the trams, buses, vans and cars each bullied for supremacy, buoyed up by the glee of the younger generation to get behind the wheel. Eddie had to shout out more than once as an old lady or gent stepped blind into the road. One man born before the first car was built didn't hear the wheeze of a Morris 10 as it bore down on him and a minute later an old woman was almost swept up by a tram that crackled past, the shock making her wobble, as if the tram's electricity line was routing through her to earth.

Eddie worked efficiently, much quicker without Bert, though his muscles tightened at tipping so many barrels off the wagon into their new homes in the beer cellars. The sweat was starting to sting on his back by the time he had finished his morning round and he was glad to be gliding back down towards the brewery.

"Blood and sand, you're quick," said Jeavons, not sure if he was pleased or annoyed.

"I'll be back by two."

"You'd better be," he shouted.

Before Jeavons had turned back to the brewery, Eddie was already running down Ecclesall Road towards Pinstone Street, where he'd arranged to meet Millie. The Moor was busy as he chugged along. Eddie slowed a little as he pulled up the street, peering in the windows as he started to think about what to wear for his performance next month. He dressed well as a rule, but the Empire was more than a single step up from his Sunday best.

Eddie skipped between the slow crowds, tugging up towards the Peace Gardens on Pinstone Street, where the Town Hall was berthed like a ship in a harbour, and only easing up when *Marsden's Milk Bar* was in sight.

Millie was inside, looking trapped and frightened in a corner. The girls behind the counter –

five in all – were busy, but not too busy not to notice Eddie or give him a smile. He'd been known to tip them before and he was fun to talk to. He gave them a sense of hope that the world was bigger than these four walls and a lifetime of Ice Cream Soda.

Eddie didn't ask what Millie wanted. She would have spent too long wishing and not wanting to be too greedy.

He traded a few quick jokes with the girls as he` carried over a Melba Split and a Sundae, laying them before Millie's wide eyes as if he was Father Christmas.

"Take your pick, but do it quick, cos I'm hungry."

The Melba was too much to resist and she grabbed at it and then gobbled. She was pretty, but just a little too urgent for Eddie. When she was done, she looked up at him with guilt and worry. She owed him something now.

"How are you, Millie?"

"I'm all right."

"Things all right at home?"

"They're not bad."

She was lying, of course. Eddie wondered why he'd asked. Perhaps because, for all his thought of how he was going to approach the subject, he didn't know quite what to say.

He leaned back and looked at Millie as if she were part of his audience. Immediately, that created a distance between them and a space to work in. That established, he started to talk about old times at school, the people they knew and the things that they did. Millie laughed at his impersonation of some of the teachers in school. She was happy as he talked about the neighbourhood and the characters they came across, grotesques for the most part, but golden hearted in some cases, good for a laugh in others. Millie was soft now.

“Did you know Mary Riley?”

“Not well, but . . .”

“You heard?”

She nodded, not looking up now.

“I don’t think she killed herself on purpose, Millie.”

Millie’s mouth widened.

“I don’t think she meant to.”

“But, why---”

Even as she said it, an idea began to form about why Eddie might be asking. He watched her face and could see the confusion build. For a Catholic girl, the guilt was always just beneath the skin and she was waiting to be exposed. Even so, she couldn’t believe that Eddie could be so callous.

“You can’t always know, Millie.”

He was going to slow things down. He was going to make her confess.

“It’s terrible.”

“You’re right.” He paused to catch a glob of ice cream. “It’s a sin.”

Millie shrank down, just nibbling at her dessert. “I know.”

“Well, that’s what they say. The Church. The priests.” Again, he paused, taking his time to dab his food with his tongue, to catch each taste of sweetness clear and distinct. “But it’s easy for them, isn’t it?”

She nodded like a twitch.

Eddie carried on.

"It's easy to say what you should do and shouldn't do. It's easy to tell other people what they have to do. It's harder to live it, though, isn't it, Millie?"

She was starting to shake a little now, the hands holding her spoon trembling, so that the metal hit the table, making a drum rattle, drawing the attention of the girls behind the counter.

"They don't know anything, Eddie." She shook her head. "They don't know how it is."

He reached out his hand and laid it over hers, which was cold. Her body relaxed and the trembling stopped.

"You do what you have to, don't you?" He smiled at her and it was so kind a smile. "You do what you're told."

She nodded eagerly.

He squeezed her fingers gently. "Did *you* do what you were told, Millie?"

Millie's eyes started to water. She had a thin body and a frail appearance and now she seemed perfectly insubstantial. She wanted to scream but couldn't make any sound.

"I'm sorry, Millie." His hand was warm and his fingers were strong and his voice sounded kind. "I need to help the family. I need to find things out."

Tears had formed into drops in her eye. Eddie watched her. He squeezed a little firmer with his fingers.

"What do you want?" When she looked up at him, her face was absolutely empty.

"I just want a name, Millie. No-one'll know it was you who told me."

He felt her fingers tighten on his. He imagined that a whole part of her life was flashing by her again: the horror of pregnancy; the pain of abortion; and the never-ending emptiness that had followed afterwards, when whichever father it was had abandoned her. Then, the slow, everyday shame of pretending nothing had happened and going back to Church and lying to the priest every time she made her confession. For a second, he doubted himself. He wondered if he was losing his touch. If he hadn't expected Millie to pop out a name with a smile on her face, he had relied on the fact that she would tell him. Now, looking at her drooping head and sunken eyes he sensed he might have lost his audience.

"Betty Wilson." Eddie was going to say something, but waited. Millie wasn't done. This was her time in the confessional. "My sister arranged it all."

Eddie smoothed his thumb over her hand, looking over at the girls behind the counter.

"Same again, when you're ready."

Chapter Seven

"Ladies and gentlemen! Prepare to be amazed!"

Eddie shook his head, which – upside down – seemed all the more portentous.

Nancy, his stage assistant, lowered him down from the makeshift hoist he had rigged up in the church hall at Our Lady and St. Thomas's.

He stared at her and frowned. "You don't sound amazed yourself."

She shrugged. "I'm saving my voice."

"This is rehearsal, Nance. Do you think I should not do the stunt? Maybe we should just have a cup of tea and a bit of cake and talk about it."

"If you think that's better."

Nancy didn't get sarcasm. Irony was a world away from her. Eddie had chosen her because she was willing, had a loud voice – a bit of a bray, but one that carried over the stalls – and legs that looked fantastic in nylon. To be fair they looked even better *out* of nylon and maybe that was another reason Eddie had selected her. He had been somewhat compromised. More than once.

For her part, Nancy still imagined that the stage act was part of a courtship. While she and Eddie hadn't had sex for some time, she put that down to him wrestling with his conscience. He was a Catholic after all. She remembered that from the time she screamed *Jesus* when he had borrowed an "Indian Basket Trick" set up from a friend and he caught her with a blade. He had looked at her sternly and she made a mental note not to take the Lord's name in vain again.

Eddie was just angry that she'd underplayed the trick. He looked at her legs again. That helped a little. Nancy was very obvious in her appearance, one part flash and one part flesh. They both worked. Even when you're stuck upside down, centre-stage, you can cast an eye to the audience and watch the middle-aged men drooling at the bits of the body they can see and dreaming of the parts they can't.

"Try it again."

He had fixed a winch so that Nancy could link a hook into the back of the straitjacket he was wearing and hoist him. She was a buffer girl in the steel industry, used to hard work and heat. Eddie saw her muscles twitch as she pushed the wheel to raise him up.

"That all right?"

"Good enough. Ready to go again?"

"Ready."

She cleared her throat, which was stuck with smoke, dust and metal filings. The sound rattled in her chest and she spat on the floor with a force. "I won't do that on the night."

"Glad to hear it."

She coughed again.

"Ladies and gentlemen!" Her voice was big, her mouth wide and her teeth were still bright enough and all her own. "Prepare to be amazed!"

Eddie could feel the blood falling through his body down to his head, where it pooled, so that his face burned. His back was already wet with sweat and his fingers itched. Even so, he couldn't help smiling at the thought of Randolph Douglas thinking this up then passing it on to Houdini.

"Watch closely as the Incredible Eddie Reynolds tries to free himself before the burning rope he is hanging from snaps and he crashes to the ground!"

Today, the rope wasn't lit. This would be an act of imagining.

As Nancy ran through her introduction – word perfect this time – Eddie steadied himself, wriggling his shoulders ever so slightly. The lock was a cheat. He had the key in his mouth, yet even that required a touch of artistry, Nancy passing it to him in a kiss. She enjoyed that part of the trick the most. Beyond that, to free himself from the jacket was all down to his ability to work his body loose through a combination of flexibility and strength. And all of that was against the clock.

"Go!"

Nancy had Eddie's watch in her hand and her eyes flipped between its face and his. Eddie looked like a fish caught on a hook, wriggling for existence with all the urgency that life demanded. The movements entranced Nancy, though she couldn't say why. Eddie seemed to be fighting against the inevitable. Then – a miracle! - the jacket was loosening and while he continued to struggle it was clear now that he would succeed. He would be free.

As the jacket hit the floor, he put his arms out wide to accept the crowd's adulation.

"How quick?"

"Ninety seconds."

He sniffed. "I could be quicker."

"That's all right."

He slumped into a chair, massaging his right shoulder, which had picked up a little tear in the exercise. The pain niggled him. Nancy sat opposite.

"*All right*?"

"Well, you know what I mean?"

He *did* know. It was *all right.* Nothing more. Despite the effort and the pain in his arm, tonight it all just felt like a trick, which, of course, in part it was. It could be more than that. At its best, it could look fantastic. The crowd liked a spectacle.

"Did it look difficult?"

Nancy nodded. "Yeah. *Really.*"

And it *was* difficult, a brutal manipulation of his joints to unwrap the straitjacket and get the key from his mouth to his fingers to work the locks. One time, he nearly dislocated his shoulder in the struggle. Houdini had sometimes done as much on purpose. Eddie knew it was an option if things got tough. Two little tricks helped, though. The first was to make sure he took a big gulp of air before the straps were tightened. Once he was hoisted, he let out the air and that gave him some wriggling room against the locks. The second served much the same purpose, catching a few fingers of fabric as he was secured, then letting them go as he was lifted up. After that, it was pure effort and most times it hurt.

Nancy put her hand on his. "You can take me out if you want. *Song of Songs* is on at The Abbeydale."

"Seen it." His eyes were miles away.

"Are you all right, Eddie?"

He snapped out of it and looked right back at her.

"Where's the excitement, Nancy? Where's the thrill? They *know* I'm going to escape."

"But it looks great, Eddie. It's exciting. There'll be music playing if we're on at the Empire. That always gives me goosebumps."

He shook his head. "No, it's tame. Houdini hung fifty feet up in the air when he did it. What will it be at the Empire? Ten feet?"

"Nobody else is doing it."

"Because it's been done. There's no danger. There's no mystery."

"Mystery?"

"Yeah. Did you see Gene Dennis when she was in town?"

"Was she that mystic woman thing?"

"That's her. She was amazing. The audience couldn't believe it. They thought she was in touch with heaven and hell. It was like she'd ripped the cover back and could see right in."

"Is she a fake?"

"She's so good it doesn't matter. People want to believe. You've just got to give them something to believe in." He looked up at the hoist. "And this isn't it."

There was a pause.

"So, do you want to go out?" She put her hand on his knee. "Or do you want to stay here for a bit?"

***

He wanted to find Betty Wilson. Nancy had gone away, more or less happy with a kiss. Eddie looked at his watch and saw that time was ticking on.

***

The Crofts was tiring as the long day lengthened towards darkness. The bodies stuck in the tenement blocks had fought as far as they could, hanging on like babies who wanted to sleep, but wouldn't sleep, but wanted to. Here was a neighbourhood that had to believe that there was more to life than waking up early, working hard, coming home and – when it was soft and warm – falling asleep at the table, stumbling to bed, to wake up again the next day and start all over again. Faces hung in the doorways. They were looking for something better.

Maggie Tasker was waiting for something worse. She didn't quite know what it was until she saw Eddie. The face that could charm the pants off dozens of ladies just left her cold. All those people were sunk in the moment. Maggie was spending her life dealing with the aftermath.

"Hello, Maggie." Eddie was gentle, almost apologetic.

She put her body across the threshold. As Eddie came closer, it became clear exactly what she was protecting. Coming from behind her, clawing out onto the street, the drunken snores of her father landed like hand grenades. Maggie couldn't do anything to stop it, except maybe take a cushion to his face and hold it there until it was quiet, at last.

"You upset Millie."

"I'm sorry."

Eddie could see that her body was tense, making her muscles firm as a way of protecting herself. It wasn't just his looks that made her want to soften. There was a light in his eyes that might just be kindness, with no strings attached and that was worse than anything.

"She's been crying."

"She's had hard a time."

"You don't know *half* of it!" The words came at him like stones.

"No."

Again, the calm unnerved her. She wanted to be angry. She wanted to hit and hurt and hate and he just bent and rolled. Nothing touched him.

"What do you want?"

"Did you know Mary Riley?"

She tutted. "Everyone knows everyone, Eddie."

"Did you know her well?"

"No. She kept herself to herself."

"But there was a man at her house."

"I never saw him. Some people said they did."

Eddie paused. He was preparing himself – and Maggie too.

"She was pregnant."

Maggie's face fell.

Eddie had her now. She was his audience.

"She drank *Lysol*, Maggie. Imagine that." He waited for a couple of seconds. "Does it ring a bell?"

"What do you mean?"

"You know what I mean, Maggie. Millie."

"I don't know what you've heard . . ."

He had to admire her courage.

"I need to find Betty Wilson. I need to know if this was one of hers."

Maggie's face was tight. "Why would I know?"

Eddie looked at her full on. He was going to be hard with her. "It could have been Millie. It'll certainly somebody else. Someone's daughter. Someone's sister." The words landed and hurt. Maggie had carried guilt for every second since she'd found that Millie was pregnant. It was Maggie who made contact with Betty Wilson, Maggie who invited her round on one of those times when she knew her father would be washing his face in beer at the nearest pub.

The thoughts made her face set. Eddie was going to have to push her.

"What happened to the father?"

She laughed. "Him? Nothing. Nothing ever happens, does it? What *could* happen to him? They do what they want, Eddie and then when it gets a bit nasty, they tell you what to do, or else." She shook her head. "It's always the same, isn't it? The men have some fun and they tell the girls to deal with the problems What was Millie going to say?"

"They could have got married."

She laughed. Her eyes were rolling and Eddie couldn't help but step back.

"Married? You don't know anything, do you, Eddie? Not since you've moved away. You've forgotten our world. He was *already* married! But just like the rest of them he's got a good Catholic conscience. They take their rings off when they're getting down to business."

The words chilled him.

"I need to know where to find her, Maggie. For Mary. For Millie."

She nodded. "And for you, Eddie, I bet. For you."

He felt the guilt rip through him. When she came towards him it was all he could do to stand his ground. And when she leaned in, he felt his skin go cold. Then she whispered in his ear.

It was an address.

Chapter Eight

Maggie had given him a street name and a number. He had written it on a piece of paper which he was holding tight in his hand. Though it was a few years since Maggie and Millie had visited, Eddie guessed that it was unlikely Betty Wilson would have moved, unless the police had shipped her out of home and into prison.

He was in a positive mood, then, as he hopped off a tram that had carried him up City Road, even though it was late and the beginning of tipping out time for pubs.

The air was dirty as he stepped onto the pavement and the road seemed to groan along with him as they both climbed up towards the house he wanted. It was too late for children, the streets mostly quiet and contemplative, coughing with occasional bursts of energy in a consumptive wheeze as people spilled out of the pubs. The streetlamps had come on, but rather than shed light they mostly seemed only to blur the endless fine ash that floated in the air to catch in the mouth, lungs, clothes, hands and hair.

As he walked, Eddie noticed a couple of men watch him warily. This wasn't the safest place to be, but Eddie didn't have anything much to steal, he could run fast and he still carried that wonderful sense of immortality that has died by the age of thirty. He had a purpose and felt it was enough to keep him safe.

He knew the area well enough from his beer deliveries. Even so, the houses all bore an unrelenting sense of monotony and sameness. The only distinguishing features were the Sheffield hills, which rolled the streets up and down. After a short time, though, he picked up the one he wanted then worked his way along.

His knuckles rapped on the door. The sound blew away down the street like a warning cry. Two boys appeared out of nowhere, stuck in their perpetual cap and shorts, as if they could never change.

"Bit late for you, lads."

"Who are you?" Asked one. There was no fear in his eyes. School days and home nights had beaten all of that out of him.

"Who do you want?" The other.

"I'm looking for Betty Wilson."

"She's in the pub."

"Much obliged."

He magicked a coin out of the air and tossed it up high into the sky, to let them scramble and fight for it – or share it if they chose.

As he turned, he heard the coin land and tinkle as it rolled, the sound of their raised voices drowning the tune it played as they tore at each other to get it.

The pub was obvious enough. The Traveller's Rest was a big lump of a building, dropped in the heart of a few thousand households ready and willing to drink when they could.

There was a hush as he entered, mutters coming from dark corners of the room. The landlord looked uneasy. This wasn't one of Eddie's pubs. He was a stranger.

"We're just closing."

Eddie leaned on the bar and looked at the landlord straight on. "That's a shame."

There were whisperings behind him. This was the sort of place where bad things were imagined and then came to life the next day across the city.

"You live round here?"

That was the landlord's way of saying that Eddie didn't.

"Visiting friends." Eddie looked at the beer on tap and winced. "You want to get *Wards* in here, mate."

"Cheeky bastard," but he was smiling as he said it. "Here." He pulled him a half pint because of his bravado.

Eddie took a drink, chugging it round his cheeks before he swung a look round the bar to try to find Betty Wilson. The place was mostly empty now, the early shift workers having shuffled off to bed for the briefest bit of sleep. There was only one woman inside. Eddie caught sight of her positioned like a spider in her web in the dark corner of the room. She was sitting with two men who would have been about Eddie's age. Her sons, he guessed.

They left as a group. Eddie gave them a couple of minutes before draining his drink thanking the landlord and wandering out again.

The evening had grown cool now, unfriendly. The dark had crept in, pulling a blanket over things, which the streetlights could never quite penetrate. As Eddie watched, the group of three seemed to split, with Betty heading towards her house and the other two continuing on. Business to attend to, maybe. He doubted that they had their own house. That didn't matter for now. What mattered was that he had an opportunity and he didn't like to miss them. As the outline of their bodies sank into the black Eddie skipped up and tapped at the door.

"Who is it?"

The words came from a voice that was full of barbed wire and vinegar.

"I want to talk to you, Mrs. Wilson."

He used her surname to intrigue her. He was treating with her respect and respect was something that she hadn't known for so many years she could hardly recall it. She was more used to the sound of hope in a young girl's voice. She'd heard it a thousand times, with a string of women who had got into trouble and needed help. She was their salvation.

The door opened just a squeak. A sharp eye pointed out.

"Who are you?"

"I'd like to talk to you."

Eddie was always easy on the eye and his smile had a way of softening things. His fingers, though, held money and it was money that mattered.

"What do you want?"

By then, she had already opened the door and he was halfway in.

The house stank of decay and lost illusions, a disinfectant fog rolling like a low mist down the stairs, staining the bits of carpet. He wondered if this was where she had performed her operations. The carbolic stench suggested that every now and then she simply doused the walls as if with holy water, to make everything blessed and better again.

"I need your help." He put the money on the table in the living room, where the walls seemed to be caving in towards them, gasping for dry days and a respite from the damp.

Betty Wilson had a thin, sharp body, like a rose bush when the bloom had dropped. Come too close and it would prick you. The skin on her face was tight with smoking and chequered with lines of age and worry.

"*You* need help."

"Yeah. Makes a change, doesn't it?"

"I don't know what you mean."

Her eyes kept steady on the money.

"Yes, you do, Betty. I know what you do."

"My boys'll be back soon. They won't have you in here, spreading lies."

"They're not lies, Betty, are they? Girls come to you when they're pregnant and you give them a way out. Sometimes it works, sometimes it doesn't. The baby usually dies and sometimes the mother too."

"I've never been convicted of anything."

"And you're not denying anything."

"What do you want, fancy boy?"

She meant it as an insult. Eddie was quite pleased to be different from her.

He put his finger on the money on the table. Betty's eyes followed.

"Tell me about *Lysol*."

Betty laughed. He was treading into her realm now, becoming a boy who knew nothing about how the dirty world worked or the things women did and had to do.

"Very efficient."

"It kills things?"

"Stops them."

"Afterwards?"

"And before for some girls." She smiled again and her mouth was like a cave.

"Did you ever tell girls to use *Lysol* as a way of getting rid?"

She shook her head, but she wasn't saying *no*. She was dismissing him.

"You don't know anything, do you?" She had an acid smile, then wiped it clean. "I'm doing everyone a favour, son. There's no food to feed the babies we've got. What are you going to do with the new ones?"

Eddie hadn't come here to be lectured. "Did you ever speak to Mary Riley?"

Her eyes were sharpening. She imagined she was close to a trap. She just didn't quite know whether she was already in it.

"Name means nothing."

"She's dead. Disinfectant. She was pregnant. Does that sound right?"

She saw *that* trap clearly enough. "I never told no one nothing. It's lies."

"What happens if you take too much? Can it kill you?"

He eased his finger forward so that the money came closer to her. She studied it hard, images coming to her of fresh bread, cheese maybe, and certainly gin.

"Might do. Depends how much you take."

"Half a bottle?"

She laughed. There was no humour it. "That'll take care of *everything*."

"Have you heard of it happening?"

A smile formed on her lips that was mirthless. It opened up her mouth to show gums that were rotten and gaps where teeth should be.

"I've seen everything, love. I've seen disinfectant, all right. It can work and it can cause a cause a mess. And I've seen hat pins, crochet hooks and knitting needles and that's a risky business, I tell you. Then there's the gin bath, if that's your poison. And there's a hundred potions out there, everyone with a promise."

"Can it kill you?"

"That's what it does, love. It kills things."

For a moment there was a flicker of sympathy on Wilson's face. Not for Eddie, of course. He was just a source of money. It was sympathy for another woman whose life had twisted and fallen and would soon be forgotten, while the men staggered on regardless.

"Was it yours?" She asked.

He shook his head. "No," he said simply, knowing that in another time and place it could have been.

"Shame," she said, as close to poignant as she'd ever get. "Might have stood a chance. Not like all the bastards I see." She sniffed. "Runts. If they were animals the mother'd let the siblings kill 'em."

Eddie shuddered and pushed the money towards her.

"Spend it wisely," he said.

"I'll spend it quickly, love. That works better."

Night-time had become total as he stepped outside and the world was altogether unfriendly. The taste of burnt air caught him again in the back of the throat and lungs and disorientated him so that, just for a moment, he lost sense of where he was. He pushed forward anyway, trusting his luck as much as his judgement. As he moved, he wished he'd paid more attention to the shifts and bends of the streets as he'd done his rounds over the last couple of years.

The benefit of Sheffield, though, was that the seven hills often gave you a glimpse down into the valley, which was something to head for. He kicked forward, with a little more confidence, all of which he lost as he started to hear echoes of his own footsteps playing in loose harmony behind him.

He twisted his neck to try to see what or who was there, but everything was blurred. The darkness of the houses, dry-coated with soot, merged with the nightlight to make everything uncertain. He faced forward again, starting to run, his heels skidding as they hit the cobbles, pitching him forward so that he almost lost his balance.

Up ahead, he saw a turning and took it, only to find that it led him upwards and back into the knot of streets that had twisted together in the shape of arthritic fingers. The footsteps behind him were quickening. He guessed that Betty's boys imagined he had more money on him. He'd flashed some for their mum and he dressed smarter than anyone in this dark part of the city. There were no police here this late at night. If you were out on your own, you'd have to live with your decisions.

At the top of the road, Eddie shook left, which he hoped would start to take him down into the valley where the centre of town was better lit and busier. Again, his feet skittled on the cobbles, where someone had thrown their slops to make the surface slick. His left leg shot forward as his arms reached out instinctively to balance him, which meant that he went into a slide at first rather than a fall, until his right leg buckled and he tumbled forward, hitting the stones hard with his right hand and then with a shake at his shoulders, where he tried to balance himself.

Right behind he could hear the boys' footsteps hitting down like steam hammers.

He jerked himself up and forward and then deep down into one of the many gennels that tied street to street. The boys were just thirty yards behind him, happier in hunting than Eddie was in fleeing. They were following the sound of his flight and it was like a beacon for them – until they turned into the gennel.

For a few yards more, they ran, tearing along the path in pack-dog mentality. Then they slowed, to listen.

There was silence.

Either side of them, the houses were stacked in slapdash fashion, leaning over them to make the darkness darker. Up ahead was blind. Behind them the streetlight had given up hope of reaching them and was letting them go.

They could hear nothing and see nothing. Eddie had disappeared.

They edged forward slowly, but less surely. This was still their time and their turf, but things had happened in the dark over the years in Sheffield. Their mother had told them about the gangs that had ruled and roamed here and beaten men bloody and blue for the contents of their wallet, or no reason at all. She spoke of them like bogeymen. They were some years gone now: just enough to have become legend.

A sight sparked in front of them, then a sound almost on top of it, the sound of a match taking flame. The match blew out and the image was replaced by a tiny gold circle of a cigarette tip, winking in the black. The light drew their eyes to hide the face behind it.

Footsteps started, gentle and steady, as if Fred Astaire were tapping out a light routine. The smell of clean cigarette smoke cut through the industrial air to tickle their noses, just as a body appeared.

"Hey, mate!"

The body stopped.

"You seen a bloke run past you?"

The body had a head and it nodded.

"He was quick, fellas. If you want to catch him, you'd better run."

Which they did. They belted their legs into a sprint and the noise ricocheted off the walls of gennel to bounce the sound into a drum roll.

Eddie took a suck on the cigarette, held it close to his heart and then let it blow out slowly. Hiding in plain sight was something he'd learned from Harry Houdini. He felt as if he had just honoured him. The thought made him happy. He smiled.

Chapter Nine

Painted Fabrics was the brainchild of Annie Bindon Carter. She'd gone to Sheffield to study art and when the War came, she'd volunteered to help out in one of the hospitals that tended the soldiers. She watched the procession of young men arrive, bloodied and battered and far too often butchered – hands, arms and legs missing. The experience jolted something in her artistic mind and she had a vision. She tied a paint brush to an amputee's stump to see if they could paint.

And they could.

Five years later, she bullied her way to grabbing hold of an old army camp – close by to where Eddie now lived – where she created Painted Fabrics, a sprawl of workshops for the outcast ex-servicemen with critical injuries and there they made screen prints, block prints, stencils and more. Annie was on a roll, roping her sister and friends into the business to create designs which the men could make.

She never rested or once let any one of the men in the workshops think that this was a charity. The designs were sharp. The artwork was high-end quality. Annie took them across country, pitching hard to bludgeon people into buying. Princess Mary took up the role as patron and before long, *Claridges* were carrying items made by Eddie's Dad and his comrades. Annie bustled on as she pulled together groups to charge up and down the land selling their wares at exhibitions and shows. She pumped the hand of anybody with influence that she knew and they listened, they saw the products, saw they were good and they bought them. Annie was selling quality.

Not that you'd guess as much as you came closer to the huddle of prefabricated huts that housed the men. They were lucky to be alive and they were glad. They never discussed the fact, focusing their energy on getting up each morning, putting on white shirt with starched collar and tie, combing their hair straight then putting on their overalls when they came to the workshops. They got their heads down and worked hard, breaking out of the huts every now and then to help paint the outside walls a regular white, or tidy up the flower beds that were tucked between buildings. They were proud people.

"Working on anything new?" Eddie asked, walking alongside his Dad to work because it was of those days where the pain showed in his eyes every time he moved.

"A couple of things. Your mother'll like them. They're bold."

He'd developed an understanding of art through his work. It empowered him. He would never forget coming across – for the first, glorious time – the inspiration for designs from the likes of Dufy, Matisse and, from them, Monet, Pissarro and more.

It was just a fortnight until Princess Mary and the Duke were due in the city to visit. The workshops buzzed with anticipation. One of Dad's *Pals* who had survived the fighting, but turned down the chance to join him at Painted Fabrics, called it a farce. He was tipping his hat in with the Communists, he said.

"Nonsense," his Dad said. "You get Royalty and you get pictures. You get pictures, you get noticed. You get noticed, you get money. That's how the world works."

"I don't know what Karl Marx would say about that!"

"No you don't, do you? Because you haven't read his books and if you had, you wouldn't understand them. *This* matters," he said with absolute certainty.

He had fallen in love with colour, design, shape and form. He knew he was ignorant and he loved the fact, because every day made him a little less so. Just last year, Eddie had bought him a book on Paul Cezanne. His eyes had dampened with tears. He didn't mind crying in front of his son. If you can lose a leg and live on, then letting yourself weep and be seen doing it was never going to be a hardship.

"What about you, Eddie? Is the brewery ok? Is it what you want?"

"It's money, Dad."

"But what do you *want*?"

"You know what I want."

"You want to be on stage and have the audience paying through the nose to see you, then cheering every move you make."

Eddie smiled. "That's pretty much it."

His Dad nodded, taking from Eddie the packed lunch Mum had made.

"I'll be there. I'll be watching." He patted Eddie on the shoulder. "I'll be cheering."

***

The thought stayed with Eddie as he tugged his way up the steady incline of Millhouses Lane, heading for the garden fete that was being held there, heralded by the energetic booms of brass from the police band, great waves of tuba rolling out from the back garden to the front. The trumpets followed them out, playing sweet and tight as if they were every one of them rising angels.

The grounds of the host house were busy and the spirits were good. The adults were loosening up, helped by the punch they were sipping. The children loved it from the moment their feet touched the lazy grass of the long lawn.

Eddie, though, was here on business. His gym club had agreed to put on a show. Though he had missed some rehearsals recently - practicing his act - the group had drilled a number of routines so perfectly that they could roll them out when occasion called. The only thing that worried Eddie were his knee and his shoulder. The latter was stiff and Eddie needed to play a key role as a base position in a human pyramid.

The pyramid was Eddie's idea. As soon as he heard about the invitation, he knew what to do. You never turn down an opportunity: no matter how few are in the audience or how small the fee, the chance to perform was always a blessing because every second in the spotlight made you sharper to your mistakes, made you wiser to what the audience wanted and made you confident. And you made people remember you. He learned that from Professor de Lyle.

Eddie said to be bold and go big. "Let's do the pyramid."

The naysayers in the group didn't have enough of his confidence to challenge him.

He was loosening up as he drifted over to the police band, which had paused for a cup of tea and a cake. Constable Dougie Mathers was slapping jam on top of cream to make his own little pyramid on one of Mrs. Denby's scones.

"Eddie!"

Eddie and Dougie had spent time at St. Vincent's together, in school during the day then in the social club in the evening.

"Hello, Dougie. You're sounding good."

Dougie had his trumpet laid in his lap as he bit so heavily into the scone that the cream surged up to give him a white moustache, covering his now-hidden black one.

"Thanks. Are you up soon?"

"Ten minutes or so."

"Good luck."

"Won't need it."

Dougie laughed. That was what Eddie had always said, when they were playing darts, dominoes, snooker, or cribbage. Eddie was the most competitive person he'd ever met. Eddie sat down beside Dougie, positioning himself just inside the lip of a marquee awning, looking out onto the crowd that busied back and forth. Without the sonorous boom of the band, the sound of the energy released in talk sprung back and forwards across the lawns.

"Where are you stationed now, Dougie?"

"Darnall way. Why?"

Eddie chewed his lip. "Do you know the boys who work round our old patch?"

"Round St. Vincents? Course I do?" Dougie put down his plate. "Why?"

"There was a woman . . died of poisoning."

"Killed herself. Mary Riley."

"Died of poisoning."

"What's the difference?"

Eddie didn't look at Dougie. He imagined he was staring into the eyes of the priests he had talked to and by implication, God. "Intent."

Dougie didn't trouble himself much with detail. His view of the world was shaped by the colour of the city: black, white and intermediate shades of grey.

"You mean she didn't mean to?"

"Maybe. Did they think of that?"

Dougie carried on chomping. These were his moments of relaxation. Unlike Eddie, Dougie was already married and trailing three little ones behind him. What with that and the job, moments of peace and quiet were hard to come by.

"They will have done."

"But they said it's suicide."

"So I heard."

"Where was the note?"

Dougie pulled a face. "What note?"

"Exactly, Dougie. What note? Where's the suicide note?"

Dougie laughed. "You've been reading too many books, Eddie. I've seen lots of suicides where there's no note." He laughed. "Half of the people couldn't write!"

Eddie chewed his lip. He wasn't going to give up.

"There was a man, they tell me."

"There's always a man, Eddie. To be fair, it's usually you."

Eddie laughed. "I just wondered if anyone had heard anything, or said anything. You know, who he was."

Dougie had picked up his plate again. He was on again in five minutes, which only left so much time to indulge. "I'll ask the boys in the band."

"Thanks. And – hey," he pointed at the trumpet, "good luck with your next set."

"Ha, ha! We *will* need it!"

By then, Eddie was already moving, smoothing his way across the grass, viewing the bodies in front of him as he viewed every audience, seeing them all and focusing on one.

She was standing just adrift from a small group of friends and relatives of the children in a girls' dancing troupe, who were parroting a routine with a mathematical sense of rhythm. Every foot was in the right place, but not always quite at the right time or the same time. They knew the shape, just not the flow.

"I've never seen anything in my life as beautiful as you are."

Ada turned and smiled at Eddie, full and happy. "*Grand Hotel?*"

She was in her element, here in Millhouses, where the money was green and real, what the Americans would call *old* money. Ada was as pleased to look at the house behind them, stretching up to all of its four-storey height, as the show before her. The show would be over soon. The house remained. Bricks and mortar, she once told Eddie, were better than diamonds. Change was in the air, she said: a chance to grab something before it passed you by. The old orders were struggling with the new world, as if they had never quite come to terms with the twentieth century. Twenty years ago, this house may have had half a dozen servants. Now it could only muster two, working regular hours and living out.

As if she sensed the same, the lady of the house lost her concentration, dropping a glass, the flute landing on a garden feature where it smashed into a thousand pieces. The sound caught everyone's ear, the sound of chaos and decay. A maid came to pick up the pieces, snagging her finger on a shard that burst the skin open and popped the blood. She glared at the glass, then over at *her ladyship*.

Eddie stood close to Ada, so that their arms touched. For a second, he thought of Louisa, who had started her trip over to Lincolnshire that morning. She would have unpacked by now and set up with some confederate bunch of girls and mothers to work the fields for four weeks, snagging her fingers every five minutes. She had soft hands. They would heal, but they would scar.

"Are you nervous?"

"I'm excited."

"Isn't it dangerous?" She squeezed his arm.

"That's why I'm excited."

He left her then, joining his troupe as they fell into costume and started to loosen up, waiting for the announcement that would tell the crowd to hush and hold their breath.

"You ready, Eddie?" The leader of the group was sharp, tense.

"I'm always ready."

A loud voice boomed across the crowd, introducing the gymnasts and asking for applause. The clapping was steady, accompanied by shrieks from the boys and girls, who guessed that they were about to see something magical. Then it began, a shift of limbs that was shapeless at first, until a pattern started to form, figures now flipping upwards into the air as a building of bodies became flesh in front of them.

Within the frame itself, muscles tightened and chests puffed with desperate clutches of air into the lungs as the effort demanded. Eddie felt his shoulder rip with pain as it supported one, then two, then three and finally four bodies above him. He smoothed his foot forward to ease the pressure on his knee, which was starting to burn.

The frame wobbled. His hands gripped to hold on. Everything was fluid for a moment with collapse as likely as anything.

Then it was done. The boy on top of the pyramid lifted his arms. The crowd roared.

When they were finished, Eddie walked back towards Ada, who was still clapping and holding a glass of lemonade for him. She ran her fingers along his bare arm and then smoothed a few drops of sweat from his brow.

If she had been preparing a speech, she never got a chance to deliver it.

"Eddie Reynolds?"

The voice came from behind him with a sense of heaviness about it. Eddie turned to see a fat frame barge into the marquee, a big body carrying a little pin head. He was wearing the band uniform.

"That's me."

"Pete Crowther." He stuck out a hand and for all Eddie's exertions, Pete's fingers were wetter. "Dougie Mather mentioned you."

Eddie didn't know Crowther's name, but he knew the type. When the police had beefed up their numbers to fill a Flying Squad, they had appealed to people happy to work within the margins of the law. That had led to blind eyes in every direction so that by the end of the last decade the local force was carrying officers who had not so much blurred the lines of the law as erased them. There was a reckoning, then then a bounty of suspensions and dismissals. Some survived who shouldn't have. Pete Crowther had the look of one of them.

"Mary Riley?"

"You know something?"

Crowther shrugged, not wanting to give anything away. "You were asking about her."

"I was asking for a friend. Was there a note?"

Crowther watched Eddie cautiously. The kid was cocky, he thought. He was asking *him* questions, knowing it should be the other way round.

"We didn't find one."

"What about what she used? It was disinfectant, wasn't it?"

"Who told you that?"

"The friend knows Mary's Mum."

Crowther sniffed. "Yeah, it was disinfectant."

"Lysol?"

Crowther pulled a face. "I don't remember, to be honest, son. Does it matter?"

"It might do. I heard there was a man."

Eddie had a way of wearing people down. Crowther had to smile.

"You ever thought of joining the force?"

"No. What about the man?"

Crowther was cautious. He didn't trust Eddie. "We're looking for him. Are you?"

"Who is he?"

Crowther chewed his lip. "The name's Billy McGloin."

Eddie sucked in a breath of air. He had a name. Crowther grunted and withdrew.

"What is it with Mary Riley?" Ada was by his side again. "Did you know her? I mean-"

"You mean, did I *know* her?" He was smiling, so she joined him. "No, I didn't. Now, let's get out of here."

They skipped out of the garden with the sounds of celebration just starting to wane, then threaded a way along to Ecclesall Woods, which was soft, almost opaque in the skewed evening light. J.G. Graves – one of Sheffield's greatest benefactors – had bound the three pieces of woodland together in the last decade to give over to the people. For the majority of city folk, it was an undiscovered gem, but for the cognoscenti it was heaven itself. Eddie knew where each path threaded, where they knotted and where gaps swelled between them. He was pulling Ada forward.

"Watch my skirt."

Ada was still checking her step and watching for thorn or bramble when Eddie caught her and kissed her. He pulled her into him and let his lips slip from her neck to her ear and her cheek and then firm and strong on her mouth.

"I'm watching it," he said as he slipped his hand down to where the hem brushed over her stockinged thighs, snicking a thumb under the fabric and tricking its way upward.

“You’re crazy, Eddie.”

But she didn’t stop him. She couldn’t.

Chapter Ten

Father Casey lined up his shot precisely. He wasn't exactly smug about his snooker skills. That would probably be a sin. He was happy to say that they gave him pleasure. He turned the situation into an occasion of thanks to God.

All of that was forgotten for the moment, as he blew chalk dust off the tip of his cue and bent down to line up the white with the black. He almost chuckled at the irony for a man in his profession. Then he checked himself and remembered how he would need to act when he won: modest celebration; no sort of gloating. He took a breath to steady himself.

"I don't think it was suicide."

Eddie's words tumbled across the baize like spiders. It was the conclusion of Eddie's conversation with Father Casey that evening, built around the gaps between shots as Father Casey played his game.

Father Casey pulled himself back. He stood for a second. "She killed herself, Eddie."

"She didn't mean to."

"Do you know that?"

"I think so."

Behind them, Friday night carried on as normal. Local "indoor leagues" built to a climax through the weeks, with every sort of sport and game competing for your attention. Father Casey's team-mate stood off to one side, watching anxiously and wondering why the priest hadn't made his shot to win the game.

"You need to know *why* she drank the poison, Eddie. And when you know that you need to ask yourself a question of whether it makes that much of a difference."

Father Casey *knew*, Eddie realised. He knew she was pregnant. And he believed that killing a baby was as bad as killing herself. Eddie, himself, didn't quite know why. His family, friends and the people at church weren't too big on unpicking the details. They just knew the rules.

"Life is the most precious gift, Eddie. We give thanks for it. We have to protect it at all costs. These things are within *our* control, when so many other things in the world today, sadly, aren't." He shook his head. The world was unravelling around him, it seemed and he was clinging on to what he could.

Father Casey was calm again as he leaned back over the table, steadying himself.

Eddie was grasping at straws. "What if she *had* to do it? What if someone made her?"

He wanted to know about Billy McGloin. The police did too. What was his story? Eddie couldn't believe that things weren't connected.

"It's too late, Eddie."

Father Casey snapped his arm from the elbow, with just a little bit of anger, which made the white ball sing as it struck. The black ball hit the pocket hard and rattled like a last breath, before sinking. Father Casey wasn't happy with himself. He'd avoided pride and substituted it for wrath.

His team-mate didn't mind, hollering.

Father Casey turned to look at Eddie.

"If you want to do something for her, Eddie, then pray for her. Pray for her soul."

Eddie nodded. That hadn't occurred to him. "Have you ever heard of Billy McGloin?"

Eddie was watching the priest's face as he spoke the name. The features were still.

"I don't recognise the name."

So, who was he?

***

He carried the thought outside, where rain was starting to spit, licking the grime off the walls and the floor, to build it into dirtballs that would roll down the hills. He thought of what the priest had said and knew it made sense. He could have taken it to heart and taken it home with him. Instead, he was skipping towards Mary Riley's house. It was too close to pass by, without just peeking.

The street was quiet as he came to it, the streetlight black from a little act of vandalism or poor repair. The two were interchangeable.

Eddie smuggled himself up to the door. He took a look at the lock.

Escapology was an act of illusion. The illusion was that you were a magician. The art was only to let the audience see what was important to them. So, the key that you had in your mouth, or up your sleeve, was a mystery to them. Eddie had been picking locks since he first watched Houdini wow the crowd in Sheffield. He spent hours practicing, till the skin on his fingers went raw, blistered and then toughened. This lock – a cheap product on a cheap door in a cheap house – presented no problems. He was quickly inside.

Already, the house was starting to smell of its emptiness. The absence of anyone to clean or sweep let the damp dig in and settle.

Without light in the house and only the smudge of dusk to guide him Eddie edged his way along, uneasy about what he would find or feel as his fingers smoothed along the walls, which were wet and lumpy. Having lived in the neighbourhood long enough, he knew the make-up of the houses. They had been dumped down with lazy brickwork to a dull design that never varied. He knew the shape by heart: the place of the parlour and the kitchen, which was where he was heading.

Some light crept in through the kitchen window and allowed him to find his way to a small pantry space. He let his hands smooth over the objects he found until he happened on a box of matches. The damp had started to eat into the box, making it soft. The first two sticks he tried he only decapitated as the heads fell off limply.

The third was a charm with the match flashing images of the kitchen to Eddie in waves.

Tidiness was all that Eddie could see - impression of someone who had tried to make a pattern in a small space, in order to make the outside world and every part of it a little more logical.

As he used his first match to light his second, he looked into the pantry to see everything as it should be. Mary Riley was a thorough, organised woman. Eddie remembered Stan commenting on the fact. Tinned food together on one shelf; sauces next; tea, cocoa and *Ovaltine* alongside; one shelf down were the health products, with a slew of items to cover every ailment: *Beecham's Powders* for a cold, self-evident *Andrew's Liver Salts*, *Yeast-Vite* for a whole host of problems and *Dr Cassell's Tablets* for everything else. Mary was one of those people who had a remedy for every situation and if they cost a little it was a lot less than Doctor Gilmartin, however good and kind he was. Eddie let that thought sink in as he looked to the bottom of the pantry, where the cleaning products were. There was a row of items and no obvious gap. He leaned in to look closer and saw an opened bottle of disinfectant sitting in the middle of the line. It wasn't *Lysol* and the question of whether it was half-full or half-empty was unresolved.

Eddie twisted round to study the kitchen, but the dark gave nothing away. He blew up two matches together to try to penetrate the gloom. The light bounced off glass in the corner. He stepped closer and the match licked up the grim blackness to make things visible. Standing away from the pantry on the windowsill was a single bottle. The name *Lysol* made itself proud in the heart of the glass.

Eddie couldn't help but think it was a strange place for the bottle to be. On the floor wouldn't have surprised him, as he imagined convulsions kicking in. Or back on the shelf would reflect Mary's sense of order. The windowsill was not in place, but not abandoned: just out of the away. As he reached out, he noticed, too, that the cap had been replaced. He unscrewed the top and didn't need to sniff. The odour came out of the bottle like a bad genie trying to find a host. The bottle was two thirds gone. That was a lot.

For a second, he simply stood there, trying to imagine how the moments must feel with your hand wrapped around a bottle of liquid as toxic as this: terrified to jump into the unknown; terrified to stay still.

Just then, the fact and reality of Mary's death came crawling all over him. He shuddered, his body trying to shake off the thoughts that followed that first imagining. He turned himself round and pushed out of the kitchen, taking a peek into a dark and dank front parlour, which was sunk in permanent damp. The room was bare and Eddie left it, picking his way upstairs, sensitive to the creaks of pain that each footstep squeezed out of the warped wood.

If anything, upstairs was a little grimmer than downstairs, the water sucking its way in through the roof then working down the walls, so that they had started an inevitable crumble into collapse. Mary had done what she could to make her room habitable, but it was a battle. There was a crucifix on the wall and a few drips of family photographs perched on top of a sideboard. The pictures gave up some of their stories simply. He guessed the couple standing elegant and upright were her parents. He imagined the older woman, who had not yet made any sense of the twentieth century, was a grandma. Then there was a young man and that was the picture that intrigued Eddie. He was smiling and his eyes had a sense of both fun and hope. Was this Billy McGloin?

He didn't know and he didn't waste time wondering, though he did lift the picture off the sideboard to tuck into his pocket. He moved now back to Mary's bed, where the sheets were neatly folded. There was an old bedside cabinet to the left of the bed. Eddie opened the drawer gingerly, to find a bible, with a bookmark to remind Mary of where she was up to. Eddie couldn't help but open it to see if there was a miraculous clue for him to find. The pages opened to the *Book of Psalms*, which Eddie imagined that Mary had returned to for comfort, night after night. The words spilled out before him with the sort of terrible beauty that made them hard to put down.

In the cabinet beneath the drawer were a few more everyday oddments; a pristine copy of *Police at the Funeral*, by Margery Allingham; some hand cream; a couple of handkerchiefs and an address book.

Eddie lifted the latter and flipped through the pages, which were mostly blank, though something caught Eddie's eye. He flicked back to confirm that there were two sets of handwriting in the book. For the most part, the names and addresses were formed in a neat and tidy hand. There were a few, though, which were a bit rougher. Was that Billy? He couldn't be sure and gently laid it down again, moving down the corridor to the second bedroom. This was barer still, but the bed was made. There were signs, too, of some sort of life. A sweet wrapper had made its way under the bed, possibly out of Mary's eyeline. There was a rug, too, by the side of the bed and it had some pattern of wear that had come from hard, heavy boots. Eddie was puzzled and he wondered if Billy had been a lodger rather than a lover, or at least a lodger at first.

His thoughts were distracted by sounds he could hear outside then just as he started to make sense of them he suddenly realised that someone had entered the house.

The footsteps were firm and unambiguous. They were confident and heavy, the sound of heel on floorboard gave the sharp impression of a stick hitting flat on a snare drum. The boom echoed down the thin passageway into the kitchen and seemed to surround Eddie.

He eased out onto the landing to peer down, seeing the edge of a shoulder as it swung into the parlour. Eddie waited and listened, not sure this time if he could as easily sneak away as he had done at Ada's. Soon, though, his doubt gave way to intrigue. He could hear heavy sounds of a chest heaving fast as it pulled and grabbed at things in the parlour, a low, long list of profanities slipping out and poisoning the air.

He took the opportunity, taking off his shoes to squeeze to the side of each stair step, so that the wood barely murmured. The front door was ahead of him, the parlour behind. He had to be calm as he pushed forward, pulled the door open and burst out.

Even as he skidded away, there was a side of him that wanted to stay and confront Billy McGloin, so while his body wound him through the gennels and passageways that tied the neighbourhood together, he found himself circling back to Mary Riley's house. He took steady and gentle steps, watching the door all the time. It was shut now and he was waiting for it to burst open like some deux es machina.

"What're you doing?"

The voice came from behind and caught him sharp.

He twisted round to see the wiry frame of the young boy with the cigarette cards. Peter was ducked into the shadows on the other side of the street. Eddie walked over towards him.

"Taking a walk. How's the collection coming?"

The boy pulled a face. "Not got any more recently."

"Did you get some from the man who was in the house here?"

The boy nodded. "A few."

Eddie squeezed the photograph out of his pocket.

"Is that the man who lived there?"

The boy studied.

"I think so."

Eddie smiled.

"I'll keep a look out for your cards."

Peter's face became happy for a moment, but the moment didn't last. Eddie was puzzled as he stared at it and then saw that the line of Peter's eyes was going beyond him. Eddie twisted round. The figure of a police constable had swung into view and Eddie decided that this wasn't the time to hang around. He would come back for Billy another day.

***

The house was quiet when Eddie got home and he guessed that Mum and Dad had both gone to bed.

"Eddie."

He was wrong.

The parlour seemed darker than usual, as if the late night had sucked a little more light out of the lamp that hung above Dad's head. The paper was rested on the arm of the chair so that it looked like Dad might have been sleeping, or dozing at least. Eddie wondered what dreams appeared to men like that, who had been soldiers, fighting at the business end of the battle. He never asked. His Dad didn't say.

"Hi, Dad. How's the cricket gone?"

He was trying an old-fashioned game of deflection and it worked for a moment.

"Bloody rubbish. We haven't got to three hundred and we're five down. Leyland's digging us out of a hole, thank God. It takes a Yorkshireman, doesn't it?"

Eddie had never shared his Dad's love of cricket, but he understood it well enough. It was warfare played honorably, for the most part. There was order to it.

"Sit down, will you?" His Dad's tone was serious. Eddie sat down. "What's going on, son?"

"It's something I'm doing for Stan Kitteridge."

"Good friend to have."

"That's right."

"And?"

And so Eddie told him what he was doing and what he knew. What he was doing didn't seem that much when he said it and what he knew seemed like nothing at all. When he'd started telling his tale, he imagined that he would close it with a statement. Instead, he had a question.

"How come getting rid of a baby is as bad as killing yourself?"

"They're the rules, Eddie."

"Oh, come on, Dad."

"We need rules, Eddie. Haven't you seen? Things are a mess. The war to end all wars, they said. It wasn't. It didn't. We need something else."

"How does that tie in with not having a baby?"

"It's faith, Eddie. And family. That's what we've got left. They can't take that from us. Cromwell sent his men to beat us back in the homeland and they battered us all right. But he didn't beat us. He didn't take our faith. So, we can't give it away."

"I don't think she gave it away, Dad. I don't think she had a choice. I think someone made her."

"And you're going to find him when the police can't?"

Eddie nodded. "Yeah. That's exactly what I'm going to do."

He was stubborn, pig-headed and arrogant.

His Dad couldn't have been prouder of him.

Chapter Eleven

Eddie put a Saturday morning work shift behind him, heading across town to the Corporation Fair Ground to meet his mum for the Sheffield Annual Dog Show. As he walked, thoughts of Louisa's letter got stuck in the teeth of his mind. The detail was factual and fairly humdrum. Louisa was no Faulkner or Fitzgerald. Her prose was tidy and steady. Perhaps she was Hemingway. The detail told Eddie of the journey in a day-to-day manner, then the arrival, setting up camp, meeting the girls, going out to work, eating, bathing, sleeping, waking again. It was utterly mundane and it choked Eddie for a moment.

As he came close to the showground he was caught up in the crowds that were starting to thicken. Eddie sank into the throng, carried away by a sense of weekend wellbeing. Inside the Fair Ground, the noise of the humans – boisterously chattering and catching up on weeks gone by – battled with the woof, howl, bark and whine of all the dogs collected there. Big money was on offer with over a thousand dogs on show.

Mum loved dogs. They had one when she was young. Percy.

"It's an odd name," Dad had said.

"He was an odd dog," she replied.

Eddie and his Mum had arranged a place to meet and Eddie managed to smooth his way through gaps in the crowd to get there early. He was almost always early. Precision mattered to him. Mum was almost always late. He didn't mind.

"Eddie!" The sound of her voice was warm. He gave her a quick kiss on the cheek.

"Dad didn't fancy it?"

"Not his sort of thing."

Eddie nodded, knowing that despite everything, his Dad had established – or acknowledged – the limits on his world. This was just too much to manage.

"I suppose he'll be getting his reports on the cricket."

"That's right. Let's have an ice cream." She didn't want to talk about it.

Eddie bought two cones then they found a spot to watch the proceedings, cheering each category, noting which breeds they liked and which they didn't, marveling at the variety on show, from Pomeranian to Pekingese and every sort of Spaniel to Samoyed.

The show built to a crescendo and Eddie noticed how people finally started to tire of clapping and cheering. Timing and knowing how much was too much was a key to the art of performance. Here, the activity was overwhelming, wearing the kids in the crowd down from feverish excitement to exhaustion. When they started to whine, Eddie began to fidget.

"Shall we get off?" He suggested to his Mum and she nodded.

"Where to?"

"I need a new shirt for the show at the Empire."

"We can try the market."

His Mum smiled as they threaded their way out, heading through town to the "rag and tag" market, which was just starting to slow down after a typical busy day of bustle and haggle. The stalls were slammed up tight to each other. Bodies had to breathe in to squeeze past, trying to snatch a peek of what was on show or on offer. The traders wore their hearts on their sleeves, doing their best Shakespearean comic relief characters, which the housewives and husbands laughed at and laughed off. When push came to shove, this was all about money. When the purses came out the smiles disappeared.

Eddie's Mum picked at a few things, which she said would suit him. He turned up his nose. They were good value, she said. They were cheap, he responded. He knew he wanted to walk into the bigger and better shops and buy quality.

***

They parted in the late afternoon. Mum was going home to Dad and Eddie wanted to see what he could find out about Billy McGloin. The pubs were the best place for that sort of thing, but he wanted to pop into the Empire first.

As he approached, he paused to take in the sight. The Empire was something to behold. The owners had pulled in Frank Matcham to design it. At the time, he seemed like the captain who was riding the wave of the theatre building boom. He made the Empire stand tall and look big, a couple of Jacobean spindles giving it a sense of largesse while the two and a half thousand-seater auditorium made good on the promise that this was a grand place to be and to be seen. With the building in his back-pocket he headed south to London for his glory years, seeing – among others - the Hackney Empire, the Hippodrome, the Colisseum and the Palladium rise up from nothing to dominate the skylines.

Back up in Sheffield, the Empire opened its doors and theatre royalty walked through: Gracie Fields, George Formby for the masses; Ivor Novello and Anna Pavlova for the upper classes and everything in-between for everyone else.

Eddie had sat inside, on the edge of his seat, more times than he could remember and if seeing Houdini in the flesh was still the greatest thrill of his life, then there were dozens of other acts who had caught his attention and his imagination. To think that he himself might tread on that same stage was hypnotic. He had picked up his escapology in earnest from eighteen onwards. In the seven years since he had been honing then hawking his act round clubs, pubs, school shows and church halls. To trade all that for this was something indeed.

His heart skipped a little faster.

He found Stan in the middle of sorting out a double-booking. He seemed relieved to have Eddie as an excuse to leave.

The theatre was starting to bustle, getting ready for Saturday night entertainment.

"Good crowd tonight?"

"Good enough."

"I like the line-up."

"It's solid, Eddie. It's not going to change the world, but hey-ho." He turned serious. "Have you got any news?"

"Yeah, some."

Eddie was cautious, needing to make it seem like he had a lot, but not giving it all away too fast. He needed that booking.

"Let's get a drink."

Stan led them through the building to the bar. Eddie savoured every stride. There was a tension in the air of people getting ready to put on a show. They were terrified for the most part, except for the old timers, who were in the bar already, sinking a few quick drinks to give them a buzz, rather than to steady them.

Putting two drinks on the table, Stan sat down and stared straight at Eddie. "Tell me."

Eddie fed his story slowly. He kept Stan on edge and kept him thinking there was more to come. He held back on giving away Billy's name at this stage. He wanted something more to share at a later date. At the end of his tale, though, Stan seemed pleased.

"Well, it's not cut and dried, is it?"

"There were no signs that she was going to kill herself, Stan. There was no note."

"But she was pregnant?"

"Yeah. Doctor Gilmartin confirmed it without saying as much."

"Reason enough? Catholic guilt and shame and all that stuff you deal in?"

"I don't think so."

"You've not found the man yet?"

"Not yet. I'm looking."

Stan shook his head and looked perplexed. "Mary, though? Pregnant? I didn't put her down as the sort."

Eddie nodded with a straight face. Most men he'd met didn't understand women or try too hard. He kept his mouth shut on the subject, which left a gap in the conversation, until Eddie couldn't contain himself.

"Have you sorted out the running order yet?"

Stan laughed. "I'm spinning plates, Eddie, you know? It's a fluid business." The metaphors didn't match, much like the ties Stan wore. He was hedging his bets.

Eddie knew that as a novice, he was likely to be on very early, maybe even first. That was never a good place to perform. "That's all right."

"Look, Eddie, I appreciate what you've done. The booking's yours. I'm a man of my word. Drop it if you want to. I'm not sure what to tell the mother now anyway. Unless," Stan bit his lip as he said it and Eddie leaned forward, "you can find the man."

Eddie straightened. "I can!"

"You think so? I'd be ever so grateful, Eddie. I really would. For her mum, you know."

Ever so grateful sounded like a good enough reason to keep on searching. Besides, Eddie already knew that he couldn't easily let go. He had a sense of commitment. He remembered the first time he had worked out how a trick was done. He had simply studied it relentlessly to discount every wrong solution until only the right one was left. When he had the money, he bought tricks to see how they worked. He needed to know how things were done. That was all for show. This was life and death. He couldn't leave it.

***

Eddie was back in the Crofts where the neighbourhood hung a cloak over him as soon as he stepped into the shadows that the buildings threw across the street. The dry air had the effect of cooking the dust and grime that collected up against the corners of buildings so that the burnt aftertaste stuck to your tongue. As ever, there was a busyness about the streets, the activity peppered with caution, which you could see writ large on the faces of the men, women and children who watched you walk by. Not everything they were doing was legal. Not everything was without sin and this was a largely Catholic community.

Up tight to the terrace slums were the workshops that played their part in the business of the city, adding their share of dirt, dust and smoke to the environment. Saturday was quieter than the rest of the working week, but never silent. The need to claw back all the ground the economy had lost after the Depression was an everyday obligation. The factory owners didn't use clocks in the same way as everyone else. Time was money so that when the small hand struck the hour it might have been ringing a cash register. Like every other boy, Eddie had put in his hours in one of the sweat shops, working with the *little mesters* in the cutlery trade, burning his fingers on molten metal or cutting them to the bone on sharpened steel.

This wasn't a neighbourhood to be proud of. Mention the Crofts and all anyone could think of was workshop and slum and to live there or work there was to know that your life wasn't going to be long and wasn't going to be pleasant.

Eddie sloped through the crisscross of roads towards the Royal Oak, where the mood inside was fluid. People weren't sure what was going to happen or whether it would be a good or a bad night. They had their drinks in their hand and they were ready for what tonight – and life in general – had in store for them. They'd been in denial in their teens, but as the years dragged on, the future became clear. They were stuck here, now stuck in the beer, spitting out arguments about sport that had been and sport to come. Sheffield United had won the bragging rights over Wednesday in the season just gone. That could make the conversation bristle.

"What're you having, Eddie?"

John Rigby was a tall, thin man who seemed to get a little taller and a little thinner every year. Eddie and his Dad used to come in every so often when they lived in the area, but in the time between John looked to have added a few inches up and lost a few out.

"I'll try a pint, thanks. Do I get a discount for trade?"

"You get a discount for keeping your hands off my daughter."

She was hovering in the background, cleaning glasses. She'd been born with the chance to be pretty and the chance hadn't quite gone yet. Another year or two of damp, dirt, poor food and hard work would start to make her chiselled face look hollow and her slender frame just skinny. Eddie hoped she wouldn't lose the flash in her eyes that darted up at him.

"What about my thoughts?"

Down the bar, the daughter looked at him and smiled. They'd shared a few moments ten years earlier.

Rigby laughed. "Keep them to yourself. Now, how's your Dad?"

"He's fine, thanks."

"He's up at that, uh-"

"Painted Fabrics."

"That's it. Going all right?"

"They've got royalty visiting. Same day that they open the new library."

"Bloody hell. That's a bit grand, isn't it?"

"It's an excuse to dress up."

The landlord laughed. "But that's not why you're down here, Eddie. Is it?"

Eddie shook his head. "Do you know Mary Riley?"

"Heard the name."

"I'm trying to find out about someone who was hanging out round her house."

"Called?"

"Billy McGloin." He pulled the picture out of his pocket.

The landlord shook his head, then nodded down towards the corner of the bar, where the light seemed to have been sucked out, only to leave darkness.

"Gilbert Rollins. Could be your man."

"How come?"

"He knows everything and everyone."

He was going to ask how but there were some things you didn't ask and when you couldn't ask you could easily fill in the blanks.

Eddie watched Gilbert as his arms played a steady up and down movement of beer to mouth, then cigarette to lips. In between times his jaw worked away to make little words come out quietly, but there was no one sitting with him.

Studying his face was a way to place him in gangland society. His eyes were cautious, darting and he bent his neck down as if he was always ready to duck and run.

Sheffield suffered bad times following the end of the war. The less money people had, the more they gambled. With few jobs to go round and only poor jobs, there were thousands of men ready to bet their weekly benefits on the chance to win. They didn't even believe that they were going to win big. Gambling employed them and that was that. To stay solvent was a way to keep working. They went out early and came back late. If they came back even, they had done well. Horse racing was a staple and dog racing too. But the creative types weren't confined by the obvious outlets. Street bookies became inventive and became entrepreneurs, leading to bare knuckle fighting, pigeon racing and even handicap races, where men who were desperate for money would become the substitute for the racehorse and pound the streets.

Of all the street betting, though, the *tossing rings* were the cash cows.

Pitch-and-toss is about as old a gambling game as there is, tracking back to ancient Greek times, when – who knows – maybe Plato took a break from philosophy to see what he could do with cold, hard cash. The Sheffield variation was simple enough. Line up three coins on the end of your first two fingers and toss them, spinning, up into the air. The bet was a balance of heads against tails.

There were up to half a dozen rings strung up informally around the city. Each one had a hierarchy.

The *toller* was at the top. They ran the pitch and took their cut. That cut paid for the *pikers* or *crows* who kept watch for any over-enthusiastic copper who might be sniffing around.

Gilbert was a piker. Eddie thought he might have seen him one time, when he'd snuck along to a ring that was held in Wadsley to watch the business go down.

The police cleaned it all out in the end, with heavy hands and truncheons when they had to. A few of the gangs served time in prison, but never very long. The others filtered back into society and disappeared. Some got jobs as the economy finally started to pick up. Others, like Gilbert, drifted forever, waiting to be called when the glory days came back.

"What's he drinking?"

The landlord chuckled. "Whatever you buy him."

Eddie led with the pint glass, slapping it down onto the table then pushing it across to Gilbert like bait. Gilbert looked up at him, through eyes that seemed too far back in his head, as if they'd been retreating into their sockets for all his life. Around the eyes, the face was empty, the skin worked rough in a way that would never be smooth again. His chin was wrapped in a permanent ten-day stubble which, every now and then, he'd attack with a tired razorblade, making the growth uneven. He had a flat cap on his head which threw some shadow on his face and he seemed happy to hide there.

"Who're you?"

"I'm Eddie Reynolds."

Eddie liked saying his name. Even as he was considering whether he needed a stage name, he liked the one he'd got. Randolph Douglas had switched to the title of *Randini* to reference Houdini and Houdini had changed his to honour his great predecessor – Houdin – and partly because Erik Weisz clunked. Stan Laurel, on the other hand, knew that Jefferson didn't fit too well on posters. Chaplin kept *his* name, though, just changing Charles to Charlie as Edward had turned to Eddie. And now he'd added *The Incredible* as his moniker.

"And what do you want?"

"I've bought you a drink."

Gilbert was born suspicious. He had come out of the womb into an unwelcoming world and he had been on his guard ever since.

"Why?"

"I'm trying to find someone."

He looked at the drink in front of him, and then at Eddie, and then at the drink again. His hand shot out and clasped it.

"Who?"

"Billy McGloin."

If Eddie had hoped for a flicker of recognition, he'd have been disappointed. Gilbert had kept his mouth shut and his face set with the biggest bruisers on either side of the law. Keeping quiet was what he did best.

Eddie laid the picture on the table.

Gilbert pulled a face, which wasn't pretty to look at. "Nice looking boy."

"Do you know Mary Riley?"

"She died." He wiped his lips. "Killed herself."

Eddie let it go. “I heard he was hanging around her house.”

Gilbert shrugged. “There’s no law against it.”

“There is in heaven,” Eddie said, mostly to himself.

“Ah, you’re one of those? Irish?”

“Well, I’m not Italian.”

“It’s all the same to me.”

“Do you know him?”

Gilbert wrapped his fingers round the glass of his pint jar as something to trust. “The police were looking for him.”

“When she died?”

Gilbert took a drink. He wanted to enjoy his moment. “Before that.”

Eddie’s breath tightened. “Why?”

“I heard he was trouble and they came knocking.”

“What kind of trouble?”

“Some sort of activist. Stirring things up. That’s why he left.”

“Where did he go?”

Gilbert shrugged. “Can’t be sure. Might have been Upperthorpe.”

The name of the area stirred something in Eddie, but he couldn’t put his finger on it and his mind was buzzing too much to be clear on anything.

“What do the police know?”

“You’d have to ask them.”

“Do you think they’d tell me?”

There was a noise behind them as someone bustled in, but Eddie ignored it.

Gilbert sniggered. "Here's your chance to find out."

"How come?"

Gilbert chewed his lip. "They're here."

Eddie was puzzled, looking round to see that the front door had opened to let a mean-spirited cool June wind sneak in and busy round the room to make everyone feel a little cooler. Two ever-so-solid bodies came with the breeze, their frames throwing shadows over the hearth. The one in front was well built. The one behind seemed huge.

They were dressed for Saturday night, smart casual in a slovenly way, clothes pulled across bodies that didn't want to be defined.

"You sure they're coppers?"

Gilbert took a bite of his beer.

"They've got big feet and big boots," whispered Gilbert, remembering them as they had come towards his head one time. The fingers he'd broken then had never quite straightened.

The first of them pushed over the threshold, almost skipping past the landlord and sliding down the bar to where the daughter washed glasses. His hair was short and sharp on his head, with a slug moustache across his lip, breaking up the jowls of his face.

"'Ey up, love. Give us a smile?"

She smiled because it was a risk to her Dad if she didn't.

The officer kept going with a few pickup lines he'd lifted out of American potboilers. They were crude and obvious, but then so was he. The girl responded gamely. He was a customer, after all. And he was a copper.

His companion leaned on the bar with his elbows, facing out into the room, studying the patrons. His gaze stopped when it landed on Eddie.

Eddie looked right back at him.

"Evening."

The officer twitched. "Who're you? I've not seen you here before."

"It's my old stamping ground, isn't that right, Mr. Rigby?"

The landlord nodded. "Oh, ay. Eddie was here as soon as he could drink."

"Not *before* he was old enough, I hope?"

The second policeman had moved himself forward. Eddie backed off a little as seventy-five inches and close on three hundred pounds of body planted itself square in the centre of the bar space.

"Course not."

The officer had lost his moment with the daughter. He turned back to Eddie instead.

"What brings you over this part of town."

"I'm looking for Billy McGloin."

The name worked like electricity on the policemen and they stiffened.

"Why?"

Eddie smiled. "I want to ask him about Mary Riley."

Mary's name did nothing to soften the two men.

"What do you want to know about Mary Riley?"

The policemen were suspicious of everything and Eddie guessed he'd touched a nerve. He wondered just what Billy had been up to.

"I'm helping a friend find things out for Mary's mother."

The larger policeman was going to say something, but bit his lip. The closer one leaned in towards Eddie.

"What've you found out?"

Eddie shook his head. "Not a lot."

The first officer softened now.

"I'm Ted Pearson. This is Wilf Magill."

Magill nodded, but didn't smile.

"Nice to meet you."

"Likewise. Now, Eddie, you need to be a bit careful round here. You'll remember that from when you lived in these parts."

"I'm always careful." He said it with a smile.

"Are you? Well, you sound a little smart, too."

Wilf Magill manouevred himself round to study Eddie. Eddie returned the gesture, taking a closer look at the brick wall of a man, with a fat face and small, sharp eyes.

Eddie brazened it out. "Are *you* looking for McGloin?"

"We might be. We're looking for a lot of people."

"Mary Riley was pregnant."

Magill and Pearson shared a glance, before Magill spoke up. "Who told you that, son?"

Eddie didn't want to overplay his hand, or betray his sources. "It's what I heard."

Ted Pearson snorted. "You've been talking to Gilbert here too long."

Eddie wasn't so easily thrown. "Was Billy the father?"

"He's a troublemaker, Eddie," Pearson said.

"How come?"

Magill stepped forward. "He's a bad lad, Eddie. Keep away from him."

Pearson pecked at his shoulder. "But if you hear anything, *anything*, mind, let us know. This is going to be a busy week, so we could do with all the help we can get."

Magill picked up the thread again.

"And just for the records, can we take your address?"

Eddie's heart skipped a little. He didn't like to give it, but he had to.

They went back to their drinks. Eddie turned back to Gilbert, who seemed to have shrunk into the further corner of the room, where the shadow was deepest. All that showed were his eyes, which glowed with a slow burn of the last coals on the fire – almost done and ever present.

"Don't trust 'em."

"Should I trust you, Gilbert?"

"If you've got any sense you will. Get out while you can. Once they get their teeth into you, you're pigfeed."

Gilbert was still nursing bad experiences over the years, from that time when the line between the felons and the flatfoots became blurred.

"I'm not so easy to catch."

"That's where we all start."

And you end up here, was the next line.

"Why are they so busy this week? What's in the air?"

Gilbert pulled a face, as if Eddie was a simpleton. "Mosley's coming to town, isn't he? And he's been trouble wherever he goes."

Mosley. Things were starting to tick and to align, like minute and hour hands on the clock. Mosley's visit seemed like an alarm setting and that gave Eddie an idea.

He drifted away from Gilbert and slid past the policemen on his way out. Upperthorpe was in his thoughts. Maybe not tonight, though. He had another line of enquiry he wanted to try tomorrow and that would require some energy.

Chapter Twelve

Sunday morning came without sunshine. Eddie took a breath of cold air as he got up and stretched. The first thing that greeted him downstairs was his Dad, bemoaning England's slow progress as they had ground their way to 440 in the first innings, before Australia's reply.

"At least they've got Bradman out," his Dad said rather bleakly.

As a Sunday treat, his Mum had toasted tea cakes. The taste of the currants sat sweetly on his tongue as he bit in, letting the warm butter spill into his mouth.

"What're you up to today? Do you want to come to St. Pat's? There's a gala on." His Mum put a cup of tea into his saucer and Eddie tapped in two spoonsful of sugar.

"I'm going out walking."

Dad bent the corner of his paper down. "Where?"

Eddie tried to look nonchalant. "Mam Tor way."

"Mam Tor? The trespass?"

There had been talk for some time of an organised trespass of the land around Mam Tor, part of a push to reclaim some common land that had been lost over the centuries. The *right to roam* was gathering pace.

"We're not trespassing, Dad. We're just walking."

"You be careful, Eddie. You're trespassing. There'll be police."

"Not as many as there are people, I bet."

"Still, Eddie." His Mum put a hand on his shoulder. "Take care."

His Dad was clucking. "Give them a reason, Eddie, and they'll take it."

"We won't give them a reason. We're just walking."

"You're breaking the law, Eddie. It's not your land."

"It *is* our land, Dad. When did God give it to them?"

"Eddie!" His Mum was tense.

"Watch yourself, Eddie. These are strange times. Who are you walking with?"

"A friend."

"Who?"

"It's all right, Dad. They're not bloody Blackshirts."

"Don't swear, Eddie," his Mum rasped.

His Dad was cool. "It's not the Blackshirts you need to worry about, Eddie. It's not Mosley." There was that name again. "It's the Communists you want to watch. You've seen what's happening with Labour. They're starting to split."

"I thought you were a Socialist."

"I *am* and I'm proud of it. I'm not a bloody communist."

"Dad, don't *you* swear either. What is it with the pair of you?"

Eddie took a drink of tea. "Someone said there'd been a bit of bother with Mosley."

"A bit?" His Dad snorted. "Don't be near the City Hall this Thursday."

As he heard the words, Eddie couldn't think of anywhere better to be. He liked crowds. They excited him.

He didn't have much interest in politics, though, except for the fact that Billy McGloin seemed to be tied up in it. He was hoping that he might find out more that afternoon, joining up with Ada and a few hundred hikers who had organised the mass trespass across the Moors. The people wanted their countryside back. He guessed that there would be some radicals amongst the crowd. One of them might know Billy.

Mass, of course, came first. The sermon touched on the evils of the flesh and for a few moments, Eddie squirmed in his seat, trying to reconcile his times with Ada – and others before her – with the rules of the Church. He struggled to see how something that felt so good could be quite so wrong, though the practical ghost of Ada's husband was more tangible than the holy one.

When the mass ended, Eddie said goodbye to Mum and Dad then checked his watch. He was early and hung around in the warmth of the church hall which was where Father Cleary caught him.

"How are you, Eddie?"

"I'm fine, thank you, Father." Eddie shuffled in his seat a little, with words of the sermon coming back to tickle him.

There were still a few hangers-on in the hall: the lonely and the limpets, droning on and draining the life out of the priests minute by minute. Father Cleary turned away from them, in towards Eddie, to shield them both and give them intimacy.

"And how've you been getting on with your problem?"

"It's complicated, Father."

"How so?"

"She didn't kill herself."

"No?"

"It was an accident."

"An accident?"

Eddie chewed his lip. "She didn't mean to."

"Ah."

The word hung like judgement. Short and sharp.

The priest laid a hand on Eddie's shoulder. "It's a hard world to live in, Eddie. It's a puzzle. I see a lot of young women struggling to know what to do and what's right. They get so many different signals."

Eddie felt he was being patronized, but he was polite. "I don't think it was her fault. There was a man."

Father Cleary coughed up a short, hard laugh. "I'm sure there was. It's an old story, Eddie, all the way back to Adam and Eve. You can't have everything you want, but people tell you that you can. There's a change coming."

Eddie was aware of the change. It was starting in the cinema with the battle for a new code of ethics. The last code settled on by the censors and the studios had been one of the greatest works of fiction in cinema history. As Hamlet might have noted, it was more honoured in the breach than the observance. Eddie didn't see the need. His motto was: let people say what they want and see what they want.

"Thanks, Father."

Father Cleary caught his arm. "Did you pray for her? Did you light a candle?"

He had done both. It didn't seem enough.

***

At the train station he found Ada, who was dressed like a film star would dress for a walk in the country: stylish and impractical.

"Is it going to be cold?" She was shivering.

"It's not going to be warm."

Despite the summer month, the weather could generously be described as inclement. Eddie didn't mind. He hadn't been out of the city for weeks and while he knew he was lucky to live on the edge of town, there was nothing quite the same as the unadulterated beauty of the Peak District as its ranges bent and bowed either side of the train line.

"Is this going to be safe, Eddie? I can't be doing with getting arrested."

"I thought you liked your causes?"

"What do you mean?" She was sharp.

Eddie shrugged. In the dull times between sex, Ada would get animated by whatever she'd just read or – more likely – just heard at one of the many meetings she went to. Self-improvement was a passion. She dedicated herself to it. Psychology was her latest pet subject. She spoke of the architects of this new science as if they were gods. When Eddie looked blank, Ada repeated the names that had stuck her head. "It's Freud and Jung and Jones," she said, in a teacherly tone. "I bet you've never even heard of Ernest Jones." Eddie shrugged. He'd never heard of Young either.

He shook his head. "Forget it."

"And why do you want to walk on someone else's land?"

He looked at her sideways, seeing how a sense of middle-class land grab had started to permeate her thinking.

"It's *not their* land and I just want to be *able* to."

"It sounds like a luxury."

"It *is*. And what's wrong with that? We should share it. The owners bleat on about their God-given rights, but God didn't give them any of this."

She laughed. "Oh, you and your god. You seem to forget him when you're between my legs."

He would usually have laughed at that, but today felt different. The words stung him. He turned away. He thought of Louisa. She was too good for him. He knew that. Ada didn't like silence. It allowed her too much time to think and that could lead to memories of where she'd come from and what she suffered, where she was now and who with and where she wanted to be: where she should be. She liked to be with Eddie because he was young, good looking and absolutely alive. For that to work, though, he had to be paying her attention.

"Am I going to be talking to myself today?"

"You can find a telephone and ask your husband to join you if you want."

That was a slap and they both felt it.

There was silence for a time. Eddie didn't feel he had much space left for any more guilt. He pushed his hand out to touch hers. They didn't always do that in public. She was married, though she took off the rings when she was with Eddie. But you can be seen and people talk.

"I'm sorry."

"No, it's me. It's *him*."

"What's he doing today?"

"What's he ever doing? He's working."

"I thought you liked the money."

"I want a *life*, Eddie. You and me meet two or three times a week and when you're done you go off to something else – and some*one* else."

"It's not all roses, Ada."

"No, but there are *some* roses, aren't there? That'd be enough."

Eddie squeezed her fingers.

***

The train bumped them along into Castleton, which was bustling with ramblers. When they fell in with the bodies that were beginning to form into a mass, he knew why he was here and what this meant. This was a performance by the public. The press would be here and the police. Something was happening. Being part of it gave Eddie a buzz. Up ahead, the chain of ramblers snaked its way across the hills. All around, people chatted. They were thrilled. They were both main act and audience.

When the rain came, it seemed like an assault that everyone had been expecting, as if God was joining the landowners and the law to see how strong their resolve was. There were upwards of two thousand in the body of the beast that drove its way up through Winnats Pass. Rain and wind wasn't going to stop it. At last, the head of the serpent rested and the tail caught up, spilling around to form a human amphitheatre. Eddie watched the crowds. There was a charge pulsing through them. They were together and connected. The police were there, but holding back. They were overawed by the numbers and a sense of cohesion. He noticed how some of the officers couldn't stop their hands twitching towards their truncheon as if the only thing to do with something you didn't understand or couldn't control was beat it to death. Meanwhile, the speakers spoke and the crowd listened and lapped it up. The rain came at them again but they were ready for it with their hats tugged down, wrapped in their macs. Eddie watched them, seeing them as an army. His Dad was right. The nation was changing. And it was moving. The police held their lines – waiting.

Even as people strained to hear the speaker, there was a continual whine of a single voice, close by. He wanted to find the person who was talking, who couldn't keep quiet and had to say what he thought. Those people were unguarded. That was what Eddie wanted. He started to move towards the voice. The sound was an irritant, insistent. He searched through the bodies to find an angular young man with a humourless round face, featured with black frame glasses and knotted at the neck with a university scarf, spitting out his thoughts to people around him, every one of whom edged away, inch by inch. That gave Eddie a space to slip into.

After another volley of disapproval aimed at the speaker, Eddie found an opening line to try. "You don't seem too impressed."

The young man turned on him, with a mixture of shock at being at interrupted and slow pleasure at having an audience. "They're not going to change anything by *talking.*"

"You think they need to act?"

"Action's everything."

Eddie wondered who had fed him that line. "How come?"

"If *they're* taking action, *we* need to take action. And *they* are certainly doing that."

"Who's they?"

The young man looked at Eddie as if he was the village idiot. "You'll see when Mosley comes this week. If it's like Olympia it could be a blood bath."

"What happened at Olympia?"

Again, Eddie received the look the young man reserved for fools. "Ask Harry Miller."

Eddie shrugged. He decided to push. "What about Billy McGloin?"

The name put a little tremor in the young man's face and Eddie shivered to see it.

"McGloin? He's trouble. Harry'd tell you if he was here. Harry knows everyone."

"Where is he?"

"Who? McGloin? I don't know. I haven't seen him recently. Harry might know."

Eddie stared at him, seeing the scarf he worse knotted at the neck, with Sheffield University crest standing proud. "Is Harry at the University, like you?"

The young man nodded. "That's right."

"Are you studying politics?"

The young man smiled. "*Everything's* politics. That's what Harry says."

***

"I don't want to go back." Ada stood in the station at Dore and hung back from Eddie.

"You've got to."

She watched him coolly. "You're so young, Eddie. You haven't grown up yet."

She said these things periodically. She thought it gave some weight to her age, when mostly she just felt a slow bitterness at his youth and the opportunities still ahead of him.

"And I've got to go."

That shocked her. "Where?"

"I'm going to find Billy McGloin to see what he knows about Mary Riley: the kid she was carrying; the fact that she's dead."

Ada jerked, almost in spasm. "Eddie, what are you doing? What are you thinking? Leave it to the police."

He thought of the two bobbies in the bar. "They're Keystone Cops."

"You'll get in trouble."

Memories of Ted Pearson and Wilf Magill came back into view. The width of their bodies filled the screen of his imagination. He didn't want to get on the wrong side of them.

"Not if I'm careful."

"Why? Why does she matter so much? She's not the first person to kill herself."

He shrugged. "Maybe because I got out of the Crofts – and she didn't."

"Is this your Catholic guilt thing?"

He laughed. "It could be."

But it wasn't.

Mary Riley's death and the circumstances surrounding it had formed a lock around the truth. And Eddie would never be defeated by a lock.

"You're going to get caught, Eddie. You can't trick your way out of everything."

"Do *you* want to get caught?" He was direct with her.

"What do you mean?"

"Do you want to leave your husband? Do you want to be with me?"

"It's complicated, Eddie. You wouldn't understand."

He smiled. "When *I* get trapped, Ada, I know that I'm trapping myself. And I always have a key."

"Life gets harder, Eddie. Enjoy the simple times."

He turned on his heels. "I am doing."

***.

Even before he got to the front door of his home, the smell of his Mum's cooking came out to greet him like happy bounding hounds.

"You didn't get arrested then?"

Eddie's Dad gave the line well, but he wasn't smiling.

Eddie turned to his Mum – and she wasn't either. "What is it?"

Mum creased a little, then turned back to the cooking. "The police have been around."

He hadn't expected that. "Why?"

His Mum turned on him. "What have you done?"

"I haven't done anything. What did they say?"

"Why are the police calling on us, Eddie?" His Dad was firm. He'd fought a bloody war, for God's sake. Taking a tough tone with his son wasn't so hard.

"I don't know. What did they say?"

"We've *never* had the police, Eddie."

Eddie guessed his Mum was twitching with neighbourhood shame and motherly worry. Ah, well.

"Who was it? I saw a couple of them on Saturday night."

"It was Ted Pearson. He asked you to go to the station when you could."

Eddie nodded.

"Eddie?"

"It's all right. It's this thing with Mary Riley."

"Oh, Eddie."

"There was a man, that's all. Hanging around. Living there, maybe."

"*Living* there?"

"It happens, Mum."

His Dad spoke firmly. "Eddie, I love you, but you're a daft bugger sometimes."

Eddie nodded. "I know."

They stared at each other and knew there weren't any words to explain. Eddie was following his head and his heart. His Dad had followed his comrades and orders and lost thousands of them and his leg with them.

Chapter Thirteen

There was a threat of rain in the air as Eddie swung out an arm to catch the handle of the tram to pull himself aboard. The weather was unsettled and Eddie was too. He had got up early so that he could call at the police station on the way to work – and he had another letter from Louisa to read. He burst open the envelope with a frustration of guilt. He still hadn't managed to put pen to paper, though the memory of it had flickered across his mind last night as his head had hit the pillow.

As he read, he noted how Louisa had a pretty hand. There was a grace to her script, reflecting the way her voice worked on Eddie and the way her body moved. Hitting him like a hangover, he wondered why he spent as much as a minute with Ada. There was no future in it. There was no love. But then he remembered how she looked when laid out on her bed, inviting. Seeing it that way, things were more complex.

Eddie tried to make images in his mind of what Louisa was telling him, but there was an everyday monotony to the pictures she was painting. He was being unfair and he knew it. There were exceptions. Louisa and a few of her friends from the Crofts had found a church to hear mass. That single line rippled across Eddie's heart and made his chest tight.

Any further thoughts were going to have to wait. His stop had come. He jumped off the tram fast to hit the pavement hard and move forward.

*****

The police station was lazily warm at that time in the morning with a steady June heat starting to make things boil. The officer at the desk gave the impression that he was behind on his work and would never catch up. He looked at Eddie with some irritation, gesturing for him to sit down and wait, which he did.

Ted Pearson breezed through a few minutes later, noted Eddie, then walked away, leaving him for another quarter of an hour. Eddie fretted. Time was important to him. He didn't like to waste it and he was never late. He tried to clear his mind to think of the performance at the Empire: what he would do; how he would do it. He always had half a dozen ideas spinning in his head, from first conception to finale. He had now more or less decided on the act. What was perplexing him now was how to add a *wow* to what he was doing. It wasn't enough to be skilful because most of the skill was hidden. Magic had to work before people's eyes. He remembered his fury when he performed his first escape in front of a collection of Aunts and Uncles. They had applauded politely, murmuring appreciation. And then he blew through a quick couple of shows of the Ambitious Card trick and they were exultant, cheering, whooping and drying their eyes from the laughter and surprise.

It was just a card trick. All right, it had fooled Houdini once, but he caught it straight away the second time. It was sleight of hand and slick, but there was nothing too it. Escape, though, was a physical challenge. It was hard to do and it hurt.

Eddie needed a pay-off for his performance.

Ted Pearson sauntered back through. "It's Eddie, isn't it?"

"It is."

"Follow me, son."

When he offered Eddie a cup of tea and Eddie accepted, Pearson rolled back in his chair and waved a hand. A woman who was working there came skipping over. He didn't even look at her as he placed his order.

"And bring the sugar," he called after her as she scampered away.

Pearson was thick set into his forties now. He'd been a copper since he got back from the war and he'd seen the turbulent times, when the Sheffield gangs got hold of the city with their fists. He hadn't made it into the Flying Squad, but he'd seen their work and knew what had to be done.

He was watching Eddie curiously, flicking his thick, black Kitchener moustache as an instinct. He'd started doing it in the trenches, as they waited for the command. He didn't know he was doing it now or what that meant.

When the tea came he tipped in sugar by the spoonful. Eddie took some, then took a sip, a little bit of leaf that the sieve hadn't caught sticking in his teeth. He worked it with his tongue as a way of exercising the muscle. The mouth was a perfect place to hold a key. He could work wonders with tongue. He smiled and thought of Ada.

"You found anything out?"

Eddie shook his head. "Not much."

Pearson nodded. "What do you know about McGloin?"

"Was he the father?"

Pearson shrugs. "Who can say?"

Eddie sat back, then leant forward again. "Why wasn't there a note?"

"A note?"

"Suicide."

"Maybe she didn't have a pen handy."

Eddie pulled a face.

Pearson scowled.

"You seen many suicides, son? Been there to sort it out? They're not pretty and there's no one way of doing it and no right way. Poison. Hanging. Cutting your wrists. If they've got a gun from the war, then you're clearing their brains off the wall. They don't all write notes. Maybe they don't know what to say, or who to. They can't find the right words."

Eddie wasn't bullied. "Mary Riley could. She was bright."

"Not that bright, was she? She got herself knocked up, didn't she?"

"And that brings us back to Billy McGloin."

Pearson smiled. "You don't give up, do you?"

"Not very often. I learned that from my Dad."

"Ah, yes. He's a good man. You should be proud of him."

"I am."

"Is he proud of you?"

Eddie paused. "I think so. Why did you call at my house?"

Pearson sharpened. He didn't like anyone to ask him questions. That wasn't the way things worked. There was an order and a pattern. *He* asked the questions. Those things mattered.

"To get you down here."

"Why?"

"You're a cheeky bastard, aren't you?"

Since the police had beaten the biggest part of the criminal fraternity out of business they'd moved with a swagger. Once they'd bloodied the lines of the law with the truncheon and knuckle-duster it became harder to see where their dominion ended. Pearson could say anything. He could do anything. The papers would back him. The public would back him. People wanted peace and if they couldn't have that, they'd settle for order.

"Sorry."

The apology puffed Pearson up. He felt that he'd soft-bullied it out of Eddie. Eddie was happy to let him think that.

"What were you doing in the pub on Saturday night?"

"I used to live round there."

"That's what you said. Most people don't go back."

"I've got a girlfriend there."

Pearson sniffed. "Things have changed since you moved."

"I suppose they will have. It's a changing world."

"You're right, Eddie Reynolds." He was firm. There was a fire in his eyes. "It *is*. You need to be careful where you go. You need to be careful who you're with."

Eddie sat back. "I try to be."

"Try harder. You don't want to be spending times with the likes of Gilbert."

"He seemed harmless."

"The people he knows aren't."

"I wasn't talking to them."

Pearson took a swill of tea. What do you know about McGloin?"

"Nothing much."

"How much?"

"He might be in Upperthorpe."

"Who told you that? Was it Gilbert?"

Eddie nodded.

Pearson smirked. "That's a bit vague. Did you get an address?"

"No."

"Did he tell you anything else?"

"No, but I was talking to someone who said he was mixed up in some political stuff."

Pearson sat up, watching him cautiously. "Be careful, Eddie."

"People keep telling me that."

"We've got that Mosley fella coming here next week. Do you know about that?"

"Doesn't everyone?"

"Are you going to listen to him speak?"

"I wasn't planning to."

"Why not?"

"I wash my hair on Thursdays."

"You're a clever dick, aren't you?"

Eddie shrugged.

Pearson started on him again. "And what about what Mosley says? What about the Blackshirts?"

He was going to say he didn't have one, but decided against it. Know your audience.

"I don't know."

"What does your Dad say?"

"He says, watch out for the Communists."

Pearson smiled. "He's a smart man."

"He survived the war."

Pearson nodded and sighed. "That's right. Where was he?"

"Somme."

"Bugger."

"What about you?"

The question triggered memories in a flood and Pearson flinched. "Arras," he said softly. "Vimy Ridge."

His mind was playing tricks with him, so that the tea on his tongue started to taste of mustard gas again. The memory triggered pictures of swollen, distorted faces when the skin was bare and an endless echo of Canadian accents tripping up and down the lines.

"I'm sorry."

Eddie had been too young to know what was happening at the time and no one had wanted to talk too much about it afterwards. His sympathy wasn't for knowledge of the places and the action, just the catch in the policeman's voice when he spoke the names.

"Who was telling you about Mosley then?"

"Someone I met out on Kinder."

"You were on that walk, were you?"

Eddie wondered if it was a trap. It had been a trespass after all. "I was in the area."

"Good answer. What did he say?"

"Just that there was someone at the University who might know."

"Who?" Pearson was pressing.

Eddie didn't like to give the name and didn't know why.

"He didn't say. Just said that he was studying there."

"Who was it that told you?"

"I didn't ask."

"You're not very thorough, are you?"

"Well, I'm not a policeman, am I?"

Pearson laughed. "Your mouth's going to get you in trouble, laddie."

Eddie smiled. It wasn't usually his mouth that people warned him about.

"What do you think McGloin's going to tell you?"

Eddie hadn't planned that far ahead and sat back in his chair for a moment, to consider.

"I want to know if he's the father and if Mary meant to kill herself or she was just trying to get rid of the baby, and if that was his idea or hers – and why he left her."

"You might want to take a packed lunch with you."

Eddie didn't smile. "Gilbert told me your lot already had an eye on McGloin."

"*Our* lot?" Pearson chuckled. "We keep an eye on a lot of people, Eddie. We might even keep an eye on you."

Eddie felt a chill. He was being warned.

Ted Pearson relaxed and his body spread out on his chair. "Look, we want to find him, just like you, for the same reasons and maybe a couple of others. That's police business. The thing is, we've heard a rumour about him."

Eddie twitched in his seat. “What?”

“We’ve heard where he might have been seen.”

“Where?”

Pearson smiled. He was using his words like casting a line and Eddie was biting. It was nice to have power. “A pub over Wadsley way.”

“Have you been?”

“What do you think?”

“He wasn’t there?”

“That’s right.”

There was a pause. Pearson was leaving a gap. He was playing with Eddie, making him wriggle.

“What’re you going to do?”

Pearson took his cup and lifted it to his mouth, sucking the tea over his lips and tea in a great swirl, so that the liquid made a whooshing sound as he drank it down.

“I thought you might want to go and have a look.”

Eddie’s pulse quickened.

“Me? Why?”

Pearson laughed.

“Because you’re not a bloody copper, are you? People seem to disappear from places when we get close.” He slapped his cup down. “And you work in a brewery, so you’ve always got a reason to go to pubs.” He grinned. “I thought you were supposed to be smart.”

Eddie smiled. “It’s Monday. I get better as the week goes on.”

“What do you reckon?”

Eddie picked up his cup, looking into the bottom, to see if the leaves would tell him anything –

and to keep the policeman waiting. Pearson was his audience now. He took a last sip then licked his lips.

"What if I find him?"

Pearson took another drink of tea. "Well, you've got a list of questions, haven't you? You could ask him those. Then you could find out where he lives - and let me know."

Eddie nodded. At the back of his mind was the idea of heading up to the University to search out Harry Miller. This felt so much more immediate.

"I'm free tonight."

"Is that a yes?"

Eddie nodded. "What's the pub?"

Pearson smiled. "Horse and Jockey."

Chapter Fourteen

Work was a stretch, physically hard and time consuming. Having started late he would have to finish late and he was going to have to skip a rehearsal with Nancy. He assumed she'd forgive him. She usually did.

The tram tugged him through town out towards Hillsborough on his way to Wadsley, where he hopped off to try to find something to eat.

Hillsborough Corner was heavy with bustle at the end of a draining day, which had heated up as time wore on then closed in on itself, hot and sticky. The thunder had never come, leaving the air in thick, oppressive waves just above everyone's heads, sucking at their lungs. Sweat pushed through the skin in stinging spots then clagged to make shirts and blouses damp. Eddie was glad to get off the tram and try draining some cooler evening air into his throat, though even now the threat of a storm hadn't entirely passed.

He stopped by a street trader and his barrow, selling hot potatoes and a cup of tea. He took the food and drink to sit down in a shop doorway, watching the men and women push by, the men lifting their hats periodically to wipe their brows. Cars jigged past, adding more heat to a hot evening, beeping on their horns as people of all ages failed to realise that a road meant something different now. He wondered what it would be like to drive (judging that the steamer barely counted). Magical, he imagined. Another car horn snapped him out of a dream. He finished his food, sloshing the last of the tea round his mouth.

He moved out into the thick stream of people, cutting across them and slicing a path through the bodies to head over Wadsley way, remembering the thrill of the tossing rings. The mix of chance and lawlessness gave a breeze of excitement to the proceedings. He recalled how the crowd had watched in steady rapture as the coins purred into the air on the spin and then clattered to the ground. Eddie loved it.

Now, he pulled up Wadsley Lane, fighting against the humidity. The road was wide with the houses grand on either side. They were strong and steady and there was a whisper of wealth about them. He wondered what Billy McGloin would be doing here.

The Horse and Jockey reflected the neighbourhood. If it wasn't a palace, it wasn't a flea pit either. Eddie could name a hundred places in the city more squalid than this one. As he moved across the threshold, the landlady and collected regulars viewed him with curiosity rather than suspicion.

"What can I get for you, sir?"

Eddie ordered a pint and sat at the bar, sipping it slowly. It tasted a little better than the tea – and a little weaker, too.

The evening was still early and calm. The landlady - probably in her early thirties - was continually cleaning up one thing, scrubbing down another.

"Has your husband left you to it?"

She smiled. "No, he just left me."

Eddie had a kind face with eyes that called to you. She came running.

"Sorry to hear it. You keep the beer well."

"Thank you. We take a lot of care of our cellar."

"Good for you. Not everyone does."

"How do you know?"

"I'm a drayman."

"Not for us?" She *would* have remembered. "Where do you work?"

"Wards."

She shook her head.

"Not my favourite." She smiled.

"We grow on you." He grinned.

"*You* can grow on me anytime, love."

She laughed.

A customer came up to the bar. She served him then slid back towards Eddie, because he was different and younger and full of promise.

"You're not from round here."

"No, I'm meeting someone."

"A lady?"

Eddie waited a second before answering. He wanted to see how much she cared.

She cared.

"No. A fella named Billy. Billy McGloin." He looked at her face for recognition. "Do you know him?"

She shook her head and showed no emotion.

"Sorry, I don't. We've been getting more people in recently. Groups of them. They come and go. Some of them local, some of them not. Have you got a special girl?" Even as she asked, she knew she was too fast and too forward.

Eddie smiled. "They're all special."

She squeezed the beer pump and pressed her lips together. “But not tonight?”

“No. I’ve just come to see Billy. He was in the other night. With a crowd.”

“Last night?”

“I’m not sure. The last couple of nights I think.”

She stiffened. “Well, I hope he wasn’t one of the ones Bob had to deal with.”

“Bob?”

“My brother. He helps out.”

“What happened?”

“Well, everything was normal for a Sunday. There was a dozen or so in, mostly regulars but a group of two or three younger lads over there in the corner.” She pointed. “And then half a dozen other lads came in, saw the three in the corner and that was that.”

“Fight?”

“Sort of. Shouting mostly and then it got a bit rough.”

“What were they shouting about?”

“I don’t know. Politics.”

“Did you call the police?”

“No need. There was a bit of flapping. A few punches and then they ran.”

“The three in the corner not been back?”

“No. I’m guessing they’re looking for a new place. What does this Billy look like?”

He pulled the picture out of his pocket and showed her.

“Hmmm” she looked it over. “Not as pretty as you.”

“It’s a curse,” he said, slyly.

"I'll bet." She leaned back and felt parts of her body twinge with the daily ache of fourteen hours' work.

"Well, thanks anyway. Maybe Billy'll turn up soon."

"If you want to know what they were fighting about, you could ask Howard."

Eddie licked his lips to clear them of beer.

"Howard?"

"Howard Jacobs. He was part of the group that came in here."

"And he's local?"

"Lives round the corner. Doesn't usually drink here, though. He's usually down the road. The Rose and Crown.

Eddie leant over the bar and kissed her on the cheek, so that she flushed.

"Hey, I'm still a married woman, I *think.*" She held up her finger with the ring on it and looked at it as if it was a shackle.

Eddie grinned. "That's why I stopped at a kiss."

***

He had a simple plan. He was going to try the Rose and Crown. If that failed he'd go back to the Horse and Jockey and squeeze the landlady a little more. She wouldn't mind. Neither would Eddie. He had the feeling that she knew her way around the bedroom.

Though this wasn't his turf, he knew the area well enough. He had delivered here. He had friends here and – just across the way – he'd spent a good few nights chasing the dogs round the track at Owlerton Park. He never won too much. He never lost too much. So, he could wend his way easily enough through the suburbs until he came to the Rose.

Even as he approached, he knew he had the right place. A crackle of voices was making its way through the pub windows to drop on the pavement like broken glass.

Eddie pushed up and inside the door, trying to take in the scene quickly. The mood was fragile. The landlord was standing, stiff-armed, staring down two sets of bodies which had taken opposing stances. One group of three was sitting still in the corner, stuck in their chairs, but tensed. The other group was stood up and hung a few yards back, edging forward, poking in, like kids at a zoo trying to get a rise out of the animals. Words came in dark, guttural snatches with a thick Anglo-Saxon flavour.

On either side, groups of locals looked on cautiously. They were working people and they were tough enough, but they'd come out for relaxation, not a fight. Besides, there was something in the air that was different from a couple of drunken punches.

The standing group edged further forward. The lads in the chairs braced themselves. They wanted to move and knew that as soon as they did it might seem like ringing a bell.

Eddie couldn't help feeling a pang of guilt from taking the chance to study their faces to see if any of them matched Billy. They didn't.

"Come on, lads!" The landlord's voice was calm and firm. He wanted to defuse the situation. "Take your problems outside."

The standing group ignored him, starting to widen their stances in the way of a trap being set. The boys sitting down looked up at the landlord for help and then at the edges of the snare they were stuck in, wondering if they could ever be fast enough to escape it.

"Chuck 'em out, Bill!" One of the punters blared at the landlord, who didn't find the comment helpful, glaring back, even as his hands slid under the counter to squeeze on the handle of broom he kept there.

One of the lads standing caught a chair as he shifted left, making a scrape that sounded like a siren. Everyone jumped, as the landlord skipped round from the bar to make a shield between the two sets of bodies, but all that did was encourage the half dozen to raise the volume and change the words to make them harder and bolder.

A few of the regulars rose to their feet. They were older men who'd fought in the war and survived the General Strike. They were here for a quiet drink, a chat and a game of dominoes. They didn't want trouble. They'd had enough for a lifetime. Now, their deep voices provided a bass harmony for the scraping insults that the groups threw at each other.

"Get out!" The landlord was bellowing. "All of you. Get *out!"*

Eddie hovered in the doorway watching, curious as to where this would go and where Howard was. He switched his eyes between the two clumps of men to try to make some sense of them. The people sitting were dressed a little smarter and their hair was a little neater. The group standing was more rough and ready. Eddie studied the way their hands agitated, needing to move but not knowing what to do. That was when he saw the knife.

"Knife!" Eddie shouted causing the older men to lift themselves up in a call to arms.

The lad with the knife jabbed forward towards the seated group and the group sitting spilled backwards in a tumble. As their bodies fell towards the floor, the standing pack moved in, which was when Eddie hit them from the side, his hands clasping over the fist with a knife, snapping at the wrist.

All the bodies knitted together to become stuck in a jumble as each one struggled to rebalance themselves to move forward or move away, just as the regulars heaved in to catch them by the collars or just lean forward with a kick.

Eddie loosed the knife. When it fell, he kicked it away hard. The effort cost him balance and he sprawled down, banging his knee and shouting at the pain and frustration. As he tried to grab hold of a table to right himself, a foot came from nowhere. It was all he could do to keep his face away, bending back sharply, spinning over again.

The bodies were bound together now, as fists punched and nails caught on skin and tugged, dripping blood out.

To his left, he heard a yelp, as a fist managed to make contact with a face, a cracking sound spinning out from the bones. Eddie saw a boot swing towards someone's head, which twisted away at the last moment, so that the foot followed through to clatter into a table, spinning it off balance and sending three drinks flying. They exploded on the floor in a tidal wave of beer that came in a wave to catch Eddie on the cheek.

Eddie pushed himself back, trying to get some distance from the sprawl and as he did so, he saw the pub door open and three policemen push in.

They had come in ready with their truncheons up. Eddie had to think that they had been waiting. He rolled away, angry at the situation, at not finding Billy and feeling that Ted Pearson might just have set him up.

Eddie had drifted right now, further into the pub, around the group, managing to distance himself as the police drove straight to the middle, truncheons flapping, ringing down with a slap on the heads in the scrummage beneath them. Each beat drew a gasp or a groan. Eddie watched the bodies subside into stillness and shock.

The regulars were working as deputies, catching bodies and dragging them clear, pooling them in a virtual lock-up, where they sat and wondered.

"Who started it?"

The obvious question led to a dozen different answers, but the only one that mattered was the landlord, who pointed at two of the now mixed group – one on each side. He was working on the basis of the ones who had spoken most, fixing them as the ringleaders. It was an arbitrary sort of justice, but it was good enough for the police, who picked the accused roughly then handcuffed them.

"And him!"

Eddie's nerves stiffened as he saw one of the regulars point in his direction.

"He had a knife."

"I said there *was* a knife!" Eddie called back.

He could see in the eyes of some – most especially the landlord – that they weren't sure that Eddie was part of it. But he had come just at that time when things started to happen and he was tied to the word *knife.* And they didn't know him.

That was enough. One of the police officers caught him roughly, slapping the handcuffs on his wrist hard, so that it hurt the bone.

"Come on."

"I'm not part of it!" Eddie shouted.

"Out." The policeman was bullying his way forward, taking a moment to turn round to call to the rest of them. "And I don't want to be back again. Else there'll be trouble."

Eddie and his supposed collaborators were bundled out onto the street, cursing and wriggling, angry more than upset.

"It wasn't me! I was trying to stop the fight!"

"Shut up, son and wait here."

The two policemen fell into discussion, deciding what to do. They moved away from the three men in handcuffs, who eyed each other cautiously.

Eddie took a chance. "Howard?"

One of the two stiffened.

"Who's asking?" This was the taller of the two, with angular features and a grazed eyebrow. The other lad had a split lip.

"Eddie Reynolds."

The name meant nothing, of course, but the confidence came as a surprise.

"Why do you want to know?"

Eddie thought for a second, to weigh up the options and the odds. Things were tight, he calculated. He had to use the chances he had. He checked on the policemen, who seemed to be in some debate as to the best place to take them.

"I was trying to find what's going on here."

"Bloody communists," said Howard.

"Bloody fascists," said the other, the words bubbling out of a split lip, with a spitball of blood.

Here we go again, thought Eddie. "I'm trying to find Billy McGloin."

They both shook their heads.

"I've heard the name," said Split Lip.

"Where?"

"Dunno."

"Do you know where he lives?"

"No idea."

Eddie whistled. Frustration was nipping at him.

"Stop talking, you lot!" one of the officers called, without turning round to see them.

Eddie nodded thanks, looking across to the two policemen. They were still turned away, wondering if it was worth carting the three men down to the cells or giving them a warning, maybe a slap or two, right here on the road. It had a been a long night already at the end of a long shift. And yet they were uneasy to let people go. They were all looking to the horizon, as if something wicked was coming. They wanted to tighten things up to make sure they never returned to the old days of gang warfare or go the way of Russia, Germany and Italy where dark politics were making their mark.

As they played out their debate Eddie looked back at the pub then breathed slowly to calm himself. He took a look at the handcuffs and then away again. The noise inside the pub had calmed again, with landlord Bill now showing the other members of the group out none too nicely. They bundled onto the pavement with mutters.

"Clear off, you lot!" One of the policemen called.

Bill stood in the doorway, watching them go, protecting his property. His name was right above the door. William Bennett. *William*?

There was a click in his mind.

"We'd best take 'em," one of policeman said. Agreed, they turned back to their captives. They stood for a second staring, then looked at each other.

"Weren't there three?"

In front of them, stood just two men in handcuffs. Eddie Reynolds wasn't one of them.

Chapter Fifteen

By the time he got to the Crofts, the sun had been squeezed out by the narrow streets. The lights that should have taken over were tired or beaten, no more than one in three trying too hard to lighten the neighbourhood. Eddie didn't mind. Darkness suited him.

Instinctively, he rubbed his wrists, the claw of the manacles still irritating his skin. Houdini had been known as the *King of Handcuffs*. With a flair for self-publicity and a habit of dripping out secrets of how tricks were done Houdini had more or less killed the handcuff act for everybody. Even so, the routines were good practice. Eddie studied hard then practiced harder, slipping them into his act to add colour, rather than as a showstopper. The crowd always loved it. They were so caught up in the moment that they put their thinking minds aside, simply gasping out how-did-he-do-that, rather than trying to work it out.

The logistics were simple. The easiest way to open a set of handcuffs was with a key. Houdini collected thousands of them. When he was setting up a trick, he'd ask to check that the handcuffs worked with the standard key, which he'd palm to his assistant. She would make the closest match she could to one in their stock then pass it back as the genuine article. All Houdini had to do was secrete the original. He used the cream in his hair sometimes to hold it in place. More than once, he used a sixth finger, which he attached as soon as any search of his upper body was complete. More than ever, it proved that people don't see what they're not looking for. Of course, the mouth was a good place to hold the key, sometimes passed in a kiss from his assistant. That was Nancy's favoured option.

Eddie remembered one performance, where he was astonished that people didn't spot the illusion. The trick required him to be shackled with five different sizes and sets of handcuffs, starting at his wrists and working up his forearm. The image was everything. He looked like Prometheus bound and the sight was astonishing. The sleight of hand, however, was staggeringly simple. Some sets of handcuffs you can snap open with your wrists if you get the pressure right, which Eddie had practiced a thousand times. Once the first set was done, all the others were wider than his wrist so would slip off easily. All he had to do was turn away from the audience and seem to struggle. When he turned back, he was free.

Outside the pub, Eddie had used the simplest method of all. Sheffield police forces had been using standard sets of handcuffs for some years. Eddie borrowed a key off Dougie Mather one time and made a copy. He carried it, with a dozen others, everywhere he went.

He smiled to himself, then pressed on.

With the time ticking late, the streets were quiet, except for the straggling husbands and fathers staggering home with a bellyful of beer. Eddie didn't envy the families their return. As he passed the houses he heard, more than once, a shout and a responding cry jump out through cracks round windows which had been poorly fitted. He slid away from the sound, down to Mary Riley's house, where the street was desolate. Once there, getting in was as easy as it had been before.

Inside the house was sepulchral. Eddie shivered. The sense of death hung over every room, infecting the air, which was full of particles of dust that tasted like ash.

He didn't waste time, skipping upstairs to Mary's room, sadder and emptier than ever before. Sparking up a match, he made his way to the bedside table and found what he wanted exactly where he'd left it: the address book. He was nervous with anticipation as he tried to hold the match steady while he thumbed the pages, the waft of each leaf making the light wobble until he came to the letter W.

His eyes searched down until he found the entry he'd seen before. The landlord William "Bill" Bennett had given him the idea. *William* McGloin: W.M. There, right alongside it - and as clear as he could have hoped for - was an address. If he couldn't exactly place the street, he knew the area, tucked away, as Gilbert had suggested over in Upperthorpe.

This time he took the book, out of instinct. With a sense of thrill he skipped down the steps, wanting to move forward with what he'd found and be out of the house. His feet slowed, though, as he passed the parlour. His curiosity made him pause, unable to forget the search that had happened the last time he was there.

What was there to be found? For a man who liked mystery, the intrigue sparked him. He dipped into the room to peer through the gloom.

The parlour was sparse, except for an old sofa, a spread of books on a walnut bookshelf, a collection of plates in a tired Welsh dresser, a table leaning at an angle and bits and pieces on the mantelpiece. Two old rugs covered the floor where they could, burnt by sparks that had jumped from the fire. When Eddie struck another match the light bounced off the glass of a picture that Mary had hung above the hearth, a cheap copy of some pastoral scene that might make you think of better things when the wind blew and the rain fell and the whole house groaned with the weight of ages and poverty.

From memory, Eddie had heard Billy's breathing, but not much at all in the way of furniture moving. Looking at the room, the obvious thing to think was that he was searching for something that might have slid down the side of the sofa. He looked up to see a candle in a holder that was sitting on the mantlepiece. He lit it, the wick giving a strong but unsteady light that bowed as wisps of wind sneaked in down the chimney or through gaps in the windows and walls. He settled the candle close to the settee as he bent down, starting to ease his fingers along the back then down the sides. After just a few seconds, his fingernail touched something solid. He pulled it out, triumphant.

It was a threepenny bit. Eddie stared at it curiously. If it wasn't going to change someone's life, he thought it strange that Billy had found it and left it. The only conclusion was that it wasn't what he was looking for. Eddie didn't make the same mistake, popping it in his pocket, before rooting down deep again with his fingers.

In the still of the evening, he could hear the candle fizz as it burned, then the wax bomb tipping from the top of the candle down to the base. The only other sounds were the ones that Eddie's fingers made as they fumbled through the fabric, finding nothing.

He sat back on his haunches, disappointed as Billy before him must have been. Resting the candle back on the mantle he looked along the sad line of objects there: a postcard from "Marie" in Donegal; a clock that had stopped for lack of winding which – Eddie guessed – hinted at the time Mary had died; a small crucifix; a cheap model of a dog with a bone; and a tea caddy, which he guessed was for bits and pieces. He looked inside to see all the parts of a sewing kit. Eddie imagined Mary sitting here in the evening, mending something of hers that was a little worn, but not too bad to throw away, brought up never to waste things. What he couldn't imagine as easily was where Billy fitted. There was no sign of him. Perhaps he'd removed everything. Or almost everything.

That's when he saw it. The door, like every door in the Crofts, was badly cut and the flooring was uneven. The combination had kept the door open and with the heat that they had been having he imagined that Mary and Billy wouldn't have minded the draft it brought. But the open door also made a dark space between its back and the wall and there - just peeping out of the shadow of black - was the thinnest gleam of metal. Eddie stepped over quickly to bend down, picking up an object that someone might look for.

It was a ring: a *Claddagh* ring. He held it up against his own fingers. The size made it clear that it belonged to a man. He remembered what Maggie Tasker had said. They take their rings off when they're getting down to business.

***

Eddie slumped into a chair opposite his Dad. "Long day?"

Eddie nodded.

"Are you all right, Eddie?"

His Dad asked that question every now and then. Involuntarily, Eddie rubbed his wrists, where the handcuffs had chaffed the skin. "I'm all right, Dad."

His Mum brought in a cup of Ovaltine and put it down beside him.

"England won the cricket," his Dad said curtly. "Verity. Ran through them. Twice."

"Well, he's a Yorkshireman."

"He's from Leeds, son, so let's not get too excited."

Eddie smiled, closing his eyes. As his Dad made his way upstairs, he called to his Mum.

"What is it, love?" She came back to sit beside him, a worried look in her eyes. He was holding his hand closed. "What have you got there?"

He opened his fingers in one big reveal. "It's a Claddagh ring, isn't it?"

"It *is*. Why've you got a Claddagh ring? What have you done?" Her eyes narrowed. "Have you made a promise?"

"Nothing. I found it. Doesn't it mean something?"

She took the ring and studied it. "You wear it on your right hand with the heart shape pointing out and that means you're single and looking for love. Turn it the other way on the same hand and someone's got your heart."

"Left hand?"

"Left hand, with the heart pointing up means you're engaged."

"And left hand with the heart pointing down means you're married?"

"That's right." She gripped his hand. "Eddie, you're worrying me."

He smiled. "I found it. That's all."

"That doesn't look cheap. You need to give it back."

He patted her hand. "I intend to."

Chapter Sixteen

There was a gap between that conversation and the one he started in the morning with his Dad, but Eddie's sleep was so deep that there hardly seemed to be a space at all.

"What does Mosley want?"

The name put his Dad on edge. "He wants an alliance with Hitler and Mussolini."

"Aren't alliances good? Don't they stop wars?"

"They didn't last time, did they? They *started* them."

Eddie had never delved too deeply into the Great War. It was twenty years now since it had begun. It was another age.

"Are you out again tonight?"

His Mum was curt with him. She was worrying and she blamed him for it.

"I need to rehearse."

"With Nancy?"

"That's right. I need to catch up. I missed the last one we'd set up."

"Keep your eye on her."

"*Mum*."

"I'm just saying. You've got a girlfriend."

His Dad put his teacup back in the saucer precisely and the china rang. "Don't overdo it, Eddie. You can't run all the time." He looked around for his pipe. "Enjoy it while you can. You know?"

Eddie looked over at his Dad, feeling a choke in his throat. He knew how much he was looking forward to the Royal visit to the Fabrics. The whole city was. There was a bustle about the people, a little more chatter. It gave them hope that they hadn't been forgotten.

"I know, Dad. I know."

He got up to go, keen to track Billy down and take the news back to Stan, guiltily aware of how much further he was trying to push his standing.

"Eddie," his Mum's voice had a hook in it, so that he had to turn. "You've got another letter."

The envelope touched his fingers as the Eucharist touched his tongue on the mornings after the nights before. It tingled. "Thanks."

He kissed her cheek.

This time he didn't read the letter. He was thinking of other things and he didn't want guilt to interfere with that. He was thinking mostly about Billy McGloin. The focus kept his eyes blank, so that he didn't see the places he passed or the people who squeezed their way up the aisles on the tram, threading to their seats to start a conversation, read a book, or just let their gaze drift out of the window to watch the city change itself day by day as the century pounded on.

The distraction meant that Eddie wasn't ready when Nancy pounced upon him.

She crashed down on the seat beside him. If Eddie wasn't quite sure how angry her eyes were, her words made it clear.

"An hour, Eddie! I waited an hour!" She glared at him. "I felt a right idiot."

"Hey, I'm sorry.

He lifted his hand and laid it softly across hers, using his thumb to brush the skin between her thumb and forefinger. He was trying to think what excuse to use, but wasn't sure he could be bothered to make the effort. Even in his heart of hearts he'd never intended to get to the rehearsal.

Then he slipped his thumb beneath her hand and squeezed. "I'll make it up to you. You free tonight?"

"You can't charm your way out of everything, Eddie. That's not how the world works."

She was – mostly – wrong.

***

The brewery was busy when he got there. Jeavons handed him a sheet with the details scrawled on.

"It's busy. You've got your work cut out."

Eddie scanned the list, making connections in his head. "We'll be fine. Where's Bert?"

"I think he had one too many. He's sorting himself out." Jeavons laughed at Eddie.

"Sooner out, quicker back." All Eddie wanted was to do his job then head over to Upperthorpe to search out Billy McGloin. "What about the *steamers?*"

"Pretty much the same as Bert."

It was the wagon and horses, then.

Bert appeared just as they finished talking, lumbering over with his eyes still trying to focus on things in ones rather than twos.

"Come on, Bert. Let's get moving."

"I'm not well."

He heaved himself up onto the wagon. The effort made his face go white. He sat down heavy and breathed hard.

"What were you drinking?"

“*Magnets*.”

“Only yourself to blame.”

Bert closed his eyes.

“Go steady.”

Eddie snapped at the reins and the horses jolted forward at a canter.

When Bert was driving the trap, he looked for the flattest routes, going the longer way round to try to avoid the toll that Sheffield’s hills could put on the horses. Eddie had other ideas. There was a cool wind which would fan them as he drove them through half a dozen shortcuts, trimming off minutes with each drop and each time he arrived at a pub he was hitting the pavement while the echo of the horses’ hooves was still bouncing off the brick tenements roundabout.

As Bert lumbered in his shadow, Eddie shifted the beer, sorted the paperwork and shared some chat with the landlords. Business was steady and everyone was calm, so it was good, easy work for the first few pubs until they tugged through the city centre, where the atmosphere changed.

Edmund Waite was a lugubrious landlord, who would complain about rain finding its way into his cellar, or say that the sun was making his beer too warm. If the delivery was late, he would have been waiting for hours. If it was early, he was never ready.

Today, though, he was taciturn, watching Eddie cautiously.

“You all right, Mr. Waite?”

Waite shook his head slowly. “It’s a funny week, Eddie.” He chewed his lip. “There might be trouble. I don't like trouble." Eddie noted that he didn't mind stating the obvious.

"How's that?"

"This rally on Thursday. City Hall."

"Mosley?"

"Aye. Could be thousands." He lifted his finger in warning. "Could be *trouble*. Might cost us some trade."

Eddie smiled. "More likely to be a good bar take. Do you want an extra barrel?"

That hadn't occurred to him and he perked up at the thought. "Aye, I suppose you're right. It'll be a stampede. What a nightmare."

Leaving the city and Mr. Waite behind them, Eddie checked his delivery run again as he snapped the horses into action, renamed *George* and *Marina* in advance of the Royal Wedding. Eddie's easy rapport with the horses had made him a natural driver at the brewery, which some of the older men resented. Eddie didn't mind and neither did the horses. He was quicker and safer than anyone else and he was popular on his route. The roads sang to the sound of their horseshoes striking sparks, a tune interrupted by the screech and grind of car engines and a moving wall of trams. He'd miss the horses when the steamers took over.

"What do you reckon about the new machinery then?" He'd asked one of the farmers on a hot harvest day the previous year. Eddie was watching the horses tug, steady and uncomplaining. They were a wonder to watch, though not quite the spectacle that "Lizzie the Elephant" had been, indentured into the steel works during the Great War to do the work of a dozen mares.

"It's a fad if you ask me. Things won't change."

Eddie didn't believe that. Everything changes. The day he had awoken to the sound of his Dad knocking gently on his door ten years ago to tell him Harry Houdini was dead was the surest sign of that. Eddie changed that day. He stopped being a fan and became a student. Every now and then he'd try a new trick on Bert. Every time, Bert would fall back in his seat and bellow, "Blo-ody hell!"

Today, though, wasn't a day for tricks, or not of the magic kind. Eddie had shaved three quarters of an hour off the morning round and was now directing the cart down the dip at Upperthorpe, checking the street names as he went.

"Where're we going?" Bert asked vaguely, happy to ride and doze when he could.

Eddie saw the street he wanted and eased the horses into the side of the road.

"I'm going to make a call on someone I need to talk to and I reckon you're heading off to the White Hart." He pointed across the road.

"It's not one of ours, Eddie."

"You're not delivering, Bert."

Bert smiled. "Gotcha."

Even when pubs were closed to the public, people in the business could always get in, where they might get a drink with the landlord or – when they were lucky – the landlady.

Eddie watched Bert amble off to the pub, where he gave his own, distinctive rap on the door, as if he was tapping out morse code. Knowing he was good for half an hour at least Eddie skipped down the road, just pulling himself back to the kerb as a car barreled past, the driver wearing an expression of worldliness and wonder all at once. The driver honked his horn because he could and because it might make Eddie jump.

Eddie carried on across to the other side, where a couple of kids were playing marbles. Dotted up and down the road housewives scrubbed their doorsteps with a sense of personal and community pride. As Eddie walked by them, he whistled "*We're in the Money*" with a grin as they looked up. As his feet rapped on the pavement, their knees cracked in response as they shifted their position.

He dipped down a quick left, studying the numbers until he found the address he'd uncovered in Mary Riley's book. The house was unspectacular in an unspectacular street.

Without quite knowing why, he glanced either side of him before he knocked and then leaned forward to rap on the wood firmly four times. As the sound bounced through the house, he stood back and waited. The first few seconds were full of anticipation. The next few were impatient. He knocked again.

By now, two or three figures had appeared on the street, watching Eddie and wondering. He didn't turn towards them. As long as they were looking at him, he held the power. Once he acknowledged them, he lost all that and this became their turf.

"He's not in."

The voice was sharp and thin. This time, Eddie didn't have any choice other than to look at who was talking.

She was hard to age. Poverty had a way of stripping years out of the skin and in and around the eyes. Eddie guessed she was in her late twenties. Her features were hard and angled. He wouldn't try his charm on her.

"Did you see him go?"

"I've not seen him today."

Eddie nodded. "How do you know he's out."

She shrugged. "Because he's not in."

He couldn't doubt her. "How long's he been here?"

"Not long."

"Do you know his name?"

She pulled a face, unsure whether or not to trust Eddie. He had too much charm about him to be completely genuine.

"Might do."

"Is it Billy?"

"Might be."

"Thanks."

She wasn't finished. "Why do you want him?"

It was a good question. "I wanted to talk to him about a woman he knew."

"Did she have any money?"

He smiled. "I doubt it." Eddie had stepped closer now. "Did you talk to him?"

She shook her head. "He had people round. Came early. Left late."

"Did you know them?"

"Not from round 'ere. Is he in trouble?"

"I don't know." He smiled. "Thanks."

He skipped back to the White Hart, where Bert was talking to Mrs. Edna Horncastle, the brains and brawn of the operation. Albert Horncastle was three quarters alcoholic during the day and snored at night.

"Time to go, Bert."

"I'm still drinking."

Eddie flashed a smile at Edna and she smiled back.

"Nice to see you, Eddie."

She had thirty-eight hard years behind her. Each one felt like a welt on her body. Work was hard and she was short of comforts. One of those was her memory and now she remembered when Eddie was eighteen years old, always pushing the boundary from his home in the Crofts, venturing further and further, trying cards tricks on customers for pennies. One night she let him help her with the glasses, when Albert had slumbered to the settee and tumbled down there. When she kissed him it was like touching heaven.

"Mrs. Horncastle." He nodded and she cherished the respect. "Now come on, Bert. I've got a call to make."

"Not another. Is it a pub?"

"University."

"Bloody hell."

Eddie made the horses move with a skip, clattering the cart over the road with a rattle. He was running out of time, but calculated he could pull it back. Barely five minutes after leaving Edna with a kiss on the cheek and her squeeze of his hand, they were pulling up past towards the Children's Hospital, Western Park and the University of Sheffield.

The University was busy, gathering up the great and the good students, spreading them across the campus and city. Eddie, ever direct, went straight to Reception.

"I'm trying to find a student."

The Administrator glanced up through tired eyes after a long day. She relented a little when she looked into his face. He was young and easy on the eye. His smile, too, worked like a key in a lock.

"Who is it you're trying to find?"

"Harry Miller."

The name hit her with a slap and she looked away. "We can't help you." She wouldn't turn back towards him, picking up papers from her desk. "I'm sorry. No one can help you."

***

Frustrated, he urged the horses to get back early, where Len Jeavons stood waiting, as if he'd never moved since the moment they left. As Bert shuffled off, Eddie was direct.

"Can I get off early?"

"Is it a woman?" Jeavons was trying to be matey.

"Sort of."

Jeavons smiled a leery smile of envy.

Eddie was heading back to Upperthorpe. The early release from work gave him time, but meant he'd lost the cover of darkness. The rain that had threatened was coming in spots now and that was helpful, as it pushed more people indoors. Eddie moved fast.

Upperthorpe had a bit more about it than the Crofts, but there was still little to keep you inside if you didn't have to be there. The damp was ever-present and the insects came all year round, burrowing in through every crevice in the crumbling walls, or scratching across the floor in gallops, buzzing from place to place to find something to eat. The street was unkind for a thousand reasons – the casual brutality now and then, the smoke all the time - and the sight of yourself reflecting in the neighbours' dirty windows did little to make you smile.

As Eddie kicked his heels along the pavement the rain started to thicken. With each house he passed he could hear windows closing and doors shutting.

When he came to Billy McGloin's address he slowed from a jog to a skip then a stride. His hand made a strong fist to rap on the door. He hit the wood hard, letting the notes sing through the house. From where he stood, though, it sounded hollow. He tried again. After two or three minutes, his eyes snatched left and right to see who was watching. The rain, though, had picked up enough to push people inside. Eddie used the cover to work his magic with doors again. He knew it was a risk. It was one he had to take.

Sinking inside, he was hit by just how dismal it seemed. The last of the daylight disappeared when the door shut and what took its place was a maw of decay. Emptiness did nothing for houses like this, that never quite warmed however strong the fire. Once the smoke died away, the cold came back and came back harder. If the house was better built than Mary's, it was no better kept and just as empty as hers. He found few signs of life in the kitchen. There was no sense of permanence, just a transitory feel.

He moved upstairs to the bedroom to find a few more signs of life. Even without a body or the heat that the body gave off, there was a sense of presence. There was no dressing table here, just a table that might have been used as a desk. A couple of books sat there. Eddie walked over to see. The title on top was *The Jungle*, which meant nothing to him. The second drew his attention, with red skull and crossbones on the front. The title was *Covenants with Death*. He wondered if it was one of the spy stories his Dad liked to read. He flicked open the pages and stiffened. There was text all right, but most of it was image: pictures of the Great War like nothing Eddie had ever seen: graphic; horrific; bodies stuck in trees from a bomb blast or buried asleep in mud. He stared without moving, trying to make some sense of what he could see, then thinking how his Dad and so many others had witnessed exactly those things, from a few feet away, for real, literally in the flesh.

Eventually, he rested the book down, taking a moment or two to breathe steadily, before looking at the rest of the desk. There was a pen, a mostly empty bottle of ink, a few sheets of paper and what looked like the contents of Billy's pocket. A few small coins, two stamps and a train ticket. Eddie wondered why he had left them and thought he might have had to leave in a hurry. His curious fingers picked up the train ticket: a return trip to Newcastle some weeks ago.

Eddie felt a tap on his cheek and flinched. The touch turned to liquid, running over this skin. He looked up at where the ceiling paper was hanging down in flags, some of the boards above it rotten as teeth. He noticed a bucket on one side of the room, which he guessed was where most of the rain fell. He took a final look around the room – ugly and unloved – then headed back downstairs.

Before slipping out of the house, he checked the windows to see if the streets were empty. Not seeing anybody, he moved outside and closed the door quickly, quietly. As he did, the sound of a shoe scraping on the cobbles behind him sent a jag up the skin on his back. He took a breath, ready with a line of patter to suit any occasion.

Spinning round, his tongue ready to talk, he lost his voice.

"Are you lost, love?"

She might have passed for thirty or more, but Eddie knew she was probably no more than nineteen. When they started working the streets at fourteen or younger, age had a way of doubling up on them. She might have been pretty once. Maybe even again, with a lot of luck. Eddie sensed that it was unlikely to happen that way. Once people got stuck on a path there never seemed to be too many opportunities to turn off or turn back. Everything was just a question of how fast you went down.

"I was trying to find Billy McGloin."

"Billy?"

"You know him?"

"I've seen him. He comes and goes."

"Did you . . ?"

She laughed. "No, he wasn't interested. He always had somewhere he needed to be."

"Have you seen him in the last couple of days?" She shook her head. "Have you ever heard of Harry Miller?" It was worth a try.

"No. What's your name?"

He smiled. "Eddie Reynolds."

The rain was starting to cause her make up to bubble, making her seem like a peculiar piece of impressionism.

"Nice name. What do you do?"

"I'm an escapologist."

She giggled. "That sounds painful."

"Not if you do it right."

He watched her. He'd had a good share of relationships in his relatively young life, but he was looking at a professional. There were many ways in which he admired her, but he knew the job would kill her, one way or another. They shared a look which acknowledged the inevitability. As an escapologist, he hated the idea that some things were inescapable.

"Good luck finding your man."

Eddie smiled. "Good luck finding yours."

Chapter Seventeen

There's no time like show time, was one of the phrases that was bandied around the Brown Bear on performance days where the buzz zipping through the theatre was almost palpable as Eddie sought out Stan Kitteridge.

Looking at the clock – as everyone did every five minutes or so – told you that there was half an hour to go before curtain-up. The foyer was starting to flood with bodies which brought a second level of energy to the performers, when rehearsal and stage fright had drained them of the first. Eddie took a few moments to breathe in a mood that was a little uncertain. Weekday nights were always harder, lacking the weekend buzz that made the audience search for the chance to laugh with their hair down. Eddie watched some of the performers run through their paces, trying out steps, checking their lines. Every one of them seemed just a little unsure of how their performance would land.

Stan was backstage, already arranging the next show or negotiating fees. There were snaps of a quarrel with some performers yet through it all, Stan was calm. *Business is business*, he liked to quote, which was another way of saying that he'd pay what he paid – like it or lump it.

Eddie would have liked it. The money wasn't important right now. He knew that the key was to be on stage and to be seen and to make an impact. Everything else followed.

As he was passing a dressing room he stopped to look in to see one part of "The Punchinellos" with his feet up on the dresser, drawing heavily on a cigarette and ever so slightly adjusting the big fat red nose that was the centrepiece of his clown's outfit.

"Is it going to be a good one?"

The clown looked anxious and the sad face suited it. "What's the crowd looking like?"

"Like it wants to have fun." Eddie told him what he wanted to hear.

He grinned. "Then it'll be a good one."

He was about to leave when Eddie noticed the Players cigarette packet on the dresser.

The clown saw him and said, "Do you want one?"

"I'm collecting the cards for someone."

"Take a look."

Charlie Grimmett. Australia. Though he never followed cricket closely he always listened to his Dad and he remembered him saying that Charlie was one of the best spin bowlers he knew. More importantly, he remembered that Peter, from the Crofts, was still searching for him.

"Can I take it?"

"Course you can. You watching tonight?"

"I'm rehearsing."

"You got a slot sometime?"

"Just confirming it with Stan."

He chuckled. "Get it in writing."

He slipped away to catch some more of the performers, taking a moment to reassure a young ballerina that things would be fine. He might have stayed longer if he hadn't seen Stan out of the corner of his eye.

"'ey up, Eddie." Stan was busy. He was always moving on nights like this. "Crowd's a bit light."

"It'll be OK."

"Time for a beer?"

"Not tonight."

Stan stopped still. "Bloody 'ell. Must be a woman."

"My partner – for the act."

"Oh," he nodded, then grinned, "Nancy, right?"

"Have you got a date?"

"Course I have. Didn't I tell you? July 4th."

"Royal visit."

Stan beamed. "That's right. What a day! Maybe they'll stop by to have a look."

Eddie could feel his nerves tingle. Just for a second, he was short of breath. Greedily, his mind now moved to the running order. Billing position always mattered. He needed to feed Stan something.

"That's great. And I think I've got an address for the boyfriend." He kept back the name for name. No sense going all in at this point.

"No kidding? Wow. I'll tell her mum." He paused, stood back and looked square at Eddie. "You're a good 'un."

Eddie shrugged. "Mary was nice."

Stan nodded. "She *was*, Eddie. Salt of the earth, you know. Meek, mild – all that stuff your Jesus talked about up on the Mount." He was maudlin for a moment, then snapped himself out of it. "So where are you headed?"

"I'm seeing Nancy at the Palace."

"Back row?"

Eddie shook his head. "It's not like that."

***

Eddie was wrong. It *was* like that, or at least Nancy led him straight to the back row and as soon as they sat down she lay her hand on his thigh. "I want to watch."

"It's going to be one of those boring ones," Nancy moaned.

"I want to watch."

He was tired. They'd squeezed an hour's rehearsal in before the cinema. Now he wanted to sit down to watch a film. He'd read good things about this one in his Dad's paper. Lionel Barrymore was leading the show as the eponymous here of *One Man's Journey* and the support was strong, with Joel Mcrea and May Robson adding solid acting chops and Dorothy Jordan the flash and colour.

"It's just a story," Nancy said, dully.

Eddie smiled. A story of one man's journey was what he wanted. A journey was what he was on. With a couple of bags of welks inside him, which they'd picked up in a pub as he passed, he was happy to settle. Beside him, Nancy fidgeted, letting out little gasping sounds, to remind Eddie that she was there and that he owed her something. He slid his arm out to wrap round her shoulder like a fur. Her head angled in towards his, pillowed on his shoulder.

When the show was done, Eddie was refreshed.

When offered to take her home she was thrilled at the idea. He hooked them both on to a tram and sat at the front, like a child.

"We've got a date for the show."

"Really?"

"Really. Stan confirmed it. July the 4th."

“Wow.” She was excited and terrified. Eddie was just excited.

“We need to rehearse more.”

“You’re telling *me*?”

“I know, I know.” He put his arm round her again and she fell into him.

“Will we be all right?”

He nodded. “We’ll be amazing.”

She smiled softly and turned her face in towards him, her lips popping open ever so slightly. Eddie shifted in his seat to turn towards her and felt a jab from inside his jacket pocket, where the edge of the envelope of Louisa’s letter stabbed him.

He closed his eyes and let her kiss him.

***

“You look tired, Eddie.”

Eddie nodded at his Dad. “I am a bit.”

Eddie sat back in his chair and with his muscles relaxed his flesh sank into the cushion. The chair was old and the padding was worn, but right then and there it felt like the most comfortable place to be in the world.

“You getting anywhere?”

Eddie was drinking a cup of *Ovaltine*. He swilled it around his mouth, letting the sweetness sink in while he decided how to answer delicately.

“Nowhere fast. I might have found the boyfriend.”

“Where are you looking?”

“He moved to Upperthorpe. I’ve been round a couple of times but he’s not in. He’s been travelling round a bit, so I hear. He was up in, er,” he paused, wondering how to skip over the fact of his breaking and entering, “Newcastle, I think.”

His Dad was puffing gently on his pipe and paused to pull a bowlful into his mouth, pausing then before letting it slip out into a soft and sweet cloud.

“What do you know about him?”

Eddie shrugged. “Not a lot. Mixed up in politics. The police don’t like him.”

His Dad took another puff of his pipe.

“When last month?”

“What?”

“You said he was in Newcastle.”

Eddie cast his mind back to the ticket. His memory was photographic. “14th.”

His Dad pulled the pipe from his mouth and let the smoke drift out. “Monday?”

“That’s right.” Eddie pulled a face, as if he was in the audience of a magician.

His Dad lay his pipe down on the ashtray with a soft clink. “Interesting.”

Eddie shifted in his seat. “How come?”

“Well, if I remember right.”

“And you do.” They both laughed. It was his Dad’s catchphrase.

“And I do, the day before that there was a bit of trouble up there.”

“Aye?” Eddie was starting to get tense.

“Aye.”

“What?” Without realizing, he was edging forward in his chair.

His Dad turned left where his papers were stacked. Every quarter, he’d archive them and he remembered that it was nearly the end of June in just a few days. His fingers worked steadily before pulling out the paper for May 14th.

Eddie was sitting forward now, curious.

His Dad nodded. "I *was* right."

"What was it?" Eddie took another gulp of *Ovaltine* just to wet his mouth.

"Crowd of five or six hundred. Quite a bit of fighting."

"About what?"

His Dad passed the paper over. The pictures and headlines told a simple story.

"Bloody hell." He looked at the headlines and pictures, then up at this Dad. "Mosley."

"What are you caught up in, Eddie?"

Eddie shook his head and experienced an unusual feeling of doubt.

"I don't know."

Chapter Eighteen

Eddie couldn't sleep. The puzzle of Billy McGloin was buzzing round in his head while the connection to the Mosley rallies was unsettling. The night was warm, too, making the atmosphere itchy and sweaty. At one o' clock he gave up wrestling and slipped downstairs, easing into his Dad's chair before lifting the weight of newspapers into a pile in front of him.

The darkness was stuffy, sticking to Eddie's back as he tried to settle and he found himself wriggling out of sleepiness into a clear and steady wakefulness. Without a wind, the night was still and the house all around him was quiet, except for the steady snatches of snoring from his Dad upstairs. One of the consequences of losing his leg was the need now to sleep on his back more often and then the snoring came. Both Eddie and his Mum enjoyed the sound. It was the sound of life.

Eddie worked methodically through the papers, setting May 14th as a start date then working forwards to track the progress of Mosley's march across the country. That done, he moved back, working towards the beginning as surely as Livingstone tracing the Nile back to its source. His eyes scanned the pages as he turned them, struggling to push through the dim light to find Mosley's name stand out in the headlines, or – more commonly – the word *fascist*, which sat awkwardly in the everyday English language of the *Sheffield Independent.*

The stories he found were ugly.

Oswald Mosley had been on the fringes of politics for some time now. Like most folk, Eddie knew the name in the way that they knew the names of the Prime Minister and the headline-grabbing leaders littered across the world: Stalin, Mussolini, Roosevelt, Lebrun, and now Hitler in Germany. They blended together till the sound of any one of them caused ripples in the equilibrium to unsettle you for moments, then hours, then days. His Dad had a furrow in his brow that seemed to be imprinted with their signature.

Even as he looked for Mosley, his eyes were struck time and again by a battering ram of economic and commercial headlines. The 1920's had been a dark time for capitalism when money had lost its value in more ways than one. The prophets of doom had started to call time on capitalism, a mood that gathered pace with the Wall Street collapse and subsequent recession. Old orders were changing and new ones were ready to wrestle them. The great crash of the last decade hadn't settled any nerves on that score. Meanwhile, Mother Russia had pressed on and on, knitting together its disparate regions into an almighty whole.

The more Eddie read, the more fragile the situation seemed to be. Names that came like an echo tickled at the back of his mind: Goebells in Danzig; the Japanese in Tientsin; assassinations in Poland. The domestic world seemed tame by comparison, but it told similar stories on a much smaller scale, wondering how and when the slums could be replaced with multi-storey apartment blocks, or else bleeding the repeated themes of industry and economy, all set to a backdrop of arms talks and national debt. Alone, so late at night, Eddie felt cold and shivered with a sense of dislocation.

Mosley warned as much. His name had been dotted through the news for a few years now, though Eddie had never paid him much attention. He had lacked real presence. That seemed to have changed this year, When the *Daily Mail* had swung behind him, giving him a voice, though the paper started to backtrack in April, around the time of an Albert Hall oration and – Eddie now understood for the first time – Adolf Hitler's policy to pluck everyone of Jewish heritage out of government office. By that time, Mosley had started a lurching tour across the country, picking up supporters while rousing an equal number of anti-fascists, it seemed. Things had got ugly in Glasgow, aggressive in Newcastle, physical in Bristol then brutal in London at Olympia, where the dogs were let loose and the demonstrators against Mosley's Blackshirts took a beating. The mention of Olympia stirred Eddie's memory from the conversation out on Kinder. His eyes hurried on to find out more.

There was momentum for Mosley. The Government seemed to acknowledge as much, headlines inked across the front pages of what they would do, even trawling back a century or so to resurrect the idea of an *anti-drilling* law, which was intended to keep militias in check. What parliament lacked, though, was unanimity or motion. While some argued that Mosley was simply giving the people what they wanted, the authorities couldn't quite agree what powers the police had. The lack of cohesion created another gap which Mosley squeezed through, slipping round the country. The Blackshirts went before him and by his side. The anti-fascists rolled up to oppose him. When he was blocked, his Blackshirts used a crowbar, or else he dipped his hands into a well of money to buy himself space, though no one quite knew who was supplying the cash.

Things had come to a head at Olympia, where the Blackshirts were unleashed, uncontrolled. They came down hard on the protesters. One of them took a real beating. He was a student in Sheffield and they put him in hospital. His name was Harry Miller.

Eddie took a breath and felt the world spin round him, a dizziness of exhaustion, light-headedness and doubt. When his eyes could focus again, he continued to read.

Mosley was coming to Sheffield. He knew that. The Trade Unions had warned against it, complaining that he shouldn't be given a platform. The anti-fascist groups were more vocal. They were going to give him the welcome he deserved.

Eddie put the papers down. The time was ticking towards two o' clock and in eighteen hours or so, Mosley would be swinging his entourage to Sheffield's bright and shiny new City Hall – a symbol of a city starting to go somewhere after a decade of depression. Sheffield's leaders had finally managed to get some impetus into building a city, rather than just letting it grow. The City Hall was a key part of that plan and the new library was another. Eddie didn't like the idea of Mosley sullying those moments.

Eddie shifted uncomfortably in his Dad's chair as he felt a twinge of pain sting in his shoulder and burn a little in his leg. He was irritated by the feeling until he thought of what his Dad had suffered and what he lived with every day. He closed his eyes, with the first of the morning sun starting to creep in through curtains then fell asleep.

He woke up cold at five o' clock. He pulled himself slowly upstairs and into bed, where he sank back into a sleep full of fast, fitful dreams, thinking of Mary Riley, Oswald Mosley, Billy McGloin – and Harry Miller.

***

Bert had been on the lash again, Len Jeavons sheepishly asking if Eddie could manage the route alone. He jumped at the chance. The steamers, it seemed, were in no better state than Bert. Eddie straightaway took to sorting the horses, running his hand down their back, making the contact of flesh on flesh that made a bond between them.

Eddie gave the delivery list a quick glance. Everyone was going to have to wait today. He had a call to make. He moved the horses along at a clip, steering away from the city centre up the hill towards Upperthorpe. The horses baulked a little at his encouragement, but made good progress at a clatter. He was going rogue, heading back to Billy's house again. Housewives stopped to watch while children skipped or just stared at this stranger.

"Have you seen him? The man who lives here?"

They viewed him as an alien, his language not theirs.

He knocked angrily, hardly knowing why he was chasing Billy so hard and hoping that it wasn't just to push his name up the bill at the Empire.

"What d'you want 'im for?"

The words dropped out of the mouth of a sour-faced man in his forties, who didn't trust anyone much on a good day, which this wasn't.

"I want to tell him his girlfriend's dead – if he doesn't already know."

Eddie used the words like a whip, for effect. The middle-aged man gawped.

"He was here last night. I heard 'em."

"Them?"

"They were arguing. Shouting."

Eddie didn't need to ask if he'd tried to find out more. It was always best to keep yourself to yourself.

***

He was running against time on his route now, pushing the horses hard up the heavy slope of City Road. A feeling of clutching at straws grated on him. He liked to be precise and certain. Now he was gambling randomly.

One of Betty's sons opened the door. His face twisted seeing Eddie. He didn't quite know what to do with someone so brazen so just stood there in a lump. Somewhere behind him, Eddie caught the sound of a muffled yelp and then a low, slow sob. The smell of carbolic rolled down the stairs towards the door in a rush to get out. Right behind the smell was the sound of footsteps, planting themselves heavily as they came.

Betty's face was torn and tired. Her eyes had a glaze pulled across them from the things she'd seen and Eddie couldn't help but notice smears of crimson on her fingers.

"What do you want?"

The crying continued some way behind them, slowing to a drip.

"Do you know Billy McGloin?" He hadn't found a way to be subtle.

"I take cash, love. I don't always take names."

Eddie stood deflated. A little spark of sympathy showed in Betty's eyes.

"The men don't get involved. Sometimes they provide the cash, but they don't come round. They're not there. They don't see. What was his name? *Billy*?" She shook her head and there was a look of disgust in her features, at the thought of Billy who wasn't there and Eddie who was and every other man besides. "Get out of here."

Eddie stepped back. "Gladly."

***

With Billy no closer, the only thing that Eddie could hold onto was the idea that Harry Miller might be able to help him, but not tonight.

He'd been losing time all day which meant that he had to drive the horses and himself hard to catch up, bearing the curses of landlords who'd been waiting all day as he shifted the barrels by himself and pushed on again.

By the time he was back at the brewery it was closing time and Jeavons was standing in the yard, anxious.

"Thought you'd got lost."

"There's a lot of stuff on the roads you get stuck behind."

"Bloody cars. Nearly did for my Uncle last weekend."

"Is he all right?"

"Bruised. Bloody thing winged him and never stopped."

"I'm not sure they all know *how* to stop it."

"You're right there. You coming for a drink? A few of the lads are having one."

Eddie shook his head. "I've gotta go."

"Date?"

He remembered Ada. "Yeah. Sort of."

"How can you sort of have a date?"

It was a good question.

Chapter Nineteen

"You look tired."

Ada's voice sounded maternal. She wondered how she might have been as a mother.

"I'm all right."

She sniffed. "What are we watching?"

"You'll see."

In fact, it was a Gymkhana which had drawn people from across the city, plugging the space with moving bodies as they worked out what to see, where to sit and whether they should eat and drink now, or maybe later. Eddie fell into the crowd with Ada. He felt that thrill of the audience, its anticipation welling up like a wave building before it spilled down from the balconies, up from the stalls onto the stage where the performer commanded it. Eddie equally loved and hated to be part of that audience. He wanted to be on the stage. The excitement helped him relax after the disappointments of the day.

"Is this going to be good?" Ada's voice had a rattle.

He was tired of her today. "You could have stayed in."

She snapped away from him, seeking out a programme seller. Eddie watched her and watched the men she walked past watch her. She was dressed sharp as ever, literally a different class to everyone around her.

By the time she was back Eddie was apologetic. "What do you want to see?"

She had skimmed the programme. Now her face beamed. "I want to see it all."

He liked that about her. Her ambition was unvaulted.

She wasn't disappointed. There was plenty to see.

Owlerton was well known as a dog racing track and the greyhounds were on show today, whipping round the course with their bodies bent against gravity, straining to achieve lift-off as they chased the hare. Ada grabbed Eddie's hand as *her dog* lost its footing and tumbled, bouncing, off the track onto the grass enclosure at the heart of the stadium.

"Will he be all right?"

Eddie chuckled. "Don't eat the sausages later."

Ada slapped him playfully, switching her attention to the trapeze, gawping at the figures as they flew through the air. As she gasped, Eddie smiled to himself, acknowledging the wonder they inspired as they sailed across the sky. Below them, a troupe of acrobats bounced and tumbled, drawing the crowd into whoops and cheers. Eddie watched Ada. She was smiling, happily escaped into a world of daredevils, strongmen, fencers, boy scout brigades and military formations. There was a sense of pride that she'd known at the start of The Great War, without all the fighting.

The spectacle made Eddie think. He had agreed to perform at the church gala and the show at the Empire was coming up fast. He had to make those performances matter. They had to be special. It was critical that people remembered him.

"Are you going to watch me at the Empire?"

"What date is it?"

"July the 4th."

"What can I tell Ken?"

"You could bring him."

She pulled a face. The thought had never occurred to her. She wondered if Eddie was being spiteful. He wondered the same. Her face tightened as she turned away.

Their attention was caught as a set of jugglers entered the stage, the audience sucking up into a mighty cheer. Ada's face lifted up like a smiling child. Her eyes widened. The images in front of her connected somewhere with her dark early days, where all she had was hope and occasional glimpses of life beyond the brutal day ahead.

Eddie squeezed out of his seat. "I'll get something to drink."

He fiddled in his pocket for a few coins then scanned the area around him to see where he could buy something. A vendor caught his eye.

She was young and pretty.

She smiled. Eddie smiled back.

He was paying for the drinks when a voice behind him caught him by the shoulders.

"Eddie!"

Michael Egan had put on some weight since their previous meeting, turning out last minute on a cold December morning as part of the St. Vincent's football team to take on the Sacred Heart. Though he'd never been a regular player, Eddie was fast. Michael, on the other hand, was – by his own admission – "a big lad". He was hard to get past. If he caught you, you'd know about it.

"Hello, Michael. You're looking well."

"*Fat*, you mean." He laughed.

"No, no."

"Yes, yes. Getting too comfortable. Stuck behind a desk all day."

Egan was twenty years older than Eddie and doing well enough, helping Sheffield Corporation run the city. Time had plumped him up, his belly pushing out to pop the hairs out of his head, giving him a bald patch in the centre, which he covered with a combover.

"How are you?"

"I'm good. Time for a drink?"

"I'm . . . with someone."

"Ah," he grinned. "Lucky man."

"What about you?"

"Oh, I'm married." He laughed. "So not so lucky."

"How's the Corporation?"

"Busy. Particularly this week."

"Mosley?"

"Spot on. It's going to be a mess, Eddie." Egan's face folded up with a frown. "There's been trouble all around the country. The problem here is there's a big socialist movement. There's going to be a lot of opposition."

"What are the police saying?"

"Hold on to your helmets. Keep away from the town centre tomorrow."

"I'll practice my routine."

"You still performing?"

"I'm on at the Empire next month."

"I'll come along. It'll be fun."

"Bring the wife."

"If I have to!"

Eddie collected his drinks and drifted back towards Ada, who seemed distracted. Her eyes were chasing all over, as if she could never settle.

"Where've you been?"

"I saw an old friend. Are you all right?"

She squeezed his arm. "I missed you."

He caught her hand. It was her left and he felt the depression on her third finger, where a ring should have been.

"Let's watch the show."

Ada smiled. She was happy. The sounds and images captured her. Eddie watched her and them and all the time thought about Billy McGloin and Harry Miller. He hadn't found Miller at the University. He would have to take his chance to try again tomorrow at the rally.

***

On the tram ride home, Ada was happy, leaning into Eddie, snuggling up to him where the warmth of his body softened her. She wasn't usually so careless. She was a married woman. People saw things. People talked. Both of them knew it was only a matter of time before word got back to her husband. It was the volcano she was expecting. Some days she simply sat on the sofa wondering what it would mean to both of them: her husband and herself. Eddie, she knew, would escape the worst of it.

It was nearly nine o' clock when they started the slow drag up the road back to her house. The evening was soft, one where you wanted to linger longer with it. Ada had taken Eddie's hand. He looked at her cautiously.

"We're nearly back."

She nodded and smiled. "Dominoes night for Ken."

Eddie clicked his teeth together. He was tired. The days – and the sense of chasing that shot through them – were beginning to drag on him. "He could be back any time."

"We could be quick," she said in a whisper.

"It's a risk, Ada."

"I thought you liked risks."

When she wanted something, she could be persuasive. Her eyes tickled with promises.

He laughed.

Five minutes later, she was stripping in a slow tease in front of him, shifting her limbs to the rhythm of a dance inside her head, locking her eyes to his all the time. Her movements were strong with the confidence of knowing the effect her body had on men. Eddie was caught as much in that moment as he ever was with any of his locks and straightjackets. He sensed as much himself, knowing he shouldn't be there or should be going but couldn't move at all. As she smoothed her thumbs into the waistband of her French knickers Eddie stiffened. He knew that he was stuck there in time.

He slid down in towards her, teasing her with his tongue on her skin so that she jerked. He felt her hairs tickle his cheek. A breath escaped her. He stopped rigid, his body tense, as he thought of Mary Riley, then hundreds more with the likes of Betty Wilson swinging above them on broomsticks. Then he thought of Ada herself, who couldn't have children. He thought of how the fact made him safe – in a way that, strangely, he didn't want. A sin without the threat of punishment hardly seemed a sin at all. Eddie didn't want to cheat.

"Don't stop," she whispered.

And he didn't. This was a performance after all, but it was cold and bloodless. He was detached, while Ada disappeared entirely underneath him, her voice at times quiet, desperate.

When it was over, they pulled apart and felt the sticky separation of sweated skin. Eddie lay on his back for a while, not speaking, Ada breathing heavily. He looked around the room that was a bedroom for a marriage that he didn't belong to, his only part of it the clothes he had had folded over an arm of a chair. As he looked, he could see his jacket flapped open, where the letters from Louisa – still unopened – popped out of the pocket.

"I've got to go."

"Not yet."

She had lost her appeal. He kissed her and it was kind.

***

Short of money, Eddie decided to walk home, knowing enough short cuts to swing him back up towards Meadowhead without too much difficulty. As he moved along, the woodlands clustered around him, the last of the birdsongs saying good night, the animals slowing down then taking to bed. He couldn't get Harry Miller's name out of his head, or the need to meet him. He wondered if Miller knew Billy McGloin and how. Then he thought about Billy again. He had to find him, but didn't know where to look. He felt that he couldn't keep banging on his door every day without things becoming suspicious – and he didn't know who was watching. After all, searching for Billy had already got him arrested once.

The train of thoughts were stuck in a loop going round and round, making him dull to the progress he was making or the place where he was. By the time he stepped into the gennel next to his home church he had only one clear thought left: he had to find Miller.

"Eddie?" The word caught his ear, just before the trail of smoke tickled his nostrils.

"Hello, Father." Eddie was surprised and a little taken aback. Father Cleary was sitting on a low wall, with the Church rising up behind him, blended into the black except for the white collar around his neck, which looked to Eddie equally like a fallen halo or a noose.

"You're out late."

"Just going home."

"Where've you been?"

Eddie's eyes wriggled away from the priest. "Gymkhana."

"Was it good?"

"Very good."

Eddie didn't know what else to say and Father Cleary was happy with the quiet. The day had been difficult. An industrial city didn't take care of its citizens very well. As night closed in he was often left sitting by the bed as they were dying then died.

"Did you ever find anything else about that woman?"

"Yes. A bit. It's complicated."

"It always is."

"Really. I don't think she killed herself. Or she didn't mean to."

"It's hard to understand why people do what they do, Eddie. I wish I *could* understand, but I've seen things you can't explain."

Eddie stood in front of Father Cleary, not agreeing or wanting to argue.

The priest tugged on his cigarette. He offered Eddie one.

Eddie saw the packet. "Have you got the card?"

"Are you collecting?"

"For a friend."

"Take it."

B.A. Barnett, Australian wicket keeper.

"Got it, thanks." He left the card, took the cigarette. They sat together without speaking for three or four minutes until the last smoke drifted away.

Eddie was about to leave, except for a sense that the priest wanted to talk to tell him things and in the telling, maybe understand something himself.

"Maybe it was all too much. We cope for so long, then the smallest thing can break it."

"The straw that broke the camel's back?"

"That's right. Maybe there was just one thing she couldn't cope with anymore. She lost two brothers in the war, I heard. And her childhood sweetheart." The priest paused, taking a big drag of air. "Then at the back of your mind you hear of these things happening locally." He shrugged. "All of a sudden the most natural thing in the world is to copy them."

Eddie didn't follow. "What things? Where?"

The priest let out a lungful of smoke. It went straight to heaven.

"The woman at St. Marie's the other week. Didn't you hear?"

"No." He was sitting rigid now. "What happened?"

Father Cleary took one last lungful of smoke. He'd heard a whisper somewhere that cigarettes might be bad for you. He had to chuckle. It was the sort of thing that the Church always said: watch out for what you enjoy. He blew out. The smoke billowed round him.

"She poisoned herself. It was a mess." He shook his head. "It was in the papers."

***

Eddie's mind was troubled as he closed the front door of the house. His Mum hardly had time to kiss him as he burst into the living room and looked across at his Dad.

"Are you all right, Eddie?"

"Someone died at St. Maries. It was in the news."

"Oh, aye." His Dad was smoking and now pulled the pipe from his mouth. "I read about that." He turned left to leaf through his mountain of papers, where he lifted one from the pile, turning it towards Eddie so that he could read the headline. "Poisoned herself."

It was some coincidence and Eddie didn't believe in coincidence. He made a note visit St. Marie's as soon as he could, but it wouldn't be tomorrow. Tomorrow was all about Mosley's visit to the City Hall – and finding Harry Miller. Eddie had to hope that he would be there.

Chapter Twenty

The working day was coming to an end. People were starting to drag themselves away from shops, workshops, offices and factories to mix together through the central streets of Sheffield. Beyond this snake of bodies Eddie noticed small groups positioned around Barker's Pool, Pinstone Street and Town Hall Square, furtive and forthright in equal measures. They were coming, not going. And they were waiting, a buzz beginning to pass between them.

Eddie had things to do before his search for Harry Miller began, but he couldn't resist a quick peak at the people forming clumps that would soon be groups then later, crowds. They were sparking. The energy made him bounce as he moved down from Barker's Pool, past *Wilson Peck* on the corner, where he peered in to see the wealthier side of Sheffield pick out pianos for their sitting rooms. One of the salesmen was sitting at the keys, working through a medley of classics for the punters that passed through. Strains of the *Goldberg Variations* pushed out of the doors when someone entered or left to give the city a sense of propriety. The music was a soundtrack for Eddie as he studied those small groups. They were waiting for Mosley.

He idled ten minutes inside *Austin Reed*, endlessly escaping the advances of an attendant who guessed that Eddie didn't really have the money to shop there. He was right, but he was wrong about Eddie's ambition. He wasn't simply window-shopping; he was making promises to himself about the future.

Eddie dug into his pockets for some remaining money, then - despite knowing he couldn't really afford it - he headed into *Davey's* for something to eat. *Davey's* was his mother's favourite store, carrying most of what you might want and a reasonable mix of things that were inside your price range (that you could have) and those outside (that you could hope for).

The restaurant had a fresh feel. The waitresses were well-trained, treating Eddie like a gentleman. They were a regular mix of the young and older, all with a smiling courtesy that made the day seem better. He had thought he might bring Ada with him one time. Being there now, though, the place lacked all pretention, so he thought of Louisa. One memory triggered another and he pulled her letters from his pocket.

He read them through. The simplicity made him bite his lip. She got up, worked hard, went home, then wrote letters before going to bed.

Every letter was sealed with a kiss. In the first one, she said she missed him. In the last, she said she loved him. Eddie sat back, took a sip of tea and looked out across the city from an upstairs window. The spaces that had emptied were starting to fill. Things were in motion and something was happening. He pulled a pen from his jacket to scribble some notes on the back of one of the envelopes. He was going to tell Louisa a story.

***

By seven o'clock the space between bodies had vanished in Barker's Pool, as an ever-moving, always rocking mass of people swelled from five thousand to six then finally to ten. Everyone was fizzing. The collective force made a warp in the early evening atmosphere that you couldn't help but sense as you joined them.

The numbers caused Eddie some concern. How was he going to find Miller in this haystack of bodies? He had no idea how or where to start. As he moved through the throng, nervous chatter came out of mouths in spats, a sense of tension keeping everyone alert.

Eddie decided to head for the people carrying the banners, on the assumption that they were more formalized than the everyday person and might know a bit more of what was going on and who was where.

The banners themselves hung above the crowd showing big, no-doubt-about-it messages. Mosley and his black shirts weren't welcome. Sheffield didn't want them. That was what the socialists said. That was what the unions said. With time ticking, the banners were helping to forge a unity across the body of protesters. They were sharing a single, focused message. Eddie wondered just what would happen when Mosley arrived.

Clumped in groups at regular intervals, or up high on their horses, the police were wondering just the same. Police vans were set at strategic points like hearses waiting to carry the bodies away. Eddie did a quick calculation, losing count when he had passed two hundred. The police, of course, had their own dark blue uniform. They were their own team. Eddie didn't quite know whose side they were on.

He was close now to one of the groups trailing banners in the sky. They were bound together in a tight knot of five, deep in discussion and full of passion. As Eddie approached, they ignored him at first. The closer he came, though, the more suspicious they became.

"'ey up?"

A standard Sheffield greeting: a welcome and a question.

"I'm trying to find Harry Miller."

The name worked a charm. Their faces sprang open.

"What do you want with Harry?"

They had been made up into a circle, but now the pattern broke so that they formed a single line to face him. Three men and two women, each one looking as if they had lived enough hard life for a whole family.

"I need to ask him something. I'm trying to find Billy McGloin." Eddie tried to keep calm, remembering those times when an audience wanted to go a different way from you and knowing that once you lost them, you never got them back. "Do *you* know Billy?"

They looked at each other, then back at Eddie. "Who are you?"

"You want to leave Harry alone."

Eddie moved closer. Audiences were pack animals. You had to treat them as such.

"I need to talk to Billy about Mary Riley."

Mary's name meant nothing and the frustration of time wasted began to sag.

"Can't help you there."

Eddie wouldn't give up. "But you know Harry?"

Again, they were tight-lipped and defensive. "You want to leave that alone, son."

The words were a warning.

Eddie slipped back into the thick of the crowd where he felt himself disappear in the steady movement of men and women. The Town Hall clock looked down and wound up the tension with every movement of its minute hand. The noise was starting to collect into waves that rolled backwards and forwards over the crowd.

Despite the previous rebuff, Eddie had to try again to cut a way through tiny gaps towards the front of the congregation, which had spilled now right to the foot of the City Hall steps. The police were striped along the way, watching for a moment when the line might break and tumble forward. They were ready and their hands were itching on the handles of their truncheons.

The moment came just as Eddie was clawing to the front. A scuffle broke out and voices that had been raised now erupted. The crowd opened up around the two men fighting, the gap allowing the police to roll in, mounted officers using their horses like battering rams, bouncing bodies out of the way. Half a dozen officers swooped onto the pair to haul them away, tugging them towards the vans that were waiting to take them to the cells. As they went the crowd booed, jeering about oppression and challenge to free speech.

Barely five minutes later, three more police patrol wagons and a police ambulance rolled up, causing those who saw it to whisper and shout. The focus caught everyone's attention, allowing Eddie to slip closer to another band of demonstrators, waving banners while spilling out chants like gunfire. They didn't stop when Eddie came close to them.

"I'm trying to find Harry Miller."

He had chosen a young woman to speak to. He guessed the she was a university colleague. She was younger than Eddie, full of big, loud words.

"Why do you want Harry?"

"He might be able to help me find someone."

"Who?"

Eddie had to think how to play this. The time he had lost and his lack of progress made him go big. "It might be one of the Blackshirts."

The words worked, jerking her head back towards him.

"One of Mosley's men?"

Eddie nodded. "Could be."

"Why would Harry know?"

"He might have seen him at Olympia."

She wasn't sure. Whatever his reputation had been before, Harry had become a hero since his beating in London. Every crowd needed a figurehead and Harry was just that.

"He'll be inside."

"In the meeting? Can I get in?"

"Not now."

The words stumped him. While he wondered what to do next a group of three middle-aged men appeared by his side and moved right up to his face.

"Why do you want Harry Miller?"

The woman who had helped Eddie was nervous now, not sure if she'd just aided a collaborator. Eddie eased back on his heels, just enough so that he could run if he had to.

"I'm not going to hurt him."

"Bloody right you're not."

A hand reached out to catch Eddie's arm, squeezing it. The movement came with a wrench which he felt in his shoulder. As the other two moved up closer Eddie could see that one of them had his hand tight in his jacket pocket. Whatever he was holding, Eddie didn't want to see it. He eased back another half step.

"I just want to ask him some questions. I'm trying to find Billy McGloin."

The name went off like a firework, all three of them sharing glances, before facing back to Eddie.

"What about McGloin?"

"You know him?"

"We're not telling you anything, lad."

"That's why I need to speak to Harry."

Another inched forward again, close enough that Eddie caught a breath of potted beef over his face. "You leave Harry alone." He said it definitively. But he had to say more. "And watch out for McGloin."

A fracture in the crowd broke up the conversation so that everyone lost their places as the body surge rippled all across Barker's Pool, accompanied by a collective cry. Eddie, like all others, turned to see what was happening and caught sight of a string of motorcoaches bullying its way towards the City Hall.

"They're here!"

The cry was animal and hunter all at once, thousands pushing forward to get towards the coaches to see the faces of the fascist brotherhood. The movement was tidal, reminding Eddie of days on the Spion Kop at Hillsborough when the ground was full and the Sheffield Wednesday strikers were sweeping forward on goal. Eddie went with the flow, unable to do anything else and keen to find out if Billy McGloin was one of the new arrivals.

The noise now changed to a loud, percussive baying, the sound hitting the glass of the coaches hard, so that Eddie imagined that the passengers sitting inside - staring out - could feel the hot breath of the mouths that shouted. The ground trembled with the pound of footsteps of protesters urging towards the vehicle, then the answering clap of horse hooves on stone, making those stones sing as if they'd been struck by swords.

As the coach doors opened, the crowd grew louder. There was anger pouring off the tongues of good husbands and wives and fathers and mothers. There was a hatred of people that wanted to change the world to suit their taste.

Eddie paused for a moment, to take it in, lost his footing, lifted up by the crowd pushing forward. Struggling with his feet he tumbled down, five hundred pairs of shoes or boots banging past him in a jungle of limbs, until he righted himself to stand up tall.

As he came back into the open air, he was exultant. Now *this* was a crowd. *This* was an audience. Like everyone else, he wanted to see what happened next. The performers were about to disembark the coach. That would be something to see.

If the crowd had been expecting fear, they would have been disappointed. If they'd expected the Blackshirts to be embarrassed, they would have been wrong. The Blackshirts acknowledged the crowd: the fact of it, the size of it, the threat it posed. They viewed it as they would have viewed an opposing army. But there was no fear. Their uniform gave them camaraderie, purpose and strength. They were here to fight a war. As they looked out across the crowd – which lacked any sense of order when set against their singular style – they felt they were the only ones prepared for it.

Eddie ran his eyes along the figures to see if he could match any of them to Billy, struggling to catch their faces as they bobbed. He couldn't make a pair, yet couldn't be certain he'd seen them all close or well enough. He pushed forward to be nearer to them.

Their resolute confidence quietened the crowd a little, until they began their march towards the City Hall, when the barracking started again, from some – safe - way back in the crowd. One or two of the leaders glared out into the faces opposing them, searching for anyone brave enough to turn insults into punches or kicks. They were ready. It was a direction they would be happy to follow.

That initial arrogance could only last so long. The men and the women facing the Blackshirts were veterans, miners, ironworkers, buffers and grinders who had worked hard and long and hurt more than enough for a lifetime. They'd lost loved ones and legs and friends and fingers in the filth of the factory and the dirt of the Somme. They weren't going to be bullied out of saying what they wanted. Threaded through the crowd were the younger faces, who hardly knew the war at all, hated the pessimism of the past, the stagnation of the twenties and the despair for the future. They were here to make things better.

Eddie took the ride with them all and found himself close to the front, staring eyeball to eyeball with a thickset Blackshirt, ready to use his fists as soon as he was called on.

As the line of black snaked its way into the City Hall, the crowd sagged, its momentum lost for a moment. The quiet was short-lived, as first a few and then hundreds more took up the call against the police, while they escorted a man down the steps from the entrance, where he had been pushing papers into people's faces to get his message across. Eddie watched how the police force and the crowd moved into waves, leaving a gap where they had been until the bodies flowed back to their regular shape.

"Communist!" someone shouted. Eddie couldn't tell if the speaker meant it as a compliment.

The incident was like a firework. Once it had sparked and flowered it was gone and the crowd was restless once more. They steamed up again, as a second foray of coaches arrived, drawing the forces of the protesters forward in a surge. Perhaps because there were only two buses this time and fewer Blackshirts spilling onto the pavement, the crowd felt stronger and bolder. Again, Eddie pressed forward and tried to discover if – just by looking – he could discover Billy.

"Billy!" He shouted, his voice barely a reed in the wind against the clatter of chants and calls. Did someone twitch? "Billy McGloin!"

Eddie couldn't be sure what he'd seen or whether someone responded. He had to get closer.

"Where's Mosley?"

The call was picked up and repeated, threading the crowd together.

Eddie guessed that – like all good illusionists – he had spirited his way into the building on the back of some grand misdirection.

His absence made the mood more brutal. The audience wanted their Jesus in front of them. So, it was hardly a surprise when the tension snapped and a fight broke out, an ugly, sharp and brutal flurry of boots and arms. The bodies around it separated which made a space for the police to sink into, swinging heavy before pulling the three men apart and away to a chorus of cheers and boos. The sound was nasty. The police saw and heard as much, swinging their horses into a cavalry attack, driving that section of the crowd apart, chasing them down Cross Burgess Street, by the Regent and Albert Hall. All the while, the Blackshirts filed forward, towards the City Hall.

It seemed to Eddie that order was about to break – and yet the opposite happened. A sense of time rippled through the crowd, a collective knowledge that Mosley would be readying himself to pour out his vision for Britain. A sort of silence followed. Eddie saw one man bite his lip, an acknowledgement of a fear that the world they knew or wanted may just be slipping out of their hands. They were in the majority, surely? People would see sense, wouldn't they? But the Great War still hung over their heads, the economic collapse of the Twenties had shaken them and nothing was certain anymore. Eddie thought of the priests pulling their Church around themselves like a coat and wondered. He thought of Ada's husband keeping his money in a box under the bed rather than the bank. He thought of the film industry taking a red pen and scissors to scenes that they had to believe no longer fitted with more puritan times. Like everyone else, while he thought those thoughts, he was quiet.

The crowd was waiting for a moment to burst that bubble of introspection. It came when a police van pushed its way towards one of the exits, just in time to meet a man being escorted out of the building. There were huge cheers for one of their own. Here was an agitator who wouldn't be silenced. He had gone in to heckle, to make sure Mosley knew that people opposed him, would fight him – with words at first and then whatever was necessary. Eddie guessed that Mosley's minders had singled him out then seen him out of the hall. As the police bundled him away, he raised a fist and waved. Ten thousand people roared.

As Eddie watched them, he noticed another little fist-and-kicks fight drawing attention to itself, with crowd and police falling on it. Their movement left the side entrance to the building bare for the moment with the Blackshirts mostly alone.

Eddie veered away from the main crowd, skipping in towards the door that the Blackshirts were steadily passing through.

The fight was a perfect misdirection. No one would be looking at him. The crowd were self-involved and the Blackshirts were shuffling with an undetermined method of marching. Eddie picked up the movement to join them at the end. With everything facing forward, none of them noticed him and no one in the crowd knew that he shouldn't be there. His confidence was the key.

Once inside the door, he sheared away from the group, hugging close to the wall before moving his way towards the back of the stalls.

The mood inside the building was fragile. A sense of imminent danger made everyone move with a twitch. Eddie welcomed the fact. No one was minded to ask him who he was or where he was going. As he paced along, he could hear a groundswell of conversation pushing outwards from the auditorium, a sound that blended into a continuous beat and Eddie buzzed to hear it. He moved forward, trying to find the face that might have answered to the Billy's name when he'd shouted it out.

Up ahead, a door pushed open and an attendant emerged, bringing with him a blast of the noise from inside. Eddie couldn't help but head towards it, slipping inside unnoticed before the door swung closed. And he was there.

Chapter Twenty-One

The place felt full, the sense of occasion tripping from person to person as they chatted, some voices sotto voce out of respect for a concert hall and some using stage whispers for just the same reason. The stage itself was busy with staff making final touches to the podium or the microphone and acting as a placemark for the lights, which were tumbling down now to pick out the centre.

Someone brushed past him and Eddie turned to see a Blackshirt move with flick-knife purpose, scanning Eddie up and down once to see if he might be trouble. Eddie smiled.

"Good crowd."

The Blackshirt said nothing.

Eddie had had worse audiences so carried on. "Do you know Billy McGloin?"

The figure wrapped in black stared straight through Eddie then moved on, pitching his eyes over the seats to see where the trouble might be. Eddie watched, to see if the Blackshirt could find Harry Miller for him. The Blackshirt finished his circuit, though, without approaching anyone in the audience. When he was done he met a colleague. They fell together into tight discussion, the second figure pointing a finger deep into the stalls. Eddie followed the line and saw a quintet of fresh-faced figures, talking nervously.

"Could you please take your seat, sir?"

Eddie twisted round to see an obsequious figure in his mid-forties practice his routine for the hundredth time tonight. This was what he did and he had been doing it for twenty years. Eddie imagined he dreamt of holidays on the East Coast as he tripped out those lines.

"Sorry, I was just looking for a friend."

Eddie turned to move positively towards an empty seat, looking back after ten paces to see if the attendant was still hovering. He wasn't. He had moved on to the next standing group, ushering them to their seats, rolling out the same lines, thinking the same far away thoughts. Eddie straightened up before continuing his search on foot.

A hush was starting to roll over the audience now as seat by seat was filled. Eddie peered into the crowd to see just who wanted to hear what Mosley had to say. He was surprised – and perhaps not – that it was an all-sorts collection of people, mostly men, mostly middle-aged but some women too and some younger faces. He looked for Harry, or Billy McGloin. He didn't find either of them.

Then the auditorium lights dipped and a collective intake of breath rolled out from the stalls up to the circle then finally the balcony. Eddie was stuck alone, still standing at the back, pressed against the wall. To his left, he could see another usher starting to walk towards him. He bent quickly, searching out an empty seat at the end of a row, tucking himself into it, a square squat man with a wig and black glasses turning to squint at him.

The whispering stopped and the crowd held their breath.

Here he was!

As Oswald Mosley strode onto the stage, Eddie heard the applause start from the place where the Blackshirts were now gathered. They pumped their hands together in a way that reminded Eddie of the machinery he'd seen in the steel mills. They were mechanical.

Mosley strode to the front of the stage, dressed in singular black, looking like a moving shadow. The lights that were wrapped around his body seemed to transfigure him. The audience clapping had changed now. It was faster and louder, moving from initial politeness to something closer to fervour.

He cut a clean figure, a thick belt at his waist, suggestive of something military or martial. The chisel moustache only added to the impression, his short-cropped hair making his face sharp and hungry. The look made his body seem like one long limb. The extensions were his arms, which he used precisely, standing hand on hips for much of the time, or carving out space with a right hand that swept outwards and upwards, one sharp finger pointing high to the heavens or out at the wider world in accusation.

Eddie was sitting forward, now listening not to the words of the speech, just the sound of the voice, which worked like a sea wave, building to crescendo, falling and rising again. Eddie caught some of the sense. He heard Mosley bay about betrayal and change and revolution. Looking round, Eddie saw all the faces caught up in rapt attention, even those – he guessed – who hated Mosley and everything he stood for. They were all waiting for the crest of the wave, where he would call for their adulation. When it came, a tiny few tried to boo, but it was drowned by cheering. Beside Eddie, the man in glasses howled appreciation, for the first time in his life able to express what he really felt.

Inevitably, the speech settled into something a little more subdued. Like all passions, you can only keep them up for so long, Eddie reckoned. He watched Mosley work his audience now, prompting them during the middle part of his oration to small bursts of applause, until building to a coruscating conclusion.

The final note was a prompt for people to rise to their feet, stamping the ground or pumping their hands together. As Eddie joined with them he looked for the people who didn't move. He picked out spots of bodies, stuck in their seat, their faces glum with the reality of an everyday fascism in their city and more than a little frightened.

As the bodies settled again, it was question time, for the most part the audience acting as the straight man, feeding Mosley a set up for all his best lines. His flow, however, was interrupted by a grating sound, a regular speckle of chanting that caught in the smooth flow of his peroration like a piece of grit. Eddie scanned the audience to identify the source, helped by a flurry of Blackshirts circling a spot in the balcony as if they were trapping prey.

Mosley continued. So did the heckling.

The Blackshirts moved in and there was a cry.

Mosley paused. "Let him ask his question."

A cold silence fell on the audience. They had wrapped themselves up in a bubble and they didn't want it burst just yet. They knew that outside of the hall were thousands of people who hated them being here. But this was their right and their night, their moment to think and say what they felt. The heckler was ruining all that.

Mosley looked up into the balcony as if he was staring at an assassin.

"Tell us your name, young man."

Eddie twisted fully to look up towards the spot to try to see the face in the quarter light of the auditorium.

"Harry Miller," the young man said in a squeak.

Eddie felt his nerves tighten.

"Do you have a question, Mr. Miller?" Mosley was calm.

"Yes, I do."

The audience held its breath.

"Can you tell me why you let your supporters attack me at your rally in Olympia and hurt me so badly that I spent a week in hospital?"

Harry Miller shouted the question, an accusation, but it came in a thin pipe against the deeper, more assured sound of Mosley.

The question made the audience bristle.

Mosley was unmoved. "Olympia was unfortunate." He smiled, thinly. "The police were unclear of their powers and it was obvious that a number of people had attended the rally in order to cause trouble."

"We were protesting! Not fighting!"

Eddie watched, biting his lip, seeing the Blackshirts hover either side of little Harry Miller, waiting for a sign.

"I don't encourage violence, Mr. Miller, but these are dangerous times. "

"Are you denying they did this? Do you want to see the bruises or the scars?"

Mosley took a moment. He was aware that the audience was sitting forward. They were watching how his leadership would work.

"I have asked the Government time and again to ensure safety for *my* supporters, who attend these events in a peaceful manner, exercising their democratic rights *and* for those who choose to oppose us, aggressively and often violently."

There was a cry from Harry Miller's crowd at that point, which prompted the Blackshirts to step in closer.

Mosley raised his hand. Everything was silent again. "I will let the law deal with all legal matters. I trust you will do the same." He snapped his head away. "Next question please! Ah, yes, the lady at the front in pink."

And with that he was done with Harry Miller and done with his audience too. They had been there to hear his speech. With that achieved, it was time to go. Before he left, he gave one final declamatory set of statements as a coda to his speech and had – most of – the crowd on its feet again, cheering someone who was able to shout loudly what they had whispered in secret for years. He had given them a voice.

As he exited the stage, the mood was bubbling. A thrill of having been present at a dramatic moment gave the audience confidence to burst out of the City Hall and face down the protesters. Feet stamped, moving forward , Eddie pushing out of his seat, trying to gauge the best way to intercept Harry Miller, all the time scanning the faces of every Blackshirt to see if they matched the one who had turned their head when he had shouted Billy's name.

It was wishful thinking.

The bodies moved in a tidal surge towards the exit doors. Try as he might, Eddie could only wriggle so far before the force of bodies bundled him out onto the steps, where the protesters waited with a roar.

Eddie couldn't help thinking that it was magnificent to see, standing aloft as he was at the entrance to the City Hall, staring down what seemed tonight like the Odessa Steps in *The Battleship Potemkin.*

That was when he caught sight of his Blackshirt again – barely a dozen yards away, braying orders at the bodies that were moving in flux. He was trying make sense out of chaos. Eddie leant forward, his head dipping as he tried to steer towards the figure, just as a flurry of fists and boots started swinging away to his right and the crowd became a wave that pushed away, carrying Eddie with them.

His feet stumbled to get a grip on the steps as bodies poured down and he had to concentrate hard not to fall, feeling a wash of limbs flood round him. By the time he was steady again the figure had gone. Eddie couldn't see him anywhere, but in his mind the face didn't quite fit.

He didn't have time to dwell on the fact as the City Hall audience, bridled by police escorts, plunged into the waiting crowd so that it felt like elements mixing in a toxic potion. Eddie tried to skirt away.

By now, things were unpicking by the minute, people beginning to revert to childhood to test where the boundaries lay and just what you could do before someone stopped you. Each time a protester broke ranks, the police fell heavy on them, then as the protesters reformed after the latest police chase, a single figure made his way to the war memorial, tugging his way up to give himself a platform to shout his grievances. A line had been drawn and crossed and the police moved swiftly, heavy-handedly hauling him down, which drew protests from people round about.

As Eddie plunged back into the crowd, he could see that the numbers had swelled even further. They had formed into a phalanx, ready to surge forward each time the police popped another protester out of the hall and into a van. They were coming at regular intervals now with the crowd ready to rush towards each one, a massive tidal sway that could lift you off your feet to carry you yards forward. Eddie felt the same buzz as everyone else, just to be part of that body.

With most of the audience now on their way home, it was the turn of the Blackshirts to make their appearance. They came out big and bold. They had just listened to their leader. His words were a call to arms. When they saw Barker's Pool full of an opposing army they reshaped and reformed, strong together and more assured than ever before that they were fighting the right battle at the right time. The police watched them cautiously, not sure if they were providing protection for them, or protecting the crowd. No one else knew either. The tension tripped from person to person.

As he tried to press forward, Eddie felt a tug on his arm. When he turned, he saw the girl he had spoken to earlier.

"How did you get in?" She was breathless.

"Magic." He grinned.

"Did you see Harry?"

"Yes, but where is he now.?"

She reached out and took his hand. "I'll take you."

***

She turned away to lead Eddie through the moving maze of people. He didn't think where he was going, just letting himself follow. As they ran, hundreds of voices joined in with another rendition of the *Red Flag*, a raucous call for solidarity that made the police shuffle their feet.

The girl took Eddie up Barker's Pool then led him to a pub that hung just off the square. The place was stuck full of people, watching the scenes outside. Eddie felt strange, suddenly, not to be part of it.

"Harry!"

Just the sound of the name made Eddie's arms tingle.

"Helen."

Eddie followed the sound of the voice – high and brittle – to the body of a young man who didn't look as if he could hold his own in the playground, but who had already been bloodied in battle and come back.

"This man wants to meet you."

Harry Miller stared at Eddie and felt the holes where his stitches had been pulling the skin tighten with tension.

Eddie put out his hand and smiled. "I need your help."

Eddie knew the landlord well enough and caught his eye while bodies swelled at the bar uncertainly. Almost before the handshake was finished, two pints of beer were standing on the counter, Eddie fishing in his pocket for money. As he passed it over, he felt a quick pain of poverty. He had to hope that Stan Kitteridge would see him right next month.

"Who are you?" Harry was cautious and right to be. "What do you want?"

He was full of energy, a restlessness making his body move, which was in part a response to the beating he'd taken at Olympia. His face was still out of shape from the blows he'd taken, the swelling making his features asymmetrical.

"Can we sit down?" Eddie wanted to calm him.

Harry wasn't in a mood to be pacified. Eddie noticed now that four or five more of the people in the pub were part of Harry's crowd and they were still buzzing from that time watching Mosley.

"Were you in the City Hall tonight?"

Eddie nodded. "I was."

"Did you hear? I asked him outright about *this.*" He gestured to his face.

"I heard you." Eddie looked into the eyes of the young pup of a person, wearing a tweed jacket, a pamphlet entitled *Why War* sticking out of his pocket like a handkerchief.

"I asked him, do you accept that *your* men, those people who say they support *you*, did this to me, in *your* name?" His eyes were moving fast, remembering the slick of fear that ran up his back as he saw the Blackshirts begin to move either side of him – like vultures – as he asked his question. "He denied it."

"Are you surprised?"

He *was*. Eddie could tell it in his eyes. They had the disbelieving look he had seen so often when an audience member sees the trick unfold but can't doubt, or quite believe it.

"He just lied."

"Or maybe he just didn't tell the truth."

"Is there a difference?"

"All the difference in the world."

Harry stared at him. "Who *are* you?"

"I'm Eddie Reynolds. I heard about your trouble in Olympia and that you lived here and I thought you might know some of Mosley's crew."

Harry nodded. "I know some of them. Some of his regulars."

"By name?"

"Yes. A few."

Eddie's breathing tightened. "Do you know Billy McGloin?"

Harry paused, pulling a face. "Yes."

"Was he here tonight?"

"I didn't see him."

"Was he there in Olympia?"

"Yes. He's been all round the country."

"Is he close to Mosley?"

"Close? No. Billy's not close." He took a drink. "He's not a Blackshirt." He put his glass down. "He's one of *us*."

Chapter Twenty-Two

If Eddie had any questions, he forgot them quickly. A sense of movement blew into the pub like the wind. Eddie looked up to see the police begin to swell around the entrance, hunting.

"I think we'd better go," said Eddie.

Harry's face was set. "I haven't done anything."

He was right. Eddie wasn't sure that mattered anymore. Perhaps they weren't looking for Harry. Perhaps they were. Perhaps they were looking for Eddie.

"Come on."

He caught hold of Harry's hand to pull him up. Harry was dumb, unsure of Eddie and uncertain of what was happening outside. He understood enough to know that he couldn't stay where he was. He guessed Eddie was a better bet than the police.

"Where can we go?"

The police were thickening round the door, forming a shield that wouldn't let anyone out. Any second now, they would enter to search table to table, person to person for what they wanted. They were coming in heavy. Their truncheons were already out.

"Tricks of the trade."

Eddie was moving as he talked, pulling Harry behind him as they headed for the sidebar then motioning to Michael Donnelly, the landlord. Donnelly flipped up the side gate as Eddie approached. A couple of quick nods between them said all that was needed. Donnelly spoke in short, sharp words to his wife, Noreen, and she turned towards the cellar. As Eddie and Harry followed, a boom of energy burst into the bar and the policemen flooded in. Up above, the shouting escalated. Down below Eddie and Harry were rattling their feet down the cellar steps, chasing Noreen into the guts of the pub.

"Good luck," was all she said, before giving Eddie a quick kiss on the cheek.

"What are we doing?" Harry was an undergraduate innocent. He didn't know that pubs had a body or that they were in the belly.

"Not now, Harry."

Eddie was the magician who knew that the art of pulling off a trick successfully was total belief and concentration. He tugged up a set of cellar steps to where the beer trap doors lay shut up and heavy. He braced himself to push as the key rattled in the lock, knowing it was always easier to lift them. His shoulder groaned as he leaned into the effort, heaving the heavy doors open.

Behind him and beneath, Harry looked up in wonder. He could see Eddie above and he could see the outside world. He would never know a better trick in his life.

"Get your skates on."

Harry responded and skipped up the steps.

As they emerged onto the pavement, the crowd was dispersing, draining away a couple of hundred at a time, but leaving the streets full of moving bodies. Each of them carried their own sense of energy, so much so that they barely noted two new bodies emerge. Harry and Eddie used the cover to slip into the crowd and drift away.

"Where are we going?"

Eddie wasn't quite sure about destination, only distance.

"Let's just walk, Harry, eh? The police wanted someone and they knew where to look."

Harry's face started to pale. Olympia was still a nightmare for him, though it helped his resolve to know he was fighting the good fight. The thought that the *police* might want to hunt him was something quite different. He could take on the radicals, with an army behind him. But the state was the state, as first Mussolini and now Hitler were demonstrating.

They walked for five minutes, through Fargate, onto High Street, then down to Fitzalan Square, the crowd beside them thinning all the time as it went home to bed, until the pavements were just steady with the last of the stragglers alongside the everyday / everynight punters, talking loud by the kerb as they fell out of pubs.

Eddie pulled Harry into the London Mart public house, which the locals all called *Marple's* in memory of the first owner. The current landlord was a steady man running a tight ship. There was never trouble so the police didn't bother him. Eddie nodded to a few faces he knew, including the cellarman, who was tasting some of the wares after a busy day.

"Do you want a drink?"

Harry nodded, still of an age where you accepted every gift that was offered. Eddie had hoped he'd say no. His money was dripping away to nothing.

"Hello, Eddie."

"Evening, sir," he said to the landlord. Eddie knew when to show respect.

"I hear there's been fun and games in town tonight."

"You hear right."

"Were you there?"

"Popped along to see what was happening."

"Fair enough."

He pushed the two beer glasses towards Eddie as Eddie fumbled for the change. He squeezed the coins onto the counter. Each one landed with a ring.

The landlord looked down on them and saw how pitiful they looked.

"How's your old man? I hear the Royals are headed up his way next week."

"He's all right, thanks. Yes. Duke and Duchess are dropping into Painted Fabrics."

"Your Dad's doing fine work up there. My Gert says they make some lovely stuff."

Eddie nodded, a little bit of a lump in his throat at pride for his Dad. "Yeah, it's good."

As Eddie put his hands on the glasses the landlord pushed the coins back towards him. "They're on the house, Mr. Reynolds."

"Thank you, sir."

He turned away. He made a note to send two free tickets – which he hoped to squeeze out of Stan – to the landlord and his wife.

Back at the table, Harry was fidgeting. An instinctive energy was rattling through him, making his body shake.

Eddie laid the glasses on the table and took a seat. "Tell me about Billy."

"Why do you want to know? Who are you?"

"I've told you. I'm Eddie Reynolds."

"Why do you want Billy?"

Eddie wondered just what the right words were. "It's to do with his . . girlfriend."

Harry took a greedy swig of beer and the drink lapped round his lips like a baby. "He never mentioned one."

That was no surprise. "Maybe he didn't, but I need to share some news with him."

"Good news?"

"Not really."

Harry seemed glum at the response. "Billy's one of us. Sort of?"

"*Sort of*? How come?"

"He was part of the RWG over in Ireland."

"Come again."

"Revolutionary Workers Party."

"Sounds radical."

Harry shrugged. "Maybe. It's radical times."

"And?"

"And he came over here because they say there's a big Irish contingent here."

Eddie smiled at Harry's university innocence and his ignorance of Sheffield.

"So I hear," he said with a smile. The Crofts was a place where they didn't go, who didn't have to.

"He heard about us and he wanted to join."

"The police seem to know about him."

"The police know about everyone, Eddie. They're watching us."

"I'm not sure they've got enough men to do that."

"It's not just the officials. They all have contacts."

"People watching at their windows?"

"That's what's happening, Eddie. No one trusts anyone."

Eddie shrugged. "I know Billy was in Newcastle. Was he in London too?"

"Yes, why?"

Eddie didn't sugarcoat the words. "His girlfriend's dead. She was pregnant."

Harry was shocked – at both statements. He took a big mouthful of beer.

"He never said anything."

Life was catching up with Harry very fast these days.

"When did you last see him?"

"It was over a week ago."

"He moved house. Do you know why?"

Harry nodded. "He was getting trouble."

"Who from?"

"The police." The two words dripped out of him. He knew what it meant to say that.

"Why?"

"Why? Because we're a threat, Eddie."

"To what?"

Harry was getting animated. "The old world. The old way of doing things. Capitalism. The Empire. The class system. Take your pick." He slurped some more beer.

Eddie looked across the table at Harry, who was still young enough to have acne and whose body he might generously describe as *wiry*. He didn't see a threat.

"There's a war on, Eddie."

Eddie smiled. "Did I miss something?"

"Do you read the news?"

"My Dad does. He tells me what I need to know."

"And what does he tell you?"

"Watch out for the Communists as much as the fascists."

Harry laughed. "He might be right. *We're* socialists."

"I thought the Germans were socialists. That's what they're called, aren't they?"

"They're abusing the term."

"That makes it hard for the man on the street."

"Their actions don't, Eddie. No real free speech, anymore. They started burning books last year. That's the beginning of the end of knowledge and democracy. It's where we start working our way back to the monkey."

"I wouldn't call them monkeys."

"You're right. They wouldn't like that. Doesn't quite fit the perfect image, does it?"

Eddie shrugged. "That's Germany, Harry. We fought a war against them. This is England, for God's sake."

Harry leaned further forward. "It isn't just about what *we* become, Eddie. It's not whether Oswald Mosley gets more votes to get to be an MP and becomes Prime Minister. You're right. That won't happen. But the louder his voice, the more people listen, then there are fewer people to challenge Hitler and Mussolini."

Eddie nodded, looking at Harry, still fresh faced, even with the battle scars he now carried with him like a passport of credibility. Eddie wondered where he'd be in twenty years' time, or thirty. He guessed he'd be a little less left leaning.

"And Billy was part of that?"

"He was right at the heart of it, challenging the status quo. Stirring things up."

"Breaking the law? Is that why the police wanted him?"

Harry squirmed. "There are grey areas."

"When did you last see him?"

"Not for a few days now."

Eddie pulled his glass towards him and poured the beer down straight. It was a skill you learned at a brewery. "I need to find him."

***

The night had come down thicker by this time. Eddie felt exhaustion strain through him but pressed on. He was walking again, his money saved for a tram ride home. He was up against the clock so he moved fast, skipping through a city that was ten times busier than a normal Thursday with the police still standing like exclamation marks at regular points. Harry had scuttled his own way home, leaving Eddie with contact details.

At last, he hauled himself back to Upperthorpe, the streets dim and quiet, the lights flickering. As he turned towards Billy's, he tipped into a darkness that worked well for him.

He knocked as quietly as he could then waited. He knocked again, watching for curtains twitching. After a minute, he slipped his hand into his pocket for his keys.

He was quickly inside, snapping a match alight to help him find his way along. He stood inside the door and felt a coolness come out to meet him and touch his skin.

"Billy?" He called quietly, afraid of waking neighbours and arousing suspicion. "Billy?"

Downstairs was dark and – despite the summer weather outside – heavily damp.

He looked towards the stairs. There was a light switch but it didn't work. He pulled out his matches again, finding a candle in the kitchen. The flame wobbled, as if it was unsure of itself. Eddie noticed an unwashed plate and cup by the sink. Billy had been back. The light skipped and danced ahead of it as Eddie moved back towards the stairs. He took them slowly, one by one, each step a creak and groan.

"Billy?"

Even as he stepped forward, he knew that Billy wouldn't answer. Even the deepest sleepers respond quicker than that. In the end, it was just curiosity carrying him forward – and something else he couldn't quite place.

The house was unlovely in every room, a slum landlord not wanting to waste a penny on houses that the Corporation might soon demolish and which the tenants would never care for, even if they managed to pay their rent on time.

But it wasn't the look of the house, that made Eddie pause as he hit the top step.

It was the smell.

Crawling out from under the door at the end of the landing then slithering along the floor, the stench was unmistakable and brutal. It was the smell of disinfectant: clouds of it.

Eddie wobbled, having to push himself forward, right up to the bedroom door that was tight shut, but not tight enough to hold the odours inside. His hand trembled as he touched the handle – and pushed.

Billy McGloin was tangled on the floor in the shape of convulsion.

The candle threw desperate patterns of light across the room to show Eddie the picture in parts: the eyes were still open and horrified; the cheeks were burned, where the disinfectant had run; a bottle of *Lysol* was standing on a bedside table, its lid screwed tight.

He stepped forward, then crouched, now ever so close to a dead person for the first time in his life. He pushed the candle forward to illuminate the body more perfectly, moving down from the face to the chest, where the liquid had burned, to his arms and then hands and down to the bend of his legs and the twist of his feet, both of which suggested agony.

***

"Eddie?" His Dad had come down to meet him when Eddie had got home at last, limping into the living room.

Eddie looked up and tried to smile. From behind him and upstairs there was a call from Mum, asking if everything was all right.

"It's fine, love," his Dad said. He sat down heavily, close to Eddie.

Eddie shook his head. "I found Billy McGloin."

His Dad didn't say anything. He knew what was coming, if not the details.

"He killed himself. Disinfectant again," Eddie said.

His Dad nodded.

"It's like the thing at St. Marie's, Eddie. People get an idea in their head."

"Do you think he meant to? Kill Mary?" His eyes were pleading and at that moment - for someone who often seemed so mature and composed - he looked very young.

"I don't know. Strange things go on behind closed doors, Eddie. " He shrugged. "Who knows?" He put his pipe in his mouth and pulled at the tobacco. "Did you tell anyone?"

Eddie shook his head. "I shouldn't have been in there."

His Dad nodded. "Did anyone see you?"

"No."

A cloud of smoke blew out into the room and made everything opaque. "Good."

Chapter Twenty-Three

Eddie stood outside the main door of the Empire under the shadow it threw. For once, he wasn't happy to be here.

The day had felt short of breath. Eddie was much the same, after a dragging day beating round the city with Bert, shipping beer and listening with half an ear to people who tried to tell Eddie what had happened last night at the City Hall. On another day, he might have been interested in how versions of the truth could vary so widely (*it was a triumph for the fascists; it was a good night for common sense and communism; Sheffield showed the Blackshirts where to go*). Today wasn't that day. He had a duty hanging over him. It made every hour drag and every minute twitch.

When the round was done, he headed into town, now finding himself back at the Empire, heading inside, where the air was cool. He was looking for Stan Kitteridge.

Stan was busy. He was always busy.

Eddie had to wait and he sat there listlessly, his attention at last pricked by a boy putting up posters in the foyer, advertising the coming events. There was a new one for the show next week. Pecking order was everything, the largest writing literally meaning the biggest name. Eddie didn't care about that. There at the bottom, small but distinct, was the simple line:

The "Incredible" Eddie Reynolds, Escapologist.

A buzz passed through him like he'd never known. That was enough to energise him and begin to blow away the images of Billy McGloin. The sense of sorrow for Mary Riley was still strong, but it wasn't everything anymore. Life goes on. His Dad used that phrase time and again, Eddie always wondering when his Dad first said it, likely to himself, as they carried the bodies away.

"Eddie!"

As ever, Stan's voice cut across the space between them like a bullet.

Eddie smiled. "Hello, Stan."

Stan was in showbiz mood, skipping over to Eddie to put an arm round his shoulder.

"Come on, lad. Let's get a cup of tea and have a talk."

The glamour of the theatre was calling out as Stan waltzed Eddie through the corridors and past the offices, the sense of the entertainment business in full swing making Eddie giddy as he moved. They both stuttered, though, approaching the office where Mary once worked. Coming to the door, they looked in to see a young girl sitting where Mary had sat.

"That's Lily." Stan choked a stage cough of embarrassment. "She's . . new."

She was also pretty. She looked at Eddie and liked what she saw. Eddie imagined sitting with her and finding out about her, yet even as those ideas flitted through his mind he could still see Mary in the background – and Billy in a heap.

"Come on." Stan pulled him along.

When they came to his office, he slid down into his chair, comfortable as a king on a throne. His secretary brushed by and he ordered tea and cake.

"Did you see your name on the bill?" Stan grinned.

"I did."

"Looked good, didn't it?"

Eddie nodded. "It did."

"So why the long face?"

Eddie thought about what to say. Nothing seemed simple. "I found the boyfriend."

Stan's eyes widened. "Flippin' 'eck, Eddie. You're good."

Eddie shook his head. "Not so good. He's dead."

"Bloody hell."

"Killed himself, I reckon, the same way he killed Mary."

"Jesus," Stan whispered, then glanced up at Eddie. "Sorry." He shook his head. "Did you get a name?"

"Yeah. Billy McGloin."

The name made Stan's eyes twitch. "*Billy*?"

Now Eddie shifted in his seat. "You know Billy?"

"No, I don't *know* him. Mary mentioned him, I don't know, once or twice."

"But I asked about a boyfriend."

"Yeah?"

"You said you didn't know."

Stan took a slurp of tea. "You said a boyfriend."

"I found *Billy*. He's dead."

The two pieces of information hit Stan like a one-two from a middleweight. He put the cup down hard so that the china cracked.

"Eddie," Stan leaned forward, "Billy was Mary's cousin. McGloin's her maiden name."

***

"Are you all right, love?" Eddie's Mum had a worried tone in her voice.

"I'm fine, Mum."

"You're very quiet."

"I'm thinking about the show this week."

He wasn't.

He was thinking that Mary Riley was dead and Billy McGloin was dead and his idea that Billy killed Mary because she was carrying his baby didn't seem quite so strong anymore. It was possible, of course. Those things did happen. Even in Catholic families. From what he knew of Mary before and Billy now, the idea didn't fit.

They were shopping in Greenhill, another of Sheffield's tight-knit nuggets of village life, stitched together into the canvas of a city. They paused at the butchers to say a quick hello to Mr. Johnson, the local pig killer. Mr. Johnson was a big man, built as wide as high, with no hair on his fat head and huge forearms. As a child, Eddie had been terrified of him and the stories they told of what he did to children when he couldn't find a pig. Now, Eddie barely even gave a nod to the house where Randolph Douglas had grown up, his mind tipping between thoughts of Billy and Mary, then recollections of what Louise had said in her latest letter. If it was mundane, it made him long for simplicity in a time of life that was becoming very complicated.

When his Mum skipped into one of the shops, Eddie turned to his Dad, who was lighting his pipe.

"Billy McGloin poisoned. Mary Riley poisoned. The woman at St. Marie's ......"

"Poisoned." Dad sucked on the smoke to let it tickle his tongue. "You don't think it's a coincidence."

"Do you?"

He shrugged. He'd mostly given up on reason on the Somme.

Eddie twisted away, frustrated.

"Eddie, you're too used to there being an explanation for everything."

He had a point. Magicians suffered from a professional scepticism.

"It just seems . . ." He didn't know what.

His mother reappeared and the subject was dropped until she went to the bakers, where the smell of fresh bread rolled along the pavements like a perfect advertisement.

Eddie was kicking his heels.

"Maybe they're not the same." His Dad wasn't looking at Eddie as he spoke.

"What do you mean?"

"You say it's the same. Is it? Is it the same disinfectant? Is it the same amount?"

Eddie frowned. "What's the difference?"

His Dad slipped his pipe from his mouth. "You said that Mary Riley might have been an accident. Maybe it was. Maybe the woman at St. Marie's wasn't right in the head and didn't know what she was doing. Maybe it was just that Billy killed himself and meant to."

Eddie pulled a face. "How does that help?"

"It means you need to ask yourself some questions, if you're bothered."

"Well, I *am* bothered."

"Why?"

He didn't quite know. Stan was happy with him. He was on the bill now, where he wanted to be. But Mary Riley wouldn't be at the show, front or backstage. She'd gone and she'd been replaced. That seemed too sudden, too complete. She'd been stuck in the Crofts and she never got the chance to get out. Everything about that jarred with him.

"It just doesn't seem right."

His Dad shrugged. He'd seen enough things that didn't seem right before they happened then seemed absolutely wrong when they were done.

"So, find a connection. Maybe the woman at St. Marie's knew Mary. Or Billy. Or both."

For a second, Eddie was angry with himself for not thinking of that. Then he was just grateful for the idea his Dad had given him. At last, he could lay this thing – and Mary Riley – to rest.

***

Leaving his Mum and Dad to make a slow trip back home, Eddie scuttled into town, chasing down Norfolk Row to the parish church of St. Marie's. Unlike the quick, brutal build of churches such as St. Vincent's – where speed mattered more than ceremony – St. Marie's had a sense of grandeur, a bold spire stretching an arm out of the cluster of buildings surrounding it, part supplication and part aspiration.

Moving off the street into the church was to slip from the cloying warmth of the late afternoon into the steady cool of the nave. At that time of day, there was little business to be done, though the church was never empty. A scattering of parishioners thumbed their rosaries in silent prayer while a middle-aged man lit a candle for his mother. Eddie stood watching them, feeling some calm after too many days racing through the hours.

"Can I help you?"

The Irish burr seemed to come from nowhere so that it appeared as if God himself was talking to Eddie. He jerked round to see a priest he didn't know. His tongue was stuck for a moment. How to ask what he needed to ask? Be bold, Eddie. Be direct.

"There was a woman who died here."

The priest's face clouded over.

"A terrible thing."

Eddie nodded. "I had some questions." Was that enough? Would he have to lie? Here, in the heart of the Catholic community.

"Ah, well, you might be wanting to ask John, who helps." He smiled. "John Lunt."

Eddie felt a buzz. "Is he here?"

"Well now, you're in luck. He's in the presbytery. Come with me and we'll see if we can find him." As he started to walk Eddie noticed how steady his steps were. He'd seen enough that nothing and no one could ruffle his equanimity.

John Lunt was busy with church affairs as the priest led Eddie in, looking up with worry above his glasses, as if he was about to be caught out. Eddie knew the type: quiet, industrious. The boy who was picked on. The boy that was bullied. Free of school, they found a place to settle then built a fence around themselves. In his case, John Lunt sat behind an old oak desk that might have fallen off the Ark when it hit dry land. Now he was an important part of the laity. He *mattered*, he kept telling himself.

"Thank you, Father."

The priest smiled and left.

Lunt looked up at Eddie cautiously. He had defined his world quite specifically. There was a pattern to it that covered place and people. Eddie was not part of that pattern.

"Do I know you?"

Eddie sat down. "No."

Lunt was holding his pen in his fingers and his grip tightened as his eyes squeezed into a stare. "What do you want?"

"I want to ask about the woman who killed herself." Lunt unwound in a moment, his body melting from rigid to jelly. "And I heard you found her."

"It was terrible."

He was confessional and he wanted to talk. He had told the police things, but everyone else had been gentle with him. They had spared his feelings and treated him as if nothing had happened. But it *had*. He had to tell people that.

"I can imagine."

"You *can't*, though. That's the point. You think you can imagine things. When they really happen, though, when you really see them, it's all so different."

Eddie knew his audience. "Tell me."

Lunt leaned forward.

"It was just an ordinary day. I'd been finishing some work in here and I heard a noise." His eyes lost focus for a second. "I don't think I'll ever forget that sound." He would hear it forever. "It was a moan and a wail," as if it had been torn out of the throat of the woman. "I ran out." The echo swept across the church, along the aisle up to the rafters.

He paused now, retracing his steps and each movement of his memory made him scared again, unready to reach the body, scared to look.

"That must have been hard for you."

Lunt looked at Eddie vaguely. He couldn't understand. "I've never seen anything like it. She wasn't dead, but she was dying. And the smell. ." That came back to him now, washing over him. "I wanted to help, but I didn't know what to do. I was in shock. She was curled up into a ball. Her face was swelling. Her lips were burning - and her cheeks. It must have poured over her." He closed his eyes. "It must have hurt so much."

"What did you do?"

"I went for help. Father Dolan came in, then Father Morrisey and we tried to settle her. Tried to help her."

"Did you ring the police?"

"Mrs. Lamkin did. The housekeeper. And we rang the hospital. But," he shook his head, "she was dead by the time they got here. There was nothing they could do. Nothing anyone could do." He crossed himself as he had done every time the memories came back.

"Do you know what disinfectant she used?"

Lunt was puzzled. Of all the questions he had been asked, this had never been mentioned. "I'm not sure."

“Would you know the bottle again if you saw it?”

“Well . . I might.”

Eddie paused. “Would you remember the name?”

Again, Lunt was hesitant. “Possibly.”

Eddie played his card. “Was it *Lysol*?”

The name struck Lunt like lightning. He almost recoiled.

“Yes! I can see it. Just by her hand as she lay there. She must have dropped it.” The image was seared into him. “I remember the name now. It was so . . bold . . and fresh . . and look what it had done to her . . to her face and her cheeks . . and her chin . . .and her hands, of course, the skin burnt raw.”

“What?” Eddie felt his throat tighten.

“What?” Lunt was confused.

Eddie swallowed to wet his mouth. “The *hands*?”

“When it came out of her mouth, it poured on her hands. I mentioned it to the policeman. He said it was a reflexive gag.” He shook his head. “All over her thumb and down to her wrist. The body just tries to reject the poison. It’s instinctive. You can’t stop it.”

Eddie gripped the handle of the chair and squeezed, feeling as if a lock had just been tightened – or loosened – round him. He wasn’t sure which. In his mind, he still held a perfect image of Billy McGloin’s dead body: his face, his chest, his legs, his arms – and hands. The face was burnt. The hands were almost folded in prayer and quite perfect.

Chapter Twenty-Four

After another close, sticky day the evening breeze was welcome as Eddie pushed across town up towards the Crofts. He drove his feet along the cobbles with a hammer on anvil ring from his heels until he got to the bigger, better housing, where Doctor Gilmartin was talking with a colleague in the garden, drinking fresh lemonade while the birds sang.

"Eddie!"

The doctor was surprised and a just a little uneasy. Eddie was breathing heavily, the sweat sticking his shirt to the skin on his back.

"I need to talk to you, Doctor."

He gestured. "I'm with a friend, Eddie."

Doctor Gilmartin had a reputation for never being ruffled. He knew just how and when to play the importance of his seven years of learning and countless years of practice and he dressed it in the soft, Irish burr which convinced most people of anything. Eddie didn't care.

"It won't take long."

"Eddie, are you all right?" He was changing tack, now, trying to be paternal. "Why don't you come see me tomorrow? I've got some time." He smiled a smile at Eddie that Uncles or Grandpas kept as their own. Then he nodded to his colleague, to assure him that everything was under control.

"You didn't tell me everything, did you?"

That stopped Doctor Gilmartin right where he stood. He didn't like to be challenged.

"What didn't I tell you?" Right away, he knew that was a mistake.

Eddie was standing above the Doctor, which gave him an advantage. He used it now, stepping a little further round so that the sun was behind him, making his body a shadow and his outline luminous.

"About Mary Riley. What they found." He paused for effect. "And what they didn't."

Doctor Gilmartin chewed his lip, then looked across at his guest, who was starting to feel nervous. The respect for the neighbourhood doctor was a sacred bond. It required two-way trust that they were doing all they could for their patients – and that their patients would trust them and, most importantly, pay them. In many ways, it was a sign of faith and – as Eddie was discovering – it could be dangerous to dig too deeply into those things.

"Can you give me five minutes, Henry?"

Henry nodded as he lifted a glass of lemonade to his lips while Doctor Gilmartin shuffled Eddie inside. Even before they had researched his room, he was talking.

"This had better be important."

He stretched out his hand to guide Eddie towards his office, his inner sanctum. Already, he felt uneasy. He wasn't doing things on his own terms. He didn't like that. He was angry with Eddie.

Eddie marched in to wait for the Doctor, who wanted to take back control, so he took his time to take his seat, gesturing for Eddie, too, to sit down.

If Doctor Gilmartin had hoped that Eddie would be ill at ease now, he was mistaken. Eddie was full of fire.

"Now, what are you talking about, Eddie?"

"I'm talking about Mary Riley."

"What about her?"

"You saw the body."

"I did."

"And you thought she committed suicide. You *said* she committed suicide."

"I did."

"And I'd be surprised if you didn't know about the woman at St. Marie's who killed herself just a couple of weeks ago."

"It . . I . . had heard something."

"Did you think it was curious?"

"Not really." He was settling now. Eddie was just throwing things at him, inching into *his* world: medicine. "People often hear of someone doing something then copy it. They know it works."

"Is that what you think happened?"

"I think it's likely, yes."

"There were similarities?"

"Yes."

"Like the burns on the mouth?"

He nodded, wise again. "Yes, that's common with this sort of thing. It's very hard to do something like this as if you were drinking a bottle of pop. Quite often, people are drunk when they do it."

"Was Mary Riley drunk?"

Slower now. "There was no . . indication. People don't *always* drink. Just sometimes."

Eddie nodded. "But whether they've been drinking or not, they usually spill some of the liquid they're using to kill themselves, or a baby they want to get rid of."

Eddie was blunt as a hammer and Doctor Gilmartin quivered ever so slightly.

"I've said so, yes."

"On their lips?"

"Yes, on their lips."

"And their chin?"

"Quite often."

"Down their neck maybe?"

Doctor Gilmartin was feeling prickly now. The questions were too easy. He didn't know where Eddie was leading him. He didn't like it.

"Sometimes. It depends on what they were wearing."

"Is it because they gag? They spit it out?"

"Or they're drunk, as I said. They're shaking. And they're nervous."

"You said Mary Riley wasn't drunk."

"Yes . . No . . You're right."

"So, they spill it?"

"Yes."

"On their lips and their chin and their neck?"

"Yes."

Eddie paused and slowed things down until time stopped ticking. "And their hands?"

There it was. The trick.

Doctor Gilmartin didn't know what to say. His tongue was stuck. "Well . ."

Eddie smiled. "There was nothing on her hands, was there? On her lips? Yes. On her chin? Yes. But not on her hands. Not a drop. Now how does that happen?"

The Doctor knew enough to know when he'd been fooled and he was ever so slightly impressed with Eddie. He almost felt he should clap. "It *can* happen."

"Billy McGloin's dead, Doctor." He let the words fall like a punch. "Same way as Mary. A bottle of *Lysol.* Did you look into it? Check the hands?"

Doctor Gilmartin smiled, painfully. "What do *you* think happened, Eddie?"

"She wasn't trying to get rid of her baby, Doctor. And she wasn't trying to kill herself. Not like the woman at St. Marie's, was it? Neither was Billy. There was no mark on their hands. But that woman in the church might have given someone an idea." Eddie paused as they both waited for him to give the conclusion. "For murder."

***

Arriving back home, he found a note to say his Mum was out with Auntie Jean, catching up on family news. He wished she'd been there. His Dad was sitting by the radio, listening to strains of the Duke Ellington band pouring out *Jazz Cocktail.* As Eddie came into the room, his Dad put down his pipe and then his paper.

"You'd be no good at cards with that poker face."

Eddie frowned. "She was murdered, Dad. And so was Billy McGloin."

His Dad was impassive. "How do you know?"

"There's no burning on their hands. Neither of them."

His Dad nodded. "Who did it?"

Eddie shook his head. "I don't know. The police were chasing Billy . . .but to kill him?"

"It sounds a bit extreme, but these are funny times."

Eddie slumped down. "Funny? I suppose. And I can't find out, can I? No one's going to tell me and I don't know who to ask. I was thinking about it on the way over and every time I ran it round my head it was the same. I don't know *anything.*"

"You know they're dead."

"Well, I know *that.*"

"You think someone killed them."

"Yes. Obviously."

"You just don't know who."

"Yes! That's the point."

His Dad sniffed. "Were the bottles still there?"

Eddie turned round on his Dad. "The disinfectant?"

"Yes."

"Yes. Why?"

His Dad lifted up his pipe again. "You could always check for fingerprints."

Eddie's eyes widened.

***

"Eddie!"

Eddie barely heard his father as he slid out of the house, back into the night. Without the money for a tram, he used the slopes of Sheffield to roll him forwards. He took comfort in the first part of his journey, the long slide down Meadowhead, taking him to Chesterfield Road, then Woodseats Road to cut across to Abbeydale Road. Half an hour slipped by without a pause to think. His mind was simple clear. He needed to collect the bottles of *Lysol* for the fingerprints.

His Dad had explained things straightforwardly weeks before. "Fingerprints, Eddie. We've all got 'em". So far, so simple. "They used 'em like signatures back in the old days."

"How old?"

"B.C."

"Bloody hell!"

"Don't swear."

"Sorry."

"That's all right. Then, who knows why, hundreds of years later some sort of Consul in India during the Empire days gets the bright idea to take a record of everyone's print."

"Why?"

"Like a register."

"Smart."

"Very. And they started using them in trials at the beginning of the century."

"Successfully?"

"Very much so."

"I've never heard much about it."

"It was in the news a couple of months back. A judge made a joke about it."

"In Sheffield?"

"That's right. He made a point of telling the police how to do their job." He smiled. "It's the future, Eddie. You can see it now."

Eddie could see it all right. The vision drove his legs along, though they were tired and heavy, finding every one of Sheffield's hills a slow drag as he clocked up four miles on foot.

Revisiting Billy's house was hard. The smell of disinfectant by now had poured down the stairs to wash its way along the walls, embalming the building to make it a tomb, but a slow stench of rottenness sat on top of it which made him nauseous. Taking a breath, he started a slow, uneasy tiptoe upstairs again, peeking into the room where Billy's body was still lying, every minute dragging the last humanity out of it until it would just be a shell, then just a skeleton. He wondered how long it would be until the smell made its way to the neighbours to make them wonder. They all knew the smell of death.

With his fingers wrapped up in an old pair of his white stage gloves, he lifted the *Lysol* bottle gently and eased it into a bag he had brought with him. As he did, he tried not to look down at Billy's body or face – and failed. A look of shock horror plagued his features. Eddie's gaze met Billy's eyes reaching back towards him so that he recoiled. He wanted to run but his mind kept him where he was. He was staring at Billy's hands. The fingers were long and slender. A pianist's fingers. That made him think of the Claddagh ring. Gritting his teeth, he leaned in towards Billy and lifted his hands to look for marks where a ring might have sat. There were none.

He emerged back out onto the street with a sense of nervousness pulsing in his heart. His body was tired, weary of chasing but knowing he still had a long way to go.

Taking his bag he pushed on, sinking back towards the shadows when a figure strayed across the street in front of him, snatching a look down to where Eddie sank in the blackness. The figure paused – Eddie motionless – then passed.

By now, one day had gone while the next wasn't quite ready to replace it, leaving just enough light to see every shadow but not enough to see anything clearly. Each body that slipped somewhere in front of him or to the side – and every sound that happened behind him in a door click, or a boot scrape or a cat cry – made him tense. The warmth had gone with the light. Eddie buttoned up his jacket against a wind that was kicking along the streets now, trying to pull a little of the day's grime off the walls and windows.

Even now, there were still some cars on the roads, wheels thumping along the uneven surfaces to make their drivers rattle. Eddie tried to catch a glance of them as they boomed along, all single men looking for something or leaving something behind. Their hands were lazy on the wheels, energy spent, eyes dilated, their blood thick with drink.

Eddie watched one approach a tight corner too straight and too fast, wondering when he would realise he needed to turn – and it was right at the last second, the rubber of the wheels digging into the road surface to tug the car round, but not without one side of the vehicle lifting up a little, only to thump down again as it turned the bend.

The sound disappeared and things were silent again. Eddie pressed on.

By the time he got to the Crofts he was exhausted, drawing on the sort of energy he reserved for the stage, when the shows *had* to go on. You did the performance. You didn't stop. He took a breath then moved, the neighbourhood closing round him like a dark pillow over his face.

Now, as Eddie skipped along the cobbles, the area slept fitfully, its whole chest full of smoke, dust and dirt. Every so often, a light was still shining. He liked to hope that someone, somewhere was making love but knew it was much more likely that a husband drunk into a seventh stage of stupor was beating up on his wife as the kids buried their heads under bedclothes, hoping it would stop or that Daddy wouldn't come for *them*.

Mary Riley's street was uniformly dark. Even so, Eddie stepped carefully, cautious as he approached the door. He couldn't explain why he took more care now, except that it seemed that things had changed and he'd changed with them. He imagined someone was watching him. When the tiredness struck him, he wondered if it was God.

Inside the house was much like Billy's: dark, unlived in, unloved and ever so desperate, rancid smells now creeping out of a pantry that hadn't been cleaned yet. Eddie shuddered, thinking of himself inside a coffin – a trick he had been trying off and on for the last six months. The trick had always worried Houdini when he tried it. There were too many variables, too much risk, not enough money. No one could quite imagine what it was like to be buried alive. Eddie had wondered. He had tried it once, with Nancy. The horror was something unlike anything he'd ever known. Nancy said it scared her. It scared Eddie more.

Now, Mary Riley's house was beginning to have the same claustrophobic hug that he'd experienced then and he wanted to get out.

He made his way to the kitchen, snapping two matches alight to give him sight of the *Lysol*. Ever so gently, using a handkerchief to keep his own fingers clean, he lifted the bottle he wanted to put it alongside the other in the bag. It snuggled down with a click of matching glass and Eddie stood up again.

As he slipped back into the streets, he saw that the night hadn't stirred during his time in the house. It was still mostly recumbent, but restless. He took a couple of steps forward, starting to breathe easier at last when a stray beam of lamplight flashed in a pair of eyes that was looking straight at him.

Eddie softened when he saw it was Peter, the boy with the cigarette cards.

"Why're you still up?" He scolded him, transferring his tension. "Your dad'll skin you."

"I haven't got a dad."

The thoughts of his own father made Eddie sadder still. Yet it might be a blessing. You couldn't tell.

"Well, then your mum'll be twice as mad."

The boy didn't respond.

"Hey, look," Eddie rummaged in his pocket for his wallet, picking out the card he'd taken from the clown at the theatre. He produced the card with a flick of the wrist.

"Charlie Grimmett!" The boy's face exploded with joy.

"All right. Now, it's your turn. Do something for me." His fingers worked in his pocket to pull out the photograph of Billy McGloin. To see the flash of youth and life in his face made Eddie have to grit his teeth when he remembered what he had seen tonight.

The boy looked at the photograph seriously.

"When I showed you this, you said you'd seen him before."

The boy nodded.

"Here," Eddie said.

Another nod.

"Was he the one that gave you the cards?"

The boy looked up at Eddie and then – very definitely – shook his head.

"Who gave you the cards, Peter?"

Peter didn't nod, didn't shake his head. He shut his mouth then looked down at the ground. Eddie could tell: he was scared.

Who was it?

***

He slipped down the road back towards town, wanting the brightness of streetlights to give him some comfort and take him out of the shadows.

Periodically, there were people, mostly in ones and an occasional two. Every so often there was a car, steady in the quiet night, with no need to hurry. All of that seemed normal. Eddie was pleased that normal still existed.

"Nah then, son."

The voice caught him by the neck. He hadn't been looking for anyone and so didn't expect anyone. The policeman now standing beside him was a surprise.

"Hello, officer." Eddie's mouth was dry.

"You're out a bit late, aren't you?"

Eddie had watched enough performers on stage to know that the key to control was confidence. Throw things back on the audience whenever they disturb your balance.

"Well, I've been, you know," the streetlights were bright enough to catch half of Eddie's face and show the eyes dance a little with innuendo, "seeing my girlfriend."

The policeman cleared his throat. He didn't want a conversation like that. He had a daughter who was Eddie's age. He didn't want to imagine what she might get up to with a lad like Eddie. "Lucky boy."

Eddie smiled. "Lucky girl."

The policeman shifted the weight on his feet, uncomfortable. "What's in the bag?"

Eddie's arm tightened. Time accelerated. He had to answer fast. If he lied and he was caught out it would be trouble and he'd been spending more time with the police. He didn't want to do that.

"Cleaning stuff." He couldn't tell the whole truth.

The policeman's face creased with puzzlement. "Cleaning?"

"I was helping her dad clean out his pigeon coop."

The policeman grinned. "Is he a racer? I always wanted to race. Never got the time."

"When you retire?"

"Fat chance. The Missus has things all lined up for me."

"It's your time. Your money." Eddie was still tight with tension, but playing the lines.

"Try telling *her* that. Or is your girlfriend different?"

An electric image of Louisa flashed through his mind. "Yeah. She's different."

"Lucky bugger. Now, get off."

Eddie smiled and turned away.

"Wait a minute!"

The voice was a fishhook that caught him in the back. He turned slowly, inevitably.

"How come you're walking?"

Eddie tapped his pockets. "She spent all my money."

The policeman laughed. "Not too different, then. Here," he squeezed his hand into a trouser pocket and pulled out a coin. "Get a tram and get yourself home. I don't want to know what she's been doing with you, but you look knackered."

Eddie collapsed onto a tram seat and let it cuddle him, fighting sleep all the way home, so that he didn't know whether or not he was awake.

As the tram hauled close to home, the conductor nudged him. "This is your stop, pal."

"Thanks."

"Get some sleep."

Eddie nodded. "I will."

Chapter Twenty-Five

Eddie's Dad looked at the two disinfectant bottles on the table, then looked at Eddie before turning back to the bottles.

Eddie watched his Dad.

When his Mum came in she looked at Dad, Eddie, then the bottles.

"What are we doing?"

Eddie looked up at his Mum. He explained the parts that he could and left out anything that would upset her more than necessary. Even so, her face was set.

"Oh, Eddie."

His Dad lit his pipe. "You need to give them to the police."

"What are they going to do?"

"They're going to do their job, I hope."

"How?"

"Check them against their records. See if they can match them up."

"How many records have they got?"

He was a little flustered. "*I* don't know. Some. A lot. Do you reckon it's one of the Blackshirts?"

"Maybe."

Maybe. But it didn't explain why Mary was pregnant.

"Well, they're wrong 'uns, aren't they? They've got records as long as their arms."

"I suppose so." He wasn't convinced.

***

The evening grew stickier as the night wore on. Eddie was at that restless stage, somewhere beyond exhaustion, which can make you too tired to sleep. He wrestled with the sheets for half an hour then dragged himself out of bed for a glass of water.

The tap was stiff. The mechanism clanked a few times before pushing out the liquid into his glass. The noise sounded like the apocalypse so late into such a quiet night. There was no wind through the windows. The world was still.

Eddie took his drink into the living room and sat down. His jacket was hanging on the back of a chair. He knew that his Mum would have wrestled over whether to hang it up or leave him to do it, as she'd told him often enough. He took out the latest letter from Louisa. He was sitting by candlelight, which meant the illumination came and went in flickers and made him have to search for the words.

Her story was straight and simple as ever. He had never been gladder of something so uncomplicated. As he finished, he found a sense of purpose tingling through him. He went to the sideboard, where the paper, pen and ink were. He lifted the first volume of the Encyclopedia Britannica from the bookshelves to rest on, dipped his pen in the ink and started to write.

He wanted to tell her his tale and in writing it he hoped that he would find some final meaning in what he'd been doing and why. The words came out fast, falling onto the paper through his tight and tidy script. He had learned it early, copying text fastidiously from Houdin, Houdini and others. Within minutes he had completed his first page, which had started with the sentence, *Sorry for not writing sooner, but I've been very busy.*

From the present minute, the story tracked back through moments that changed his life, when the mystery of magic came so close to him that he had to reach out to touch it. Every one of his heroes was a latter-day Prometheus and now he, too, had become one. He was childlike in the honesty of his excitement and unusually frank about the things that scared him. He knew – as Houdini had always known – that the closer you came to perfection, the closer you came to death. Houdini had ploughed his way through the travelling shows spending time with shucksters and rounders, working the simple tricks, trying out the psychics for size – watching the audience gawp in wonder at the obvious fraud – before settling on escapology, *because it was real.* Yes, it was a show, yes, there was sleight of hand, there was distraction, but at the end of the day, Houdini and every other escapologist – Eddie included – had to free himself from the ropes, chains and locks. If they didn't, they died. It wasn't magic. It was art. Or – to put it another way – it was real magic. That was what the audience wanted. They wanted something to believe. That's what Eddie had to give them. That's what he would do at the Empire and at the summer fete for the church. He would perform a miracle. He thought of Jesus, then. Not healing the sick, or driving out demons.

Walking on the water. Rising from the dead.

He sat back with four pages written when he realised he hadn't put down a word to say that he missed her or that he loved her. He added those as footnotes then sealed up an envelope, scribing the address on the front. He leaned further back in the chair, which had never seemed so comfortable. At rest at last, he drifted away into sleep.

***

At some point he woke again. It was light by then. No one else was up yet, so he tugged himself upstairs to bed and fell straight into sleep until the sound of his Mum shouting him started bouncing off the walls.

"You need to look after yourself." His Mum poured him tea then pushed the bread and jam towards him.

He nodded.

"Are you going to go to the police?" His Dad's voice was brisk.

He shook his head. "I can't, can I? They'll ask how I got them."

"How *did* you get them?" His Mum asked.

Eddie looked up at her and then over at his Dad, who chewed his lip.

"Oh, Eddie," his Mum said.

"I'm going to take them to Father Cleary. Ask him to give them to the police."

His Dad whistled. "It's not a bad idea."

"It's the best I've got."

His Dad looked at him cautiously over the corner of his paper.

Eddie avoided his eyes. He buttered his bread, wanting to load it then with jam. The jar was almost empty. He guessed that his Mum had gone without in order that he could have some. He pushed it away.

"What's wrong with it?"

"I'm sweet enough already." He gave her a grin she couldn't resist.

Outside, the world was working away, steady, unexceptional. The weather was warm to the skin, with the promise of more to come and the ground was starting to gasp for lack of any real rain.

***

Father Cleary smiled when he saw him. With mass just finished he was busy in the sacristy, hanging up his vestments.

"Back again?"

"Bad penny."

He chuckled. "What's in the bag?"

Eddie bit his lip. "Evidence."

Father Cleary's face screwed a little. "Evidence of what?"

Eddie couldn't help himself. Father Cleary hadn't moved a step, but his body was leaning inward. Eddie had drawn him and controlled him now. He had the power of magic in his voice. This was what everyone waited for: the reveal.

"Murder."

He almost expected a gasp – and then applause.

Instead, the priest laughed. "Well, thank you, Sherlock Holmes. Let's take a look."

Father Cleary led him down the corridor, past a breakfast room, where two other priests were chatting in their steady start to the day, sharing stories of the night before. They watched Eddie as he passed, curious.

The room Father Cleary found was small and stuffy and Eddie, still tired in a heavy, drowsy sort of way, felt breathless.

The priest sat opposite him, studying him. "Now, what is this, Eddie?"

Eddie lifted the bag onto the table. The priest pulled it towards him and looked in.

He looked up at Eddie with a smile.

"We don't pay deposit on bottles, Eddie. Try the off licence."

"They're from Mary Riley's house – and the house where her cousin was staying."

"Cousin?"

"Billy McGloin."

"I don't think I know him. What's he like?"

"He's dead."

That stopped the smile.

"They were both poisoned, Father. Just like the woman at St. Marie's poisoned herself, but this was done *to* them, not *by* them."

"And how do you know that?"

"There was no spill or burning on the hands, because it wasn't *their* hands holding the bottle."

"How do you know about the burning?"

The image of Billy's body flooded back to him. "I asked Doctor Gilmartin about Mary."

"And Billy?"

Eddie paused. "I saw him."

Father Cleary sat back and pulled a couple of breaths into his chest. The early heat of the day was getting to him now. He felt muddled. "Why have you got the bottles?"

"They've got fingerprints on them."

"Fingerprints?"

"They can show who was holding the bottles."

"How?"

"It's the new science, Father. My Dad told me."

The priest nodded. Frank Reynolds was a sound man. He said what he meant and what he meant, he knew. "And what do you want me to do with them?"

"Give them to the police."

"And not say who gave them to me?"

"I'd rather you didn't."

"That could be awkward."

"Murder's like that."

"Eddie. . ."

"Father, please."

"It won't change anything, Eddie. She's been buried now."

"It might change what people think about her."

"It might." Then he nodded. "All right, Eddie. I'll do this. Then will you leave it alone?"

Eddie nodded. "There's nothing else I can do."

"You won't go chasing anyone?"

Eddie shook his head. "I don't know who to chase."

"Good. But you've done well. I'm proud of you. You fought for her."

"Someone had to."

Eddie walked into work, three and a half miles of pavement giving him time to wake up more steadily and think more clearly. As he sauntered into the brewery, he felt for the first time in a while that things were becoming simpler.

He was wrong.

***

When he arrived home, he was aware that there was a problem. The house was unusually quiet. His Dad liked to listen to the radio whenever he could, searching the airwaves for music. The sound was usually an accompaniment to the smell of baking or cooking, his Mum getting ready for an evening meal or a weekend of scones, or parkin.

Walking through the door there were no sounds, no smells.

"Mum? Dad?"

There was a pause before an answer came.

"We're in here, Eddie."

Eddie shuffled through, his heart tight. His Mum and Dad were sitting rigid in their chairs. They looked up at him as he stood in the doorway.

"The police have been again."

Eddie couldn't stop a flash of doubt shooting through him that Father Cleary might have betrayed him. But he couldn't believe that. And he couldn't believe the police had scared the information from him. Eddie had never seen anyone's eyes glisten so much as when Father Cleary told the story of Jesus being tempted in the desert by the devil. He was a strong-willed man.

"What did they want?"

"They wanted to know where you were. When you were coming back."

"What did you tell them?"

"The truth."

Eddie was still feeling tense, his arms stiff. "And then what?"

"They're coming back."

"Tonight? I'm rehearsing tonight."

"You'll talk to the police first." His Dad's voice was tight and strict.

"If I'm in."

"Eddie." His Mother was tart.

"I haven't done anything wrong."

"You broke into two houses. Houses of people who are dead."

He had to acknowledge he *had* done that. He changed tack. "*They* don't know that."

"They're not stupid."

"They're not smart, Dad."

"It's not a good time to get cheeky."

"It's not a good time to get nervous."

"Eddie, this is serious, love."

"I *know* it's serious, Mum. Two people have been killed. They've been murdered. They've already buried one in a pauper's grave and the neighbourhood are saying she committed a mortal sin by killing herself and maybe another one by being pregnant. Her cousin's dead. God knows why! Now it's with the police. They should be investigating. If they can use the bottles, that's good. If they can't, that's that. Stan Kitteridge asked me to look into it, see what I could find. Now I've done that I'm finished. I've got a show next week and me and Nancy are doing something at the church garden party. I need to focus on *that.*"

His Mum and Dad looked at him long, but not so hard. Their love was always so close to the surface that they couldn't be angry with him. Besides which, he was right.

"Just be careful."

"I will. If I need to. It's over for me."

Once again, he was wrong.

***

The family were just sucking on boiled sweets when the sound of footsteps slipped in through an open window. They looked at each other and waited – until the pop of knocking on the door answered any question they might have been asking themselves. Eddie started to move, but his Dad put up his hand, pulling himself up, some of the strain showing on his face. He stood up straight.

Eddie watched him make his way to the door. Work had been busy for the last couple of months as preparation for the Royal visit added worry and time to the weeks.

"Good evening, Mr. Reynolds." It was the voice of Ted Pearson. Eddie bit his lip.

"We were hoping to have a word with Eddie."

"He's busy tonight, Constable."

"It is quite important."

There was a moment of quiet.

Eddie's Dad felt it pass between them. Each one had their own understanding of waiting for the next thing to happen. For him, it would always be waiting for the officer to blow the whistle before the charge began.

"He's busy tonight. You're not wanting to arrest him, are you?"

"Oh no, sir, it's just routine."

"Well, he can catch you on Monday then, can't he?"

Another pause.

"I said I'd call back later, Mr. Reynolds. You didn't say I shouldn't."

If he'd expected Frank Reynolds to blink then he didn't know him very well.

"I didn't know that he was going to be out again. He's rehearsing. He's an escapologist. He's got a show on at the Empire. And he's performing at the church summer fete in Graves Park tomorrow."

There was a pause.

Eddie imagined his Dad was looking at Pearson eye to eye. Pearson was a big man, much bigger than Dad. He knew, though, that his Dad wouldn't shift. He wouldn't wobble. The thought made his eyes wet and his throat tight.

"Tomorrow would be better, Mr. Reynolds. I'm on the beat, so I can call by. First thing'd be good."

"We've got mass first thing. It's Sunday, Ted. Are you forgetting?"

Pearson coughed. "Of course."

"And we'll be at the memorial at High Hazels after that. Are you not going?"

Pearson sniffed. "Like I said, I'm working, I'm afraid. Otherwise I'd be there. "

"Of course. After that then?"

"I can drop in around lunchtime. It's on my way. Will you tell him?"

"Of course I will, Ted," he used his Christian name like a tool to irritate him. Once you'd been in the army and seen service, the rank of a police officer didn't count for much. "And thank you, Ted, for the job you do."

"Good night, sir."

"Good night."

The door shut.

Eddie and his Mum said nothing as his Dad came back and sat down, slowly, heavily.

Then he looked at Eddie. "I thought you'd got a rehearsal to go to."

***

The rehearsal went badly. Eddie was struggling with his shoulder and trying just a bit too hard. His movements were stiff and tight and more than once he forgot his lines. When Nancy fluffed a word, he snapped.

"That's not it, Nancy. That's not right!" He jerked himself out of his bonds and landed heavily on the floor.

"I'm sorry, Eddie."

Her face was creased with worry. She was always afraid that he would get someone else. She loved to be on stage, with the audience wanting to be her or be with her. Two hot tears were squeezing out of her eyes, making them wet.

Eddie took a big breath. "Hey, I'm sorry. It's not your fault." He straightened up. "It's not you. It's me. It's this stunt. It's the way we're doing it." He shrugged. "It's not exciting. There's no danger."

"There *is*, Eddie." She skittled up beside him. "There *is*. You're upside down. The rope's burning."

He shook his head. "They know the rope won't burn through – and if it does, so what? I drop ten feet onto the stage floor."

"That could really hurt."

"Yeah, I could break my collar bone." He rubbed his shoulder. "I'm not going to die, am I?"

"I don't want you to die, Eddie. Don't say that."

"No, I don't want to die either. But I want people to think that I might."

"Why?"

He thought of Mary Riley and Cousin Billy. *They* were dead. Someone had tricked them and everyone else. He wondered what Ted Pearson was going to ask him.

"Because that's all that matters. Life and death."

Still thinking of Mary, he hardly noticed that Nancy had taken his hand and was holding it in hers, leaning in towards him, now resting her head against his vest.

"There has to be more than that, Eddie." She looked up at him. "There's got to be."

The words caught him, more for the sound and the feel of her breath on his neck. He bent his head to stare down at her, where her eyes were opening. The wetness from the tears made them gloss. Her free hand reached up and held his arm, feeling the tightness of muscle where the biceps were.

"You haven't told me what we're doing at the fete tomorrow."

He lifted a finger to brush away the tears that had dripped down to her cheek.

"It's a surprise." He kissed her forehead. "It'll be fine."

She squeezed his arm and closed her eyes, waiting for him to make the next move, leaning further into him. As she did, a sound started up – the first few tentative notes of choir practice, dripping out of the church. Eddie looked down at Nancy. He inched away.

***

Dusk was rolling down the hill from his home to meet him, covering the park as he strolled up through it, the air beginning to clear at last, but still a little warm with a taste of tar to it. He was heading back to his house, but taking in the area that had been marked out for the church summer fete.

He stood back, took a breath then studied his *stage.*

He felt with his feet, testing the earth to see how firm it was. The hot summer air had dried it to turn some of the soil to dust. He bent down, pushing his fingers into it, so that it crumbled and that pleased him. From his inside pocket he pulled a knife to mark out a space. Looking at his watch, he saw that time was ticking on, but he had an idea of what he needed to do, breaking into a quick skip to the edge of the park, where it skirted the gardens of houses that backed onto it. He ran down the line until he saw what he wanted, bouncing over a low wall to lift a spade from a tool shed, before heading back to the place he had marked. He worked for an hour, stopping when he was satisfied with what was possible and before the work tired him too much. He had things to do tomorrow.

He laid the spade back where he found it and strolled the last few hundred yards home.

Chapter Twenty-Six

Eddie didn't sleep much, walking the house at three o' clock in the morning. His body was tired but his mind wasn't. At six he managed to snatch a couple of hours dreaming.

After that it was time to get up and get out. As his Dad had told Ted Pearson, church was first, then a journey all across the city to High Hazels Park, where a service was being held to remember those who had died in the war.

The park was on the Rotherham side of town, which meant a couple of tram rides to get over there. That was hard on Eddie's Dad. His leg was playing up, though he wouldn't say anything. The pain, though, held the muscles of his face like puppet-strings and there was no hiding bolts of agony that came and went. His Mum watched him cautiously, not sure if the event itself was part of the problem.

A swarm of bodies had already started to pack out the park, spilling either side of the paths to watch the local branch of the British Legion march past to lead the way. Twenty years had passed since the Great War broke out, when the Sheffield Pals Battalion had been formed on a wave of populist support. Eddie's Dad was first amongst the volunteers, with his brothers and his friends. None of them knew it at the time, but they were treading along the fault line of an earthquake that would change everything. The day Dad signed up, three of his brothers and four of his friends were with him. Two brothers and two friends never came back. He saw them all, die or dead. As the clergy led the crowd in prayers, the memories of their faces and their bodies and the person that they were all came back to him. He wanted to cry. He tried. The tears wouldn't come. Battle had stopped things up and they would never start again.

The Vicar of Carbrook spoke passionately on a simple, singular theme: peace; international peace. He was trying to make things shine again so that they were obvious and clear. His words invoked the past, but the purpose was to wave a warning about present times and the dangers that seemed to be creeping up on countries again. All across Europe, radios were starting to chatter with omens of war.

The dignitaries at least had enough sense to avoid ostentation or make the occasion a steppingstone for their careers. A light wind skipped through the park to make arms shiver. The feeling seemed to match the mood. When the services were complete, the collected crowd splintered into smaller groups, yet something still connected them. Part of it was memory and reflection of that battle on the Somme, eighteen years earlier. Part of it was newer and fresher. Word was dripping out of Germany of things that had happened over the last two nights. News was sketchy, bound up with rumour, but the mood was grim. His Dad's face was dark. For the first time in years, Eddie stood back to see a man who had been shattered and was now –quite literally – less than he'd been. Everyone ignored it most of the time. But there it was. Or there it wasn't. Eddie realised for the first time ever that his Dad was a greater exponent of distraction than anyone. That included Houdini.

"Let's get back," his Dad said.

"There's no rush, Frank, love. You can stay and talk to your friends."

He shook his head. "We've done what we came to do. Time to go."

***

"You know what these are?" Ted Pearson dropped the disinfectant bottles onto the park bench between himself and Eddie, where they were sitting on a warm Sunday lunchtime. The noise was jarring, as Eddie watched Pearson's fat fingers smudging the glass. The moment felt suffocating, though they were in the most open space imaginable.

Looking at them Eddie couldn't shift the reflection of Billy's face in one of them. "Empty bottles."

"Smart."

Pearson eyed Eddie cautiously. He'd slap him if he had to, but he didn't really want to. There was a look in his eye of Eddie's Dad that worried him. He knew that he hadn't seen as much as Eddie's Dad. Never would. And never wanted to. They were out in the open, too. Witnesses could always be as much of a hindrance as a help.

"They were dropped off by a priest. You might know him. Father Cleary."

Eddie nodded.

"You *do* know him?"

"Yes."

"He's the priest at your Church. Which you go to every week."

"I go with my Mum and Dad."

"Course you do. You're a good Catholic lad, aren't you, Eddie?"

Eddie shrugged. A memory of Ada staring back at him through her dressing room mirror as he pushed heavily from behind came back to him hard. "I know right from wrong."

"That's a good start. And lying's wrong, isn't it?"

Eddie shrugged. "I don't think Jesus said much about it."

Pearson laughed. "It's one of the commandments, son, isn't it?"

"Not one of the ten."

"Are you a smart-arse, Eddie?" Pearson's patience was tightening, thinner all the time. "Have you seen these two bottles before?"

Eddie shook his head straight away. "No."

"Do you know where they came from?"

Another shake. "No."

Pearson sat back. Eddie was convincing. He was certainly confident.

"One was taken from Mary Riley's house. We think the other was taken from Billy McGloin's."

"Why?"

Pearson didn't like the question. "What do you mean?"

"Why would anyone take them?"

Pearson shifted in his seat. "You don't need to know that." He knew it was a weak answer and his mouth had to say more. "Does it matter?"

"It might help me understand why you want to know if I've seen them."

"That's not important."

"Are the bottles important? What's happened to Billy?"

Pearson twitched. Part of his game was to see if Eddie knew that Billy was dead. Eddie was playing what his Dad would call a straight bat. Nothing was going to get past him.

"He's dead?"

Eddie sat back on the bench, then looked away. While he was acting out a role there was a truth inside his head that made his face genuinely pale. Even so, he had lines to deliver.

"How did he die?"

"Poison." Pearson was starting to feel the mugginess of the day. He'd had a skinful the night before and wanted an easy Sunday morning to drift through, before a gentle afternoon then hair of the dog that night at the local. "But let me ask the questions, son. Mary Riley and Billy McGloin. Two people you were asking about."

"I didn't find Billy. But *you* found him?"

Pearson couldn't find a way out of the little traps Eddie kept setting, while Eddie himself just seemed to skip over the ones Pearson laid out. "We found him. In Upperthorpe. A neighbour gave us a tip."

Eddie's body tightened. Which neighbour? What did they say? "I don't know how I can help you."

Pearson snapped. "Did you give Father Cleary the bottles to bring to us?"

Eddie kept his eyeline constant with Pearson. "Did he say I did?"

Pearson just wanted to punch him. It was so much easier. He'd lived through the glory days of bludgeoning Sheffield's gang members into a bloody submission, then hauling them into court. Instead, he shut his eyes. When he opened them again, they were hard and mean.

"If I find you're involved in *anything*, Eddie Reynolds, I'll come down on you so heavy you won't see daylight for days. You understand me?"

"Perfectly."

Pearson nodded. "Get off home."

Eddie walked straight and steady along one of the many paths that criss-crossed the park, keeping his steps balanced for as long as he could. As he approached the entrance though, his resolve gave way, a jelly feeling of weakness flushing through him, making him reach out his hand to grab hold of the cast iron. He realised, for the first time, that it wasn't breaking and entering that Pearson was threatening him with. It was murder.

***

Dropping down the hill, Eddie stood on Chesterfield Road and took in his surroundings. The Woodseats Palace sat across the road, boasting its forthcoming screenings of *Sealed Lips*. One for Ada, he noted. Close by was the Chantrey, which made Eddie think of Stan, who lived just up the road. He had things to do, but time enough to call on Stan, he reckoned, turning up Stan's street before dipping down the passage between Stan's house and the next. As his feet echoed in the dark tunnel, he could hear laughter from the garden. The loudest voice was Stan's.

"Eddie!" He called out Eddie's name as if he was introducing him on stage.

Stan was sitting with his wife, Charlotte, their two girls and their neighbours from both sides. There was a table between them replete with bottles already opened, sandwiches, cakes, a teapot, cups and saucers and teacake.

Stan, as ever, was in full flow. He had a cigarette permanently on the brink of tipping out of his lips, but never quite slipping. In between snappy bites of conversation he took a draw on the tobacco and let the smoke soothe him.

"Are you ready for Thursday, eh?" He turned to his audience. "He's a star in the making this one, you know?"

The collected audience gave an *aah*.

"What do you do, love?" This was one of the neighbours, blousy and blonde.

Before Eddie could say anything, Stan was on his feet.

"Ladies and gentlemen, may I present to you, in his first major performance in Sheffield . . . The *Incredible* Eddie Reynolds, Escapologist," then he gave a stage wink to the ladies, "and womanizer!"

Eddie dropped his head with a grin, as the ladies cheered.

"An esca-what?" Here was the husband of the blonde.

"An escapologist, Dick, you berk!" Stan remonstrated. "Like Houdini."

"Oh, right!" He laughed loudly as he belched back some of the fizz of his beer.

"That sounds like some act. Escapology *and* womanizing." The blonde woman was staring intently at Eddie, looking out from the greyness of her marriage into the blue of his eyes.

"He doesn't do that at the same time, Iris," Stan laughed. He was standing now, coming over to Eddie "Are you joining us, Eddie?" Even as he said it, he put his arm round Eddie's shoulder to turn him away.

"No, I was just passing, Stan."

"Shame, shame. Ah, well. It's going to be a busy one, Eddie."

"That's always good."

"What do you need to know for Thursday?"

The basic question. "When am I on?"

Stan paused to give his cigarette some proper attention. They both knew that, by any reckoning, Eddie should go on first. He wasn't a name and he didn't have much experience behind him. They also knew that the first act was more or less a sacrifice. Half of the audience were still arriving, still sorting themselves out. Those actually seated were talking or looking forward to the main act, the reason they'd come. Only a few were attentive.

"What are you doing?"

"It's going to be good, Stan." Eddie went on. "Not what you'd expect."

Stan sucked a breath through this teeth, then nodded. "I can put you second."

Eddie beamed. That was all he could ask for. A zip of pleasure ran through him, followed by a line of cold. He wondered how much he'd used Mary Riley for his own purposes. She was still dead. She was still in an unmarked grave in the city cemetery, away from her Catholic family.

"Thanks, Stan. I'm on at the Church gala up at Graves Park later if you're interested."

"Well, I might be, indeed, Eddie. . . I might be." He smiled affably.

"All right. Well, I might see you then."

"Yes, you might. You might."

Stan wasn't going.

Eddie didn't mind. He had what he wanted: not to be first on stage. With that sorted, he walked along the way to call in on Nancy. Her house was busy, her mum still making adjustments to her outfit for the performance this afternoon, her dad cutting the hedge in their pocket garden. He was proud of what he had, his little estate. He smiled when he saw Eddie, seeing someone he could show it off to. He started to chat, until the sound of Eddie's voice brought Nancy out, skittish with nerves.

"What're you doing here, Eddie Reynolds?"

Eddie smiled. "What are your brothers up to?"

"Trouble," her mum said, chasing Nancy with a handful of pins for her outfit.

"Why?" Nancy asked.

"Do they want to earn a bit of money?"

A scurry of feet brought two of them – fourteen and sixteen – banging to a stop in front of Eddie. "Yes, please!"

Their mum laughed at their eagerness – at last – to do something they were asked. Money was the key. "Right. Come on," said Eddie, "and bring a shovel."

"A shovel?" Nancy might have said more if her mum hadn't accidentally pinned her, drawing a sharp cry.

"You look lovely, Nancy." He kissed her on the cheek. "I'll see you later." He turned to her brothers. "Follow me, boys."

Chapter Twenty-Seven

Eddie dropped back at home looking tired.

His Mum fretted. “Are you going to eat something?”

He looked at her a little lost, with an expression that asked: *are you going to make me something*? She spoiled him. She knew it. He knew it.

With a quick bite to eat inside him, he hurried into his performance clothes, pulling a light mac over it all for concealment.

As he skipped along to the garden fete, he could see how people from the parish and from nearabout were beginning to filter into an area of Graves Park that Sheffield Corporation had allowed the church to use. Two of the more officious parishioners had done a sterling job of roping off the area, though Eddie couldn’t quite see the point as there was no admission fee and surely the Church wanted as many people attending as possible. Father Cleary didn’t look comfortable with the arrangements so it was no surprise to Eddie that, later in the day, he found more than one stretch of rope unhooked from its post.

Eddie saw Nancy’s brothers leaning on their spades, sweating heavily, looking expectant. He smiled, waving at them. They came running for their money.

As the day warmed up the atmosphere was beginning to bustle. Say what you want about churches and Christians, they knew how to throw a social party. They had their business down pat. The organization was faultless and they made sure that the mood was fun. Eddie watched it all from a distance. He could feel the butterflies start to flutter in his stomach. Nancy was standing beside him, leaning into him.

"Do you think they'll want to watch us?"

She was asking a fair question. There was a lot going on, stalls of all sorts, from baked cakes to best home-grown vegetable to any variety of games to play or ways to lose your money from (moderate) gambling. Eddie studied three boys trying their luck at the coconut shy then looking to sneak an extra ball when the stallholder was collecting the ones that they had already thrown. His Mum was at a drinks table, pouring out squash while talking to friends, neighbours and punters. He looked for his Dad. It took him a few minutes to find him. He was sitting alone, smoking his pipe. His face was heavy.

"They'll watch us."

Today would be something different for them.

"Are you sure?" She was dressed and made up to appeal to all the men who wanted to be close to a young girl but not so immodest to have the mothers and wives curl their lip.

"I'm sure."

"Are we doing the usual?"

They had a routine down pat for occasions like this. It was ready off-the-shelf, which meant that they knew it well enough to spend all their time working up the audience.

"I want to do something different."

He felt her hand on his arm. "Eddie?"

"It's all right. It's going to be fine."

She didn't get a chance to respond. Father Cleary waved a big hand in a sort of blessing as he came over, to stand side by side with Eddie. Nancy slipped away to get a drink.

"There's a good crowd."

Father Cleary shook his head. "They're not buying, Eddie. They're talking, all right and they're moving round. But they're not spending their money."

"There's time yet."

He shook his head. "It's a lot of effort, Eddie, for not much money."

Religion was a business. Father Cleary knew that. Eddie knew it too. Faith and prayer fitted in somewhere, but the pounds, shilling and pence were their own holy trinity for a church still trying to re-establish itself in the country.

"It's going to be all right."

Father Cleary laughed. "You're telling me to have faith."

"I am. I'm going to put on a show like they've never seen. They need to pay for it."

"How are you going to do that? We're a little limited with stage props."

"We're all sorted." He nodded towards an area away to the left of the crowds, where a sheet was laid on the ground. Nancy, back with a drink, noticed it for the first time.

"Eddie? What are you going to do?"

"Something special." He grinned. He watched as Nancy took a few tentative steps towards the space that had been marked out, where her brothers were now idling. She stopped short, then turned to look back at Eddie, her face white.

"What's it worth, Father?" Eddie asked.

Father Cleary stood back a little. Eddie, he knew, could be precocious. Even so, the priest felt he should get more respect than this.

"God's thanks, Eddie. Isn't that enough."

"A Catholic burial would be, Father."

"That again?"

"That again."

"Eddie, we've talked."

"You know she was murdered and you know how."

"And until the police say that that was what happened, then we *don't* know how."

"I thought we were working to a higher law."

"That's up in heaven. We're stuck down *here.*"

Eddie stared at him. "I'll do my part, Father. I'll leave you with yours."

Eddie might have said more, if Nancy hadn't tugged so hard on his arm that it turned him away.

"What *are* we doing? And what's the sheet? What's under it?" She was starting to fluster. "Is it what I think it is?"

"It's all sorted, Nancy. Don't worry."

His voice was soft enough to calm her. She quietened as he changed his focus to the crowd in the background. They were loose, drifting. He told Nancy to start to put out the message. He needed to knot them together.

His attention was caught by a slice of glamour approaching the event with a swagger in her walk. Ada was done up, as they said, like a million bucks. Her Sunday best was better than anyone else's. Then, dragging two yards behind her, looking quaintly distracted, came Morris. Eddie could tell that Ada had dressed him. The suit was smart, the shoes were sharp, the hat was new. He didn't know how to *wear* any of it, though. His stomach sagged and his gait was slovenly. The clothes just hung on him. Eddie could only imagine how much Ada hated to walk beside him, maybe consoling herself with the fact that his money had paid for her perfection. Maybe. Perhaps that was what grated the most.

"Hello."

Eddie smiled. Ada was playing the game perfectly today. She couldn't stop her eyes twinkling, though, responding to Eddie's body head to foot then everywhere in between.

"It's Eddie. Eddie Reynolds."

He put out his hand and they shook formally.

"I'm Ada. This is my husband." She was looking at Eddie directly, eye to eye. "Ken."

Eddie turned to Morris with a smile. Was he a bad man? In the eye of the Lord, perhaps he was better than Eddie himself, though Eddie wondered how, when Jesus scored the sins, he judged between adultery and love of mammon. The Old Testament was harder on Eddie. Perhaps the new one was kinder.

"Hello, Eddie. Ada says she's heard that you do tricks."

"He's an escapologist!" Ada tugged her husband's arm, like she might a child who should be able to answer better in class.

"Oh, well, that's something, isn't it? Like Houdini? saw him at the Empire."

"1920?"

"1911."

Eddie nodded. “He did the milk churn escape.”

Morris warmed at the memory. “That’s right! Bloody impressive.”

“Language. These people are *Catholics*.”

“Sorry, Eddie.”

Ada interrupted. “What are you going to do for us, Mr. Reynolds.”

Eddie smiled at the use of his surname. Memories of things she’d whispered in his ear came back to him so that he heard them again.

“Something appropriate for a Catholic show.”

“Sounds intriguing.”

“It is. Get ready to be generous with your donations.”

“We will.”

She tugged her husband’s arm. “Oh, yes. We like to support things,” he said.

When they moved on, Eddie walked over to his Mum, who was pouring lemonade and squash by the bucketload.

“Any chance of a free one, before I go on.”

She smiled at him as passed him a glass.

“Is it something special?”

He nodded. “It is.”

“Have you done it before?”

“Not properly.”

“Well, you’ve got Nancy to help. She’s very competent, I’m sure.” Her voice was tart.

“I talked it over with Randolph.”

“Randolph?”

“Douglas. *Randini*. I’ve told you a million times. Lived in Greenhill. Lives in Castleton.”

He remembered the conversation perfectly. Cups of tea in hands, sitting at the table in that dreamlike cottage in Castleton, where Douglas and his wife had built their museum of wonders piece by piece. Douglas talked, Eddie listened, knowing that he was sitting at the feet of a master. Douglas was a scholar of the art, which is why Houdini had pressed him when they had the chance to meet. Eddie wondered how great Douglas might have been, if only illness hadn't cut his career in half.

As they talked, Eddie's eyes had flicked around the walls, skipping over the display of handcuffs that Douglas had amassed over the years, some of them a direct gift from Houdini. His focus then stuck on a picture of the two men together, taken the last time they met in 1920, when Houdini was performing at the Empire. Douglas was backstage, lending a hand and moral support. Houdini was going to perform the Torture Cell. It was a showstopper.

"This isn't easy, Eddie," Douglas said. Knowledge turned magic into a science which only attracted Eddie all the more. It also meant that when he frowned, there was no mysticism about it. He was worried.

"I know."

Douglas had looked him up and down. "But you're strong. Good upper body."

"Thanks."

Douglas smiled. "You know the risks."

"I do."

"The only question, then, is: are you ready?"

The sound of Father Cleary's voice startled him out of his reverie, a perfect echo to what Douglas had asked him. "Are you ready?"

Eddie was brought back to the present moment. He nodded. As he walked towards the priest, Nancy came running, sliding up against him.

"Eddie? I looked under the sheet! What are you thinking?"

"It's exciting, Nancy."

"Are you sure about this? We've got your other stuff. We could do anything."

He looked around and though it took a few seconds, he picked out Ada, who was pretending to be admiring floral bouquets, but whose eyes kept searching for him.

"We're doing this."

Father Cleary came up smiling.

"You've generated a bit of excitement all right."

"Good."

Father Cleary raised an altar bell high to ring it, the sound working in Pavlovian style on the people gathered there. Eddie turned to Nancy and whispered.

She beamed then turned to the crowd. "I need two strong men to help me out!"

That brought some laughter. After a certain sheepish prodding and jostling, two men shuffled forward, urged on by their wives and children.

"Thank you, gentlemen," said Eddie. "Nancy." Just the one word was the prompt for her to go to their bag of tricks, which had been sitting off to one side. Nancy had picked up the Gladstone bag through the family. Its age and weather-beaten look gave it some eminence. You might imagine that the whole history of magic was contained within. She took her time to pick out the items she needed, making it seem bottomless.

As she pulled out straps to bind him, Eddie turned to the crowd, which was now leaking towards them from every stall across the site.

"Today, I am going to perform a stunt that you are unlikely ever to have seen before."

That brought a healthy gasp.

"And one that you will *never* have seen performed. . . . . . successfully."

Now there was an *ooh.* The crowd stuttered forward. Eddie was Svengali to them.

"The great Harry Houdini himself tried this trick." He paused for effect. "And failed."

That brought a gasp.

The audience was starting to mutter now, the little snatches of conversation timid or uncertain. This was more of what they'd wanted from their religion: a little spice of mystery and wonder. What did Eddie have that their priests couldn't muster? Did he have a closer connection to God than they did? They had to hope so.

Father Cleary was glaring at Eddie. His eyes were fixed, his face set. He knew that he was staring at another demagogue, one of the many that were sweeping up populations with the clearest of messages and the greatest of promises. Eddie felt the power himself. For these moments at least, he commanded these people.

"These two fine gentlemen," he created a gap for the audience to laugh, "will guarantee that the ties that bind me are as tight as they can be. And then. . . " He paused, again. But in fact he stopped. What he would say next would be something entirely new. There was no continuity. It was change and revolution all at once. He waited and gave the audience a moment to anticipate.

"They will bury me alive."

Chapter Twenty-Eight

Eddie could sense the shock that tripped along the line of the watching crowd. He looked out to see their faces, to find his mother, then to find Ada. They were stiff and still. The last face he caught was Nancy's and it was full of horror, even though she knew what was coming. She had the look of someone who had sat at the bedside of a dying lover until they had finally seen them pass.

Eddie turned now to the two men: amiable and affable, Sheffield born and bred, dressed up smart, squirming against the collars and cuffs. Both showed fine cuts to their skin where they'd shaved when they'd been told to.

"And who do we have helping us today?"

"Bill," one of them muttered, who got a cheer, which drew a smile.

"Pete Handy," said the other, more confident.

"Well named, Pete. I hope you *are* handy."

They smirked. The crowd laughed.

"And what do you two fine gentlemen do?"

They looked at each other sheepishly, as if it might be a trick question.

Eddie knew before he asked. Their hands told their story, nail-end brown with dirt that no soap could wash away, skin polished like leather at the tips and their hands cut every which way from blades they had handled. One of them had lost the tip of his index finger, when he was younger and didn't see why you had to concentrate so hard. They were little mesters and did the smaller, no fuss jobs on the finer items of steel or silver, while the big behemoths just worked on tonnage.

"Gentleman, please step forward."

The crowd was swelling as passers-by from the park were drawn in. While Eddie was strapped and bound there was a sense of ritual which caught the eye. Something strange was happening for a Sunday. People who saw it knew they had to get closer.

"As you can see," Eddie called out, making sure his voice carried well beyond the front row, to draw more people into him, "the ropes are tight and the locks are secure." He winced – theatrically – as Bill grunted to pull the knot fast. "Would anyone like to check?"

On cue, Nancy skipped out to the crowd to pull two women forward.

One of them was Ada.

The other was a young girl, made to look older by starting work at thirteen to support the family. She wasn't sure, anymore, how many options she had left to her. With a father dead and mother mostly absent, she hadn't quite given up hope, but didn't spend much time on dreams. Eddie, though, was something to wish for, still so young, pretty and strong with it. Yet old enough to protect her. She barely looked at the knots or the locks. She looked into his eyes. When he smiled at her she lost a breath.

Ada was more reluctant. She gave the first girl space, knowing how Eddie could affect you. She recalled the first time they had met, at the wedding of a couple with ties to both of them. The affair was a simple, Church Hall event with warm beer and home-made food. Ada had gone with her husband, who quickly found someone who liked to talk business. Left alone, Ada felt the atmosphere of fun swell around her. People were happy .They were dancing. They were laughing. She could see it but not be part of it. Then Eddie appeared and offered her a drink. In all the occasions she thought back to those moments, she replayed the idea time and again that she had seduced him. He had been so young. Now, though, she wasn't so sure.

"Would you like to put your hands on the ropes to test them?"

She looked at him hard and fast. All of their times together jumbled. She recalled everywhere she had touched him, how he touched her, with fingertips, tongue, sometimes the palm of the hand in a soft slap, sometimes just the lips. She had a flash of memory of the night he'd dragged her along to see *The Mask of Fu Manchu*. The ripples of sensuality that ran through the film made her wriggle in her seat. When she took him home, she was eager to tie him and be tied. She smoothed her touch along the rope lines to the knot.

"Is it tight?"

She nodded.

"Is it tight enough?"

She pushed her finger into the space between the rope and his shirt and felt the squeeze of his muscle. "I think so."

They shared a glance and in the background Eddie was aware that Nancy was watching them. He guessed that his mother was too. "Thank you."

As she started to turn away, she looked back. "Is this safe, Eddie?"

"When did that ever stop us?"

Her face sharpened, then she left him.

"Thank you, ladies." He nodded to the girl, who was still hanging beside him. "Thank you, gentlemen."

He paused to let the audience understand what they could see: a man bound. That was intriguing, but hardly a mystery and hardly magic.

"Now all we need is a place to confine me." He was dark, then light again. "But this is a park, not a church yard. Surely, there's no grave around here!"

After a fraction of silence, one of Nancy's brothers piped up. "Over 'ere, Mister!"

The boy pulled the sheet away, jumping down into the hole he'd helped to dig until he all but disappeared. Gasps popped out of mouths as the boy fell.

Beside him, Eddie could feel Nancy tense and he noticed Bill and Pete rock back on their heels. Eddie had the momentum with him. He wouldn't lose it. He gestured to Nancy who skipped behind him. With a suitable flourish he gestured for the crowd to close in round the shallow grave that had opened up.

Bodies jolted forward, beginning to press up towards Eddie, a Christian crowd, drawn by a burial chamber. Where the sheet had been was a deep hole dug out of the earth, started by Eddie the night before and finished today by Nancy's brothers, who sweated hard for the money they earned.

The reality of the situation was now beginning to alarm some of the observers. The mutterings were growing louder. Eddie liked what he saw, catching Father Cleary's face, which was torn between pleasure and pain. Eddie smiled.

People were starting to clog around Eddie now, studying his strapped-up body with some wonder and then looking down towards the hole as is they were looking at some gallows, with a hanging on the way.

"Ladies and gentlemen." He shouted the words, just to still them. "We are ready."

The words sent a chill through the crowd – and a thrill.

Nancy scuttled beside him, turning away from the crowd. "Are you *sure*, Eddie?"

The hunger from the crowd convinced him. He nodded.

"I will shortly enter the grave." He chose the word carefully. "I will lie down. A board will be placed on my back." He paused between sentences to let the implication sink in. "Then the earth will be thrown down on the board until the grave is level with the ground." Another pause. "When the sound of the ground being stamped down is finished, I will start my escape. Time is everything." He stared at the crowd. Every one of them was staring back at him. "They say no man can hold his breath for more than a minute." He was exaggerating on the low side, knowing that they would check their watches. He was comfortable with ninety seconds. He'd practiced in the bath for years.

Father Cleary skipped up to him. "Is this safe, Eddie?"

He smiled, turning back to the crowd. "If I'm not free in *two* minutes Nancy will signal these men to try to rescue me, alive – or dead!"

Father Cleary stepped back conflicted. He wanted to believe in Eddie. Yet he knew it was dangerous. Something in Eddie's eyes told him, too, that there was a brag in the suggestion that he could hold his breath so long. But Father Cleary wanted the money that he thought people now *had* to give. This was something special. For a Christian man, this was akin to the miracles.

Eddie noted that the crowd was still growing, words being passed on person to person. Not only had most of the stalls come to a temporary halt, more and more people were coming into the arena. Mostly dressed in summer colours, a darker shade caught his eye.

"We may need a couple more volunteers to help these gentlemen put the earth back."

The dark shade was thickening and coming closer. At first it seemed like a swab of black, but as Eddie's eyes focused he could see that it was – though darker than dark – blue.

He saw a hand go up, a slash of navy that stood out across the lights and whites of summer clothing. The hand was thick, solid, the legs pushing forward with pace.

"Hello, Eddie." Ted Pearson smiled as he approached, Wilf Magill lumbering up beside him.

"Hello, Constables." Eddie's breathing stiffened.

"Do you need a hand?"

"Thank you, gentlemen." He kept his expression still. The performance was everything. But he had to turn away. Nancy saw his face.

"Are you all right, Eddie?" She put her hand on his arm. For the first time he felt just how tied and trapped he was.

"Yes. Come on."

Turning back to the audience, he looked sombre.

"The moment has come. Gentlemen, take your positions." Then, turning to Nancy he whispered. "Don't let them stamp the ground down too flat. It *has* to be loose."

Eddie stepped towards the grave when the sound of a voice caught him in the back.

"Have we checked the straps?"

Slowly, Eddie turned, to see Wilf Magill staring right at him, pinning him eye to eye.

"Would you like to check again, officer?"

Magill's face didn't break. "I would."

Eddie smiled, as ever. "Then please step forward."

Pearson came with him, as if the two were part of one body.

Magill leant his face forward to inspect the knots. His eyes were brutal, poring over every fibre of the rope. Not quite convinced by one of them of the knots his hand came out to check. Eddie had to stop himself stepping back and tumbling over.

The hand that came towards him showed skin that had been scorched.

It might have been a fire that did it.

It might have been a scald in the kitchen.

But Eddie knew right away that the burn was caused by the acid that pours out of a disinfectant bottle when you're pressing it up to the mouth of someone who doesn't want to drink it and when they retch, the acid catches your skin to mark it red.

"Looks all right," Magill said, stepping back.

Eddie didn't move for a moment.

"*Eddie*," Nancy whispered.

His lungs were snapping in his chest. He knew that he needed to be calm before he started the performance. He *had* to control his breathing, but he couldn't.

"Eddie?"

"It's all right." He nodded, mostly to himself. "Let's go."

He could feel the bodies of the four men lumber towards him as he stepped down into the ground, the crowd letting out gasps as his body began to disappear, then vanish completely. Up above, he heard the stamp of footsteps as the crowd surged in like a wave of water coming to fill a space.

Despite the warmth of the weather of previous weeks the earth this far down was heavy and damp, the dank stench of soil coming on him hard. He knelt and felt a shiver of worry.

Slowly as he could, with no arms to support him, he lowered himself down and then levelled his body. His muscles tensed.

The next moment a darkness fell over him as the board was lowered down, covering his whole back. He pressed up a few inches on his elbows, leaving himself wriggle room before the earth started to fall.

In the blackness he could only see his mind's eye and that brought back the image of the acid burn skin on Constable Magill. Had he killed Mary Riley and Billy McGloin? At least onc of them. Probably both. He couldn't begin to understand why.

Now Magill was standing over Eddie, about to help to bury him.

Eddie's breath was caught in his throat with his chest tight. Keep yourself calm, Eddie. Save your energy. These were the moments of stillness.

He took a long, slow breath.

The earth was starting to compact, pressing the board against him, squeezing through his back into his chest and making his lungs start to pop. He wanted it to end. He wanted the earthfall to stop, so that he could start his escape proper.

The sound now was peculiar. Not the sound of earth falling, just a sense of pressure on his ears and a noise that was unknown, unfamiliar and yet all encompassing.

His thinking started to blur so that he had to force himself to pull a last, good lungful of air into his chest before he began to work the knots in his suit.

A moment of panic made him gasp as he felt oxygen pour out of him, remembering the fact that Houdini had never managed to perform the trick that he was now attempting. He made himself slow again, sucking some of the remaining air out of spaces around him then feeling it dribble, thinly, into his lungs.

He started to wriggle, but not in a way to work the knots lose. His body was jerking compulsively.

Eddie! Slow yourself down. Be steady.

The light was gone. Sound was gone. The air was disappearing, leaving Eddie with three feet of earth on top of him, Constable Magill standing above, pressing the ground down, Eddie imagined. Trapping him in. Sending him down to hell.

"Keeping calm is the key, Eddie."

Randini's voice came to him from nowhere - a conversation over a cup of tea.

"And the amount of earth. Three feet, not four." Douglas had placed his cup down. "Harry didn't measure well enough. He gave himself too much to do. He had more than four feet of earth on top of him and it was wet. Dryer earth is what you need. Only ever try the trick in summer." Eddie's breath steadied. "And three feet, not four."

His body started to move like a fish, working from his legs up, through his waist, on to his shoulders and arms, pushing at the knots to shake them free. As he struggled, he tried to keep his breathing steady and his mind still, only focusing on the actions his body was taking. Just as he pushed, though, the board above him slipped, the soil uneven above it, sloping it down onto his calf.

"Never panic. Breathe steady," Randini had said. "There'll be air around you, under the board and some in the earth."

But he couldn't not panic. His leg was trapped. When he tried to compensate by using his arms harder the ache in his shoulder shattered into pain to blank his thinking. The seconds cost him control. His breathing stuttered, his lungs taking the chance to try to draw more air in, working too hard and too fast.

The knots hadn't loosened as time was falling away. Eddie was trying to count steadily, but kept losing his place. The loss of patterns made him panic again. His body reacted by working into spasm. His leg was still stuck while his shoulder was weeping at him.

The lack of air was starting to fog his thinking as his brain gulped on any oxygen he could find. Out of nowhere, images of other times and places looped around his mind like a cinema reel. He saw his Mum, Dad, Ada, Louisa. They seemed far away from him – or him from them and he didn't know why there was a difference or what the difference meant. Their faces were stretched, or incomplete and they were unclearly lit, the darkness all around him inside his tomb sucking away the light, like colour from a lolly. For a second, he floated.

In that moment - that seemed to stretch time - he could see the end of things. His body could only be strong so long. Randolph Douglas didn't have the stamina to continue with his magic and in the end Houdini's demise was a failure of the body. They weren't alone. The amazing David Devant had succumbed to palsy, The Great Lafayette died on stage in the flames of one of his signature tricks and Chung Ling Soo took the bullet he was meant to dodge.

He gasped.

A knot was loose! He urged himself against it, freeing an arm, then a hand and the hand drove through the dirt to another knot to free it and another; two arms now free to push against the earth to free his leg, to let him kick and start to drive up at last. His fingers clawed through mud that had compacted. Every inch felt like a foot, every foot like a chain. He urged himself up, his breath almost gone and the banging in his lungs now a banging in his brain of blood boiling along its channels.

He saw Louisa again. She was an angel and she was calling him.

"I'm not worthy."

Then there was Mary. Then there was Billy. Mary was vague. His memory played tricks on how well he remembered her. Billy was vivid, wearing his death mask. Mary would be with God now, somewhere up high. In the meantime, here he was digging down low, heading towards the devil.

He thought of his Mum and Dad, imagining them up above, wondering and full of worry. His Dad! Who fought through hell for peace, to see his son lost in such a stupid, meaningless way on a middling Sunday afternoon. Was that what Eddie wanted? What *did* he want? What did he want to be? What did he want to do?

Now, his mind showed him Houdini, his hero. Beside him was Professor de Lyle, his inspiration. Then Randini, his mentor. De Lyle had tried to steer him away from this trick. *It's not a trick at all, Eddie. It's showing off.* Randini had simply warned him: Houdini couldn't do it, why can you? What makes you different?

What did he want to do? He wanted to do *this*! He might have said it out loud, because he was aware, suddenly, of taste: the taste of dirt on his tongue and now down in his throat, tickling him to cough.

He pushed again. How much further could it be? How far was forever?

He pushed harder and found space. His fingers were free. Another heave lifted the board off him completely. Earth tumbled down. That might have made him panic again a moment ago, but now he was back in control. The movement of the earth created space and it was space that he needed. Through the pain in his shoulder he drove himself up, his back battering against the soil. As he pushed he wrestled his body round so that he was facing up.

Free fingers became a free hand, then two. He pushed his arms wide, opening the gates back into life. Even now, the ground resisted so that he almost fell back with exhaustion. One more surge split the earth apart, daylight flooding down onto his face, even as soil tumbled across his skin.

He could hear cheering. He could see the faces of Nancy and Ada, staring in and staring down, full of care, want, need and some love.

He was still thinking of Louisa as a hand grabbed his to pull him up.

He saw the skin. Burnt.

Eddie emerged out of the ground, only to fall to his knees. He was on the point of passing out, but he could hear the crowd and they were cheering. He had to do what he had to do. He turned to them, held up his hands in triumph.

Ted Pearson took his arm and pulled him up, so that he was sandwiched by the two officers. "That was a close shave, Eddie."

He couldn't speak, just nodded.

"You want to be careful, son." Wilf Magill said quietly in his ear.

Chapter Twenty-Nine

He should have gone home. He'd just performed an act that Houdini never mastered and he'd risked his life doing it. That had to be enough to justify some rest. But it didn't.

"Where are you going?" His Mum was anxious and urgent.

"I just need to see someone."

The fete was burning down to the embers on a late Sunday summer afternoon. Father Cleary was relaxing now. He hadn't done much, but he'd worried. Now he could smile. The money had come. He gave Eddie a wink. He knew he had part of a bargain to keep.

"I won't be long, Mum."

"Eddie-"

His Dad put his hand out and caught her arm. "Let him go."

***

The Crofts was uncertain when he arrived, a mood of suspicion hanging on the faces of people who watched him go by, leaning out of their houses because the dry sun was better than the dark and the damp. Eddie walked steadily, but without energy or drive. He moved as if he was part of a funeral procession.

Maggie Tasker saw him coming. She was ready for him, as if she'd been expecting his return from the first time he called. She was a good Catholic girl and knew what retribution meant. Eddie stood back from the doorway, the threshold that he wouldn't cross and Maggie would continue to defend as long as she could.

Their eyes met briefly but couldn't hold. They had a sense of pain and shame that were different and the same.

"It was Wilf Magill, wasn't it?"

The name was enough to make Maggie twitch, her body reacting even as her mouth tried to stay shut. "I never said that."

"With Millie? You don't need to." Eddie had a cigarette in his hand. He needed something, taking a long drag, letting the smoke pour into his lungs to sanctify them. "Just as long as you don't deny it."

She dropped her head.

Eddie continued. "And then Mary. How many more around here? I mean, who's going to stop a policeman?" He shook his head. "Who's going to try?"

"Billy McGloin?"

The words came out hot. They shook Eddie where he stood. They told him what he'd guessed. He looked at Maggie to see that her body had softened. She couldn't shut her mouth anymore.

"Do you *know* that?"

She laughed at him.

"I don't know anything, Eddie, except hunger, thirst and poverty. Everything else is a guess, but what do you think?"

He nodded.

"I think you're right. I think Billy had a mark against his name and they came looking for him."

"Wilf Magill at the front of the posse."

"Sounds likely. Billy was out. Mary was in."

Maggie sucked at her lip, as thoughts of Magill with sister Millie made her blanch.

"And we know what happens next."

The words were cold and simple.

Eddie blew out a breath of the same dirty air that he'd sucked in. "Magill got her pregnant?"

"That's what men do, Eddie."

"And what happened?"

"Magill didn't want to pay, I'd guess. He'd seen it done before and reckoned he could cut out the middleman."

"But he used *Lysol* and he *knew* that could kill. He'd have known about the woman at St. Marie's."

Maggie's face was blank. "That works, doesn't it? Either way, the child's going to die. If the mother dies too, it's not a tragedy. All loose ends tied up."

"Except Billy."

"He came back. Or he got to hear. That's what people are starting to say. I didn't know that last time you called."

Eddie could piece together the rest. Magill had found a way of killing that worked and looked like suicide. Billy came back causing trouble. He needed to be sorted.

"Did he say something to Magill?"

She shrugged. "Maybe. Or Magill just got to know that he knew something."

"That's a bit of a risk to take."

Maggie laughed. "Billy's Irish, Eddie. He's poor and he's a nobody, except a troublemaker. Better off dead as far as most folk are concerned."

He looked away. The words meant something to him. He took them home with him, where he found his Dad sitting alone, the radio silent.

"Where's Mum?"

"She's in bed. She's tired."

Eddie nodded.

"Before you sit down, can you get us a couple of bottles from the pantry?"

Eddie brought back two bottles of beer, presenting them to his Dad with a glass, as you might a peace offering.

His Dad smiled and snapped the tops off with a bottle opener. "There you go."

He held one to Eddie.

Eddie shook his head.

"Go on. You need it."

"Thanks." Eddie fetched another glass.

"What's on your mind, Eddie?"

Eddie stared at his glass and then at his Dad. "One of the policemen did it."

"Did what?" He had to ask.

"Killed Mary Riley. And Billy McGloin." He paused. "I think."

"So, it'll be his fingerprints on the bottles?"

"If he hasn't got to the bottles already. And he'll know someone's found him out."

His Dad nodded.

"You believe me, don't you?"

His Dad smiled. "I never doubted you, Eddie."

They sat for a minute of silence as if it was a remembrance.

"What are you going to do, Eddie?"

Eddie shrugged. "What can I do?"

His Dad had long since given up on trying to achieve the impossible, or explain it.

"Keep your head down. Don't cause trouble. Leave it as suicide."

"Pauper's grave? No service? Nobody knowing the truth."

"God'll know."

"Is that enough?"

"Sometimes it's all we've got."

Eddie took a long drink of beer until the glass was empty.

"Get to bed, son. Sleep on it. It might be better in the morning."

***

It certainly wasn't better in the night. Eddie's bedroom was sticky with the heat that was hanging onto the city and wouldn't let go. The airlessness made him gasp, keeping him awake, with his body needing the comfort of sleep, while his mind raced all the time. Exhaustion had kept him from thinking clearly so that now he lay with his thoughts jumping, crowding on each other and bumping together with the first steps of dreaming.

When he sat up in bed it was two o'clock. As his breathing slowed and his eyes got used to the dark his thoughts became sharp to a point.

He thought of Mary, then of Magill, brutalizing his way into her house and pinning her there on the sofa, pausing only to take off his ring before he unbuckled his belt. Eddie wondered if Billy had caught them in the act and thought of the shame for Mary, as well as the pain. Billy? Full of ideals. Full of principles. Not yet smart enough to know that there weren't laws enough to look after Mary and her kind.

That was it and it was done. Eddie dragged himself to the window to see if the city had any answers for him, knowing that there were none left.

He sat back on the bed and then laid down.

His journey was over. Perhaps things would start to get better in the morning and he could start to look ahead to his performance at the Empire.

***

Judging by his Dad's face, things were very much *not* any better in the morning. Eddie was stiff in every part of his body as he struggled downstairs, but at least hoped for smiles from his parents. There were none.

"What's wrong?"

His Dad didn't look at him straightaway and his Mum put her hand on his.

"The news isn't very good, love."

He looked over at his Dad, who was silent.

"What is it?"

Dad looked up at him and then splayed the newspaper onto the table, where the headlines looked like bullet holes.

Eddie slipped onto a chair and buried himself in the story.

Adolf Hitler had made his move over a weekend that was starting to be known as the *night of the long knives*. He had moved beyond democracy, taking his next logical step towards absolute leadership with a team beside him to help plan the strategy and a mob militia to deliver it. The first step was to snuff out every challenge that was close to him. The heavy presence of the Schutzstaffel was obvious in every action, as any sort of threat was hunted then summarily executed.

"He's killing his own men, Eddie." His Dad was holding his pipe, unlit and empty, just something to touch. “He’s killed Rohm. That was *his* man. His gofer. Van Schleicher, too.”

Van Schleicher had been Hitler’s predecessor and recommended Hitler to replace him. He was shot where he stood. His wife as well. They weren’t alone. There was a long list. As they’d hoped for with Rohm, a lot had died by suicide. The others had mostly been shot. They didn’t even know the numbers.

“He’s in full charge now,” his Dad muttered. “No one can challenge him. No one can stop him.”

The sound of his Dad’s voice worried Eddie. When he looked over, he saw his Dad’s eyes, his gaze floating outwards, without purpose. He was defeated.

“It’ll be all right, Dad.”

His Dad didn’t listen.

“Eddie’s right, love. Don’t get yourself worried. It’s a big week this week. We’ve got royalty coming.”

“And I’m on at the Empire,” Eddie offered.

His Dad snapped out of his reverie. “Are you up to it?”

Before he answered, Eddie’s body felt a quick flood of pain from every muscle, from his calves up to his neck. “I will be.”

“Take care, Eddie.”

The words were sombre. For the first time in his life he wasn’t sure that taking care of himself was in his control.

***

The Monday morning tram ride was a relief. Passengers were bustling, full of chatter. The sound broke Eddie’s concentration, so that he didn’t think too hard about the trick yesterday, or Wilf Magill or Mary Riley.

Eddie was angry. He wanted to do something. Run, jump, punch something. At least his mind did. His body wanted relaxation. Yesterday had drained him to the point where his nerves seemed to be floating at times during the day, as he put in a steady shift and let the basics of barrel-delivery occupy him.

By lunchtime he was ready for a change, or a sleep. He took the former, heading down a busy Ecclesall Road to knock on the Professor's door.

"Eddie!" George Fox's face was alight with excitement. "I've heard amazing things. Come and tell me."

They sat in the garden and drank lemonade.

"You did it? You did the coffin trick?"

"I didn't use a coffin. Just a board."

"Still . . .What was it like?"

Eddie let his mind trip back to the moments in the hole, with the earth solidifying around him. "I don't plan to do it again in a hurry."

The Professor laughed. "Very sensible. But what about Thursday?"

Eddied nodded. "That's what I wanted to talk about."

The Professor poured another glass. "Then let's talk."

***

The conversation energized him and he started to look at positives. He *had* performed the coffin trick. He had the show coming up this Thursday and *wasn't* on first. And while he had stirred something of a hornet's nest with the *Lysol* bottles, the police didn't *know* that he was the one to get hold of them. With those things to reassure him, he made the logical and sensible decision to leave the police alone.

They, however, didn't reciprocate.

His Mum's face was ashen as he came back home.

"What?"

"The police have been *again*."

"Why?"

"They want to talk to you." She had been crying.

"What about?"

"They wouldn't say." Eddie moved inside, where his Dad was back in his chair, solid and still. Eddie turned round to his Mum, who shook her head and whispered. "Let it be, Eddie."

"You all right, Dad?"

"Don't tell them anything, Eddie."

"I've got nothing to tell them."

"Good."

His Mum snapped. "He's got to help them, Dad. He's got to say what he knows."

Eddie put his hand on his Mum's arm.

"He doesn't know anything, Mum. He can't help them."

His Dad was fighting again. It was a different battle and it was harder.

"I'll see what they ask me." That pacified his Mum. "But I can't tell them what I don't know."

Chapter Thirty

The station was sticky, as Eddie found himself in a poky room towards the rear of the block, summer heat flooding through the cheap bricks to pool in every part of the building. Eddie was itchy and twitching, sensing the presence of Wilf Magill. He had been sitting there for twenty minutes when Ted Pearson finally appeared.

"Thanks for seeing me, Eddie." Pearson smiled. "That was quite a trick on Sunday. How do you do it?"

"Magic."

"I don't believe in magic, son. I believe in facts. Flesh and blood." He paused. "Mary Riley. Billy McGloin."

Eddie was ready for him. "They committed suicide, didn't they? That's what you said."

"But you knew them? Strange that."

"I didn't know Billy."

"You were looking for him."

"You told me where to look. And I didn't find him." Alive.

"Why were you looking?"

"To tell him his cousin was dead. Stan Kitteridge asked me to find out what I could."

"Why would he do that?"

"He knew Mary's mother. I think he wanted to help her out. She was grieving." He explained about the situation with the Catholic burial. Obfuscation was part of the art of magic: confuse people with information.

Pearson sat back in his chair. He was used to smart-arses. Eddie was a little smarter than the norm. Not much, though and it didn't make a difference.

"It doesn't look good for you, Eddie. You've got your fingers dirty."

Eddie looked at his fingernails, still ridden with soil. "That goes with the territory."

"If you know anything, you need to tell us."

"I will."

Pearson nodded and chewed his lips. He was working out what question to ask next and how to phrase it. The wait made Eddie sweat.

"There are some things missing from the houses, Eddie."

The words chilled him and his muscles stiffened. "I didn't go in in the houses."

Pearson smiled. "I didn't ask you if you did."

Eddie shuffled in his chair, memories of the address book and the ring stinging in his mind, as well as the *Lysol*, of course. A picture, too. The book might not matter, or the photograph. But the ring? By his reckoning that belonged to Will Magill. "I'm just saying."

Pearson stared at him, then slowly lifted himself up. "I'll get you a cup of tea. Let you have a think about things."

As he left the room, Eddie wilted. The exhaustion from Sunday was still crippling him in moments while the tension of the weeks was now taking its toll. He realized the mistake he'd made, badgering people not to believe that Mary had committed suicide. He had made it a murder now, which would need to be investigated. That could be problematic. Almost on cue, the door opened. Eddie was ready to be apologetic to Ted Pearson, say he didn't know anything and that it probably *was* suicide or say anything else that might have smoothed things over.

When he looked up, though, it was clear that nothing at all was going to help. When he looked up, he saw Wilf Magill. The sight of him sharpened Eddie. His nerves stiffened.

"Hello, Eddie."

Magill sat himself down heavy, happy and proud at the weight of his body. It was part of his power. He rested his elbows on the table between them and folded his hands, as if in prayer. Eddie couldn't help but look down at the scorched skin across the back of Magill's hand and fingers. He pictured the liquid burning into the flesh as it spewed out of Mary's mouth or Billy's. He noticed, too, where a band of pale skin sat on one of the fat fingers – protected from the scorch of the sun by something shaped like a ring.

Above the hands, Eddie saw the forearms bound inside the uniform, thick and strong. He imagined the grip on Mary's jaw as he'd poured the liquid down. And Billy wasn't a big lad. He was no sort of force against the three hundred pounds of weight that Magill could throw around.

"You're in a bit of trouble, Eddie Reynolds. Your fast tongue won't get you anywhere."

Eddie stared at Magill, trying to see if the eyes would give away the secrets of what he'd done.

"I'm just answering questions. Trying to help you. You seem to be struggling."

Magill's hand snapped out in a punch, but it was slow, letting Eddie rock out of the way, so that the arm crashed back down to the table. The hand landed hard with the fingers splayed out, showing the acid burn on the skin like the dark legend of a treasure map.

Eddie was standing up now, moving back, skipping round towards the door.

Magill bounced his chair backwards then hauled himself up. "We can put you at Mary Riley's house easy enough, Eddie. There're people there who'll say they've seen you."

Eddie flushed hot, feeling again the claustrophobic panic he'd felt in the grave, trapped and buried. "That's a lie."

Magill came at him again, lumbering. Eddie skirted round the outside of the room – keeping his distance.

"That's not what I hear. You've got a girl down in the Crofts, don't you?"

Eddie blanched and Magill smiled to see him do it.

"Louisa, isn't it?" His whole face curled into a leer and – seeing Eddie lost for a moment – he sprang forward fast, using his forearm to batter Eddie backwards, up against the wall, his free arm now slipping up Eddie's chest to leave his hand at his neck, the skin of which seemed to wobble with the burns that had taken hold there.

Eddie tried to say something, but couldn't. He was suffocating – and trying to hold his breath to stop from choking.

"It's my patch, Eddie. That's my territory. You moved out. I moved in. I'm part of the parish, Eddie. I'm part of the flock." He grinned, increasing the pressure. "I'm watching you, Reynolds. And my friends are too."

They stood a yard apart, neither of them quite knowing what Magill would risk here in the heart of the police station. Magill had contacts and confidence, but liked to choose his moments. He didn't like to be disturbed. Ted Pearson would be back any minute. He could explain a punch and a slap, but his intentions were deeper than that. He let his arm go loose. Eddie slid down the wall to his haunches, catching his breath, watching Magill.

Magill was smiling now. "Just watch yourself, wherever you go. If you ever go down a dark alley, just make sure you can see what's at the other end. You might not like it."

"Is that what you said to Billy?"

Magill lunged again and Eddie had to lean fast with a twist to avoid him, reaching for the handle of the door, just as Magill's hand caught his jacket sleeve to try to haul him back. The pair of them wobbled across a tipping point as Pearson opened the door with two cups of tea and stared, wide-eyed, at the pair of them.

"You all right, Wilf?"

Magill pulled himself up straight.

"I was showing him out. He's not going to say anything, are you, Reynolds?"

Eddie stared at him, then at Pearson. He shook his head.

***

After a jittery day, Eddie was pleased to be back home. He needed to get his head straight to make sure everything was meticulous for Thursday night. He was rehearsing his patter when a knock on the door surprised everyone. Eddie and Mum and Dad looked one to the other and then at the door. His Dad started to pull himself.

"I'll go, Dad."

This time his Dad didn't argue.

As Eddie opened the door, his breath was stuck in his throat.

"Oh . . Hello, Nancy." Eddie hung his head. He'd forgotten that they'd agreed to rehearse. "Come in."

"Hello, Eddie." She was beaming, dressed a little too bright and short for his Mum.

"Are you ready?" Nancy asked.

Not on any level, Eddie thought. His body still ached with a rhythmic pain and the exhaustion had settled in his head so that it felt full of cotton wool. But he picked up his jacket, kissing Mum goodbye. She squeezed his hand. His Dad patted his shoulder.

"Don't be late."

They rehearsed in the church hall. Nancy was sharp, Eddie was dull, going through the motions, feeling his nerves shear with each movement. This was a different trick, but it was the same muscles. As he hung upside down, the blood pouring into his head, he was only aware of memories of the grave. They were dark and terrifying and stopped his breath as they flashed through his mind: but they were exciting. As he lowered himself down, he remembered his conversation with Professor de Lyle then thought ahead to Thursday.

"It needs more work," Eddie said. "I'll check the hall's free again tomorrow."

She bounced up to him, catching his arm to pull him in for a kiss on the cheek. He felt the warmth of her skin, soft and comforting.

They packed up, shared another peck on the lips, Nancy hovering just for a moment to see if anything else was on offer. Seeing there wasn't, she went, leaving Eddie went to search for his priest. He found him in presbytery, sipping a sherry and reading *A Man Lay Dead*. When Eddie knocked on the door, he looked up.

"Eddie. Are you finished? Sit down."

He flopped down into a chair.

"That was quite a show on Sunday. A little risky, I thought, but it certainly caught the crowd's imagination."

"Did you make much money?"

"Does that matter?"

"Yes. They need to pay, to show how much it meant."

The priest smiled. "We did very well, thank you."

"Good."

"You look tired. And you're performing again on Thursday?"

"That's right. Do you want a ticket?"

"That'd be grand."

A silence spread out between them, a gap filled with a shared knowledge of what they should be talking about. Father Cleary edged round the subject.

"Is everything . . *else* all right?"

Eddie thought of Mary again, Billy again, Wilf Magill, Ted Pearson and then thought of himself, his Mum, his Dad.

"It's a bit of a mess, Father."

"The police couldn't help?"

Eddie looked up with a smile. "I don't think so, Father."

"What are you going to do?"

The thought had been ever-present since he had seen the mark on Wilf Magill's hand. It was the greatest trap of his life – and he had no idea how to escape it.

"Do you think prayer could work?"

***

Wednesday morning brought some brightness. Eddie was pleased to see his Mum smiling, though less so when he saw why. She was holding another letter which she handed to him like the eucharist. He took it gingerly, wondering where he had laid the *one* letter that he had written but not yet posted. As he read, his mind drifted over to the coast where Louisa had teamed up with three down-to-earth girls called Mabel, Betty and Pippa, who she worked, chatted, laughed, ate and slept with, talking about boyfriends no doubt. She wondered what Louisa said about him. Eddie tried to think back to such innocent times but found that the past was hidden from him. It was a long stretch back to school days and school friends. Where they had they all gone?

"How is she?"

"She's fine, Mum."

"Do you miss her?"

“I do.” He said it unreservedly.

His Dad had finished breakfast early. The Royal visit was just a day away with activity at Painted Fabrics reaching fever pitch. Annie Bindon Carter was everywhere, calming nerves, geeing up the staff and making sure that the whole enterprise was a perfect shop window to the world that would see it tomorrow.

“Do you need a hand, Dad?”

“No, you get off.”

Eddie was happy to be busy and the horses were pleased to see him as he entered the brewery yard, the steamers having broken down again the day before. Len Jeavons was in a good mood too and with the weather continuing to steam Eddie felt some sort of relaxation slip into his muscles and mind. Even Bert was in reasonable shape. He’d been fighting a summer cold, which had limited his beer intake by half a gallon so that he was as close to bright and breezy as he’d been in twenty years.

“Take it steady, lads,” Jeavons called out as they drove away, pulling out carefully into traffic lines of cars, vans, trams and other carriages.

The city was burning, flags of smoke hoisted high out of chimneys then floating free across the skyline, falling ever so gently into clothes, hair, heart and lungs. The forecast promised another dry, humid day. It couldn’t be long until the rain came, Bert said. Maybe today or tomorrow. By the end of the week for sure. Eddie hoped it wouldn’t be tomorrow. He wanted the day perfect for the Royal visit then dry to persuade the undecided to take a trip to the theatre. Bert sparked up a cigarette, offering Eddie one. He took one, even though his chest was still tight from the burial and coughing hurt.

The round was unspectacular and painful in parts, Eddie's muscles still at straining point. He managed well enough, taking his time and taking opportunities for a chat with the landlord or a cup of tea or a drink of lemonade with the landlady. By the time they approached the brewery gates Eddie was calm again. He stayed that way until he saw Jeavons standing on the threshold, with a strained look on his face.

"You all right, Len?" Bert said. "Look like you've seen a bloody ghost."

Eddie hopped off as Jeavons approached. "What?"

"The police have been here, Eddie."

"What did they want?" His skin was crawling as he asked.

"They wanted to know what you've been doing."

"What do you mean? I've been working."

"Well – there was that day last week you wanted to leave early….."

"You told me to get off!"

"I know, I know. It's just--"

Eddie stepped back and closed his eyes. A sense of claustrophobia came over him and he felt like he was being buried again. "Thanks for sticking up for me."

"Eddie!"

But he was already gone.

***

Four hours later, he was hanging upside down again, the aches of his body making his movements slow, irritation turning to anger. He snapped at Nancy when she fluffed a line.

"It's *tomorrow*, Nance!"

"I know! I'm nervous."

"Don't be nervous. Be better!"

His arm was stuck and he lost his composure, jerking when he needed to be precise, a couple of muscles bouncing like rubber bands. Eddie could feel the sinew fray. The knot came loose and he let himself down, looking over to Nancy to see a tear in her eye.

"Look, I'm sorry."

She came over and fell into him, her head sinking into his chest and her arms reaching round him. She smelt cheap. But also hot and vital. When he looked down he saw just how tightly her outfit hugged round her curves, pushing them out towards him. His hand slipped to her waist where it was warm. She leaned up her head, her lipstick far too obvious, something that would work perfectly on a stage, but close up made her look like a doll in a shop window. He kissed her anyway and felt her tongue slip inside him, as her hand slid away from his back to his hip, then his thigh and then towards the zip on his trousers.

That was the moment to stop things. Eddie knew that. Right then and there, though, he was in the audience and no longer in control. He felt her fingers searching as his own hand slipped onto the warmth of her thigh then started to slide.

Chapter Thirty-One

"Where's my shoes, Maggie?"

"What do you mean *shoes*? You only need one!"

Eddie kept his head down when his parents started bickering. Thursday morning was the worst he'd known. His Dad was anxious and his Mum was anxious for him *and* for herself. Eddie was just excited. For a few hours, at least, the worries of Mary Riley, Billy McGloin and Constable Wilf Magill were behind him. Royalty was coming to town and he'd been allowed a day off to go with his Mum and Dad to Painted Fabrics, Len Jeavons still wriggling with guilt that he hadn't looked after Eddie better. That also gave him an easy time to prepare for his own show that evening.

It was going to be a big day.

Yet another letter had come from him from Louisa, simply wishing him good luck. He sat at the table staring at the words, remembering a frantic flash and bang in the Church Hall the previous evening with Nancy. He closed his eyes and shook his head.

"Are you ready?" His Mum threw the question at him like a plate.

"Two minutes."

"You'd better be!"

Eddie didn't understand the rush. They were going to be hours early. Still, he loved them enough that it didn't matter.

The weather was more than generous as they started their walk, Eddie's Mum buzzing with thoughts of the day ahead. The news was that the Duke couldn't make it: some injury to his hand. That left the Duchess in charge. Her itinerary started with the Library. Eddie was happy with the idea of the library. He liked the thought of knowledge being close to hand. He still had so much to learn.

As they approached the workshops everyone seemed to have a bit more of a bustle about them. The weather helped, softly warm with a promise of a fine day ahead. The three of them fell into line with a number of others heading the same way. The mood was brittle with excitement.

Given that the Duchess wasn't due until the afternoon there was a lot of nervous energy to expend in the hours until then. To Eddie's eyes, everything looked perfect by ten o' clock. He offered to help where he could, but it was hard to find anything that really needed doing.

"Do you need me?" He asked his Dad.

"Somewhere to be?"

"I thought I'd catch the Duchess in town."

His Dad nodded. "Are you coming back?"

Eddie smiled. "Course I am."

It felt good to slip away, free of the jittery tension at Painted Fabrics, away from work, away from home, where he couldn't help fearing that Wilf Magill or Ted Pearson might appear at any moment. And, with a tense night ahead of him, he welcomed the chance to sink into the crowds that were starting to thicken along the pavements in the city centre, jabbering with talk of what the Duchess would be wearing, where she would stop, whose flowers she would accept, who she would acknowledge ("she was looking at me when she waved", they would shout). The mood was jubilant. The Duke and Duchess had become favourites of the Sheffield crowd, visiting often enough to show the sort of commitment that could persuade a distant northern city built from steel that it hadn't been quite forgotten by the Big Smoke. Eddie guessed that the likes of Harry Miller might say that it all reeked of the landowners nodding to the household staff. He might have been right. Even so, the mood of the crowd suggested that they welcomed the change. Today, even the factories had taken notice, the chimneys quieter, spewing out less of their daily belch, making the air cleaner and sharper. Eddie enjoyed taking a breath then letting it swill round his lungs.

A thrill of tension tightened as the clock ticked on with delays in timing only heightening the sense of anticipation. Eddie thought of the crowd gathered and how different it was from a week earlier at the City Hall, all the anger dissipated into a feeling of warm generosity. He picked up some chestnuts from a seller, working his trade from a cart, his horse standing alongside, taking pats and tickles from passers-by.

As he ate, a murmur trickled through the crowd.

She was coming.

A communal intake of breath seemed like the sea receding, before it came back with an almighty crash as the car that carried her emerged onto the street, the crowd surging forward in one continuous movement. Eddie felt himself carried along and loved the motion, reminding himself time and again that *this* was what people wanted. He had to carry that into his show that evening.

***

Eddie followed the progress of the Duchess to the library, then went his own way as she headed to the hospital for another event and he headed back to make sure he was in place at Painted Fabrics before her convoy arrived.

"How was she?" His Mum was almost trembling as she asked.

Eddie smiled. "She was grand."

Looking around, everything at the site seemed perfect, but that didn't stop teams of people doing last minute preparations – Annie rallying them all the time - right up until the moment someone hollered, "*She's here!*"

Eddie hung in the background with his Mum, who clenched his hand tightly, her eyes moist or openly wet for most of the time of the visit.

There she was! The Lord Mayor was standing just off one shoulder and an officer (of course) from the workshops bowing in front of her.

The Duchess moved like a dancer, her dress perfectly cut in a blue that seemed to match the sky. Annie had a route planned for her which she followed for as far as politeness required, before swinging off to drop in on "Taffy" Llewellyn at his home on the base, engaging him in gentle conversation, then repeating the trick with *Barnsey* – as Dad called him – another disabled veteran, who swelled to have been selected for attention. Eddie's Mum muttered that the Duchess could just as easily have picked Dad and Eddie smiled, feeling the same.

The Duchess picked up the tour again, spending good time in the workshops, sharing some words with one of the administrators, then getting her head down to select several items for her collection.

"What's she got?" Dad asked.

Mum peered above the gathered line of spectators to see. "A cushion. For her car."

His Dad nodded. "Anything else?"

"Bedspread."

His Dad smiled. "Could be one of mine."

She squeezed his hand.

As the Duchess finished her tour, the sound of a violin made the Summer day seem more lyrical still, a group of children of the staff performing a dance they'd been learning for weeks now. As she passed along, a second line of business started up, picking up a number of orders from her entourage, including an altar cloth that his Dad was particularly pleased with. As Eddie watched his Dad he felt pride squeeze his throat.

The Duchess handled herself well. Eddie liked the way the old royalty and the new (Hollywood) conducted themselves. They understood the distance between themselves and the rest of the world. They knew their role. Elizabeth had come into the royal family with a fine pedigree and knowledge of what lay ahead. Her face had an easy smile, but the muscles could harden against the toughest times and when Eddie tried to see what was in her eyes, he saw a reflection of turbulence. Like his Dad, she saw the threat from abroad. Closer to home, the relationship of her brother-in-law and Wallis Simpson caused sleepless nights.

Barely forty minutes had passed between her arrival and her departure, but you'd be forgiven for thinking that time had stopped for the workers and families at Painted Fabrics. Annie was floating: hugging, kissing everyone. Eddie's Mum just hugged Dad and held on and Dad smiled, smiled, smiled.

Eddie enjoyed the moments as he passed out a few last tickets he had for the show that night. Then, giving his apologies, he had to run.

***

Preparation was everything and tonight was critical to what he was going to become. He met up with Nancy and they ate a light tea together, both bubbling with thrills of the night ahead.

They were at the theatre by half past five to find it alive and kicking. Activity was brewing slowly, bubbling in every part of the building, the ladies who ran the ticket office swilling cups of teas or chatting with the doormen as they arrived and then the ushers.

Stan Kitteridge bounced along with the flow of the evening. He gave the impression that he was the glue that would keep the evening together. There was something in that. He had booked every act after all. Now he wanted to see them settled in, wanted to check that they knew the running order, had everything they needed – and were ready. He wanted a good show. This was his reputation as well as theirs.

"Eddie!" Eddie got the showbiz smile. "And Nancy!"

She got a leer. She simpered.

"Follow me."

He led them through the maze that started behind and beneath the stage and stalls. Eddie was thrilled to be part of the world that night, not just watching it. The ways were narrow so that it was hard to walk more than a dozen yards before someone was pressing against you, passing the other way, always sharing a smile or a word of encouragement.

The dressing room space was cramped yet felt like luxury. Eddie sat himself down then looked around.

This was it.

Nancy was busy straightaway. She had to look perfect. Every extra second could help. She sat herself down in front of a mirror and began to prepare, stripping off her clothes without attention to who might be close by. Her lack of inhibition made the number swell. Eddie looked around to see a middle aged man gawping as her legs were pared down to perfect skin that was too good not to touch. He caught Eddie's eye, twisting away.

Eddie picked up a cup of tea, starting a slow drift through the dressing and rehearsal rooms. He knew the bill backwards, but wanted to put faces to names. He wanted to see the competition. First up was Clara Monaghan. She had a loyal following, but she came from over the Pennines. The Sheffield crowd always liked their own a little better and the Lancastrians a little less. Eddie spent a few minutes chatting with her. She was nervous and liked his company and his soft confidence.

"Are you the magician?"

"Escapologist."

"Like Houdini?"

He smiled at the comparison. "That's right."

"Isn't it dangerous?"

"Only if you do it right."

He thought back to the burial trick, his mind racing with what he'd achieved. That only served to remind him how tame things could be tonight.

Eddie passed along, now sitting down for ten minutes with the *Assassins of Sorrow*, Cyril Hatton and Jack Herbert. Eddie had seen them before. He knew how funny they could be. Jack had an effortless rapport with the audience which seemed to connect to a direct line of his personality. He was sitting, half-dressed, half made-up, throwing off one-liners to anyone who would listen, cranking out stories that he'd picked up over twenty years of performing. Brother Cyril laughed occasionally, inbetween trying to drag Jack back into rehearsal mode. Every show was an end in itself for Jack, but for Cyril it was a step onwards and upwards. Their career was heading in the right direction. They'd even been on the BBC more than a few times. Even so, Cyril couldn't relax. Jack could.

"'Ey up, lad. Pull up a chair."

Jack pushed one over to Eddie.

Cyril turned on him. "You that escapologist?"

"That's right."

"You're on before us. Don't get 'em too excited."

"I'll do my best."

"You want a smoke?"

Jack offered a cigarette, which Eddie took, noticing the *Player's* pack then thinking back to Mary Riley and the times that she would have scuttled around the building here, just keeping things going, quiet and unnoticed. Now forgotten.

"Thanks."

"What else have we got tonight?"

Eddie thought back over the bill. "A juggler. Some midgets. A few singers."

Cyril pulled a face. "Sounds all right."

Eddie took a long lungful of smoke. "You'll be fantastic."

Cyril turned on him. "You can never take it for granted."

The words hit Eddie.

Jack nodded. "You're right, Cyril. As always" He cackled. "But don't forget that the audience *wants* to have a good time. They've paid for it. Our job is to let them do it."

Eddie nodded and smiled.

Time to get ready.

Chapter Thirty-Two

Stan had blessed Eddie by not throwing him out there at the opening. Nancy, though, was twisting her body with nerves, wanting to get on as soon as possible to get off again.

"Do I look all right?"

"You look fine."

"*Fine*?"

"Stunning."

"Really?"

"Really."

Eddie didn't get worried in the same way, though he knew he needed to start feeling a thrill in his skin. That's what would give him an edge.

They were standing in the wings where the response from the audience was splashing onto them from across the stage. Even though it wasn't Saturday night, the crowd was boisterous. The sun had shone hot on them all day while the Royal visit had threaded a sense of well-being all across the city. As Jack had said, they thought they deserved to have some fun. The hungry audience was always the one you wanted, but you had to feed them well.

"I'm so nervous, Eddie."

"You'll be great."

"How's your shoulder?"

"It's all right."

"You should have been resting this week."

"You didn't say that when you got on all fours, did you?"

She giggled and blushed, punching him playfully.

"Ladies and gentlemen. . ."

The words were like a calling.

"The *Incredible* Eddie Reynolds!"

Eddie felt his body swell. Before he knew it he was striding onto the stage, hands held high with Nancy, then bowing together and letting the first wave of audience anticipation roll over them.

Eddie played his patter well, running the line along the front of the stage to engage the punters, who whooped and cheered. He knew that the greatest art of the performer was to understand then manage space and time. He made the stage big, the clock slow. He even slipped in a quick joke that Jack Herbert had whispered to him when Cyril wasn't looking. The audience bellowed.

Then, like flicking on a switch, he turned to the action as he began to take every spectator on a journey to a darker side. He laid out the escape he was going to perform and made clear the dangers. As he talked, Nancy called up a happy, hungry young man to help her soak a rope in paraffin. This was going to hold Eddie aloft as he tried to make his escape, bound upside down in a straightjacket with the straps locked tight. The smell of paraffin sank into the stalls, making people squirm. You don't play with fire.

Nancy wasn't finished. She pulled another two men eagerly up onto the stage, happy to squeeze beside her in her skin tight, high-cut costume and feel the flesh of her arms and the stocking on her legs. These were the men to bind him.

Eddie stared into the audience as he dared them to doubt him.

They didn't.

A minute later he was suspended. The crowd gasped just to see the spectacle. There was something ghoulish in it. For those who knew their Tarot here was the Hanged Man.

The straps were tight enough that Eddie could feel them cut into him as Nancy called to him to ask if he was ready. She was beside him, holding a long, lit taper.

"Light it!" He shouted – and she brought the flame close to the rope.

The audience shrieked as the fire took hold. It seemed to explode. They shuddered, not sure that they weren't witnessing an immolation.

Eddie wriggled and struggled.

The crowd were quiet.

His shoulder hurt and his body was tired. Even so, the lads had been lazy in their knots. Everyting was too easy. If the rope lasted as long as it should, then he had more than enough time. The crowd had given him their sense of wonder when he started. What else did they have left?

A sense of fidgetting was starting to fall on the front rows. There was something of a thrill to see if Eddie would manage his escape before the rope burned, but they guessed he would.

That was when the unexpected happened.

Out of nowhere, the trap door on the stage flew open. It created a black hole in the ground – directly below Eddie.

Nancy looked over in horror, shocked at the disturbance, then the danger.

A head poked out – and looked bewildered.

The audience trickled out a giggle, that tripped into a bellow.

Eddie wriggled.

The head apologised and pulled at the door. It didn't budge.

The look on the faces of the stage hand started to quieten the audience. A slow intake of breath began to sound across the auditorium. Nancy glared at the stage hand, then up at Eddie and then – involuntarily – at the audience. Her face was white beneath the make-up. Eddie stared down deep, where the hole dipped twenty feet into the dark.

That was a long way to fall.

The stage hand pulled himself up onto the stage, trying to work the door from the top. He shouted out acoss to the wings.

The audience were tipping forward in their seats when the stage manager and assistant came on from the sides. They heaved at the door, without any success.

Eddie struggled as he looked up towards the fire that was unpicking the rope, strand by strand.

"Get him down!" The stage manager shouted at the stage hand.

The audience gasped.

The stage hand looked dumb, then started to move, but knew it was too late.

The fire was taking its last chomps of the rope, as Eddie threshed against the knots.

As the stage hand ran to the pulley, the first strands of rope snapped, Eddie's body rocking side to side to make the crowd groan.

Perhaps he could swing himself free, the audience thought. Perhaps he was safe.

There were only seconds left. They said they didn't want to watch, but had to – and wanted to.

The fire bit in and the rope split.

Eddie was falling and as he fell, his arms came out at his side in crucifixion - - catching the stage either side of the trap door hole, staring all the way down the steps to the world below. A sharp line of agony ripped from his shoulder all down his body so that he almost fainted with the pain.

A moment's pause was followed by yelps and whoops and cheers.

Eddie was on his feet, Nancy tucked into his side. She was crying.

They bowed then bounced away.

"Don't ever do that again, Eddie Reynolds."

He smiled, Jack Herbert slapping him on the back as they passed.

"Nice one, son."

Eddie smiled, seeing Stan rush up to the stage staff to congratulate them on the way they'd played their part. He sat down backstage, took a cigarette then a drink to watch from the side. Most performers would hurry away to hide, keeping a little bubble of themselves and their performance as perfect as possible. Eddie wanted to watch and learn. He laughed all the way through Jack and Cyril's routine. It was slick in a way that made you wonder why everything couldn't be that smooth.

When the show was ended, everyone barreled out onto the stage for a final bow. Eddie felt the cheers like kisses on the cheek or pats on the back.

Nancy was in ecstasy, hugging close to Eddie to begin with before sinking into other embraces with a backstage crowd that wanted to be tactile.

"Oh, Eddie!"

His Mum was nearly in tears again. It had been an emotional day.

"Bit close with the rope," said his Dad.

"Did you doubt me?"

"Part of the plan, was it?"

Eddie grinned. "Everything's part of the plan."

His Dad was right, though. The trap door had been a late decision. Nancy was cautious, but Stan could see how it could work and backed Eddie, corralling the stage crew to set it up. The idea had come, of course, from Professor de Lyle.

Stan blew through, shaking everyone's hand, passing out the money. Eddie enjoyed the moment. He rifled through the notes, slipped some to Nancy, palmed a few himself and then reached out to his Mum.

"Buy yourself something nice."

"Eddie! You should be saving that. For a house. Or a wedding."

He slipped the money into her bag.

"I'm planning to elope."

She laughed. "Don't you dare."

When his Mum and Dad left and other hangers-on had drifted away, a core group of performers rolled out to the Brown Bear, where they were soon stuck in beer and whisky. Nancy started the session tight beside Eddie, but as the flattering comments came her way she drifted towards the sound of them. As Eddie was finishing his drink, Stan caught him.

"Mary's mum was there tonight."

"How is she?"

"She's holding up. I've told her what you told me. I think it helped."

"That's good, I suppose."

"Do you know who did it?"

Eddie bit his lip. "It's hard to say."

The image of Billy rolled back into view. Eddie couldn't stop himself shuddering. As the memory passed, the sight of Wilf Magill's hand replaced it.

"Are you all right, Eddie?"

"I'm tired."

"Fair enough."

"I'm going to get off."

Stan pulled a face."Don't you want to celebrate?"

"I'm working tomorrow."

Stan patted him on his back.

"You were good, Eddie. They liked you. Keep practising."

"Thanks. I will."

He slipped outside. While the June evening was still balmy, it felt fresh after the fug of the pub. As he passed the Town Hall he looked up to see the clock. The time was just before half past ten. The tram was a little late and so he leaned on a wall, letting Sheffield's night trade pass him by. He closed his eyes and only saw the darkness.

Chapter Thirty-Three

"How did the show go?"

Ada had an affectionate feel, to such an extent that even as they climbed the cinema stairs to get to the screen she was holding his hand.

"It went well. Thanks. You should have come."

"I was tied up." She missed the irony. "Was it dangerous?"

"I thought it was safe enough. I got out."

"It's a matter of time, Eddie."

"Isn't everything?"

Ada didn't want to row tonight. She was in a wistful mood. The film they'd chosen carried her thinking into farther and wider directions, as they watched Edmund Lowe and Shirley Grey drape a romantic thread across the wonder of India in *Bombay Mail*. The film dripped with a sense of the exotic. Ada gripped Eddie's arm at every opportunity, slipping him kisses in the darkness when she could.

Outside, the evening was dark but warm. The heat was still hugging the city, the rain building but not able to break through yet.

"Are you coming back?"

"Is it safe?"

"I thought everything was dangerous."

"You have to make a judgement."

She stopped, so he stopped too. "What's your judgement then?"

He didn't get a chance to answer, a shape in a shadow falling across his face as someone blocked out the light as they passed.

"Evening, Mr. Reynolds."

The sound of the voice came on him like fingers on his throat. He was too choked to speak, looking up to see Constable Wilf Magill.

Ada froze, staring at Eddie, then more slowly at the constable.

"And who's this young lady, Eddie? Your fiancé?"

Eddie bit his lip.

"Cat got your tongue?"

"Is there a problem here?" Ada was sharp.

"You tell me, sweetheart."

"I'm not your sweetheart."

"More's the pity."

She glared at him, about to speak when she felt Eddie's hand on her arm, squeezing.

"We were just watching a film, Constable. That's allowed, isn't it?"

"*That's* allowed, Eddie. *That's* allowed."

"Thank you."

"Safe journey home, then."

Ada sneered, as Eddie steered her away. His breathing was fast. He moved her forward twenty steps before he spoke.

"Be careful."

She pulled away from him. "What happened to the incredible Eddie Reynolds?"

Eddie paused for a moment, then spoke calmly. "He got buried, Ada. It gave him time to think." Think things like: what was Magill doing there, on this side of town? What did he know? How did he find out?

"I won't be spoken to by lugs like that."

"Watch him, Ada. He's dangerous."

"Dangerous? He's supposed to be protecting us."

They were walking along Abbeydale Road now, the pavement making gentle loops up and down on a mostly flat – for Sheffield – highway.

"Come back with me."

"Where's the old man?"

"At the Club. Getting drunk. Chasing girls."

"*Does* he chase them?"

"Not very far and not very fast, but he'll give them a nip if he can. That's all he's good for." She was maudlin. "All he's bothered about."

She was sullen for a time while Eddie was silent, but she brightened as they pushed up her road – no longer holding hands – towards her door.

"Maybe not tonight," Eddie said simply.

Ada stopped where she stood.

Eddie was suddenly very tired of his life. There was an urgency to it which was beginning to wear him down. He thought of Louisa and wanted her back. He wasn't worthy, of course. He knew that.

"I'm not a toy, Eddie."

She opened the door and pushed inside, leaving a gap. He trailed behind.

He didn't look at her, letting thoughts flow round in his head. So, what was this, then? One more performance? Perhaps. A physical act. Even though his body was tired he knew he was strong enough. He wanted to sleep, though. He wanted to rest. The meeting with Constable Magill only reminded him how far he was from stillness. And it had been such a long week.

She took his hand. "Come on."

Ada was hurried, where she was usually just eager. And she was demanding, much more than expectant. There was a rush about her, stripping her clothes too quickly, leaving them where they lay. Eddie knew they were too good for that. He lifted them up and placed them on a chair by her bedside table, while she pulled herself round to face him.

She snapped open her bra to let her breasts fall out and they bounced with the same sort of energetic need he could see in her eyes. She was kneeling on the bed, her fingers flicking at her garters to loosen her stockings, which she rolled down smooth, fixing his eyes all the time.

Eddie stared as she pared down to her briefs. She was performing for him. She was trying to outdo him, trying to better his show at the Empire.

"I hope you've got some energy, Eddie."

She slid down her panties and held them towards him.

Eddie glanced towards the window and pulled the curtains a little closer to. Behind him, he switched off the main light, so that only the lamp by her bed lit them. She put a smile on her face and let it roll across her lips.

As he came closer to the bed, she reached out to him to catch his shirt, popping open the buttons before helping him to tug it off. She pulled him onto the bed, kissing him urgently, her hands spreading out across his chest, down to his trousers. As she worked her fingers at his belt, she took his hand to lay it on her thigh, which was soft and hot.

"Come on, Eddie." She nibbled at his ear, dipping her tongue into the gap. "Come on."

The seconds tumbled after that, as she got quicker and Eddie harder. She pushed him back down on the bed and slid down his stomach.

Eddie breathed out to empty his lungs. He looked across the room and wondered if this was all that wealth meant: a better made wardrobe; a better made dressing table; carpets on the floor. Ada heaved herself up to drop down on him. The mattress dipped and the springs groaned. A better bed, Eddie added.

She wasn't looking at him at all. Her head was up. Her eyes were closed. She might have been anywhere. He could have been anyone.

She didn't hear the front door at all.

Eddie did and jerked, which shocked her eyes open.

"What?"

He put his hand up to her lips – waiting. He didn't have to wait long.

"Ada!" The voice was flung upstairs like a hammer.

"*Eddie*!" She was frozen.

"Ada!" The voice came again, louder, harder. It felt like punches.

Ada rolled aside, and Eddie was aware of a circularity that had brought him back to where he seemed to have started. He stared at the window. *Only go back to the tricks that always work for you.* That's what Randini had said. Eddie knew he would never try the coffin trick again. He wondered why, then, he had come back here.

"What are we going to do?"

Eddie was pulling at his clothes now. "Call down to him. Say you've got a headache."

He threw her a nightdress and moved to the window, tugging at the curtain to peak out. He was looking for a clear route away from the house.

He wouldn't get one. Standing fat and proud in the middle of the road was Wilf Magill, making good on a promise to make Eddie's life hell. It took Eddie a few moments to understand what that meant. This wasn't bad luck. This was planned. Magill was hunting him down, cutting off his escape routes. Even so, he tugged the window open.

Ada was still flustered, for the first time ever full of panic.

"I think he's coming upstairs."

Eddie gripped Ada's arm and pushed. "Go to the door. Don't let him come to you."

When she didn't move, he pushed her forward.

As she opened the door, the sound of her husband's footsteps on the stairs were starting to sound like drumbeats getting louder. Ada fell into the doorway, still puzzled.

"Ken, love. You're back early."

The footsteps stopped, halfway up the stairs.

"Got talking, didn't I?"

"Talking? Who to?"

"Doesn't matter, does it?" His words had a whisky slur to them.

"What were you talking about?"

There was a pause.

"*You*."

Eddie watched Ada as her body stiffened.

"What about me?"

"Where you were. What you were doing. Who you were . . .doing it with."

"I was at the pictures. I told you." Ada was going to fight.

"Who with?"

"With Margaret."

"Really?"

"Yes. Now what's this all about?" She wanted to manage him, in the way she had done a hundred times when he had had a drink too many.

"What're you doing in bed?"

"It's late. I'm tired. I've got a bit of a headache."

The steps started again. They stamped Morris up to the landing. The light threw a shadow from his body that came into the room, searching for Eddie.

"You weren't with Margaret, were you? You were with a bloody man!"

"What are you talking about?"

The sound of his hand hitting her cheek struck Eddie in the heart. His breath stopped. He knew that he should run out there to defend her – and he knew he wouldn't.

Ada gasped. "What? Ken, I don't know what- -"

He hit her again and it pushed a cry out of her.

Eddie stiffened, his skin tingling.

"If I catch you with anyone, sweetheart, you'll be out of here and back where you came from before you know it. Don't treat me like a bloody idiot."

She didn't say anything now.

The seconds stretched, then the footsteps started again, becoming softer and more distant as Morris blundered back down the stairs.

Ada turned, moving slowly back into the bedroom, closing the door.

She didn't look at Eddie, who stood in a pool of shame, trying to argue what he knew to be true: he couldn't confront Morris– for her sake. He was right and she would have said the same. It didn't help.

"You'd better go," she said quietly.

"I can't get out, Ada. There's someone watching. They told your husband about us."

She turned on him.

"What are you doing, Eddie? What have you done? You've ruined everything."

When he reached out to touch her, she turned away.

He slipped to the door, opening it a crack to check that her husband was gone. Taking the opportunity, he slipped down to the bedroom at the back of the house and to the window there, easing it open to look down towards the garden.

The lawn below was bordered by flower beds, which ran close enough to the house for Eddie to drop onto. Even so, as he looked down through the half-light, he reckoned he had less than a square yard to aim for over a twenty-foot drop.

He pushed his hand down hard on the outside sill, to check how secure it was, his mind calculating the options, knowing that they were limited.

As he considered, he heard a knock on the door.

He couldn't help himself standing up stiff.

"Hello, Constable," said Morris.

The words made their way upstairs to haunt him.

Though he strained, he couldn't hear the whole conversation, just the sound of Morris's voice, which was fattened and amplified by drink.

"Yes. Take a look around. I'd appreciate that."

By then Eddie was squeezing through the window, feet pressing against the sill to keep a grip as he twisted his body round – his shoulder groaning at the strain – so that he was now facing the glass and could start to lower himself down, fingers tight on the sill. He needed to reduce the fall as much as he could so he was taking a six-foot bite out of it by lowering himself as far as he could, but the weight of his body made his shoulder weep with pain so much that he wondered if the muscles might just snap. Nearly at full stretch, he twisted his neck back to look down at the spot he was aiming for. Fourteen feet down to concrete didn't look good. He needed to swing a little to make sure he landed on lump of grass.

Even as he hung there, though, he could hear the thump of Wilf Magill's footsteps beat down the side of the house to come towards the garden.

Eddie rocked as best he could, side to side, then let go – and flew.

He landed awkwardly but on grass, tipping over to one side before landing in a heap.

The fall disorientated him so that when his head cleared, the sound of thick lungs pumping air was almost upon him, Magill just yards away. Eddie rolled up and skipped away, running fast down the garden, then jumping forward and up without thinking, into the mass of a hedge.

The hedge was a spiky jelly of branches. His arms flailed through its quicksand to tug him forward and through. Behind him, he felt a grip catch his calf. He wriggled his leg to snap it free, pulling on with a clinging, swimming action, which seemed to get him nowhere until – thanks be to God– he tipped down on the other side.

Magill's voice burst through the hedge, but it was blind.

He couldn't see Eddie.

Eddie stood still staring back, regaining his breath.

Then he turned and walked quickly away.

***

The knock on the door came ten minutes after Eddie had entered.

His Dad opened up, to see Wilf Magill's frame fill the doorway.

"A bit late, isn't it?"

"I'm looking for your son."

"He's in bed. Can't it wait?"

Eddie, whose door was just ajar, could hear every word.

"When did he get in?"

"An hour and a half ago." The half was true enough. The hour was a lapse of memory.

"Where's he been?"

"He went to the cinema."

"Who with?"

"I didn't ask."

A silence followed. Upstairs, Eddie closed his eyes. Though he was shaken and frightened, it was pride for his Dad that made him start to cry.

"He needs to be careful of the company he keeps."

"I think we all do, Constable."

His Dad shut the door.

A few seconds later, his Dad appeared at his bedroom door. "He's gone."

"Thanks, Dad."

His Dad stepped into the room, seeing Eddie curled up on top of his bed. Right then and there he looked just like a boy who had been caught out. "Was that him?"

Eddie nodded.

His Dad wanted to say something else. He wanted to reassure Eddie or advise him. What do you say? He'd seen too much to think anything meant anything.

"Get some sleep."

Eddie did what his Dad had told him and stayed in bed. He re-read the letters from Louisa. In between times thought of Ada. He felt he should do something: comfort her; confront Morris. He wasn't sure he could easily do either. His body was tired, the buzz of his burial trick last weekend and the performance at the theatre was long gone, leaving him empty.

He thought, too, of Nancy and the laziness of his behaviour with her and by implication towards Louisa. It wasn't quite a dark night of the soul, but he slept badly, had bad dreams, woke up tired and wearily ashamed of himself.

The weekend passed slowly, the clawing summer heat not letting up, with the prayed-for rain never even on the horizon.

Work was a slog through Monday, with the dullness of days spiking on Tuesday as he entered the gates, seeing the thick frame of Wilf Magill blocking a doorway, trapping Bert inside as he slapped him with questions. Eddie hung back, watching from the side until Magill had gone.

Bert looked beaten up as Eddie edged towards him..

"'ey up, Eddie," Bert grinned, best as he could. "You've just missed yer mate."

"What did he want?"

Bert sniffed. "He wanted to know if we'd been around the Crofts. Maybe stopped there. And Upperthorpe – same thing."

Eddie's mouth was dry.

"What did you say?"

"I said we delivered there. Every week. Rain and shine. Nothing unusual about that. Nothing untoward."

Eddie felt tension slide out of him with the sweat on his back. "I owe you one, Bert."

"You can *buy* me one, son.

If he'd imagined that things were sorted, he was quickly disappointed.

A further police visit to the house had the neighbours twitching curtains and his Mum not able to eat the dinner she'd made. Eddie felt guilt as much as worry as he watched her. He was called into the station again and went as ordered.

They left him in a room by himself this time, dark and hot, with the heat outside rising by the minute. He felt he was buried again. His only hope was for someone to open the door to let him out, knowing that the hand on the handle could be Wilf Magill.

The thoughts began to clog in his head, which combined with the heat to prickle sweat across his skin in itches and stabs. He got up, just to move, trying to resist a feeling of suffocation. His mind skipped back to the burial trick in Graves Park. He almost had to smile at the irony of his current situation, stuck in a hole with no obvious means of escape. Then Eddie felt the air shift as he turned to see the door opening, his heartbeat skipping.

Ted Pearson stepped into the room looking straight at Eddie.

"Now then, Eddie." Pearson sniffed. "Someone says they saw you near the place where Mary Riley died."

Wilf Magill's prophecy had come true. Eddie went cold. He tried to breathe steadily. "I know people there. My girlfriend lives there."

Pearson nodded. "And someone said they saw you asking questions in the neighbourhood where Billy McGloin was found."

Keep calm, Eddie. It's just another trap. Don't fall into it.

"Where's that?"

Pearson smiled. The kid was cute. "Upperthorpe."

"We deliver beer there."

"You weren't on the cart."

"I might have been stretching my legs."

Pearson didn't believe him, but he wouldn't give up on him yet. "Eddie, if there's anything you need to tell me, now's the time." Then he held out the olive branch. "You can trust me."

Eddie shrugged.

Pearson didn't let go. "I told you that someone broke into Mary Riley's house, didn't I?"

"It's a dangerous area."

"They seemed to be good with locks. Couldn't see a mark on the door."

Eddie met Pearson's gaze. "Maybe it was Billy. He lived there, didn't he? He had a key. Maybe he took the things you said were missing."

The ring. The address book. The photograph.

Pearson leaned back. "Something's not right, Eddie."

Eddie's eyes shifted, imagining exactly where he had hidden the address book and ring in his room. The photograph was in his pocket. He could feel its edge nibbling at his skin. Those things had all seemed so safe – until now.

Eddie stood up. "Yeah, something's not right. Two people are dead."

The reminder made Pearson sit up. Death had lost some of its sting when he was fighting in Paris. He had to remember how much life mattered. He stared at Eddie and could only wonder at his energy, his vitality. He envied him those things, but only so far. Eddie would get himself into trouble. And then there would be worse people than Ted Pearson waiting to deliver some punishment.

"Be careful, Eddie."

They both knew what he meant.

***

Things didn't improve at work. Len Jeavons was hanging in the yard when Eddie got there, a hangdog expression on his face.

Eddie guessed the answer even before he asked the question. “What is it?”

Jeavons sniffed. “The police again. They wanted to check which days you were on the wagon.”

“Why?”

Jeavons looked sheepish.

“They want to check a link to some robberies that have happened on our route.”

Eddie took in a breath of air, feeling a sense of containment trapping him. Wilf Magill was slowly closing down his world.

Keen to try to change his mood a little he skipped into town after work, sinking himself into the cool calm of the Empire, where he caught Stan Kitteridge holding forth about what makes a great show to a couple of new secretaries, who listened politely because they wanted to get on and had heard that Stan favoured those he fancied. They were prepared to flirt as much as they needed to. Eddie’s Mum would have condemned them as hussies, but Eddie could see how the world worked for them.

“Eddie!” There was no smile on his face.

“Hello, Stan.”

“What are you doing here?” Stan came up beside him, ushering him out of the room.

“Well, I just came to have a talk about the show last week. And maybe another. .”

Stan was shaking his head. “Small steps, Eddie. Small steps.”

He had guided Eddie into a corridor, which was quiet.

“What’s wrong, Stan?”

“It’s nothing, Eddie. Nothing.”

Stan was still trying to move him along and Eddie shrugged his hand off.

"What's going on, Stan?"

Stan put his hands on his hips, pursing his lips before speaking.

"Someone lost something at the theatre last Thursday. They reported it to the police. Thought it might be stolen." Stan looked away. "The police called round. They, uh . . .asked who was on the bill and . . .they seemed interested that *you* were."

Eddie felt a chill, starting a tingle in his arms.

"You know that it was nothing to do with me."

"Of *course*, I do, Eddie. Of course I do."

Eddie wondered whether to tell Stan about Wilf Magill and Mary.

"Stan-"

"Eddie, we're friends, aren't we? You've done me a big favour with Mary and her mother. I owe you one." Then came the kicker. "Let's just wait a few weeks, eh? Pick things up again in August maybe."

A few hours later, Eddie sat on his bed, the claddagh ring tickling his palm. It was the only evidence he had. And, with the address book and photograph, one of the things linking him to Mary Riley's house.

It was all very simple.

He had to put them back.

Chapter Thirty-Four

All through the following day Eddie was simply waiting for the evening. When dusk crept along – still hot and dry and throat-stuck with smoke – it found him slipping into the Crofts again. Eddie felt the address book tucked in his pocket – photograph inside, then looked at the ring in his hand, which seemed to burn his skin when he touched it. He slipped it inside his pocket. As he came closer to Mary's house his nerve started to fail. The daylight was still thick enough to light him up, burning up the streets so that everything was clear. Within minutes of entering the neighbourhood, Eddie felt as if a dozen pairs of eyes had spotted him, with a dozen mouths whispering their words to Wilf Magill.

When he closed in on Mary's house, he slowed to a stop, jumping when a voice shrilled behind him.

"They're watching."

He twisted round and there was Peter. He was, as ever, hovering, trying to get out of the world he was in but not knowing where to go. Eddie moved over to him. "Who?"

Peter was uneasy saying more. "Men."

Plural. That wasn't good. "Where are they?"

The boy rocked on his heels. "They're everywhere."

"What are they doing?"

Peter was finding the words harder each time. They seemed to stick in his throat. "They're looking."

Eddie pulled out a cigarette and lit it. "What for?"

The boy was studying the cigarette pack in Eddie's hand. Eddie pushed out the card that came with it. "You."

Inside his jacket pocket, the ring and address book seemed to burn.

He turned around, heading home quickly.

But he didn't go home directly. He carried on along Abbeydale Road until he came to the junction with Ada's road, which spurred up right. As he walked up the steady incline, he was slow. His ankle had started to hurt again, the impact of the jump from the window having compressed it. He was walking on the opposite side of the road to Ada's house. When he drew level with it, he paused to sit on a garden wall opposite, watching.

Time slid by. Eddie couldn't put a number on the minutes that passed. He was waiting for something to happen, but he didn't know what. Of course, that wasn't true. He was waiting to make himself make a move, but couldn't. He didn't know if it was fear, lack of confidence or loss of motivation. All he knew were the people that passed him by as he sat and watched and waited. Some said hello. Some didn't. None of them made him move.

Then, with the luck that persuades people they made the right decision, the door to Ada's house opened and Morris strode out. He called something as he walked, but he didn't look back or wait for an answer. For a moment, Eddie thought Morris might see him. He hoped that he would and might make a connection. More than anything, Eddie wanted resolution. He wanted to beat Morris for what he'd done to Ada. But Morris had other things on his mind as he walked down the road steadily with a purposeful stride.

Eddie watched him go then dragged himself across from one pavement to the other, his steps faltering as he came close to the door. His knock was timid. The wait for a response took forever.

The door opened to show Ada in the shade. It was only when she stepped forward that the bruising on her face shone more clearly. Worse than that, though, were the eyes. They were beaten.

She wasn't either surprised or worried to see him.

"What's he done to you?"

There was no need to answer. Most of it was visible. She dropped her head.

"I'll kill him."

He said the words, without really feeling them. He imagined what Jimmy Cagney would have said and then done. She shrugged.

"Look, I'm sorry."

She reached out a hand and put it against his cheek. "Isn't this what your God believes in?" She was far more sad than bitter. "Punishment for things you've done wrong?"

He shook his head. "I don't think so."

She almost smiled. "That's a shame. I could believe in something like that. It's simple." Eddie was about to say something when she shook her head. "You'd better go."

He nodded, backing away.

She looked up at him with a smile, some glimmer of joy still managing to twinkle at the side of her eyes to provide a little light against the shadow of the bruising. She was going to tell him that she loved him, but what was the point?

Eddie walked home, hot and tired and ate a little of what his Mum had kept aside. As he finished it, she ran her hand through his hair.

"It'll be better tomorrow, duck."

***

She was wrong. It was worse.

The police were back at the brewery, with a bullish Wilf Magill at the front of the representation.

The talk was all bluster, citing complaints about the wagon. There was no substance to it, but it was enough to get Eddie taken off his round and pushed into the brewery proper, where he did what he could but where it was obvious that he couldn't do much. At the end of the day, Len Jeavons took him aside for a quiet talk.

"We can't carry you, Eddie."

Eddie nodded.

Jeavons continued. "We need you on the wagon or . . . we don't need you."

Eddie felt the ring inside his jacket like a cattle brand burnt on him. It sat alongside his other aches and pains. Weeks of chasing and exertion had left him perpetually tired, so that when work finished he bundled himself off home, determining to have some food before heading out again. His plans were disturbed by Nancy.

She called just as he was finishing his tea. "Do you want to rehearse?" She touched her lip with her tongue to let him know that it might be a euphemism as instinct made her push her chest forward.

First instinct was to be angry at her, but it was just deflective guilt for his own shame. He hadn't treated Nancy well. She deserved better. That seemed to be a pattern for him.

"I can't tonight." He wriggled his shoulders. "I need a few more days."

"Do you want a walk?"

Without the energy to shake her off and giving in to her company on a hot summer evening they headed to Graves Park, where the hole he had dug showed fresh wet soil. Though he felt some pride at what he'd done he could still imagine himself down there.

"I was worried when you were down there, Eddie."

She took his hand. The skin on skin was a comfort.

"It was just a trick, Nance." He smiled, absently. "That's all it was. There are bigger things."

Tomorrow, he told himself, he had to put the ring back.

Chapter Thirty-Five

Something changed in the night, so that when Eddie woke it was like he was trapped in a hot fog. The air was thick and solid, making him dizzy as he walked. The weather was knitting together, creating fat swabs of humid air that dulled him as he headed downstairs.

Another letter on the table from Louisa didn't help. The sight of it came on him like a whiplash.

"It's muggy," his Dad said.

"Could be a storm," his Mum added.

They were portents of doom as he sat beside them, weary before the day had begun.

His Mum nudged him and nodded towards the letter. "Are you going to open it?"

He looked at the letter and saw his name written in the soft roll of Louisa's hand. Where he should have felt happiness he only felt guilt.

"I'll read it on the steamer." He hadn't told them that he might not be riding it.

He put it inside his jacket, next to the ring where just the touch of the metal made him shudder. As he ate his breakfast, he couldn't stop himself wondering whether he would hear footsteps on the path outside or a knock on the door. He didn't and scuttled off to work.

He sat on the upper deck of the tram, gazing out onto the city as it woke up to take its first puffs of smoke. Hot air tightened around the population so that they wheezed. He thought about the day ahead, resigning himself to dull, but simple graft. He knew that he needed to summon up the energy to make an effort.

Just five steps into the yard, though, changed everything. Len Jeavons was standing waiting for him, shifting the weight in his feet with a relentless restlessness.

Had the police been again? Already?

"Eddie!"

Eddie felt himself stiffen as he came closer.

"Bert's gone and done it, hasn't he? Got so drunk this time he fell downstairs and didn't realise he'd broken his leg." The consequence wasn't a long time coming. Jeavons pursed his lips. "I need you to cover the round."

Eddie nodded. "That's all right."

"Eddie, I don't know what's going on, but keep an eye out." Jeavons was anxious. "Don't do *anything* that might set the police off. They've got their eye on you, so just be careful." The phrase was coming back again. "And you're on the horses. The steamer's buggered again."

Eddie wondered if his luck might be changing. He had the ring in his pocket and now a free ride on the wagon. And though he was a little worried about how his shoulder and ankle would hold up, this was as good a chance as any to get things back in place.

The horses were pleased to see him again. They skipped out at a trot, Eddie careful to rein them in to keep them close, with the morning now clammy with heat. The roads were already starting to rattle with trams, cars and vans and he drove steadily.

The work was hard and hurt him. Some of the landlords helped, some didn't. Every now and then a landlady would try to get someone to give him a hand, but that could work against Eddie. No landlord was keen to help if they saw a light shine in their wife's eyes gazing at the young drayman.

Eddie was pushing himself hard. The round was a heavy one, meaning he had to work even faster to carve out some space to call in at the Crofts. He was nervous too, which tired him. All the time between drops he was looking up and down the road for a sight of the police. One time, he had to jerk to a stop as a vehicle careered towards him and he could only breathe again when he saw it was the city's new fire engine, black, shining and nicknamed the *Pig*. It was heading out towards Ringinglow, maybe to slow down a fire that might have started on the moors. It was that sort of day. There was a smell of smoke to it.

The weather was starting to close in, wrapping the city in a ball of humid heat, which only made the soot feel tighter in your lungs each time you breathed. Eddie was wheezing heavily, sweating cobs as he pulled the horses and the wagon to a stop, a little way off from Mary Riley's house.

He left the horses by the Red House, with the landlady squeezing his hand as she said she'd keep an eye on them.

"I won't be long," he said with a smile.

"You'd better not be." She nodded towards the skies, where the clouds were clumping together in dark masses. "There's rain on the way."

The rain would be a relief. Eddie was hot as he walked, having to keep his jacket on to hide the address book and photograph. He kept his hands in his pockets, his right clutching tightly to the ring as he pushed on, feeling a pain with each step in his ankle. The jump from the window was still working its way out of his body.

The throbbing was a distraction, making Eddie unusually unfocused as he weaved his way through the streets. He didn't spot the policeman until he was less than twenty yards away, having to twist to his right to slide down a gennel to keep himself hidden.

He didn't know what to think or quite what to do, staying motionless for minutes, his thinking not as sharp as the pain in his ankle.

"They're waiting for you."

The voice made Eddie jolt so that it was a moment before he regained his calm to see Peter standing in the shadows of the houses, watching him closely. His face was dirty, but it was plain and open and Eddie welcomed that.

"How many?"

"Four, I think."

"Do you know them?"

The boy nodded. "One of them."

"Burn on his hand?"

Another nod.

"The one who was at Mary Riley's and gave you the cards."

Eddie didn't even bother to phrase it as a question. Wilf Magill was watching for him, waiting.

"He gave me this." The boy put his hand in his pocket, pulling out a whistle.

"And what's that for?"

The boy looked up at Eddie. His eyes were full of pity and shame.

"He told me to blow it if I saw you."

Eddie stiffened. "You don't want to do that, do you?"

"No."

"Why not?"

The boy looked at him eye to eye. "You used to be one of us."

Eddie stared at his face, cut short and tight by so little food and so few nutrients. It wasn't a long stretch for Eddie to see himself there.

Eddie pulled a penny from his pocket and placed it in the palm of his hand. He let the boy touch it to feel its weight. Then he took it back, closed his palm and when he opened it again, the coin had gone. The boy squealed. Eddie himself looked surprised.

"Where's it gone?"

Peter shook his head.

"Wait a second." As he said that Eddie leaned forward towards the Peter's ear, clicked his fingers and the coin reappeared. He smiled. "Blow that whistle in five minutes. And give that to your mum." He slipped the coin into the Peter's pocket, then he turned his face towards his destination.

Five minutes.

He could have asked for ten, but the moment was everything. He needed the impetus. He skipped back to the streets, hugging close to the near side of the road, where the sun could never quite reach. More or less invisible, he slid along the buildings, keeping his eye on the one policeman he could see, who was dawdling and disinterested, chatting to the women he saw. They were talking idly about the weather, just how soon the rain would come, sticky with heat that seemed to be closing around them as the air grew tighter.

Eddie eased himself up to the front of Mary Riley's house, softening the door open with a gentle click. After the clammy heat of the outside world, inside felt funereal cold, drying the sweat on Eddie's skin. He lost a breath as he stood in the house where Wilf Magill had raped Mary Riley he didn't know how many times, then later murdered her.

His plan was to put the ring back, stuck somewhere out of sight in the parlour, where Magill might reason that he had never looked. He would slip the address book on a shelf, unsure if anyone knew it was missing. If it wasn't the best idea in the world, it was the only one he had. He moved forward to put it into action.

He was too purposeful.

His footfall wasn't heavy, but the floorboards were old and tired and creaked. He wouldn't have noticed it too much if the sound hadn't drawn a corresponding scrape of footsteps from upstairs. Eddie turned quickly, ducking into the parlour, dropping the ring into the last ashes of the fireplace, leaving the address book on the mantelpiece. As he pulled back out of the room, the footsteps were already starting to hit hard on the stairs.

"Reynolds!"

Eddie looked up left to see Magill fill the space at the top of the stairs, now tumbling down towards him unstoppably.

Quick as he could, Eddie spun round, heading for the door, his legs just starting to move him forward when he felt a fat hand land on his shoulder, squashing the flesh to knock him off balance, so that he tripped, banging down to his knees. Behind him, Magill's breath poured out like a dragon, wheezing with the effort of movement and giving Eddie his only hope – that he could outrun the constable.

Even as the thought came to him, the flat of Magill's boot caught Eddie in the back as he scrabbled forward, lifting him up against the wall with a thud. Another blow or two like that, Eddie knew, would stop him dead. He'd be easy pickings for Magill to lean over and lay into. He gritted his teeth then pushed himself forward in a spring, giving him just a little distance from Magill's swinging boot, enough for him to scramble to his feet.

Behind him, Magill lurched forward, his right hand pulling out his truncheon to give his arm extension. He reached out in a swipe, catching Eddie's back hard enough to make him gasp. The blow didn't stop him, though. He had just enough energy to continue forward. He ducked down, pushing hard towards the door then tearing into the knot of streets that made the Crofts such a maze.

As if responding to the moment, the light across the city had darkened as the clouds gathered. Eddie didn't have time to stop to wonder what that meant, leaning forward into a sprint that would carry him a little way from Mary's house then allow him to circle back to his wagon. He bent left up the hill so that Magill wouldn't see him so easily as he bundled his way out of the door in pursuit.

Almost immediately, Eddie's ankle was flaring with pain. Every footstep that landed with a twist on the uneven cobblestones shook it looser, making the nerves sing. He tried to clear his mind of the feeling, tried to just keep focused on running, now shifting right down a side street, praying that he knew the area better than Magill. All he could be sure of was that he couldn't hear footsteps behind him. He didn't waste time to turn to look.

He was zig zagging through the Crofts, faces at doorways and windows casting an eye on him and then on the sky and back to him again. They knew what it meant if someone was running that fast. They wondered if they should intervene. To help the police could make their life so much easier. Without pausing to study, he could see it in their eyes and then – just once or twice – he saw a sign of a wish for him to succeed. Eddie was one of their own, after all. Or at least, he used to be.

He had cut a tight path through the knot of streets with just one more turn ahead of him, which would bring him out opposite the Red House and he committed to it, forcing himself forward, while his ankle screamed with pain.

Then he stopped with a jolt. The wagon was ten yards in front of him, but two policemen were standing either side of the horses, stroking their manes.

The crash of Eddie's heels on the street broke them out of their reverie, but the breathless air made them slow to make sense of what they could hear and see. They were starting to move, starting to edge towards where Eddie had appeared when the sound of a whistle cut through the fat air to make them pause, then turn towards the sound to chase it.

God bless you, Peter!

Eddie didn't waste the opportunity, taking a sharp turn to steer away from them, though immediately he could now see Magill lumbering towards him. If it was a comfort that Magill was slow, it was balanced by a swelling that was starting to clamp over Eddie's ankle like a leg iron. Eddie let gravity roll him down Solly Street, branching down into Hollis Croft, his breath now exploding in his chest.

Ahead of him, he saw St. Vincent's church. It seemed so natural to go there, an instinct that tugged him. Sweat was now bleeding out of him, sticking his shirt to his back while his throat rasped with the hot breaths he had been taking. He limped towards the church, pushed through the door, into a sepulchral cool and calm. Despite its newness, the church had a centuries-old feeling of sanctuary about it. The impact was a sedative to Eddie. He slowed.

"Eddie?" The voice came from nowhere, but it was calm and soft. Eddie turned to see Father Casey. "Eddie, what are you doing?"

Eddie could barely breathe and to speak was beyond him for a moment.

"Wilf Magill!" That was all he could manage.

Father Casey was close to him now. "What about Constable Magill?"

Hearing the priest using Magill's official title chilled him. The priest was venerating him.

What could Eddie say? Father Casey dealt with certainty. Some things were just matters of faith. And this was Magill's church now, not Eddie's. There was no safety here, he realised. He pushed himself up.

"He's chasing me, Father."

"What have you done?"

Eddie shook his head. "He's not chasing me for what I've done, Father. He's chasing me for what I *know.*"

"Now, Eddie—"

Eddie looked around him and the sense of sanctuary began to slip away. This was just a building. Four walls and a roof. It wouldn't save him. It wouldn't try.

When he opened the door, the air had grown thicker still and the sky had blackened, sucking up the light to make the whole day dark. Eddie tumbled to the other side of the road, feeling abandoned by God.

For a few moments, he thought his luck might have changed. He could neither see nor hear a policeman. He could start to walk steadily and a little more certainly. Even so, he wondered where he could escape to. Being free today was only postponing the inevitable. How could he hide forever? The thought made him gasp and his eyes started to water.

He thought of his Mum and Dad. He pictured his Dad, heaving himself upstairs every night, the pain of the effort picked out bold in the features of his face, most of all in his eyes. You have to try, Eddie. You have to try.

The thought gave him fresh strength. He started to push back to where he'd left his wagon and horses. The air was heavy as blankets now, hot, thick and hardly allowing enough air to keep his lungs moving. The sky had blackened deeper when a first, tentative, exploratory drop of rain tickled the skin of his cheek to roll down in a tear.

The sensation jolted him, making him aware of his surroundings again. His eyes searched through the gloom to see if there was trouble ahead, just as his ears picked up footsteps from behind: hard and fast. He twisted to see the figures of two police officers emerging a hundred yards down the road from where he was, starting to shift up a gear, wondering if they'd found what they wanted.

Eddie wasn't running. He had to make a choice. To run now was to admit his guilt and wave a flag. Also, he didn't know where Magill was, but he knew he was out there somewhere in the knot of streets.

Despite his instincts, he managed to walk steady, the footstep sounds softening behind him as the police officers eased into a march.

Eddie breathed easier for just a second until a crash to his left announced the body of Wilf Magill emerging from a side street, building up momentum to propel himself forward. Glancing behind, Eddie saw the two officers recognise Magill and jump, as if he was their puppet master. They were starting to move.

Calculating fast, Eddie had few options open to him. He certainly wouldn't have time to get the wagon moving before someone caught him. For the rarest of moments, he panicked and froze, too tired to react anymore. He looked up towards the Red House, which seemed so close, but in the corner of his eye, Magill was barely forty yards away with the two offices starting to kick up a drum roll behind him.

That was when the whistle blew again. Eddie had to smile at the way Peter was playing the policeman, making them jig. The sound was sharp enough to cut through the thick, hot air like a knife – stopping the two police officers where they stood, spinning them round, Pavlovian, to head towards the sound.

Even Magill stumbled for a step or two, dumbstruck by the noise. Reynolds was *here*, he wanted to shout, but his breath wasn't strong enough to give any weight to the words.

Eddie saw his chance, whipping his head round to see that the road was clear below him. The street was now a long tumble down towards Broad Lane. Eddie started to run again. Despite himself, he turned to look behind to see Magill coming at him at a steady pace, maybe even gaining a little as the slope and his weight gave the impression of an irresistible force. Eddie stared ahead to look for some sort of way out but couldn't see one. The road would take him straight down onto Broad Lane then right out in the open, but what then?

He was halfway down when he felt the rain drops slap hard against his face. They were fat, heavy, full of portent. His eyes skimmed upwards where the sky was black. The drops started to thicken and accelerate.

Then the rain came fast and hard, like a volley of bullets. Eddie was twenty yards short of the junction with Broad Lane and it seemed like the apocalypse had started.

The rain was falling down vertically – stair-rods his Dad used to say – hitting the ground hard before bouncing back up.

The sound was monstrous, taking away any sense of whereabouts.

All Eddie could do was flounder forward, his clothes already sagging about his body, clinging to his skin as if he was washed in blood.

He could barely see as he leapt off the pavement, turning into Tenter Street, invisible to anything that was passing and blind to it, too. Each step, all he could think of was a need to move forward, always with the expectation of a hand catching his shoulder, pulling him back.

He pushed forward onto the road, only aware of the lights and sounds of vehicles in the abstract, though he sensed that they were there.

He hit the other side of the road as the sound of a car howled past, the tyres kicking up a wave from the water that was already running rivers down the road.

The shock made him pause and at that moment he heard the wet squeal of wheels trying to get a grip on a road surface that was playing like ice. The sound was ugly, but followed by a thicker, more sickening thump, before both sounds were washed away by the drown of the rain that continued to pour down.

When Eddie turned, he saw a car skewed across the wrong side of the road and there in the centre, a big, dark lump of a body.

A tram that had been passing ground to a halt, conductor and passengers leaping off to run towards the figure, voices trying to make themselves heard above the relentless rattle of the water that pummeled them all.

Eddie just stood and watched.

The body didn't move.

Nor did Eddie, unable to pull himself away, eyes drawn to the frame of Wilf Magill, lying still and solid on the ground as bodies busied about him. The bodies were urgent, insistent. They were arguing for life and battling the rain. The quickness of their movement reflected a need to keep fighting for as long as they could. But the rain was going to outlast them all. It wouldn't stop, wouldn't slow.

Magill didn't move.

His stillness defeated them. After just two minutes – which might have been days – they, too, slowed down to stop.

He was dead.

Eddie stood under the canopy of buildings and watched, the water thickening and deepening by the second, blurring every image, filling space with its sound.

***

Eddie climbed back up the hill slowly, unsure what to expect or what anything much meant to him. The policemen had gone, though and the horses were hunkering down against the rain, twitching when the thunder started to rumble. He patted them, dragging a hand through hair that was sodden. The water cascaded past him. The city was drowning. Roads were pouring water down into the valleys and flooding them.

"Let's get back, boys," Eddie said and climbed back aboard.

***

The rain didn't stop. Roads became rivers as the city took on the shape of a series of waterfalls, pouring stormwater down into the flats where it spread out in all directions, its fingers feeling for flood gaps then filling them up. Eddie battled his way back to the brewery, where the shock of the storm was changing to a slow panic. Len Jeavons stuttered for ten minutes, uncertain what to do, before sending everyone home. Eddie tried for a tram, but there was no easy way to travel so he put his head down to walk, the roads and pavements before him blurring into an ever-shifting liquid mass. By the time he got home, the rain had settled into a rhythmic beat and from the top of the hill he could look down safe enough, but was too tired for any sense of comfort.

His Mum bullied him out of wet clothes while he laid on the sofa, a blanket over him and a mug of tea steaming by his side. The warmth quickly dried out the damp that had sunk down to his bones. He started to drift in and out of sleep, waking with starts when dreams of uncertain things started to blur with reality. Then he lay still, pulling out Louisa's latest letter, which was damp and ink smudged. He could make out enough. He knew what it meant. It told him she was coming home.

After dinner, he sat at the table with paper and pen. Off to one side was the letter he had started. He left it there and began again.

He told her he missed her. He told her about the trick with the grave and said that it scared him. He hoped she was happy. He hoped she hadn't hurt herself. As he wrote those words his throat was stuck with worry. He thought of far away and couldn't help thinking of his Dad in the trenches in France. They were so very different in so many, but not so different after all.

He told her about the show at the Empire and how well it had gone.

He paused and looked around him. His Mum was cleaning the dishes as his Dad turned up the radio and lit his pipe.

Eddie turned back to the letter and looked at the things he was saying to Louisa.

He told her he loved her – and asked her to marry him.

He put the pen down and fell fully asleep.

Chapter Thirty-Six

Friday was busy with talk all over town. Eddie tried to keep out of the way at work, wondering just what would happen next, but nothing did. The storm took all the headlines, squeezing Wilf Magill's death in as a footnote, a tragic consequence of the treacherous weather and the appalling driving conditions. Just what Magill was doing in the Crofts that day no one seemed to say and no one asked. Perhaps the policemen who had been with him had never known why they were. Perhaps they *had* known and wanted to keep it quiet. Eddie reckoned that Magill couldn't have told them *too* much.

Eddie's Dad had given up the passive life when he gave up his leg. He hobbled down to the station to ask Ted Pearson if he was going to need to speak to Eddie again.

Pearson shook his head. "No need, Mr. Reynolds, thank you. I think that's all sorted."

By which he meant that they would blame Billy McGloin for the pregnancy, the murder and his own suicide. Or rather, they would just bury him and all associated stories with him.

Eddie slept well and waited for time to pass, until he found himself walking straight and steady with no real pain in his ankle and no sort of niggle in his shoulder.

It was a Saturday afternoon in summer and he was smiling. He couldn't do anything now about Mary and Billy and Wilf Magill and he didn't try to, or tried not to think about it. He didn't think about Nancy much. He needed a break, he said. He wanted to head over to Castleton to talk to Randolph Douglas again, for new ideas. He didn't think of Ada much, either. Where he had once felt guilty about his desire for her, now he felt some guilt about his lack of desire. Today, he had one purpose, which was to head down to the coach stop at Abbey Lane, to meet up with the bus that was bringing Louisa home.

He was early and found a wall to lean against, letting the sun cover him softly. He felt its healing. He had the letter in his pocket that he had written for Louisa. He hadn't yet decided whether or not to give it to her. He had options and he liked that. He might gift it to her as part of his apology for not writing sooner, though that felt like too much of a play. He didn't want to dissemble with Louisa. He wanted to be honest. She deserved that much and he didn't deserve her. He'd never known it more clearly and – because of that – had never wanted her more. She offered him a different way of living: comfort, safety and happiness. He found it strange that it wasn't obvious to him that that's what he wanted. But then this was someone who buried himself voluntarily. He had to smile at that.

All around him, Saturday business was taking place and people were in a good mood, skipping along towards Millhouses Park and the lake and the lido, or heading up hand in hand into Ecclesall Woods. Eddie looked up and down and he saw some sense of peace and order and happiness. They didn't notice him. All of a sudden he wanted to shout out: *hey, look here. I'm the Incredible Eddie Reynolds.*

Perhaps he wasn't today. He hoped that he would be again. When he thought that, he thought of Nancy. Then he thought of Ada.

And then he *saw* Ada. And Morris beside her. The image struck him.

They were walking on the other side of the road, coming from their home in Dore towards Eddie and towards Millhouses, Morris in front, pulling, and Ada behind, lagging.

Eddie stared at them, unsure which one worried him more, before realizing that it was the sight of them both together that disturbed him most.

As he stared, the cough and splutter of the coach tugged between them, Eddie looking up when he heard a banging and saw Louisa's palms slapping against the glass, her face radiant with pleasure to be back and to see him.

The coach pulled past and Morris and Ada were five steps closer, Ada now looking up at last, seeing Eddie, recognizing him, the realization making her feet stutter, so that Morris had to slow. He glanced back at her and then up ahead, over the road, towards Eddie.

The coach had stopped now and the bodies were bundling out, riding a wave of noise from the conversations that had rolled across the seats from the flats of Lincolnshire back to Sheffield, flushing with emotions of having been sisters in arms for four weeks and now happy and sad to be de-mobbed.

Louisa appeared at the door and turned towards Eddie.

Eddie smiled, sneaking a glance down the road, where Ada and Morris had now stopped and were considering what to do next, edging to the kerb as if they might come across: Ada, he knew, wanting to; Morris perhaps feeling that he needed to.

"Eddie Reynolds!"

Eddie shook his head and closed his eyes for a second, asking himself the age-old question: just how am I going to get out of this one?

More by Laurence Green

Books in the Charlie Baxter Series

Introducing Charlie Baxter

In the beginning, Charlie Baxter is an everyday Joe called Charles Backley and working a dull IT job in a city school. Things change when he comes home one day to find three men trying to break into his house. He is scared by that and terrified by them. He soon discovers that they don't want him because they've got the wrong house. When he finds the right house he also finds an enigmatic and charismatic character called Kris, who asks Charlie to find out who the three men are and why they're chasing him. Charlie takes on the guise of Charlie Baxter, Private Investigator, as he gets drawn into a neighbourhood turf war with community leaders, business chiefs, local drug lords and the police. With only the mysterious Maya and friend, Gil, to help him Charlie is racing against the clock towards the anniversary of a local shooting that rocked the community and looks likely to tear it apart this time.

Charlie Baxter's Boxers

Times are hard for P.I. Charlie Baxter, so when he gets the chance to run an adultery case and a search for a missing dog together he thinks his luck has changed. And it has: for the worse. It doesn't help that his client is a local boxer with a history of stepping off the straight and narrow. Charlie finds he has as much work to do protecting his client as he does finding the client's dog. And he finds that the world of pet theft is big, ugly and very, very brutal.

With help from a seasoned dog-walker called Jess he has to find the boxer's boxer and keep the boxer out of harm. The journey takes Charlie from boxing ring to dog pit and he finds himself just where he doesn't want to be: centre stage.

Charlie Baxter's Cold Hard Cash

When an anonymous client leaves cash for Charlie to follow a client, he is intrigued. When the person he is tracking is chased to his death, Charlie is worried and when he finds out that the person who died was carrying a box of cash from a security van raid he begins to wonder if he's out of his depth. As well as the client and the police, two rival gangs are also searching for the missing money and Charlie is caught right in the middle. When he finds the money, things only get worse and more deadly. Charlie has to work out the smartest and safest thing to do with the cash, before the net closes in on him.

OTHER BOOKS

Vision

When Ben meets Jenny it seems for the first time that he can start looking to the future. Things change completely when Jenny sees a huge explosion at a bridge on television. It seems like a report, but there has been no explosion – and Jenny had never even turned the television on. The incident takes her all the way back to a past she wanted to move away from. No one can explain just what she's seen, yet everyone is keen to try and the help they are all offering might be just what destroys Jenny if she or Ben can't make sense of things first.

Keep up to date at:
losgreeninc (jimdofree.com)

Laurence Green at Goodreads

Laurence Green Author Page at Amazon

Printed in Great Britain
by Amazon

41950894R00229